"His lordship has ordered you brought here," said Rodney.

"Yes, but the servants . . ." Mary peered out the window at a Roman-nosed butler appearing at the front door. "There will be questions—like who am I and why am I here? What am I to say?"

"They shan't question you," he told her. "I shall tell them that you are a friend of his lordship's sister, Lady Langfield, and that you are here for a repairing lease in the country." Rodney suddenly looked thoughtful. "In fact, that is what you are to tell anyone, no matter what their identity."

"But my clothes!" protested Mary. She clutched at her seat and shook her head as the chaise rolled to a halt. "I cannot pass as a lady."

"That is why you shall stay here in the privacy of the country while you learn to become one," he said, and his voice allowed no further opposition. "You have recently been rescued from debt and poverty. Tell people you have now come into a sufficient fortune to establish you comfortably. No one need know anything else. Now, come. There is nothing here to be frightened of."

She looked at the elegant house with a flock of servants to see to her needs. The novelty of this position, combined with the beauty of the house and its furnishings, all at her disposal, quickly overcame her. Suddenly, she was glad she had not fled, for then she would never have had this brief chance to savor luxury such as she had never known . . .

A Love So Wild

DEBORAH CHESTER

BALLANTINE BOOKS • NEW YORK

Library of Congress Catalog Card Number: 79-11874

ISBN 0-345-28773-8

This edition published by arrangement with
Coward, McCann & Geoghegan, Inc.

Manufactured in the United States of America

First Ballantine Books Edition: July 1981

With gratitude, to Bob Duncan and Robbin Hawkins

Chapter One

MARY CLAMPTON huddled on her pile of straw deep in the hell that was Newgate Prison. Through the tiny barred window of her door she could see the wall torch flickering a feeble light about the rough corridor, but as it sent no illumination into her own cell, she had no interest in it. She guessed it to be night out in the world that had been forbidden her for countless months. The meal had been served with a hunk of stale, crumbling bread, and bread was always brought at the end of the day.

A tremor shook her, but she forced down the nausea from the fear each successive day aroused. Shifting on the straw heap that had been filthy when she first arrived and had not been changed since, she put her elbows on her knees and covered her face with her grimy hands to pray for one more day of strength to endure this horrible, degrading existence—but the squeaks and chittering of the rats fighting over the remainder of the food that she could not quite choke down distracted her thoughts until she gave up to sink into a stupor of despair.

She would never be released, she thought dully, her mind stumbling around the same old thing. Hope had left her weeks, months ago. Somehow she had been forgotten; there had never been a trial. Her hands clenched from the fierce sense of unfairness, of gross injustice which was the only thing left within her, besides fear, that still had passionate life. No, none of it was fair. Her hands slowly unclenched, but she took no heed of the pain her nails had made by digging into her flesh. Forgotten—no release, ever.

A rat skittered past her, and she flinched away, shutting her eyes to avoid its malevolent gaze. Why did she not kill herself and escape this? Daily the temptation pricked at her, but she had no means save by refusing to eat. And so far she had never failed to try to swallow down as much of the foul stuff as she could. Suicide was her means, but she miserably knew she was too much a coward yet to take it. How she managed to endure, day after endless nightmarish day, was beyond her comprehension.

Then suddenly, through the quiet of the wet stone mass about her, above the quarreling of the rats, came the sound of echoing footsteps. Drawing in a ragged breath, Mary rose to her feet and ran to her door to listen. Across the corridor, other gaunt unkempt faces appeared at the little windows like ghosts with straining eyes. No one spoke. It was quiet enough here at this end of the corridor for Mary to hear the muffled flutter of the wall torch as it leaped in the drafts of cold damp air.

Her heart began to hammer faster and yet faster, until each thud brought pain. She drew in another long breath and leaned her perspiring forehead against the cold rusted iron of her door, willing herself not to give way to panic. Perhaps it was only the cripple-backed jailer making one last round for the night. She must not let her fears make her think otherwise.

But there were too many footsteps coming. Her ears strained to hear past the blood pounding through her head. Yes, they were brisk rapid feet—not the jailer's halting ones, which she could hear too. The jailer was bringing someone—a man.

She bit down upon her trembling lip and tried to look out again. But the angle was wrong to see very far, and even standing on tiptoe did not help. Her thoughts and fear battled on. She was the only woman this way, but surely it was just the lawyer coming again to argue with the old man in the cell to the right of hers.

But fear was too strong. It forced her to stumble back a few steps from the door. The footsteps halted just outside, and she stood petrified with ears strained to listen to the crackle of stiff paper and the jailer's mumble of, "Aye, 'ere's the Clampton wench."

Almost instinctively she snatched at her only defense, which was to feign insanity. All this time she'd kept up the pretense—until she sometimes half-believed it was true—as a poor sort of insurance against any possible assaults on her virtue. But now, it seemed, was to be the first true test of her ploy.

Choking down a sob, she broke out into wild song, deliberately roughening her voice. The rats chittered angrily. She heard them scurrying about and raised her voice until it cracked of its own accord.

"Don't be afraid, my rats," she chanted. "Stay and play with me. I'll keep my little ones safe."

The lock turned in her door. She yanked in her breath with a sob and fled to the rear of her cell. The door swung open with the slowness of infrequent use, and she heard the jailer say, "It's account of the damp, m'lord. Rusts up the locks and 'inges somethin' fierce, it does."

Mary bit her lip and clenched her hands to stop their trembling. The jailer poked in his head and raised the lantern high. Its light licked at her tattered skirt, and she shrank back farther against the rough wall. The damp surface against her back made her shiver.

"Come on up ter us, so's the gentlemen can see yer face."

Mary found it difficult to breathe. Her heart pounded, and she seemed to be made of straw. Another moment and she would faint; then there would be no hope for her at all.

"Hie! Come on 'ere!"

"Never mind, jailer," said a quick, well-bred voice. A slender young man stepped to the doorway, his features in shadow from the light behind him. "I'll go in. Give me your lantern."

"No," said the hardest voice Mary had ever heard,

from someone she could not yet see. It was clipped, cultured—the voice of a gentleman. "I shall go in."

"But, my lord—" protested the man at the door, half-turning.

"If I am not satisfied with her, then everything is off. I'll take that lantern, thank you. And you will close the door behind me."

The first man in the doorway was pushed aside by a larger, taller figure in a caped driving coat. Though he was all in shadow, such an air of ruthless authority emanated from him that Mary almost collapsed in complete despair. She was already sliding down the wall when one last thread of strength tightened within her. Like one dazed, she shook her head in silent, horrified protest. But he advanced steadily inside, with the lantern casually in one hand.

She threw up a shaking hand to dash the perspiration from her brow, then suddenly, almost mindlessly, shrieked and whirled herself about in a wild dance, flinging her arms up over her head and flailing them with an insane fury.

"Come out, little rats. Come out and play," she sang, her voice cracked with terror.

"Good God, my lord, *stop!* Surely you can trust my judgment?"

"Not in this." The man in the driving coat shook his head.

"Sirs, she's daft as a loon tonight," said the jailer, wringing his hands. "I told yers she's gone binky over the rats. Are yers sure yer don't want ter see another?"

"Yes, my lord!" The smaller man gripped the tall one's arm. "Let us try another. She's quite mad."

Mary flung herself back against the wall, panting. She dared not yet hope, but just perhaps . . .

The lord pulled free of the hold on his arm somewhat impatiently. "We both know what folly this scheme is, Rodney. I agreed to see this one. If she is not suitable, we will not seek another in this pestilent hole." He coughed and threw up a handkerchief over his face. "Gad, what a stench! Stand aside, Rodney."

Mary closed her eyes a moment against this final dashing of any chance for her. Then she bit her quivering lip and eyed the lantern in determination. Somehow she must seize it and set fire to herself—or him.

The door swung shut behind the lord, and to her it was the slamming against all escape. Still holding the handkerchief to his face, he glanced all around before setting the lantern on a rickety stool—her only piece of furniture. She hugged the wall with her face averted.

"Come here so that I may see your face properly." He looked up sharply. "Come!"

Reluctantly she pushed herself away from the wall and approached him on unsteady feet. Her heart continued to thud hard and fast, and her every breath almost choked her. She came up just within the circle of light, clenching her hands within the folds of her tattered skirt to hide their trembling. His hair was dark, and he was so tall her head came but to his shoulder. His caped driving coat covered him from the white cravat gleaming at his throat to the glossy toes of his boots. Shadows yet hid his face, but he seemed completely sinister and cold-blooded. She dared not raise her eyes above the floor.

But he had no reservations against staring at her. She became very conscious of his scrutiny and trembled more. He must not see my fear, she told herself desperately. He must not.

"Hold out your hand," he commanded.

Mary flinched from the harshness of his voice and tightened her lips. If he touches me, she thought, I shall do it. But her will shrank from smashing the lantern and setting fire to herself.

"Are you deaf, wench? Do as I say."

Slowly she extended her shaking grimy hand. But to her surprise he did not take it; rather, he produced a quizzing glass and squinted through it at her chapped, reddened fingers with their broken dirty nails. In sudden shame she drew her hand back. He said nothing, but continued to eye her through his glass until her face and throat were aflame. She jerked up the ripped shoulder of her dress and was grateful the bodice was not cut low.

"Gad, but you're filthy," he murmured. Suddenly he

made a gesture of disgust. "Get on back to your corner. I've no need of you."

Her knees nearly gave way beneath her in overwhelming relief. "Thank God," she sighed involuntarily.

He whirled sharply. "What was that?"

She forced a shrill laugh, cursing herself for making such a stupid mistake. "My rats are coming. Shall you see them?"

In two strides he had her firmly against the wall. She struggled against strength that was as immovable as her cell door.

"Please, no," she whimpered, jerking her head away from the face so close to hers. "No!"

He seized her chin with a cold hand and forced her head back against the wall. "I'm not the one to pretend your madness to."

She shot him a look of fury. "And I'm no Haymarket ware!"

He released her as though burnt and stepped back in obvious disgust. "Do you think I'd come here for that?"

"Why else?" Putting her hands to her face, she turned away and fought down tears and nausea. "Women are cheap here—just the jailer's bribe, I think, and no one for protection."

He coughed angrily. "Damn this infernal stench! Have I not just said I didn't come for that? What is your name?"

She choked down a sob of relief. It seemed he was going to leave her unharmed after all.

He snapped his fingers. "Come, come. Answer me."

"My name is Mary Clampton," she said, unable to trust him yet. "But the jailer has told you that; why do you ask me?"

"To hear the quality of your speech."

Such an odd answer made her dare to meet his eyes. The indistinct light hid their color, but she could see a bony, aquiline nose and a hard chin. He coughed again and put his handkerchief back to his face.

"The jailer told us that you are a thief," he said, watching her closely.

"It isn't true!" she flashed.

"Isn't it?"

His soft mockery heated her cheeks. She frowned, then glanced away with her mouth set. "They owed me money and wouldn't pay. I was facing debtor's prison."

"I can't see that you improved your lot." His voice was dry.

"I had to take the risk. I lost." She shrugged, calm enough now to wonder who he was and why he'd come. "Now I shall never get out."

"Should you like to get out?"

Her heart leaped—rescue at last! Then she caught the sudden intentness in him and forced herself to be wary. If the charges against her had been dropped, he would have said so at once. She shook her head. "No."

"Why not?" His voice was sharp, perhaps surprised.

She eyed him in suspicion. "Because there would be something you'd want of me in exchange."

He nodded. "But my price for freedom is not so high as you might imagine."

"What is it?"

"Marriage—to myself."

The man was insane. She turned away at once. "No!"

"I admit the prospect does not appeal to me, either." He took the lantern off the stool and spread his handkerchief over it. "I trust you don't object if I sit down? No? Thank you. The marriage would be in name only, and hardly permanent. I most certainly have no designs upon your . . . er . . . person, such as it is. You will forgive me if I tell you that you are hardly attractive to a man of my tastes."

"Then why want to marry me?" She forced out the words, unsure if she was dreaming or if there really was a madman here before her.

"Because I require a—shall we say, talented?—wife to assist me. This season's debutantes are hardly suitable for my purposes. As a thief, you are. You have more incentive to succeed for me than someone who has never seen the inside of a prison. You would not wish to return here, would you? I think not. Now, you will enjoy all the advantages my name and title can offer—that is, during the period of our contract. You will have pin money, clothes . . . perhaps a few jewels. If we should be successful, or shall I say, *once* we are successful, then you may go abroad—perhaps to Vienna—with a sum sufficient to maintain yourself comfortably for the rest of your days."

"But that explains nothing!" she cried.

"Come," he said with a great deal of coldness. "Do you suppose I would expose any delicately reared lady to the danger involved? You have risked thievery and heaven knows what else. That shows an intrepid spirit. For you, the risk in my plans is certainly a small price to pay for such future security as I offer, and we need never see each other again." He paused. "In fact, I should most certainly never want to see you again."

"You are not very polite," she said stiffly, with her back still turned. Why did he offer such things? This could not be real.

"This is hardly the occasion for drawing-room chit-chat," he said almost in a drawl. "I prefer to speak bluntly and escape being misunderstood, and I warn you that I am out of patience with any more questions concerning my reasons. I know what they are; you needn't, at this point. Tell me your decision."

She made herself face him and tried not to think of what he'd said. There was a trap here. He had a tongue like silk, yet he told her nothing. Nor did she forget his passing mention of danger. "I do not withdraw my refusal. You must find another to help you." The words, however, were almost impossible to say. She swallowed with difficulty, helpless before her inner warring of caution and of longing to be free.

"Very well." He rose with easy grace. "It makes little difference to me if you prefer to spend the rest of your days singing to rats."

The trembling seized her again. She fought down tears, putting her hands to her cheeks. "I can't," she whispered. "Oh—"

"Make up your mind. I can't afford to dawdle here forever."

"Why?" she demanded, stung by his air of indifference. "Are your horses having to stand too long?"

"I assume my tiger is walking them. But actually I prefer my curricle not be seen outside Newgate. It's terribly bad ton." He bent and picked up the lantern. "Well?"

Her thoughts whirled frantically. She must decide, but how? How could she trust what sounded too wondrous? She could not; it was too much like an absurd fairy tale to be true. Then suddenly, irrationally, she remembered the clean smell of him and his clothes when he had held her against the wall, and she knew only that he was offering an escape from this hell of filth and degradation. Surely there would be little to prevent her from escaping this man, too. If she had to live here like an animal much longer, she knew she would die. A new sense of life suddenly surged through her. She would go.

"You make it impossible for me to refuse, sir," she said.

"Precisely. Have you any belongings?"

"Only what I wear."

And the dress was not even hers. What persuasion she'd used to borrow the dowdy old ball gown from the clerk's wife next door! But it didn't resemble finery anymore. No matter. She drew a deep exhilarated breath and followed his tall figure out of the cell. Freedom at last!

The short jailer squinted at her and slammed the door. Her heart jumped. How many times had she heard that door slam? But this time she was on the right side of it.

"She . . . will do, Rodney," said the lord to a pleasant-faced young man in a brown coat. "Here is the permit for her release, and the money for a post chaise."

Rodney took them absently, glancing at Mary with a frown. "Are you certain, my lord?"

The lord's lips curled in a kind of mocking smile Mary did not trust. He did not look at her, but now, in the better light, she could see a harshly handsome face with two deep lines bracketing the well-shaped mouth.

His vivid blue eyes glinted at Rodney. "With some flesh on her bones and a bath, she will pass. Thank God she has educated speech!"

"But her madness—"

"A ruse, my boy." The mockery intensified in the lord's face. "But it is time you set to your task of making her presentable. We cannot afford to do things at our leisure."

"Yes, my lord." Rodney frowned, then nodded.

The lord started to stride away, then paused and glanced back at Mary. "Take her to . . . no, the Hall will not do. My mother is apt to take a country holiday there at any time, if Bath grows too dull. Take her to my new property north of Brighton. When she is presentable, write to me, and I shall come view the result. Take care, Rodney."

He handed the lantern back to the jailor and strode away, his coat swirling darkly about him.

Chapter Two

THEY ALL STOOD there a moment, watching his powerful figure disappear into the gloom of the dimly lit corridor. Mary drew a deep breath, not realizing until now, when the sound of his footsteps was fading, how much his presence had drained her. But freedom! She barely restrained a skip of joy and told herself to be careful. It was unwise to let herself feel too much joy yet here in the dank bowels of Newgate. She would wait a few more minutes—wait until she walked outside into the London streets. Then she would know for certain that this was not simply a cruel trick of her imagination.

The young man looked at her, sighed, and said, "Allow me to introduce myself, Miss Clampton. I am Rodney Tavers."

"How do you do," replied Mary almost in a whisper. It seemed so strange to be curtsying and conversing politely again.

The jailor spat at a cell door and peered up at her from beneath heavy, low brows. "So you ain't loony, eh, lassie?"

His dark malevolent eyes and rotten teeth revolted her, but she threw up her chin to face him with new courage. "No," she said. "I am not mad in the least."

Anger contorted his greasy face, and he lifted a fist. "Watch yer saucy tongue, wench!"

Rodney grabbed his arm and forced it down. "Have done, fellow! She's not at your mercy any longer.

11

Now, get along. We don't want to be in here forever."

With a sullen glance at Mary, the jailer held up his lantern and hobbled along to lead the way, his crooked back throwing out a grotesque shadow. Mary walked silently along beside Rodney, but each step she took had more spring and vitality to it. He had spoken the truth; she was free! Free of this hideous, stinking place and the poor wretches within it; free of fear and filth; free from this evil jailer, who had delighted in saying things to frighten and torment her before she had hit on the idea of playing mad and so kept him at a distance. At long last she was being rescued. The fact that her rescuer was a stranger didn't matter—not at the moment. Her blood began to sing through her veins, and her heart to beat in wild excitement.

It took but a few minutes for Rodney to sign a paper in the jailer's room of business and drop a few gold coins into that eager grimy palm. Then the double iron gates were unlocked, and Mary stepped out into the street for the first time in—how long?

She turned eagerly to Rodney. "What is the date, Mr. Tavers? I have lost count."

"August the thirtieth." He waved at an approaching hackney.

Mary stood stunned a moment. *August,* she thought numbly, putting a hand to her forehead. She had entered the prison gates the third night of November! Had it been so long? It did not seem possible.

Rodney handed her into the hackney with the attention suitable for a grand lady, but she scarcely noticed. Then the sudden jerk of the carriage brought her out of her daze.

She half-rose from the seat in shame. "I am so filthy!" she cried, clenching her skirt in her fists. "You cannot wish to be near me."

Rodney met her eyes, then suddenly smiled. "Please do not distress yourself. I am taking you to a small inn just on the edge of town, where you may clean up before we start our journey to Brighton. But if you do not mind, I shall leave the window down."

The breeze coming in was deliciously cool against

her face and smelled of—if not exactly pleasant ones
—at least the odors of London which she'd never
thought to wrinkle her nose over again. She glanced
once at Rodney. His air of grave civility made it hard
for her not to regard him with lessening distrust.

After crossing the river and speeding through the
fashionable west quarter—where Mary caught a few
brief glimpses of elegant town houses and broad, well-
lit streets—they soon reached a posting house on the
outskirts and stopped there. Mary was slipped in a
back way, to—as Rodney quickly explained—spare
her the glances of the curious sitting in the taproom.
A few words from Rodney into the plump landlady's
ear, accompanied by a gold guinea, brought a nod of
understanding and an offering of the serving girl's
Sunday dress. By the time Mary finished a hot bath
and a meal of roasted chicken, he had hired a post
chaise. They set out upon their journey without further delay.

She had never traveled in this manner before, and
she thrilled to the luxury of riding in a private equipage with postilions in smart livery. Rodney did not
tax her with conversation, and she spent the time gazing out the window at the lush countryside, first
splashed by silver moonlight, then the next day bathed
in brilliant sunshine that sparkled over dew-washed
meadows and jaunty flowers lifting their pert faces in
the road ditch.

It was as though she'd been blind for years and
years. She had not realized how starved she'd been for
sunlight and the blue sky like a robin's egg and dust
and singing birds and the homely plop of horses'
hooves. She longed to ask that the carriage be stopped
so that she might run out among the trees and the
grass and pick a few flowers, but Rodney was napping
in his corner and she dared not wake him to make the
request.

He slept until they halted at an inn to change
horses. Inside the private parlor, Rodney ordered
some lemonade for her and sherry for himself. Mary
sipped down the cool, tangy liquid and decided it was
time she dared ask some questions.

"Do you know what his lordship plans for me?" She blurted it out nervously, gripping her glass.

Wariness peeped out from his regular-featured face, which was open and friendly by nature rather than practice. His hair and eyes were brown, and he dressed in a plain but fashionable style. She thought his manners quiet and well-behaved, and suspected his momentary caution came from a healthy respect of his master.

When he gulped down the rest of the sherry and did not immediately reply, she tried again. "It does not make any sense to me. Why must I steal something for—"

"Please." He set his glass down hurriedly. "I . . . you need not distress yourself over that yet. This scheme of his lordship's is not . . . He may yet change his mind."

She was not reassured. What if this fine lord did change his mind? He did not seem to be in full possession of it in any case. She frowned and set her glass upon the table before circling the room. The breeze was fluttering the home-sewn draperies, and she stopped there at the window.

"So," she said flatly. "I have no guarantee of—"

"Miss Clampton," he interrupted just as flatly. "I am not permitted to discuss these matters of his lordship's."

Something in his stiff face stopped her. She lowered her eyes. "Who is your master?" she asked, unwilling to give up completely. "He did not tell me his name."

Rodney unbent slightly. "It is his way to forget such things. He is Lord—"

"Excuse me, sir." The landlord poked in his bald head. "You said to tell you when yer carriage was ready. That'll be five shillings, twopence for the parlor and refreshments."

On their way once more, Rodney promptly dozed off again, and Mary was left alone with her rising doubts. She must wait and see if his lordship really meant to fulfill his offer. And if he did mean to, then she would decide whether to . . .

She suddenly jerked up her thoughts in horror at

herself. What was she thinking of? To decide whether to steal for this lunatic indeed! Had greed gone to her head? Of course she would not steal—not for him or anyone else. She was not a thief, whatever her prison record might say, and he would not force her to do any illegal act.

Then why, she asked herself, was she going placidly along to Brighton? There had already been several opportunities to escape Rodney, but no, here she sat in the chaise, still going on her way toward whatever folly this lord was planning. Forcing herself to be truthful, she decided that she wanted to test his word, to see if he really was rich and able to give her all the things he had promised. But of course she would take nothing. She would not listen to any feeling of gratitude or obligation toward him for securing her release from jail. To do so would be utter folly, and she wanted none of it. Still, it would hurt nothing to go along a little further.

In the middle of the afternoon they turned off the main road onto a gently winding lane that was paved with smooth white cobblestones, and passed beneath the shade of ancient yews up to a stately manor built in the classical style. Mary caught her breath at the beauty of its fluted columns and simple lines. The grounds were informal, a careful riot of flowering shrubbery and fragrant blossoms of every variety.

"Am I to live here?" she asked before she could stop herself.

Rodney smiled at her. "Yes. Do you find it pleasing?"

Her face lit with delight. "As though I could not." Then she recalled her resolves and frowned. "But no, this is madness. I am a stranger. To move so freely into someone's home—"

"His lordship has never set foot in the house above one time," said Rodney. "And he has ordered you brought here."

"Yes, but the servants . . ." Mary peered out the window at a Roman-nosed butler appearing at the front door. "There will be questions. Who am I and why am I here. What am I to say?"

"They shan't question you," he told her. "I shall make the necessary explanations."

Mary wasn't satisfied. Sudden nervousness made her clammy all over, and she longed to shout at the coachman to drive on. "Yes, but—"

"I shall tell them that you are a friend of his lordship's sister, Lady Langfield, and that you are here for a repairing lease in the country." Rodney suddenly looked thoughtful. "In fact, that is what you are to tell anyone, no matter their identity."

"But won't Lady Langfield mind? What if she hears?"

"His lordship will tend to that," said Rodney soothingly. "Now—"

"But my clothes!" protested Mary. She clutched at her seat and shook her head as the chaise rolled to a halt. "I cannot pass as a lady."

"That is why you shall stay here in the privacy of the country while you learn to become one," he said, and his voice allowed no further opposition. "You have recently been rescued from debt and poverty, and now you have come into a sufficient fortune to establish you comfortably. No one need know anything else. Now, come. There is nothing to be frightened of here."

She rubbed her perspiring hands together and sat stubbornly in her corner. She could not climb out of the carriage, not even when Rodney got out and then reached in his hand to assist her. This is the time to leave, she thought in panic. She could not allow matters to continue further. The lord was wealthy enough to own a house he never visited; she had lost all desire to learn anything further about him. Now she must go. To get out of this chaise was to put herself in a position that might be difficult to escape. It was better to avoid it altogether.

"Come out, Miss Clampton." Impatience was in Rodney's voice now.

She looked at his face and read there the determination to drag her out by force. No, she did not want that. With a sinking spirit she realized that she should have not waited until now to back out. But there would still be chances to get away, and it might be better now not to cause any trouble. Swallowing hard, she forced herself to climb out, gripping his assisting hand with desperate fingers.

Within minutes Rodney was gone, and she was alone, temporary mistress of this elegant house with a flock of servants to see to her needs. The novelty of this position combined with the beauty of the house and its furnishings—all at her disposal—quickly overcame her fright, and she was left a little giddy and awed from it all. Suddenly, though she tried to suppress the feeling, she was glad she had not fled, for then she would never have had this brief chance to savor luxury such as she had never known.

Chapter Three

EVERYTHING ABOUT THE HOUSE bespoke taste and elegance, from the small gilt pedestal supporting a priceless Ming bowl in the library to the stately peacocks promenading about the terrace. But Mary felt dwarfed by the hushed spacious rooms. The polished floors hidden by silk Oriental rugs seemed to forbid her to tread upon them. Bronze cupids leered at her from the ceiling in all the most unlikely places. And the dining table, which seated fourteen comfortably and upon which her meals were served, awed her to the point of embarrassment. After two days, however, she became more accustomed to her surroundings and to being waited on by courteous, efficient servants, and began to enjoy herself.

She was wandering about the garden after breakfast, listening to the warbling of songbirds in the shrubbery and glorying in the spaciousness of the outdoors, when the downstairs maid came to inform her of callers.

Dropping a curtsy, the maid looked at Mary with huge brown eyes. "If you please, miss, there's Mr. and Miss Tavers come."

Mary had seen nothing of Rodney since he'd deposited her here, but though she did not mind seeing him again, she was not anxious to meet Miss Tavers—whoever she might be. Controlling the urge to bolt over the hedge and head for the wide meadow beyond the park, Mary reluctantly followed the little maid to the library. A woman's clear laugh carried to her before she was quite to the doorway, and she stopped there, abruptly conscious of her now clean but poorly dressed hair and the chambermaid's best dress that she was wearing. She hesitated and was again strongly tempted to flee. Then Rodney looked up and hastened forward with a warm smile that melted away some of her self-consciousness.

"You are looking very well today, Miss Clampton," he said in his sincere manner. "May I introduce my sister?"

Mary and Miss Tavers exchanged polite greetings; then the latter broke out with a low chuckle.

"Oh, it is too droll for us to act like stuffy matrons," she said merrily, and came forward with her mittened hand extended. "I wish you would call me Rebeccah. We might as well be friends from the first. Don't you agree?"

"Yes, of course," said Mary. Such an instant warmth from this elegantly dressed stranger put her a little at a loss. Shyly she shook hands and sat down on one of the striped Queen Anne chairs, wondering why Rodney had brought his sister.

Rodney seemed to sense her thoughts, for he sent her an apologetic smile. "You are probably wishing us at Jericho, but actually Rebeccah is not here to indulge in idle curiosity. She's—"

"I'm going to take you in tow," broke in Rebeccah. "That is, if we deal well together, and I think we shall, don't you? I never stop chattering, but I do know society, and Rodney says you want to enter it."

"I . . . yes," Mary stammered, glancing helplessly at Rodney.

Rebeccah regarded her a moment with her bright brown eyes set in a pretty heart-shaped face, and a faint smile hovered about her full lips. "What a task you've set for yourself. You're quite a little dowd." She sighed and sent a grimace Rodney's way in response to his frown. Then she glanced back at Mary. "I hope you have a great deal of money, for I am very expensive."

Mary dropped her eyes away from those faintly

contemptuous brown ones and gripped her hands together in her lap until her knuckles ached. She supposed she must look awful to this young woman, but it was unkind for Rebeccah to barb her.

"As a matter of fact," said Rodney, "Miss Clampton has just inherited an easy competence." He frowned. "I thought I had told you that."

"Fie." Rebeccah snapped her fingers. "How am I supposed to remember everything you may say? But if she has money, that is excellent. We shall have to hire a house, and there must be new clothes for both of us, and . . ."

She chattered on, listing a number of things that made Mary's head almost spin. She unhappily remembered her resolve to take nothing from his lordship, but the clothes and parties Rebeccah was talking of were the things she'd dreamed of all her life. For so long she had ached to dress in pretty gowns and go dancing and have the gentlemen compliment her; now these things were coming within her reach, and it was unbearably difficult to hold to her decision.

There must be something hideous planned for her to do in exchange, else she would not be tempted with so much. But her eyes could not tear themselves away from Rebeccah's appearance, set off to such perfection by a morning dress in the new slim style, with little puffed sleeves and a silken yellow sash caught high under the bosom. And how charmingly that jaunty little chip straw bonnet framed Rebeccah's face. Rodney was likewise dressed fashionably, with two fobs dangling from a striped waistcoat, and neatly polished ankle boots upon his feet. Mary studied both of them and sighed to herself. Was she not foolish to give up genteel company such as theirs when she could have it? No. She bit her lip to make herself hold firm. She would not be an idiot for all the pretty clothes in the world, no matter how wonderful it would be to have just one dress such as the one Rebeccah was wearing.

Suddenly she realized that Rebeccah's chatter had stopped. Mary looked up with a guilty start, to find them both staring at her. Warmth flashed across her face.

"I am sorry," she stammered. "I did not quite hear that last—"

"I asked," said Rebeccah with the faintly superior smile back on her lips, "if it is agreed that I shall take charge of you."

Mary held her breath and wondered where her heart had gone. Now was her chance to speak her mind and stop this before things got out of hand. She swallowed, fighting the urge to wipe away the dab of perspiration on her chin. They were still staring at her. Mary swallowed again and thought she would speak then, but the words stuck in her throat. Despair sank through her like a stone falling through water. She was just too weak. Inside she knew she was doing the wrong thing, but she could not bear for Rodney to turn her out with nothing but this borrowed dress to her name.

"Yes, of course," she said in a voice that sounded odd to her own ears. "I would like that very much." And that was the truth, but she knew that what she wanted to do and what she should do were not at all the same. She knew that she was making a mistake, but she could not help herself.

"Well!" said Rodney abruptly, jumping up from his chair. "I'll pop out and give the order for your trunks to be unloaded. Then I've got to return to London. Must be there by tomorrow. If you'll excuse me?"

He bowed to both of them and went out with a quick step.

Rebeccah removed her hat. "We may as well start at once. You look abominable," she said in a sharp, censorious tone so different from the one she had used only moments before. "Come along."

And without further delay she led Mary upstairs to be measured. Her eyes took in every detail of the house, Mary noted, and she even peered a moment at the bottom of an ivory-colored vase standing on the dressing table in Mary's room. She caught Mary staring at her and set the vase down somewhat quickly.

"How I hate the country," she said with a deep

sigh, ringing the bell and wandering over to gaze out
the window. "One must admire the flowers, but to be
obliged to deal with these tedious rustics for servants
is the outside of enough." She frowned and turned
away from the window. "I wonder how you bear it."
Without waiting for Mary to reply, she began wandering about the room again, restlessly rearranging all
the delicate bric-a-brac that Mary so far had not
dared to touch lest something end up broken.

Almost at once the door opened to show the meek
downstairs maid panting on the threshold. She bobbed
a curtsy, her eyes wide.

Rebeccah turned lazily from her examination of the
workmanship of the draperies. "Ah, so *you* are Miss
Clampton's abigail. I confess I had wondered, Mary,
if you were to prove deficient in this quarter as well."
Her smile flashed at Mary and was instantly replaced
by a frown for the maid. "Get in here at once, you
lazy wretch! We've been waiting an age."

Annoyed, Mary stepped forward. "But she is
not—"

Rebeccah held up a hand as though she were a dis-
tracting child and glanced haughtily at the maid. "If
you can ply a tolerable needle, fetch a sewing box
and any decent bolt of cloth in the house." The maid
vanished, and she glanced at Mary with her head
tilted. "How glad I am that you have a servant," she
said, smiling. "My own had to be dismissed only this
week, so here I am, having to make shift for myself."

Mary was beginning to revise her first impression of
this young woman. "But, Rebeccah . . ." she said impatiently, not liking how swiftly Rebeccah was seizing
the reins of complete authority. "The wench is—"

"Oh, pooh, you needn't tell me." Rebeccah laughed
as she took down a book of fashion plates from a
small corner bookshelf. "I *know* you don't mind sharing. What is her name?"

"I don't know." Mary hastened on at the expression
on Rebeccah's face: "I have been trying to tell you
she is not my abigail. She is the downstairs maid. I
haven't any personal servant."

"I see." Rebeccah raked her over again with hard

brown eyes. Mary tightened her lips, irritated that Rebeccah could make her feel ashamed with a mere glance. "Then we shall make her an abigail in any case," said Rebeccah with a little shrug.

Mary was startled. "But won't his lordship object to our taking one of his servants?"

"My dear child!" Rebeccah burst out laughing, but Mary found it not laughter in which she could join. She shifted uncomfortably beneath Rebeccah's frankly condescending gaze. Rebeccah chuckled again and shook her dark curls. "If you are so green as to think that Menton knows more than a third of his servants, then there is no hope for y—"

Her heart stopping with a sudden painful lurch, Mary rushed up and gripped Rebeccah's arm. *"Whom* did you say?" she blurted out through stiff lips.

Rebeccah stared at her as though thinking her gone suddenly mad. "Gracious! What *are* you about?"

Mary gripped her arm harder. "What d-did you call his lordship?"

"Menton." A line appeared between Rebeccah's finely arched brows. "What makes you stare like that?"

Mary struggled away from the numbing fog that threatened to devour her. She was suddenly too warm, but a chill tickled up and down her spine until she feared she might faint. "The old devil!" she whispered savagely, stumbling away from Rebeccah, to cling to the thick oaken bedpost. "So I have been tricked again."

"My dear, you are overwrought," Rebeccah's arm were suddenly around her, leading her to a chair and pushing her into it. The maid reappeared at that moment beneath the double load of a bolt of cloth and the housekeeper's large sewing box. Rebeccah dispatched her off at once for a glass of water and some hartshorn. Then she knelt before Mary, who was staring ahead at nothing. "There, there, Mary dearest. What has put you in such a taking? I declare, if you are not the very replica of a ghost!"

The scorn and mockery were gone from her rich voice. Mary looked up with a gulp and read only friendly concern in her heart-shaped face. Desperately, hardly able to think of what she was doing for the panic that pressed in upon her from all sides, she gripped Rebeccah's hand. "Oh, please! Are you telling me that this is the Earl of Menton's house?" Her voice shook with every word, and indeed it was an ordeal just to utter the question for the horror which filled her. That she had fallen again into the clutches of this man was unthinkable!

Rebeccah eyed her with open puzzlement. "Why, of course it is. But you know that. You know the earl well—"

"Oh, yes," said Mary with bitterness that half-choked her, and thought of the malevolent-faced aristocrat with the silver hair who had sent her to the hell of Newgate without the faintest stirrings of mercy. "I know him all too well."

"Fie! You make no sense," snapped Rebeccah in impatience, pulling free of Mary's grasp. "First you do not know him, then you do. And why you should speak of him with such loathing, I cannot fathom, for though he is the veriest wretch toward his brother, he is everywhere liked. He sets the fashion now that he has put off his black gloves and—"

"Black gloves for whom?" asked Mary with a frown. "His wife?"

"Wife!" Rebeccah stared. "Certainly not. He hasn't got a wife." She suddenly nodded. "Oh! I see. You are thinking of the dowager countess. No, no, she is in perfect health, though she would rather die than admit it. It is the *late* earl they have been mourning. The eighth Earl of Menton. I am referring to his son, the *ninth* one."

Mary started from her chair. "He is dead?" she asked, and a great weight seemed to fly from her heart. "How long?"

"Since January. It was a very sorrowful occasion," said Rebeccah in a repressive tone. "Rodney has remarked several times on how Aubrey has changed since succeeding to the earldom. Of course—do sit back down, Mary!—of course it was a great blow to

him, I've heard especially since he was abroad at the
time and learned the news by letter."

Mary sank back down in her chair, no longer listening. She had noticed no sons at the ball that had been
her undoing, so it was unlikely that this present earl
knew anything about her. Unless . . . unless he had
learned about her imprisonment and decided to have
mercy upon her. She frowned, clenching and un-
clenching her hands together in her lap, unaware of
the maid returning with some water for her. For if the
new Lord Menton—if that indeed was the name of
the man who had struck that bargain with her—knew
who she was and had come to release her, why had
he made such a contract at all? Surely he could not
know of her connection with his father. She could not
believe the old scoundrel willing to repeat the details
of her own father's disgrace at his hands to anyone.
But, again, what was the son about? Either he had
chosen her by chance, or he knew exactly who she
was and thought to find her more willing to fall in
with his plans.

If she had been distrustful before of her new circumstances, she was decidedly uneasy now. With a
cold lump sliding down into her stomach, she realized
that she had indeed stumbled into a trap and that it
was much deeper and more frightening than she had
feared.

Chapter Four

MARY MIGHT HAVE fled the house—never to return—
at that very moment rather than face the pit of uncertainty yawning at her feet any longer, but by the time
Rebeccah dismissed her for the day, her initial panic
had calmed. She began to think less of fleeing and
more of how she might turn her present circumstances
to use. Detesting Rebeccah's arrogance, Mary nevertheless realized that here was a chance to acquire the
more refined social graces. Since Rebeccah had been
brought here to teach her those things, why not stay
and learn them? Lord Menton owed her something for
the wrongs done her father and herself at his sire's
hands. Why not accept the sojourn here in this elegant
little country manor as payment for those wrongs? She
would, of course, make her departure before he could
come to fetch her away to London. Surely, if she was
quick to learn, she could qualify herself to take work
as a governess. That was genteel employment, and
anything was to be preferred over doing whatever
Lord Menton had in mind. Yes. She gave herself a
nod. Her decision was made.

The very next day a dancing master was hired to
come every morning from Brighton, and Mary was
thrilled to be learning all the steps to reels, jigs, and
all the other country dances now the rage in London,
as well as the more difficult cotillons and the fright-
eningly intricate minuet. Mary had watched gaily
dressed ladies and gentlemen speed by her on their

way to balls and parties, and she had long dreamed of tasting the excitement of the dance floor. Now her shyness melted away during the morning sessions while the dancing master drilled her over and over with the utmost politeness, to Rebeccah's indifferent accompaniment on the pianoforte.

Gradually the days began to assume a rigorous but pleasant pattern. After dancing in the morning and a cold luncheon, Mary spent the lazy fall afternoons sketching whatever Rebeccah deemed suitable, learning how to ride in Rebeccah's old riding habit, and studying the languages of French and Italian. In the evenings she was made either to sing—the thought of which made both her and Rebeccah shudder—or to practice the pianoforte. Despite tiresome conflicts of personality between them, Rebeccah's chatter was always filled with the social customs and taboos of the ton, and she was diligent in correcting Mary's slightest mistake in deportment.

Then came the afternoon early in October when it was raining and Mary could not go out riding. Rebeccah set her to embroidering a new chair covering for her room, but she spent more time dividing her gaze dreamily between the small but cheery fire of the drawing room and the rain-washed view through the large window. Rebeccah was reclining on the satin-backed sofa, looking at fashion plates. Everything was cozy and quiet.

"Mary," Rebeccah said suddenly, breaking Mary from her pleasant abstraction.

Mary looked up with a guilty start and picked up her needle. "I am sorry," she said at once. "I daydream too much."

"Yes, you most certainly do, and worse stitches I have never seen. Don't pull them so tight."

Her head down, Mary nodded and began setting stitches as rapidly as she could.

"Mary," said Rebeccah again, putting down her book and yawning. "It is time that we depart for London."

Mary's embroidery slid to the floor, and she stared

at Rebeccah with a chill draining down through her.
"What did you say?"

"Oh, pray, spare us one of these spells," said Rebeccah with irritation. "You know I have no patience
with—"

"But London!" said Mary in a choked voice. "Now?
Why?" She could not keep her fright hidden.

Rebeccah eyed her with impatience. "Really," she
said, tapping the sofa arm with her tapering fingers. "I
wonder if anything this last month has pierced your
cloud. Why, indeed." Her lips curled in plain irritation
and she swung her feet down to the floor. "The season
will be beginning in another week. How could you be
such a pea goose as to forget it?"

Mary was scarcely listening. She had forgotten it
and everything else for greed. How could she have
been such a fool? Now that she had allowed herself to
taste a finer life, it was going to be much harder to
force herself to pull back. How cruel fate was to make
her deprive herself!

She glanced at Rebeccah. "Lord Menton has written to you, has he not?" The words were like ice
within her; she could barely hear her own voice for
the buzzing within her ears. "When shall he b-be coming?"

"Why, Menton is not coming here." Rebeccah
smiled. "What droll thoughts you have. And, no, certainly he has not written to me. Why should he? We
shall surprise him and everyone else." Her brown eyes
sparkled. "How amusing it shall be. No one will know
who you are, but won't they all be curious to find out
when Menton sends a nod your way! You shall be the
mystery miss from Brighton, and perhaps even a minor rage—unless you poker up. Then, I warn you, I
shall have no patience with you at all."

"Fudge," said Mary in an unsteady voice. She
jumped to her feet, unable to stay in her chair any
longer. "I do not have the least desire to join the . . .
the ranks of giddy debutantes half my age!"

Rebeccah frowned, the expression in her eyes going
suddenly sharp. "But of course you shall be presented
and attend all the parties. Otherwise, what is the rea-

son for all this work? I declare, almost you could make me vexed. Already I have written my dear friend Katherine Ellsford, and she has been so kind as to send us both an invitation to one of her routs. I am sure she must be the most obliging person in the world, so very kind, and always so willing to be pleased."

Mary twisted her fingers together over and over during this speech, wanting desperately to break in with some statement that would rescue her from this trap without arousing Rebeccah's curiosity. "But, Rebeccah, I am not yet ready to face—"

"Nonsense." Rebeccah also rose to her feet. "Now, listen to me. I have not absented myself from society this past month and more to relegate myself back to the schoolroom on your behalf, only to have you take fright at the last moment." She frowned. "You are the most unnatural person. I do not believe I have ever seen a female fall into such a panic over the prospect of entering society. And I was brought here under the impression that you wanted to—"

"It is a wrong impression!" said Mary wildly. "I do not . . . I mean, I should like to, but not . . . Oh, you do not understand at all!" She whirled away to the window with a heaving bosom and a strong urge to cry.

"No, I do not understand." Rebeccah walked over and seized her by the arm to whirl her around. "But there is no need whatsoever for this disgusting display of hysterics. You have been starry-eyed for a month; I see no reason for this about-face. Tomorrow, if it is not raining, we shall go to Brighton and see about purchasing dresses enough to last us until we can have new wardrobes made up in London. That is all, Mary! You may calm yourself at once. I have no desire to see another of these fits. And do not believe for a second that I shall give over this scheme, for it shall send my place in the ton soaring with a protégée of Menton's under my wing. You may be assured that is the only reason I weary myself with you!"

Turning on her heel, she stalked out of the room, leaving Mary alone at the window in an agony of fear and self-mortification and uncertainty. What should she do now? Blindly she struck at the cold windowsill with her fists, then buried her hot face in her arms. She was an utter fool, she thought furiously, too overwrought now for tears. The only thing to do was to pack up her few belongings and leave.

But now she knew that she must have references to gain employment as a governess, references which she had no means of obtaining. If she had not been so careless, she would have realized that her time was dwindling rapidly and made adequate preparations. Since everything they purchased was charged to Lord Menton's account, she had no money; if she did run away, she would be stranded here in the country, where there were no prospects better than the situation she was now in. That left the notion of working as a servant, but every sensibility within her rose up in outrage at the thought of slaving as a menial the rest of her life. She was the granddaughter of a baronet, though everyone might think her the most wretched guttersnipe, and she would not bring herself so low again. Newgate had been enough humiliation; she could not bear any more. She clenched her fists, furious at being so neatly captured in Menton's net. How she wished she had never crossed the path of that man and his accursed family!

The following day did bring clear skies, and they spent most of it in an assault on Brighton's best shops. Returning in the late afternoon, the carriage overflowing with their purchases, Mary escaped while Rebeccah was directing the butler and footmen in the unloading and ran upstairs to throw on her riding habit. It took but minutes to find her crop and slip down the servant stairs and out of the house to the stables. Her groom was visibly reluctant to let her ride out alone, but she dismissed him with an angry stamp of her foot and allowed the stableboy to boost her up into the sidesaddle. Reining her mount around sharply, she rode out through the park at a brisk trot.

The mare was a small nimble chestnut she had named Jewel, and was so gentle-mannered that Mary had no fear of riding out alone. She desperately wanted a few moments to herself away from Rebeccah, who never made the least attempt to understand her. And the shopping and warmth of the ride back in the open carriage had given Mary the headache. She relaxed slightly now in the cool depths of the oak park and let Jewel amble through the stately, moss-covered trees in any way the mare preferred. Jewel lowered her small head and blew at the soft pale grass, while overhead birds chirped and called to one another.

It was all so quiet and foreign to the bustle of London. Mary was not at all eager to return to the sprawling rough metropolis, even if Lord Menton had not been hanging over her head. She had never had many chances before to visit the country, but she thought she much preferred it to London's breakneck pace that never slowed, even in darkness.

All of her thinking yesterday had been useless. It only muddled her further and had given her no solution other than that she must confront Menton and tell him to his face that she wanted no part of his schemes. Her spirits sank as they always did when she thought of this. Yes, she was afraid of him, though surely he could not be the ogre she thought him. But his father had been utterly heartless, and the son now held her firmly in his power.

No. Her fingers tightened on the reins, making Jewel's ears flick back alertly. Mary set her chin in determination. He would find himself much mistaken if he thought her cheaply bought or easily bent to his will. Though she loved this peaceful countryside, she was a stranger to it and had no idea of how to go on here. But in filthy, brawling London, she could slip out and hide forever if she had to—if he would not release her from that odious contract. It was impossible now to remember all the things he had promised her, but she was glad of that. She did not want to be tempted further.

Suddenly she thrust away all of her jostling thoughts and sent Jewel into a canter. For a few minutes it was heavenly to fly along through the trees with the breeze in her face and thick hair. The danger of whipping branches kept her busy ducking and guiding the mare, so that for a blissful moment she was released from her worries. Then they were out of the trees, with the road just ahead. She found an opening in the hedge bordering the ditch and forced the mare through for a slow amble homeward.

Rounding a small bend, she was startled by seeing a country gig approaching her at a brisk trot. Unwisely she had allowed Jewel to walk in the center of the road, and now she reined the mare to the left as fast as possible. The gig, which was occupied by a youthful-looking couple, made no effort to slow. Mary was tempted to shout at them in annoyance, when one of the wheels suddenly flew off with a loud crack.

Mary gasped; the gig bounced and tipped, spilling its occupants; and the horse pulling it half-reared and kicked at its traces. At once Mary spurred Jewel forward to cut the horse off before it could bolt and cause more damage by dragging the gig through the ditch. She jumped down, soothed the frightened beast, and tied her mare's reins to its bridle.

"Oh, *please!* Do help me!"

The young lady, who looked to be about seventeen, stopped waving her lace handkerchief over the face of her unconscious companion long enough to implore Mary's assistance. Mary hurried to her side and knelt beside the young man.

He was hardly more than a boy; Mary thought he must be no more than twenty. He was also obviously an aspirant to a sort of dandyism that seemed to be limited only by lack of experience. From his insufferably high shirt points and elaborately tied cravat to the jaunty gold tassels on his Hessians he looked complete to more than a shade. She winced at the half-dozen fobs attached to a waistcoat of very broad green stripes and a coat with a nipped-in waist and too much buckram padding at the shoulders.

"Why do you stare at him so, doing nothing? He is dead, isn't he? Oh, dear!" The young lady broke into a flood of tears that her little handkerchief seemed totally incapable of handling.

A bruise purpling upon the young man's temple beneath his golden curls seemed to be both evidence of the cause of his unconscious state and his only injury. Mary loosened his cravat and regarded the young lady with some irritation.

"I do hope you're not such a watering pot by nature."

Enormous blue eyes lifted to glare at her. There was a defiant sniff. "I'm sure it's very easy for a total stranger to be so heartless. After all, it isn't your cousin who is lying dead at our feet."

"He's only out from a blow to his head. There certainly may be some more serious injury, but he is *not* dead!" Mary pointed. "You have only to see his chest moving to discern that."

Unwillingly the large eyes examined the young man's chest, which was indeed rising and falling regularly. A faint tinge of pink appeared in the fair cheeks, then abruptly the blue eyes sparked, and she crumpled her handkerchief angrily.

"What a wretch he is! I was quite prepared to be sorry for making him take me driving, but as usual, he is not worth the effort."

Mary glanced at the back of the gig. Good, there was no portmanteau strapped to the back. She was relieved that she'd not chanced into the middle of a thwarted elopement.

"You aren't up to mischief, I trust?" she asked anyway.

The blue eyes fell beneath Mary's gaze. "Well, it is not mischief exactly. Harton has been so obnoxious these past days, I had to do *something* to take him down a peg." She glanced at the young man with such loathing that Mary had to hide a smile.

"I must say I think he has been sufficiently lowered."

The girl colored. "I had no notion that the wheel would break. I made him drive me out so that we would become lost and Grandmama would give him one of her famous scolds. But now she shall only make over him more because of this wretched mishap."

"You aren't hurt yourself?"

She shook her head. "No-no. I daresay later on I

will be a little shaky on account of the scare." She suddenly frowned at Harton. "Shouldn't he be awake by now?"

Mary confessed a slight uneasiness. "Perhaps I had better ride on for help."

"Do you live nearby?" The young lady looked at her in considerable astonishment. "But I've never seen you before!"

"Certainly you haven't." Mary smiled, a little thinly, she thought. "I am a guest of Lord Menton's." How easily the name came out, despite all her trepidations in uttering it.

"Gracious, how odd!" The large blue eyes widened. "Grandmama *will* be vexed not to have known they are here."

"They aren't," said Mary, hating the feeling that she was guilty of lying when she really was not. "They are letting me use the house for a short time."

"Oh! Why, how very kind! Tell me, is the house very grand inside now, since Lord Menton has purchased it? All of Brighton has been dying to see what changes he's made, but he's such an old fustybudget, no one's ever been invited to call. Of course, that's of no moment, since he's never visited it *once*." She broke off abruptly and blushed. "I am so sorry! I should not speak of him so before *you!* I mean, he is your host, and . . ." She bit her lip and sent Mary a helpless smile. "Grandmama says I have the most unruly tongue. Please forgive me!"

"Yes, I will," said Mary in amusement. It was so refreshing to talk with someone who had no thoughts of using her. "If I should ride on, will you mind staying here alone with your . . . er . . . with Harton?"

"Well," said the young lady reluctantly, "I suppose someone must, even if he is odious."

"Good," said Mary, moving back to the mare and mounting herself with difficulty. How handy a groom is! she thought, gathering up the reins quickly as Jewel tried to step out. Mary glanced down at the girl, still kneeling in the ditch. "I shan't be gone more than a few minutes."

And indeed, it did not take long to canter back to

the stables, give a brief explanation to the head groom, and ride back behind the slightly old-fashioned coach.

The young lady greeted her eagerly. "You weren't long at all, just as you promised. How good you are!"

At this moment Harton responded to the groom's feeling for broken limbs by a long moan and an abrupt awakening. "Good God! Who the devil . . . ? No, by Jove, I won't be robbed!"

"Oh, for heaven's sake, Harton, do be quiet," ordered the young lady. "There is no need to set up such a howl. You're getting quite enough attention already."

"Arabella!" cried Harton furiously, "You little minx, I ought to—Ow!"

"Bit of a puffed ankle, miss," said the groom to Mary. "Like as not, the young gentleman's sprained it some."

"Now, see here!" said Harton in great alarm. "You'll not cut off my boot! I just bought this pair last week! Took the very last of this quarter's allowance."

"I'm sure none of us care about your silly boot," said Arabella. "And if you don't stop raising such a grand fuss, these kind people will like as not get a disgust of you and leave us to ourselves again."

Only now did Harton really bother to take in his surroundings. He saw Mary and had the graciousness to look a little contrite.

"Excuse me, ma'am. I didn't see you before."

"Yes, that is quite clear," said Mary with a smile to take the reproach from her words. She stepped forward to him. "If you will endeavor to be quieter, I think your head may not pound so much."

"Lord, yes, it hurts like the very devil." The frown returned to his round face. "But your man there won't cut off my boot, will he? If it's only a sprain, I can wait until I'm home, and Jacobs can pull it off."

"No, it can't wait, miss," said the groom in response to Mary's glance. "If it ain't brought off now, it'll be twice the devil later."

"There, Harton, you see?" said Arabella in what Mary considerd unfitting satisfaction.

"Perhaps the boot can merely be pulled off now," suggested Mary.

The groom shrugged. "Aye. It may pain the young gentleman a bit, but—"

"Do it at once!" commanded Harton, snapping his fingers. "And try not to get too many finger smudges on the gloss." He sighed. "Jacobs is going to have a rare blue fit anyway—*Ouch!*"

"Sorry, sir," said the groom apologetically, and tugged again.

Harton clenched his hands and howled until the boot at last came off.

"All right," said Arabella. "It's off; you can stop screaming. I declare, Harton, you're worse than a stuck pig."

"Never mind," said Mary hastily, for Harton was very drawn around the mouth. "If you will but give your direction, these men will drive you home."

The whistling stableboy finished untangling Harton's and Arabella's horse from its traces and tied it to the rear of the coach before helping lift Harton inside.

Arabella turned gratefully to Mary. "Oh, thank you so very much again. It is too bad that we should meet *now* when we are about to go to London. For my come-out," she added naively. "I should like to see you again." She brightened. "But how silly of me! Of course you shall be going to London too. Won't you?"

"Yes," said Mary before she thought.

Arabella clapped her hands together. "Then may I call on you there?"

There was nothing to do now but continue with a lie. "Certainly, child," said Mary with an attempt to smile. "But mayn't you tell me your name before you go? I am Miss Clampton."

"How do you do?" Arabella curtsied politely, with her cheeks pink. "Please! I am so sorry. You will think me so rude! I am Arabella Monteforte. What is your London address? Oh, goodness, never mind! I'd never recall it. We shall meet at all manner of places."

Relieved at being spared the admission that she had

no idea of what her address would be, Mary was content to agree quietly.

"Arabella, *do* come on!" said Harton from within the coach.

"He is a wretch!" whispered Arabella fiercely. "He does not thank you, so I shall for him. Good-bye, Miss Clampton. How glad I am that we met you!"

She climbed into the coach and stuck her head out the window to wave her handkerchief until they were out of sight.

Mary rode home slowly, conscious of a renewed lump of gloom witin her. Arabella was such a sweet, impetuous imp; suddenly Mary longed anew for that season in London. How she wanted to go to the assemblies and meet more people like Arabella! Surely everyone in the ton was not arrogant like Lord Menton or false like Rebeccah. Mary sighed, suddenly wondering if there might yet be a way to experience the pleasures of society.

Not until she performed whatever task Lord Menton had set for her. The words swooped up out of nowhere and locked themselves into her mind. She gritted her teeth in rage. How she hated him! He was a fiend to torment her by offering all the things she longed for. But she could not pay his price. It was wrong; it must be against the law. She bit her trembling lip and dredged up a shaky sense of determination. Whatever it would cost, she must not give in again.

Chapter Five

WHEN MARY ARRIVED, she was alarmed to see a groom in the stableyard walking a team of matched bays hitched to a gentleman's curricle. She reined up short, with her breath caught in her throat. Could Menton be here? Involuntarily her hands tightened on the reins, and Jewel backed a reluctant step. Swallowing, she battled the sense of panic that urged her to flee at once. No, she told herself, tensing all her muscles, so that Jewel sidled and tossed her head; no, she would not do anything so foolish.

Not giving herself further time to hesitate, she beckoned to a stableboy, who hurried at once to seize Jewel's bridle. Mary stared down into his tanned, respectful face. "Who is our guest?" she asked, hardly able to speak normally for the dryness of her throat.

The lad touched his forelock. "It's Mr. Keath come, miss. 'Is lordship's brother."

She frowned, unsure of what to think about this piece of news, and dismounted quickly. Deciding the visitor would most likely be found in the library, and having no wish to encounter him, she swept her train over her arm and hurried across the terrace to let herself into the drawing room.

"Mary!" Rebeccah turned back from the door, where she had been in the process of escorting the gentleman out. "My dear, we've been waiting this *age* for you."

She did not bother to conceal the annoyance in her

rich voice. Mary glanced swiftly into a wall mirror and perceived with dismay that her hair was frowsed and that her face was covered with dust. Rebeccah seized her hand and led her over to the gentleman waiting politely in the doorway.

"Mary, may I make known to you the honorable Thomas Keath? Menton's brother, you know. What a pity you did not return sooner. He is just on his way out."

Had she been in a calmer mood, Mary might have easily been dazzled by the tall young man turning politely to greet her. He had the golden locks and chiseled profile of a Greek Adonis and needed only to exchange his buckskins and top boots for a chiton and sandals to make the vision complete.

He bowed over her hand. "I am delighted not to have missed making your acquaintance after all, Miss Clampton." His voice was pleasant if somewhat unremarkable, but she caught a hint of underlying indifference that made his words ring hollow.

Flustered, she withdrew her none-too-clean hand from his cold grasp. Unable to think of any reply, she gave him a stiff little nod and turned to Rebeccah instead. "It is wrong of me to be coming in so late," she said, twisting her whip between her hands and wondering if Lord Menton had sent his brother here to inspect her progress. She lifted her chin in defiance. "But there was a gig overturned on the road, and I was obliged to lend what assistance I could."

Rebeccah's eyes narrowed and she started to speak, but Keath was quicker.

"Overturned?" he asked with raised eyebrows. "Was the occupant a slender gentleman wearing a brown coat and a belcher neckerchief?"

She shook her head, searching his face for a resemblance to his brother, whose features she could not at all recall well.

The spark of interest faded from Keath's face. He pulled out a lacquered snuffbox from his pocket and proceeded to help himself to a pinch with graceful turns of his wrist. "I trust the wreck has been cleared away by now?"

"No, sir." Mary decided she did not like his eyes, which were of so pale a blue they seemed almost colorless. "But it is half in the ditch and will not obstruct your way."

"Good," said Keath, and shut his snuffbox with a snap.

Rebeccah snorted. "No doubt it was only some moon calf trying to play top whip with his father's best horses. Perhaps this will teach him to avoid such larks." She sniffed and laid a hand on Mary's arm. "You cannot conceive how vexed I was to find you had gone out. Especially after Mr. Keath was so kind to pause here a moment on his way back to London."

Keath bowed with an amused glance at Rebeccah that told Mary they were better acquainted than she had first supposed. "Yes," he said, his face alight now from some private joke that Rebeccah obviously shared. "But tell me, Miss Clampton, are you really an acquaintance of my brother's? Since we have . . . er . . . grown apart these past months, I am not always known to those of his set, but I fancy I should have met you before."

A little chill sliced through Mary, and all at once she was distinctly uneasy before his gaze. He was frankly studying her now, and an angry flush rose up her throat into her cheeks. "You are mistaken, sir," she said coldly. "I am quite positive that we have not met before. Nor do I find anything the least remarkable in that." Rebeccah's fingers tightened painfully on her arm, but Mary added: "I acquainted with your brother, but I am not a member of his set."

Rebeccah's face had paled in annoyance, but Keath seemed unruffled.

He smiled. "Of course, you are right. Forgive my presumption. Ah," he said then, as though suddenly remembering, and glanced at Rebeccah. "Do bring Miss Clampton along to my little dinner party on the twelfth, Becky. I am sure she would enjoy it." He turned back to Mary. "It will be a select group, with cards and perhaps a little dancing for entertainment. You do dance, don't you, Miss Clampton?"

"To be sure, she does," said Rebeccah. "And I have slaved long enough to see to it that she—"

"Then will you come, Miss Clampton?"

Mary hesitated. She should not accept any invitations, since as soon as they were in London she meant to confront Menton with her desire to have done with his scheme. He would be furious, of course, but he could scarcely force her to go against her own wishes. In the light of this, she was reluctant to lie to Keath by telling him she would come.

She glanced up at him to make her regrets and was startled by the sharpness of his gaze. At once, with a chill of dismay she realized she had been too openly hesitant. Now he was offended. Rebeccah jabbed her in the ribs.

"I . . . yes, certainly," Mary stammered. "Thank you." Smothered in mortification, her face aflame, she turned and hurried away to the open terrace doors, where she stopped and scolded herself for being such an idiot. She wished he would go and take his starched cravat and his insufferably polished manners with him.

In a moment, after receiving his caped driving coat, gloves, and beaver hat from Roberts, and declining an invitation to dinner from Rebeccah on the grounds that his superior would take it amiss were he to delay in making his appearance at Whitehall on the morrow, Keath took his leave with a bow to Mary and a careless wave to Rebeccah.

She sank down on a blue-damask-covered chair with a sigh. "You are the most vexing, spiteful-tongued creature, Mary! I particularly wanted you to enter into Mr. Keath's good graces, but what must you do but fly into the boughs and deliver quite the rudest set-down I have ever heard, then follow it up with that horrid show of making up your mind over his invitation!" Rebeccah thrust herself from the chair and began to pace. "I declare you to be utterly impossible. Really! Running off this afternoon without the least word of your whereabouts, and *then* coming in with your hair all blown and your hat askew. There is even dirt on your face." She threw up her hands. "He will have such an idea of you. I shudder to think on it."

Mary decided that if she was obliged to hear one more scolding word from Rebeccah, she would give way completely to her surging emotions. She turned swiftly from the doorway. "I am sorry," she said with a snap. "I tried to avoid meeting him."

"Gammon!" declared Rebeccah. "And what purpose, pray, would that have served? He can be most beneficial to us in London, for he knows everyone and is received everywhere."

Gripping the doorjamb, Mary looked up in anger. "Must you put everyone to use?"

Rebeccah jerked around as though burnt, and for a moment Mary was glad she had been able to sting her. Rebeccah took two hasty steps forward and clenched her fists. "What an odious, ungrateful wretch you are! Thomas . . . Mr. Keath, I mean, is a particular friend of mine, and I . . ." She stopped suddenly, and visibly mastered herself. "If you had only come back at once and sent the head groom to see to this odious wreck—"

"There was a young lady involved," said Mary, determined to be unrepentant. "I felt I could not withdraw my support from her without appearing callous." Mary paused a moment to study Rebeccah's stormy face. It was very odd. She had thought anger would render Rebeccah's type of beauty magnificent, but instead, her air of elegance vanished, making her seem plain and shrewish.

Now Rebeccah's lips curled scornfully. "Dear, kindhearted Mary. I am sure you would stop to aid even a filthy tinker."

"It happens that the young lady's name is Arabella Monteforte!" said Mary, stung. "She looked to be of unexceptional—"

"Monteforte!" A complete change flashed through Rebeccah's face. She stared at Mary with a sudden smile of incredulous delight and clapped her hands. "What a perfect stroke of fortune! You are *made* now, for I should never have been able to bring you into Lady Monteforte's sphere. She is the most odious old woman, with a tongue like a whip, but she will have to acknowledge your assistance to her granddaughter. Then, of course, it shall be no task at all to get vouchers to Almack's, for between Lord Menton and Lady Monteforte, everyone shall be eager to receive you." She laughed, to Mary's astonishment, and performed a few light steps of a lively reel. "Provoking creature! Why did you not tell me this news at once? Then I would not have been obliged to read you such a scold. Run along upstairs now. You haven't much time to change before dinner."

Mary had no liking of being dismissed in the manner one would use with a child, but escaping to her room was precisely what she wanted to do. She hurried out and ran up the stairs, ringing for Jenny as soon as she entered her room, then dismissing the little maid upon her arrival moments later. Mary struggled to unhook her riding habit and paced round the small room as she undressed, leaving things where she happened to fling them.

More than ever she distrusted Rebeccah. She was not sure why, exactly, but she thought that Rebeccah's artful tongue and facility at hiding herself behind a facade had to be part of it. The sooner they reached London, the better it would be, for they certainly could not stay here much longer without falling into constant cap-pulling.

She lifted her chin, her hazel eyes sparkling green from behind their golden flecks. Her breeding was irreproachable, and now that she was better dressed, she was pleased to think that it showed. Satisfaction began to glow within her, and she savored the vision of his chagrin when he saw that she was a lady of breeding, and not the common thief he thought her. Yes, she would thank him in her prettiest manner for securing her release from prison, but she would not consent to whatever foul scheme he had in mind.

Dressed and ready for dinner, she was walking to the door when the horror of the implications of what she had already agreed to quite suddenly pierced through her confident thoughts. Her hand fell numbly away from the knob. How could she be so doltish as to imagine Lord Menton would allow her to walk out on him, bearing the knowledge that he intended to do something quite against the law? If it was serious enough and important enough that he was willing to *marry* what he thought was a thief to carry it through, he would fulfill his threat to see her back in Newgate if she tried to make a bid for freedom now.

She stumbled over to the bed and sat down on the edge, stunned, her heart pounding so rapidly she could scarcely draw a full breath. How stupid she was not to have thought of the obvious earlier! She had blundered into his clutches like the veriest gudgeon, and now the trap was shut firmly about her. Mary clenched her fists in her lap and shut her eyes in despair. The man was a fiend. She was cornered from every side into doing his will.

Chapter Six

THE RIDE TO LONDON was made in the comfort of a hired chaise and four. Their trunks were strapped to the top, and the wide-eyed maid, Jenny, sat bolt upright in one corner for her first ride in a fine carriage. For Mary the hours passed slowly, for she could not keep an interest in the scenery forever. The day was cool, and she huddled within the first warm pelisse she had owned in years, mulling unhappily over the ordeal facing her in London. But after a while she wearied of even that and pushed the matter as far out of her mind as possible. She decided she must simply wait and see what was going to happen to her next.

That evening they put up at an inn some ten miles short of London, and the following morning proceeded into the metropolis at a leisurely pace. For the first time Mary found the bustle and noise distasteful. She stared out the chaise window at the filth of the streets and the closeness of the grimy buildings and wished she were back in the clean spaciousness of the countryside.

But London was her home all the same, and she could not stay aloof from the excitement for long, especially when the chaise reached the fashionable West End. It was a bright morning, and Mary glimpsed a few exquisitely dressed members of Quality in the act of descending their front steps. Despite her nervousness, she began to be caught up by this novel experi-

ence of riding through the streets in a respectable
equipage just like any other lady of breeding.

Rebeccah's eyes glowed. "How good it feels to be
back in town." She sighed happily and began straightening her hat. "I always feel quite wasted in the country. And won't Lord Menton be surprised to find us
here without a word? I am determined he shan't discover us except at someone's party." She laughed,
then leaned back against the green velvet squabs and
sent Mary a sly glance.

Mary glanced out at the street they had just turned
down. "Where are we going to, that we must wind
about forever? I thought we were to stay at Grillon's."

"Goodness, not a hotel." Rebeccah pretended to
shudder, and reassumed her smug smile. "We have a
house hired here on Bruton Street."

Mary blinked in surprise. "But how has this come
about? I thought you did not mean to let Lord Menton
know—"

"He is completely in the dark, I assure you." Rebeccah's smile widened, and she drew on her tan kid
gloves. "I wrote Rodney and bade him find us a place
with the strictest stipulation of secrecy."

"Fudge," said Mary, grabbing the seat as they
jerked to a rather abrupt halt. "He is Lord Menton's
secretary. He could hardly be expected to—"

"Oh, little Rodney does whatever I tell him," said
Rebeccah serenely. A footman came out of the small
house they had stopped before and opened the carriage door for them. She shot Mary an arch look. "He
has ever been devoted to me, and you must agree that
this is a perfectly harmless whim."

She allowed the footman to hand her out. Mary followed with some reluctance and stood a moment in the
street. "I still prefer that he be notified," said Mary
with her mouth gone dry at the thought of meeting him
again. "As my benefactor, he should—"

"Oh, pooh, you have no notion of fun." Rebeccah
turned her back and entered the house, greeting the
aged wisp of a butler and requesting he see to the payment of the postilions all in the same breath.

Mary hastened after her, not bothering to really

take note of her new abode. She caught up with Rebeccah in the hall and surrendered her pelisse to the parlor maid.

"Rebeccah," she persisted, wanting—now that she knew she must face the man—to get the unpleasant business finished as quickly as possible. "Are you sure it would not be better—"

"Yes, I am quite sure," snapped Rebeccah. "I am determined to see if you can take on your own merit or whether we must depend entirely upon a push from him. Of course, we shan't discount him completely, for that would be a great mistake. His position as a leader of fashion is unsurpassed. Men try to copy his cravats continuously, and he is a veritable nonpareil in all sports, even that loathsome boxing."

"He sounds odiously high in the instep to me," said Mary, attempting to sound unimpressed. She wandered into a small parlor, still in holland covers, and gazed all around.

"He is, of course." Following her, Rebeccah suddenly altered her tone. "I find him utterly the most disagreeable man I have ever met. No one dares put him in his place because he is so wealthy and well-received, but I should like to."

Something close to hatred was in Rebeccah's voice now. Mary turned from the window to look at her in surprise.

"Why do you hold him in such active dislike?" she asked, eager to learn more about her enemy. She was glad to know he was as bad as his father, though it did not make her position any better.

Rebeccah shrugged, picking up a piece of bric-a-brac and tracing its outlines with her finger. "He is a horrid man. I know of no one more cruel or black at heart."

Mary's blood chilled. She took an involuntary step forward. "How do you know?" she asked, her heart thumping.

"Everyone knows the heartless way he has treated Th . . . Mr. Keath since the death of their father." Rebeccah's eyes blazed. "As soon as the title passed

into his hands, he showed his true colors, cutting poor
Thomas off without a penny."

Mary started to ask more, but Rebeccah abruptly
seemed to recall herself and demanded they explore
the house. Mary found herself delighted with it. The
arrangement of the rooms, the selection of furniture, and the respectful demeanor of the servants all
pleased her. She was relieved that she was not to be
thrust immediately into an imposing town residence.
This house was small and cozy and private. She felt
safe here.

Rebeccah looked bored. She removed her hat,
swung it by its blue ribbons a moment, then tossed it
onto Mary's bed. "Tomorrow we shall have your hair
cut in the latest mode, then spend the rest of the day
shopping, for you simply *must* have a suitable ward-
robe. And my gowns are all looking positively
shabby."

Mary glanced up. "But won't clothes here be much
more expensive? I mean—"

"My dear, of course. That is half the fun of buying
them." Rebeccah sent her an arch glance. "Don't you
agree?"

Yes, why not? thought Mary decisively. She need
have no scruples against taking advantage of this opportunity to array herself in the first style of elegance.

Accordingly, the following afternoon they set out
for the shops of St. James's Street with the footman in
attendance, for, as Rebeccah explained repeatedly to
Mary, no lady must *ever* set foot on St. James's in the
afternoon *alone* if she did not wish to find her reputation in shreds. "Besides," continued Rebeccah, drawing her over to a milliner's window, "it can be *so*
disagreeable to be ogled by every vulgar rake who
strolls by. Do look at that poke bonnet in the corner!
I am persuaded it would be the very thing for driving
in the park. Don't you think so?"

The bonnet was indeed a vision, in palest blue, but
Mary could only feel its high crown would badly ac-
centuate her narrow face. "It's very fetching, I admit,
Rebeccah. But the color would not be the most becoming—"

"Not becoming? My dear, wherever are your thoughts? I have been said to look charming in blue."

Mary looked quickly back into the window to hide her confusion. She should have remembered that Rebeccah's first thoughts were always for herself. "Yes, yes, of course you are right," she said, striving to maintain a normal tone. "How stupid of me! It would suit you very well."

"Then I shall buy it," said Rebeccah with a nod. "Do you not see anything for yourself?"

Mary glanced back at the hats in the window. "I—"

"Well, perhaps there shall be something inside that you will like better."

Rebeccah swept inside the shop, leaving Mary to follow. "Yes, most certainly I shall take it," Rebeccah said, pointing out the bonnet to the assistant, who had come to them immediately. "I suppose it is shockingly expensive, but since his lordship is standing the nonsense, that is of no matter."

Left to her own devices, Mary lost no time in squandering his lordship's money by selecting a chip straw hat with a pink ribbon that made her look remarkably younger and carefree, and a charming little creation of green velvet that would match her new riding habit to perfection.

Rebeccah gave the shop assistant their address in Bruton Street for the hats to be delivered later that afternoon; then from the milliner's shop they set off down the street again. Turning into a dressmaker's establishment, they spent the majority of the afternoon choosing materials and being fitted by madame's deft assistants before at last setting out for Bruton Street with the footman carrying their various small parcels.

"Good afternoon, ladies."

Mary withdrew from her thoughts to return a civil greeting to Mr. Keath, who had halted his curricle beside them—to the severe detriment of passing traffic.

Rebeccah sent him her most charming smile. "Why, Mr. Keath, how mischievous of you to have crossed our path already. We but arrived in town yesterday."

Mary frowned at her in puzzlement. Didn't she realize that Menton's brother would be the best person to tell him of their presence here? But if Rebeccah had capriciously chosen to give up that absurd notion, then it was fine.

Keath bowed, holding in his impatient team with a casual hand. "Shopping already? You never change, Becky. But tell me." His blue eyes suddenly narrowed. "Are you on your way home yet, or is there still something you are in quest of?"

Mary stepped out of the way of a hurried portly merchant carrying a long cane and looked up in time to see Keath nod meaningfully at Rebeccah. To her surprise, Rebeccah suddenly stamped her foot.

"How foolish of me to have forgotten," she said in vexation. "Had you not made mention . . ." She turned on Mary. "Dear Mary, the silliest thing. I had quite forgotten that I meant to take out a subscription at the lending library."

Mary blinked, too astonished to speak. She did not understand; Rebeccah never read anything past an occasional few lines of a poem. It made no sense for her to desire a subscription from the library.

His perfectly cut mouth betraying a faint smile, Keath announced that he happened to be going in that direction and declared himself ready to be of assistance.

"The very thing!" said Rebeccah, clapping her hands. "How very kind of you and always so obliging."

"Not at all. I have quite a full hour to put at your disposal." The pale blue eyes swept over Mary. "But how remiss of me to be in my curricle! I'm afraid you ladies will be rather squeezed even if we leave John behind." He nodded at his tiger, now standing at the spirited horses' heads.

"Yes, isn't it disobliging that curricles only hold two comfortably?" Rebeccah turned to Mary. "Love, you look a little tired. It would be quite too heartless of me to make you come along to the library when I daresay you don't care to go at all. Tell me you don't mind to go on home alone? There is the footman as adequate escort."

Mary stared at her in disbelief, struggling to put

down rising anger. Of all the obvious, manipulative things! Going to the library was only a ruse for Rebeccah to be with Keath, and while Mary cared nothing about that, she did find it exceedingly heartless of Rebeccah to leave her, especially after chattering all day about how damaging it was to walk alone about the more fashionable streets at this hour. Such audacity from Rebeccah was not to be borne!

Looking up from the pavement with stormy eyes and flushed cheeks, Mary started to say that she did not consider the footman a suitable escort in the least, but Rebeccah was already climbing into the curricle with Keath's aid. Mary clenched her fists with a little shudder of rage. "Rebeccah," she said sharply.

Rebeccah paused in the act of settling herself on the seat to send Mary a sweet smile. "I knew you would not mind."

Keath gathered up the reins in his gloved hands. "Let go their heads, John. You will see that Miss . . . ah . . . Clampton arrives home safely." He tipped his beaver to Mary.

The curricle swept away into the traffic, leaving her on the sidewalk in the not-at-all satisfactory care of the footman and the tiger. Biting her lip and glaring after the disappearing curricle, she barely overcame the urge to indulge in a tantrum there in the street.

Chapter Seven

BUT SINCE SHE had been so heartlessly deserted, there was nothing to be done but make as hasty and as dignified a retreat back to Bruton Street as possible. Drawing in a deep breath, she set off down the street at a steady pace, keeping her eyes rigidly straight ahead and resolving to make no acknowledgment—however involuntary—to any gentleman who might be rude enough to hail her in passing.

She was so intent upon lashing herself into increasing rage with every step and thinking up scathing remarks which she would like to deliver to Rebeccah that she did not at first pay any heed to the carriage drawing up beside her.

Then a youthful, merry voice called out in surprise: "Why, it *is* Miss Clampton! Oh, Grandmama, do have the coachman stop. Hello!"

Startled, Mary jerked to an abrupt halt and stared at the smiling face of Arabella Monteforte. Dressed in a narrow gown of sprigged muslin and a dainty chip straw hat, she was sitting in an impressive-looking landau with an elderly eagle-faced woman who gazed at Mary with stony gray eyes. At once Mary's heart plummeted. Her position was quite bad enough at present, but to encounter such a highly ranked member of the ton as Lady Monteforte when she was out here alone set the seal upon her humiliation.

Arabella beamed. "Is it not wonderful that already we have found each other? I must make you known to my grandmama." She turned to the elderly woman. "This is Miss Clampton, who so kindly rescued us from that dreadful accident."

The hard gray eyes swept over Mary, who read in them open disapproval. Lady Monteforte nodded curtly to her. "You have my thanks, Miss Clampton." Her still-strong voice was icily formal.

It stung at Mary, and she almost choked in swallowing back a hasty retort. This was someone she dared not speak back to, no matter how great her degree of enraged mortification. "You are m-most welcome," she forced out, wishing the warmth in her face would die down so that she might somehow find a remaining shred of composure to grasp.

Arabella suddenly frowned and leaned slightly over the side of the landau. "But surely you aren't walking *alone?*" she asked.

"No," said Mary quickly. She glanced behind her and with relief noted that the footman and Keath's scruffy-looking tiger were still with her. Nodding at them, she said, "These servants are my escort."

Lady Monteforte took a fresh grip on her black cane and snorted.

Mary's temper slipped, and she threw up her head to look the old woman directly in the eye. "You are quite right to disapprove, ma'am. I do not find it in the least a satisfactory or comfortable situation, and so I am attempting to make my way home at once."

"Indeed." A faint haughty smile appeared on Lady Monteforte's wizened lips, and Mary was suddenly aware of an arrogance here far superior to Rebeccah's, for this was the attitude based on actual excellence of lineage rather than on mere conceit. "Tell me, then, Miss Clampton, why you permitted yourself to be placed in such a damaging position by walking out in this way?"

It was a question like a rapier thrust, but Mary was too angry with Rebeccah to be confounded by it. Once again she raised her hazel eyes, and this time they flashed slightly. "I have no wish to be thought one of those odious people who are forever laying the cause of their woes upon someone else's shoulders, but when I left my house I was in the company of my friend Miss Tavers. She has abandoned me, however, for the company of another acquaintance. Therefore, ma'am, I am forced to—"

"Yes," said Lady Monteforte without the least sign of unbending.

Arabella's clouded brow cleared. "How dreadful! You must get up into the landau and let us take you home. Mayn't she, Grandmama?"

"No, thank you," said Mary stiffly, afraid of receiving the additional insult of refusal. "Bruton Street is not much farther. I shall—"

"You shall make an utter fool of yourself," snapped Lady Monteforte. "Get in."

It was hardly a gracious invitation, but Mary took no heed of that. She stared in surprise. "But—"

"Oh, yes, do," said Arabella, swinging open the door and moving over on the seat. "There is plenty of room for you."

Mary did not understand, but she did know that to stubbornly refuse would indeed be foolish, as Lady Monteforte had said. She glanced back at the footman and was reassured by the relief in his homely face as he hastened forward to assist her into the landau. Lady Monteforte poked her cane into the coachman's back as a signal to go on.

"Poor Miss Clampton," said Arabella, giving her hand a reassuring squeeze. "I wondered why you were looking so vexed."

"Was I?" Mary smiled reluctantly. "That was very bad of me to show my feelings in the street."

"But, you must own, the provocation was great. I do not know this Miss Tavers, but whatever came into her head to leave you in such a heartless fashion? She must be a thoughtless creature."

"Arabella," said Lady Monteforte reprovingly, and looked at Mary. "Is this your first visit to London? I do not recall having met you before."

"No, ma'am. I have lived here most of my life, but this is my first season." Though she hated to say the words, Mary could not completely ignore the tingle of excitement that they brought.

Arabella clapped her hands. "Just like me! Shall you be having a come-out ball too?"

Lady Monteforte frowned, but Mary quickly shook her head.

"I plan to have a quiet social life."

"Then you aren't attempting to storm the highest doors of the ton?" asked Lady Monteforte with the faintest hint of scorn.

"No, ma'am." Mary made herself smile. "I have neither the hope nor the inclination."

"But how else shall you make a good match?" demanded Arabella.

"Arabella!" Lady Monteforte thumped her cane against the bottom of the carriage. "You shall *not* be speaking in such vulgar ways. You are to please remember the conduct of a proper young lady."

"I am sorry," murmured Arabella with pink cheeks.

"I should think so." Lady Monteforte tightened her withered lips and glanced at Mary, who was distressed to see Arabella so sternly reprimanded. "My granddaughter is, as you see, Miss Clampton, sadly spoiled. Is this your house?"

Mary looked up in relief. "Yes."

The coachman pulled to a halt, and Pitt, the aged butler, opened the door.

"How charming it is!" said Arabella, looking up and down the street, her blue eyes bright with curiosity.

"I like it very well," said Mary, climbing out. She stood in the street and looked up at Lady Monteforte. "I am most grateful for your assistance, ma'am."

Lady Monteforte snorted. "Daresay. Well, at least you're not the mushroom I thought at first. Good afternoon."

She poked her cane into the coachman's back, and the landau went on with a merry wave from Arabella. Mary stared after them for a moment before going up the steps past Pitt, who was holding the door open for her.

He blinked. "Miss Tavers is not with you, miss?"

"No. She went driving with an acquaintance." Mary could not hold back a sigh of irritation. Inside she still fumed, though now that was overlaid with new satisfaction at having met Lady Monteforte and being taken up in her carriage.

Rebeccah returned in time to dress for dinner, and they sat down for a silent repast—Rebeccah haughty but amused, Mary too resentful to dare trust herself to speak the merest commonplace. She decided she would not mention her encounter with the Montefortes, for she had no desire to discuss anything with Rebeccah. Anyone who could be so utterly selfish and inconsiderate ought to be soundly taken to task. But the evening wore on, and she said nothing about it. With unusual tact, Rebeccah restricted her topic of conversation to fashion, and made no mention of Keath at all. By the time they retired to their separate chambers, it was as though the incident had never occurred. Mary was still dissatisfied, but there seemed nothing she could do about it now except promise herself never to trust Rebeccah again.

Late the next morning she attired herself in a new straw-colored walking dress and tied up her dark curls with a matching ribbon á la Diana before taking her embroidery to the front parlor. Scarcely had she threaded her needle, however, before Rebeccah swept into the room, attired for the outdoors in hat and pelisse.

"Mary! Whatever *are* you doing? You know very well we are to call at Lady Ellsford's at eleven."

Mary rose slowly, her resentment fired on the instant. "No, I did not know it."

"Certainly you did, for I told you myself yesterday." Rebeccah drew on her lavender kid gloves. "I daresay you've forgotten. Really, it is too bad of you not to attend to me, for here in town you cannot allow your mind to wander for an *instant,* lest you say or do something perfectly outrageous, as you always did in Brighton. Now, *do* go and put on your pelisse. The day promises to be chill, and we must not be late. Kitty Ellsford is a dear in every way, but she cannot abide tardiness."

Lady Ellsford proved to be a tiny, vivacious matron of perhaps thirty, with twinkling dark eyes. She greeted them with a friendly shake of the hand. Then they sat down for the most boring half an hour Mary had ever endured. Since the conversation confined itself to clothes and gossip, neither of which Mary knew much about, she folded her hands in her lap and forced herself to sit patiently in silence, staring in horror at the hideous gilt crocodile supporting their hostess's settee, and murmuring something only in reply to the occasional remark Lady Ellsford addressed to her.

"Oh, it is too bad that London is yet so thin of company," complained Lady Ellsford. She sighed. "But at least Menton is in town for the season. George heard him say at Boodle's that he has no plans to go abroad this year. You can be sure we hostesses are excessively relieved. It is never so dull as when he is not here to keep us enlivened with his flirtations, and besides, that silly war has made the Continent dreadfully unsafe." She smiled in her dazzling way. "But, Becky dearest, are you going to procure vouchers for Almack's this time?"

Rebeccah nodded. "We have not yet started plans for—"

"But of course you must have them!" Lady Ellsford passed Mary the plate of macaroons. "Sally Jersey will be among my guests on next Tuesday. Do come then, both of you." She laughed. "We shall all of us conspire against her so that she shall be unable to refuse Miss Clampton a place in the assembly rooms."

Rebeccah made a gracious acceptance, and in a few moments they took their leave. Mary was glad to be gone, and she loosed a little sigh of relief inside the hackney carriage.

"You have done as well as could be hoped for," said Rebeccah, giving directions for the lending library to the jarvey. The hackney started up at a sluggish pace. "Of course, Kitty is ever easily pleased. It's only the cits whom she can't abide. But do not let this morning go to your head. Sally Jersey is the most capricious woman alive, I'm sure. You must be perfect in dress and deportment to please her. And I cannot stress the importance of gaining entry to Almack's too much."

In the face of her anger over being abandoned like an abigail in the street yesterday, Rebeccah's admonitions only heaped on the coals. But Mary bit back the temptation to say something that would set them at real dagger-drawing, and instead restricted herself merely to: "I shall do my best, of course, Rebeccah."

At the library, Mary overcame much of her irritation by becoming engrossed among the volumes, but Rebeccah strolled restlessly about the rooms.

"Oh, this is too vexing," she said at last, coming up to stand beside Mary. "I especially desired to see . . ." She frowned suddenly. "Do not tell me you mean to take out *all* of those books!"

In puzzlement Mary looked at the two slim volumes of poetry and the novel in her hands. "Whatever is wrong with these? They are authors that you recommended."

"Yes, but not so many at once. You mustn't acquire the reputation of being bookish." Rebeccah craned her neck around a tall bookshelf, then drew back with an exclamation of annoyance. "Why doesn't he come? There is no one here but the merest cap acquaintances. I am so bored."

"Why didn't you say at once that you have an assignation with Mr. Keath?" asked Mary, in the mood again to pick a new quarrel. "Surely you do not want me to play gooseberry today."

"Don't be absurd—"

"Ah, is it Miss Tavers?"

Rebeccah whirled in startlement, discomposed for the first time Mary had seen. "Wh-why, Lord Menton!" she said to a tall gentleman who had stepped abruptly into sight from behind a long shelf. "How very delightful to see you again."

But he was returning Mary's frightened gaze and paid no heed to her greeting. He lifted his quizzing glass and leveled it at Mary, who suddenly recalled that other such leisurely scrutiny in her prison cell. She flushed fiery red in shame and at once dropped her eyes, but her curiosity was stronger and soon made her lift them again. She had to see this odious man who held her so firmly in his power and thus raised

her chin to bear his insolent study of her with all the
outward composure she could muster, though within,
her heart was hammering so she thought she might
suffocate at any moment.

In the clear light, his hair à la Brutus showed raven
black, his deep-set eyes a sharp, vivid blue. His coat of
blue superfine was molded exactly to broad shoulders
that needed no buckram padding. Pantaloons of the
palest buff hue hugged long muscular legs without
wrinkle, and his Hessians shone with a brilliance that
made her blink. The cravat at his throat was of the
snowiest starched muslin, tied in an impeccable Wa-
terfall. His thick dark brows flanked the arrogant,
somewhat bony nose. A well-etched mouth was
marred by the cynical set of his lips. Those lips
twitched into a mocking little smile, and the quizzing
glass was allowed finally to drop.

He bowed. "Am I correct in thinking this is Miss
Clampton?"

Rebeccah's brittle laugh helped shatter the moment. "Fie on that shocking memory, my lord! Of
course you know it is her."

His cold eyes flickered to her briefly, then returned
to Mary. "Miss Clampton's looks are much improved
since I last had occasion to speak with her."

Mary summoned up a polite if slightly awkward
curtsy, though she feared that if she dared move,
her knees would give way beneath her. "My lord is
very kind." She eyed his unfriendly face and decided
with a sinking heart that Rebeccah had been wrong
not to inform him of their arrival. Clutching her books
tightly with perspiring hands, she swallowed hard.
How she wished they were not in so public a place!

"Well, well, what a charming scene." Keath strolled
casually up and made his bows.

At once the contrast between the two brothers was
apparent. Primarily, one was dark and the other fair,
but that was not the difference which struck Mary most
forcibly. It was, however, more difficult to define,
and she at last decided that it had something to do
with how they seemed to take instant hostile stances
against each other. Menton's dark face did not shift

expression all that greatly, but from the cold sweep of his dark blue eyes over his brother it was plain that he felt the same displeasure as that which showed plainly upon Keath's pale, classical features. Both seemed to resent the other's obviously unexpected presence.

Mary caught a glimpse of fright on Rebeccah's face, quickly suppressed by one of her bright smiles. Mary could not think of what might make her afraid, but meanwhile Keath was greeting his brother—rather carefully, she thought, and was puzzled.

Menton eyed him now in visible displeasure. "What brings you out of your office, Thomas?"

"I always spend my luncheon hour on Bond Street in the hope of seeing acquaintances." Keath turned to Rebeccah and Mary with an air of defiance. "I hope you ladies haven't forgotten my invitation to that dinner party I'm giving?"

"I wasn't aware that you were acquainted with Miss Tavers and Miss Clampton, Thomas." Menton's hard voice was dangerously casual.

Keath's expression stiffened. "That is none of—"

"Why, my lord, surely you cannot have forgotten that I've been known to your brother since nursery days?" asked Rebeccah quickly. Too quickly, it seemed to Mary, who although glad Menton's immediate attention had been distracted from her, was uneasy at the suspicion that she was perhaps too close to the middle of possible crossfire from fists or sharp words.

"Ah, yes," said Menton with his mocking smile. "But my wretched memory does not often attempt the harrowing journey back to early youth. Thank you, Miss Tavers, for nipping away that budding misunderstanding. And so, Thomas, you've already had the occasion to meet Miss Clampton also. How very energetic of you. I am spared the tedium of introductions. But tell me, am I invited to this dinner party of yours?"

"You know quite well that you are not," snapped Keath, his face flushing brilliant against the white of his neckcloth.

Menton nodded. "Yes, but one can always hope for a change of heart." The insolence in his drawl seemed deliberate.

Keath took a hasty step forward. "I warn you, Aubrey—"

"Come," said Rebeccah sharply. "If the two of you would stop baiting each other, we could all be more comfortable."

Both men glanced at her, and Menton bowed. "Of course you are right, Miss Tavers. There is no need to be dagger-drawing in public." His eyes slid to Keath. "Don't you agree, Thomas?"

Keath turned livid. "By God, Aubrey—"

Rebeccah seized Keath's arm. *"Please."*

Menton laughed softly and turned to Mary, who was watching with a frown of puzzlement. "Miss Clampton, will you go driving in the park with me later today? The air is rather chill, but I promise not to keep you out long."

The politeness in his voice was a thin mask for the anger she quickly sensed was underneath. Wishing the gripping knot would leave her stomach so that she might be able to think more clearly, she was suddenly afraid of him, afraid of being alone with him.

Quickly she shook her head. "No . . . thank you, no." The words seemed to catch in her dry throat. She swallowed in haste. "It is very kind, but I fear I am fatigued and—"

"What fustian," said Rebeccah. "We have made but one call this morning; you cannot possibly be tired." The bright smile flashed toward Menton. "You must not mind her, my lord. The chit is absurdly shy at moments. I have no doubt but what she is really willing to go driving with you and only craves further persuasion."

Mary's fingers curled into fists. She glared at Rebeccah, longing to give her a sound box upon the ears. Why must she always meddle? Now Menton was staring Mary's way again, his brows lifted. She suspected that his civility was only for show, that he had no intention of allowing her to refuse. The old sensation of being trapped began to strangle her again.

She only just managed to meet his eyes, then let hers fall immediately.

"I . . . I should be most pleased to go out driving with you, my lord," she whispered. "Thank you."

He scarcely waited for her to finish before glancing at Rebeccah. "And you, Miss Tavers? Should you care to accompany us?"

Rebeccah declined with her most winning smile. "I fear I have another engagement for this afternoon."

"Not with my brother, I hope." Menton's deep blue eyes met his brother's pale ones. "He is not a good sort, you know."

Keath stiffened despite the restraining hand Rebeccah placed on his arm. "I'll thank you, Aubrey, not to go about sullying my character!"

Menton shrugged and raised his quizzing glass. "I'm told you lose no opportunity to sully mine. It really does you no credit. I'm a favorite of the ton, you must remember. Where did you find that waistcoat?"

Keath almost shook in an effort to control himself. "I beg you will tell me in what way it offends you?"

"Oh, it doesn't offend me, dear boy." Menton raised one dark brow. "It's just not the best match for that coat." He sighed and lowered his glass. "Daily I dislike your valet's judgment more. I wish you would turn the fellow out. Good day, ladies. Until this afternoon, Miss Clampton." With a meaningful glance at her bowed and strode away without a further word.

Chapter Eight

THE THREE OF THEM stood in silence a moment. Rebeccah looked up at Keath with a worried expression and took his arm. "I beg you will take no heed of him. You know he ever delights in taunting any person, not just you alone."

"No, Rebeccah," he said, drawing a deep breath, "you will not coax me into brushing off the matter. I am expected, I suppose, to accept his remarks, along with everything else, but that I refuse to do!"

To Mary's surprise, Rebeccah's face took on a pleading expression. "You must not do anything rash! Only think of the scandal before! It has but just died down. You—"

"I have not forgotten," he said in a bleak voice, his pale eyes narrowed at a spot in the distance.

She gripped his sleeve. "Thomas!"

He looked down at his arm and gently removed her hand. "I can't afford to have creases in my new coat." If the words were light, his tone was not. The sentence hung flatly in the air. He raised her hand and kissed it almost absently. "I must be going back to my work now, but I shall be free later in the afternoon." He glanced briefly at Mary. "Your servant, ma'am."

He strode away a little hastily, one hand still in a fist. Rebeccah stood staring after him with her hands gripped tightly together; then she heaved a sigh and glanced around, to catch Mary staring at her.

Mary took hold on herself and shook her head. "Rebeccah, I don't—"

"Come, let us be away from here." Rebeccah glanced about the busy room, her manner impatient. "We've been here long enough."

They stepped outside, where a portly gray-haired gentleman kindly took the time to hail a hackney for them.

Rebeccah leaned back against the squabs with a loud sigh. "Heavens, what a scene! I was ready to sink with all of those people staring at us in the most vulgar way. Menton can be the most odious creature alive."

Mary looked directly at her, curious to know more about this. "I am all at a loss. Why is there such animosity between them?"

Rebeccah waved a vague hand. "Oh, it is a great deal too involved to explain, but they have been at each other's throats since the death of the late earl. Of course, it is all Menton's fault, since he delights in baiting Thomas at every opportunity. He knows very well how uncertain Thomas's temper can be!"

"Has there been a public quarrel between them?" Mary frowned. "I cannot see anything particularly scandalous in two brothers forever at loggerheads."

Rebeccah eyed her in some exasperation. "I cannot imagine where you have been all these years not to know any *on-dits* at all. Thomas—I mean, Mr. Keath —quite lost his temper some months past and called Menton out. Naturally Menton had been at his usual habit of mocking Thomas's every word. They were both a trifle foxed, I believe, and engaged in deep play at White's. Menton refused the challenge, of course, as was proper, but it was very bad of him to make Thomas embarrass himself so. Now it is always so very uncomfortable whenever their paths cross. I trust you took notice that I was careful to avert another quarrel. Why Menton must be so unbelievably cross-grained in the presence of his brother, I cannot imagine." She raised her slim hand to her eyes. "Pray, do not ask me anything else. I have the headache coming on."

They rode in silence the rest of the way to Bruton Street, where Rebeccah left Mary to pay the driver and rushed into the house. She went at once upstairs to her room and did not emerge again until that afternoon. Mary attempted to eat her luncheon, but it was all tasteless to her. She picked through her food for a while, then gave it up. More than anything she wished for the headache too, so that she might be able to send her excuses to Menton, but try as she might, she could not produce one. She wandered away to the drawing room and stood before the fire, rubbing her cold bare arms. Her dress was too thin for today's chill, and she shivered, dreading the approaching winter.

Why was Menton angry with her? The question spun again and again through her mind. It must be because she had come to London without his knowledge. How doltish of her to have heeded Rebeccah! She shoved herself away from the mantel and wandered about the room with her hands to her temples. It was time that she thought clearly and avoided more blunders. But what to say to him?

She clenched a fist suddenly with a spurt of defiance. She would not beg his forgiveness, if that was what he wanted. No, she would find instead the answers to her own questions. He had kept her in suspense for over a month; that was quite long enough. Nodding to herself in determination, she went upstairs to change into her riding habit. A sort of desperate defiance made her want to look her best. Then word was brought to her that Lord Menton was waiting downstairs.

Dropping her comb, she donned her new green velvet hat, arranging its short veil to a nicety, and barely remembered to snatch up her gloves on the way out. Being tardy would not improve his annoyance with her. She hurried downstairs with the inward feeling of a dog slinking up to its master to be whipped.

Dressed in buckskins and top boots, with several whip points thrust through his buttonhole, Menton was seated in the drawing room with his quizzing glass leveled at one of the books she'd brought from the lending library. He glanced up at her hasty entrance and rose in his unhurried way.

"Shall we go?" he asked with a bow, his blue eyes

without expression. "I have a great deal to discuss with you."

The cold words fell upon her like leaden drops. Her insides quailed, and she forgot everything save the need to escape going out with him. "We should have told you that we were coming."

"Yes, but that does not concern what I have to say to you. Come."

With a firm grasp of her elbow he ushered her outside and assisted her into his curricle. It was rather plainly decorated, with none of the bright colors she had seen on several other equipages. His leggy horses, however, had the look of plenty of spirit, and Mary had no doubt of his ability to handle them. She settled on the seat and folded her hands together tensely.

"I would rather you speak at once and not keep me any longer in suspense," she said in a rush, too nervous not to be blunt.

He kept his attention on his driving, moving them out into the street at a spanking trot, but she saw one of his thin brows go up. She waited, but he did not reply.

"Please, my mind is quite worn out trying to think of what you want me to do. Or why you have picked me, of all people."

He glanced at her briefly. "What acquaintances have you been allowed to make besides my brother's?"

She frowned at his changing of the subject and said uneasily, "The Montefortes and . . . and today Lady Ellsford."

"Kitty Ellsford is a fool," he said flatly, one muscular arm brushing hers as they rounded a corner in prime, high-stepping style. "How did you meet the Montefortes? But first tell me if you mean Lady Monteforte?"

"Yes, and her grandchildren Arabella and . . . er . . . Harton."

He frowned. "I do not understand. Miss Tavers has no access to Lady Monteforte's set."

Mary explained about the gig accident.

He glanced at her in some impatience. "But has Lady Monteforte herself recognized you?"

"Yes," said Mary with her chin up. "I have ridden in her landau, and she herself told me I was no mushroom."

His sudden crack of laughter startled her.

"Why do you laugh?" she asked, staring at him in irritation.

He shook his head, unable to completely repress his smile. "You would not be amused."

"I see." She bit her lip, but the words could not be stopped. "Do you always take your amusement at another's expense, my lord?"

The laughter died from his face. He turned his unfriendly eyes full upon her. "You had best take more care with that tongue of yours, my girl."

She clenched her fists. "I am not your girl!"

"Oh, but you are. I am paying for your season, your dowry, and your bridal trousseau."

She drew in her breath. "Then you still plan to marry me?"

"Of course." His voice was like steel. "As soon as enough time has elapsed for such a decision to be made, we will be wed."

She gripped the edge of the seat with both hands, panic spreading throughout her. "Why? I wish you will tell me why!"

"It is of no importance for you to know why."

"You are wrong. It is of every importance that I know what scheme you plan to involve me in."

"You are a thief. I shall require that skill." He cracked his whip smartly over the left horse's head.

"But you must tell me more than that," she said, making her voice a plea.

"No. I do not trust you yet, Miss Clampton. You will not persuade me to take you into my confidence."

"I only want you to let me go!"

"Let you go?" He frowned and nodded politely to a man hailing him from the other side of the street. "You forget, Miss Clampton, that I have procured your release from prison."

"Yes, but this eternal suspense is hardly better. I beg you to give up your plan and let me—"

"No, matters have gone too far." He sighed, the

bored drawl back in his voice. "Calm yourself before I begin to think you do not wish to marry me."

"I do not," she said with spirit.

His cynical expression became more pronounced. "Am I seriously to believe that you do not want to live in the luxury and position I offer? Come, Miss Clampton, you must not expect me to swallow that Banbury tale."

"Of course I should like to live in luxury," she retorted. "Who would not? But you do not really offer me that life. You want me as an unquestioning tool."

"Precisely. Really, I see no reason for all your objections. But," he went on, ignoring her desperate attempt to interrupt, "I will tolerate no more. We made an agreement in your cell, and I intend to hold you to your part as much as I intend to hold to mine." He paused. "Dependent, of course, on whether society will accept you. Your appearance is well enough, if a little plain."

"Thank you," she said scathingly, but he seemed not to hear.

"What invitations have you received? No, don't bother to include the one from my brother, since that one has already been made known to me. What others?"

"There is Lady Ellsford's rout next week." Mary could not smother the resentment from her voice. "Lady Jersey is likewise to come, so perhaps I may approach her for vouchers to Almack's."

He waited a moment, then raised his brows. "Is that all?"

A sudden gust of wind made her snatch at her hat in the most awkward and undignified way. She gripped at the brim, with her cheeks flaming. "Yes, that is *quite* all," she said, angrily straightening her hat.

"Don't tug at it so," he said in his calm way. "You are creasing the velvet." He took one hand from the reins to smooth the crown. "There, that is better."

A purple-and-yellow tilbury whizzed past them, mere inches from grazing the wheels.

Mary gasped and shut her eyes. "I wish you would give your attention to your driving!"

"Prinny is the accepted terror of Hyde Park with that tilbury of his. You need not worry about him. All of us know how to get out of his way."

She opened her eyes to stare after the vanishing tilbury. "Was *that* the Prince of Wales?"

"Yes." The bored drawl was back in Menton's voice. "But you must participate in the season's activities on a much more involved scale. I am surprised Miss Tavers has not made more push on your behalf."

"Perhaps it is because she is too concerned with her own affairs." Instantly Mary wished for the petty words back, but it was of course too late.

Menton frowned at her. "Jealous, Miss Clampton? Then you must learn to curb that quality. I do not like it."

Stung, she bit her lip and looked away, unable to reply.

He cleared his throat. "You, Miss Clampton, are to concern yourself *only* with society functions. I wish to see you better dressed. I wish your every evening engaged. You must prove yourself worthy of my attentions."

"*I* must prove . . ." She glared at him, hardly able to believe his conceit. "And why should it matter to me, when I do not in the least wish to receive your attentions?"

"This will be a marriage below what is fitting to my position." His mouth tightened into a harsh line. "I do not wish the rest of the world to be aware of that fact. As for you, Miss Clampton, please keep in mind that it would take the slightest of efforts to have you returned to Newgate, should you fail to do your part."

Her heart stopped with a painful lurch, and she stared at him in desperation. "But you promised me—"

"Only if you succeed, Miss Clampton. That is all."

Her mind raced to find something that would arouse a stirring of mercy within him, but as she looked at his harsh profile her heart sank and she knew there was nothing she could say. There was nothing she could do but obey him, for she could not doubt that he had no qualms about sending her back to Newgate. She clenched her hands and shook with rage born more of fear than of anger.

Within another silent five minutes they returned to Bruton Street. He helped her down with a detached air of civility. "Remember my instructions, please. I have no doubts as to the excellent state of your memory. Good day, Miss Clampton."

He drove away, leaving her fuming on the doorstep. She entered the hallway, removing her hat with violence enough to tear one of its ribbons. Lord Menton was the cruelest, most odious man she had ever met in her life, with the possible exception of his father, and that amounted to about the same thing. How dare he insult her and demand excellence in the same breath! She hated him; he was a monster to taunt her with luxury, knowing well she'd never willingly do anything that would cause her return to Newgate.

And now he demanded that she enter the finest and most-difficult-to-open doors of society. Dazedly she began moving up the stairs, dragging herself up by the banister, her feet stumbling as though belonging to someone else. How could she do what he demanded? At every turn Rebeccah scolded her for awkwardness and her boring conversation. How could she, who did everything wrong, hope to succeed in a group which insisted upon polished excellence? He expected too much of her; the mere idea of attending an assembly left her frantic. The *haut* ton was a foreign world to her; she would never fit in. She would fail, and he would fling her back into prison without an ounce of compassion.

Mary gripped the banister with aching fingers, then angrily picked up her skirts and ran to her room. Slamming the door, she buried her hot face in her hands and threw herself weeping across the bed.

Chapter Nine

THE NIGHT OF LADY ELLSFORD'S rout came too soon
for Mary. She had been to the opera last night
and to a play the night before that, but this evening
was her first true social engagement. She felt exhausted, and it had not yet commenced. For the hun-
dredth time she studied her reflection in the mirror.

"Please, miss, if you would just be still," said Rebeccah's maid. "I've just these last curls to arrange."

Obediently Mary became rigid. She hoped her dress
would meet approval. It had a mint-green slip with an
overdress of aged lace and it was cut low across the
bosom. She did not personally care for it, but that
scarcely mattered, since it was at the height of current
fashion. The maid finished arranging her dark hair in
one of the simple classical styles, leaving one long
curl to fall down upon her pale bare shoulder. Mary
drew in a shaky breath and pulled on her long gloves.

Jenny waited at the door, holding a carefully folded
shawl. She smiled at Mary. "Oh, miss, you do look
lovely."

"Thank you, Jenny." Mary suddenly was warm
inside. At least here was one person who was devoted to her.

She took her shawl and draped it about her shoulders, glad she was not prone to cold-naturedness. At
the head of the stairs she shivered suddenly and
knew that it was from her nervousness. Rebeccah

stood at the foot, impatiently arranging her own pais-
ley shawl.

"Do hurry up, Mary. We do not want to be the last
persons to arrive."

Mary swallowed a retort and came quickly down.
At all costs she did not want a quarrel with Rebeccah
this evening. Her whole body seemed brittle, as
though one loud word would shatter it. She followed
Rebeccah into the carriage, and wondered yet again
how she was supposed to impress Lady Jersey.

By perverse chance, their carriage pulled up at Lady
Ellsford's door at the same time as Lady Jersey's. She
alit from hers first and stood staring while Rebeccah
and Mary were handed out by a footman.

"Is that Miss Tavers?" she called in a rich, rather
low voice. "How odd that we should arrive together,
when I daresay you came just to snare me for vouchers." She laughed, holding up a slim gloved hand at
Rebeccah. "No, no, do not go into introductions here
in the street. There will be opportunity for that inside."

Mary's first impression upon entering was one of almost overpowering warmth. Her second was of a confusing mob of brightly dressed people all talking and
laughing in a tremendous hubbub. A short, slightly
chunky man in a puce coat came up to them.

"Hello again, Rebeccah." He had a soft, cheery
voice. "We've got a frightful squeeze, eh? Look at us,
all squashed up, and nobody minding a bit. Dinner
was scarcely enough to feed us all, and now there are
more coming every minute. But that's my Kitty." He
smiled indulgently. "She always fears half-filled rooms
and invites thrice the number they will hold. Someday
my house is going to burst."

Rebeccah smiled somewhat thinly. "Sir George,
may I introduce Miss Clampton? I am engineering her
come-out this year."

"How do you do?" He shook Mary's limp hand.
"Should you like a tour of the ground rooms?"

"I . . ." Mary gulped uncertainly. "Yes, very much."

He took her arm in his. "Good! Have you any interest in Chinese art?"

"I'm . . ." She glanced back, but Rebeccah had already drifted away to greet someone. "I'm afraid I know nothing about it, Sir George."

"That's all right, my dear. I'll be able to show you my collection without betraying any of my own ignorances on the subject." He laughed and led her toward the open doorway, stopping every few feet to greet someone, and never failing to introduce her.

Mary began to feel swallowed by so many faces. She had always imagined a rout to consist of a smaller, more select group. This seemed to her almost like a ball, save that there was conversation for entertainment instead of dancing.

"You look bewildered," said Sir George at last. His middle-aged face seemed kind. "Don't be, my dear, for I assure you, we shall none of us eat you."

"I am not so sure," said Mary, and was rewarded by his laughter.

"I feared as much," he said. "Is this your first function?"

"The *very* first. Is . . . ." She looked up at him shyly. "Is it so obvious?"

He shook his blocky head with an encouraging wink. "A little nervousness shows, but that shall only be attributed to Sally's presence. I guessed your secret, you see, because it is Rebeccah's invariable habit to bring the chits she's launching here for their first major—"

"Oh!" Warmth flashed through Mary, and she hardly dared meet his eyes. "I am so sorry. I did not know, or I should have never let her bring me. I—"

"Shush." He patted her numb hand. "I do not mind in the least. Always let Kitty invite whom she wants. She has unerring taste in company; that's why we always have such squeezes. But there, you look much improved with some color in your cheeks." He chuckled deep in his throat. "I am glad I made you blush. Ah, this is the library." With slight difficulty he made a way for them through the crowd gathered in the doorway. "Excuse me. Excuse . . . Tom! Dashed good to see you! Heard your boy caught a French ball. Oh, just in the shoulder? Then he's going to be all right, ain't he? Good! We shall all be glad to see the end of this cursed war, I daresay. Here they are, Miss Clampton. Now, you must tell me what you think of my little collection of treasures."

He stopped triumphantly before a glass case which held two delicate bowls, a vase, and an assortment of tiny lacquered boxes. Mary hesitated, wondering how she could best praise them to give him pleasure.

"But there," he said, "all the candles are glaring off the glass so that you cannot see in properly. I'll open up the case for you. Wait while I fetch the keys."

Mary glanced round at once. "Oh, please, do not trouble . . ." But he was already gone.

She sighed and glanced around a little self-consciously, wondering what she should do while she waited. None of the other people seemed to be taking any heed of her, and she began to relax after a few moments.

"Hello. Have we met each other before?"

Mary started and glanced up into brown eyes belonging to a rather thin young man in the resplendent uniform of a hussars regiment. He instantly looked apologetic.

"I am so sorry," he said. "I startled you. Please forgive me. It's been so long since I've been to a party, I've nearly forgotten how to act." He stopped shyly. "Well, this is my first one since I returned from fighting Boney. Shall I go away?"

"Oh, no!" Mary managed to find her voice at last, thankful he was no haughty overbearing person. She had been fearing such a one would approach her at any moment. "No, please do not. I am so nervous I am not really myself tonight."

"You too?"

They smiled shyly at each other; then he sketched a bow.

"I am Lieutenant Viscount Langfield—Charlie to everyone. Would you care to sit down before we are squeezed to death? There is an empty sofa right over there."

"Thank you, my lord."

"Oh, no, don't call me that," he said, leading her over to the sofa and sitting down at her side. "I daresay your manners don't like to let you call me Charlie right off the crack, but people don't know me in any other way."

"It still would not be seemly for me to call you by your Christian name after a few minutes of conversation." She sent him a glance of mild reproof. "You know I cannot."

"All right," he said grudgingly. "But you have not told me your name."

"It's Miss Clampton." She stared out at the crowded room without really taking notice of anything.

"So I must call you that?" he asked with a mock frown.

"Yes." Thawing, she looked down to hide the smile beginning to peep out from the corners of her mouth.

He sighed. "Such nicety of manners! You quite put me to the blush. Tell me, was Sir George trying to show you his stuffy old bowls?"

"Yes, he's gone to get the key to the cabinet."

The young viscount grimaced. "Oh, Lord, the most boring, fusty old stuff. As though someone cared a fig for his Chinese art. He shows it to everyone. I suppose you told him you didn't know a thing about it?"

"It is the truth." She looked at him questioningly.

The viscount shook his head sadly. "A mistake. A direct mistake. You should claim to be an expert, and when he shows the cursed things, you should remark on how blue the paint is, and he'll mark down your every word as gospel. That's the only way he shall ever leave you alone."

"But I could not lie to him. He is very kind."

"Certainly he is. But everyone wiggles out of his art collection one way or another. I've given you the easiest route. You really mustn't waste your chance."

Mary glanced hopefully toward the door. "Perhaps he won't come back."

"Oh, he will. He never forgets someone who is panting over one of his Ming bowls."

"There is a Ming bowl at . . ." Mary abruptly realized what she was saying and stopped.

"Where?" His brown eyes twinkled at her. "Finish your sentence, please."

"At Lord Menton's residence near Brighton," she said in a rush, wishing she'd not brought the matter up at all.

"You've been there?" Langfield's whole body became more alert. He stared at her. "Or are you bamming me?"

"No," she said cautiously. "I spent a short time there this summer. You see, I am an acquaintance of Lord Menton's sister, and he most graciously allowed me to use the house as my own during my stay at Brighton."

An odd expression crossed his face. and it was her turn to stare at him. "What is wrong?" she asked.

He shrugged lightly. "Nothing. I was just trying to remember if Uncle Aubrey had mentioned letting you use the house. Please tell me if my mother has ever invited you as a guest when I have been around. I should hate to be making a cake of myself by not recalling you."

Mary could have struck herself. Viscount Langfield . . . Lady Langfield . . . of course! What a dolt she was! "No. You aren't. I . . . I mean that, no, we've never met before. I am sure of it." She wanted to sink into the floor, and was immensely relieved at Rebeccah's sudden appearance.

"Mary! I've wandered for an age looking for you." Rebeccah snapped her fingers. "Come at once. Lady Jersey wants to meet you now."

Mary jumped to her feet, eager to face a new gorgon as long as she could get away from the one that had just opened its mouth to devour her.

"I must go, as you see," she said hurriedly to the viscount. "Perhaps we shall meet again some other time." Hoping it would never occur in a million years, she hurried away at Rebeccah's side before he could say a word.

"Do stop looking terrified, Mary!" whispered Rebeccah. "It makes you look like a perfect fool. Who was that young soldier?"

Mary stopped and stared at her in surprise. "Don't you know him?"

"Certainly not." Rebeccah shrugged. "Why should I?"

Mary studied her a moment, mulling over this new revelation that Rebeccah was not quite as knowledgeable of Menton and his relatives as she liked to claim. "He is Menton's nephew."

"I see!" Rebeccah's face set itself slightly. "The dowager viscountess does not recognize me, so I have no knowledge of any of her offspring. She is older than Menton and Mr. Keath by some years." Rebeccah suddenly smiled and beckoned. "Lady Jersey! I found her at last. May I make you known now to Miss Clampton?"

Lady Jersey nodded coolly, and Mary tried for her best curtsy. She had practiced in her room for days, but she could not tell now if it was acceptable.

"I am told you are shy," said Lady Jersey with a a bright smile similar to the one Rebeccah affected. "Who is your family?"

"They are all dead, ma'am."

Lady Jersey's finely arched brows rose. "I am very sorry to hear that, but I should still like to know who they were."

Mary lowered her eyes before the rebuke. "My father was Andrew Clampton. My mother's family name was Montgomery."

"Any connection to the Montgomerys of Hertfordshire?"

"Yes, very distantly, I believe." Mary's heart began to thud. She hoped this woman had not known her parents in the days before her father lost all of his money.

"Well, I cannot think of anyone I know now." Lady Jersey smiled faintly, her sapphire necklace winking at her white throat. "You are rather older than the usual debutante in her first season."

"Yes, ma'am." Mary swallowed. "It was not possible for me to have a season before now."

"So you are all the more anxious to enter the doors of Almack's."

Mary swallowed again. "Actually. ma'am, I fear to be out-of-place among girls scarcely seventeen."

Lady Jersey laughed. "Well said! But you needn't worry. The assembly rooms are not filled solely from the nursery-party set, I assure you! Very well, Miss Clampton, we shall see." She excused herself and turned away.

"Ah! Miss Clampton, you wandered away." Sir George hurried up to look at her reproachfully, then smiled in forgiveness. "Come along."

"No, really, Sir George," began Mary, but he grasped her hand and led her firmly to the library. She looked about swiftly for the viscount, but he was not in sight.

Rebeccah followed them in with a smile on her face. "Are you going to show us one of your exquisite bowls, Sir George?" she asked merrily.

He nodded happily, busy unlocking the cabinet. Mary drew in a deep breath and tried to look genuinely interested. A few others laughingly gathered round too. Sir George took out one of the tiny boxes lacquered in red and held it up so that it glinted in the brilliant candlelight.

"This is my newest addition," he said proudly. "Lady Ellsford had it purchased for my birthday last month. I believe it to be of the finest craftsmanship, though you all know that is but the opinion of an admitted amateur." His audience applauded with more laughter. He bowed and replaced the box, then with extra care brought out the vase.

Mary caught her breath in wonder. It looked so fragile she feared the slightest touch would shatter it. "How beautiful," she whispered.

Sir George beamed, and lovingly forced it into her hands. "There," he said, stepping back with an admiring glance. "A lady's palm as the ideal pedestal."

There were a few murmurs of assent all around. Mary grew warm at being the unexpected center of so many eyes.

Suddenly there was someone at her shoulder and a hard voice said into her ear: "Well done, Miss Clampton."

Menton's voice so close, so unexpectedly, startled her tight nerves. She jumped involuntarily, and the vase slipped from her timid hold. The tinkle of breaking porcelain seemed, to her ears, to be the sound of her insides all shattering at once. She stared aghast at the floor.

"Oh, no," she whispered.

She stared up at Menton's face in a daze. She saw him frown, and his hands gripped her arms. It was beyond her power to even glance in Sir George's direction. She was going to be thrown back in Newgate, she thought wildly. Menton was here, and she'd managed to create the ultimate of social solecisms. She should have known he'd be present to witness it.

He shook her. "Miss Clampton!"

She covered her face with her hands, then quietly fainted away.

Chapter Ten

MARY AWOKE to find herself in bed with afternoon sunshine streaming in her window. For a moment she was surprised to find herself abed so late; then the memories of last night flooded in upon her. She closed her eyes quickly, but the mental picture of the porcelain fragments at her feet and the horror upon Sir George's face only became clearer in her mind. She could not shut off her thoughts. He had been so kind to her, and this was how she had repaid him. Mary pulled the covers over her face, and tears welled up, hot and salty. She supposed she should be at the window soaking up as much sunshine as possible; there could be no doubt that Lord Menton would return her to Newgate without delay—probably tonight, when there would be the darkness to cover his movements from the rest of the world. She wished now she had been more eager to participate in his mysterious scheme. Had she not set up his back by making it plain she had no desire to deal with him, then perhaps he would have shown leniency with her. But now she had no hope of it.

Her pillow became cold and soggy from her tears. At last she could bear it no longer and threw the pillow from the bed, just as Rebeccah entered the room. They stared at each other in silence. Mary frantically tried to gulp down the rest of her tears, and nearly choked herself.

"Please do not start any of your reproaches,"

pleaded Mary. "I am all too aware of what I have done. Sir George—"

"—should have quite a disgust of you," said Rebeccah between tight lips. "Your looks were wild enough last night . . . I should have guessed you would cause some disaster to occur."

"I did not intend it to happen." Mary was unable to stop herself from trying to mask her shame with anger. "There is no need to imply I planned to drop the vase. If Lord Menton had not—"

"Menton?" Rebeccah's lip curled. "You will put the blame on his head, I see. Or why not mine? I was present too."

"Oh, stop it!" Mary put her hands to her damp cheeks, unable to bear the churning of emotions within her. "I—"

"There is not the slightest need to scream at *me*," said Rebeccah. "I am not the one that broke a priceless *objet d'art*." She paused a moment. "It has been made quite clear to me that you are an impossibility. I do not know why there have been all these lies told me about the eligibility of your background. It is obviously common—"

"No!"

"In fact," continued Rebeccah as though she had not heard, "I should not be in the least surprised if you are not a bold little servant trying to pass yourself off as a lady."

Mary gasped. "How dare you!" She threw herself out of bed and ran up to shake Rebeccah. "How dare you say that to me when you are not in the least bet—"

Rebeccah slapped her. Mary stumbled back, holding her stinging cheek.

"Do not ever dare touch me again," said Rebeccah. She drew herself up. "My trunks are being packed now, and I shall be leaving within the hour. Do you hear? I am washing my hands of you."

Mary thought how good it would be to be free of Rebeccah. She raised her chin. "I am glad to hear that," she said coolly. "I would not wish you to remain when my company has proved so very repugnant to you."

"Don't, I beg you, try to play Miss Top-lofty with me. You may be just as relieved to be rid of me as I am of you, but I shall ask you now how you expect to continue in society without my assistance." Rebeccah laughed scornfully, making no attempt to hide her pleasure at Mary's disgrace. "Do you expect to enter society's doors without a chaperon or a female companion? Do you think you have only to present yourself, and everyone will hasten to accept you? Oh, yes, I am sure that you have now achieved notoriety, but do not expect that to weigh with any hostess."

"Please leave." Mary's voice shook from the fury piling up within her to the exploding point. Her hand clenched around a hand mirror.

Rebeccah saw the action and read the intention in her face. Her eyes widened. "You would not dare."

"Get out," said Mary. Her temples were pounding up a headache. "And it is no use smirking at me, because I do not care a snap for the effort you've made trying to bring me into society. I think you are the most selfish, most odious female alive, and I shall be overjoyed to see you go!"

Rebeccah's face whitened. She forced out a strained little smile. "You will see. *Adieu!*"

The door slammed shut behind her, and Mary hurled the mirror at it with all her strength. The breaking glass was the vase shattering all over again; she cringed away from the sound. Menton's cold eyes haunted her from every direction. She sank sobbing to the floor, wishing she were dead.

There came a cautious tap on the door, and Jenny peeked in. "Oh, miss!" She hastily set down an ewer on the dressing table and took Mary's shoulders. "Oh, there, miss, don't take on so. You'll only make yourself ill."

Mary shook her head; the tears would not stop coming. Jenny jumped up to fetch her a clean handkerchief. It was a new one of fine cambric. Mary tried to give her a smile of thanks and failed, then gulped down her tears and defiantly blew her nose. Jenny coaxed her into being wrapped in a dressing gown and put her into a chair.

"Just you have a drink of this water, miss. We can be happy now, since *she* is goin' away."

The water seemed to strip away a little of the numbness her tears had brought. Mary drank it all down and wiped her burning eyes one last time. Jenny was a good little creature: already her simple chatter was making Mary feel calmer.

"Which dress shall I get out for you, miss?"

Mary thought a moment. If this was to be her last day of normal life, she might as well get maximum use of it. "I shall wear that walking dress of pink sarcenet and the pink ribbon I bought yesterday for my hair."

Was it only yesterday that her biggest worry was gaining Lady Jersey's favor? Mary gave her head a little shake and got up to dress. When her toilet was at last complete, she looked at herself in the mirror with resigned satisfaction. She was complete to a shade from the ribbon woven through her unpowdered curls to the pink satin slippers on her feet.

"Would you want something to eat now, miss?" asked Jenny. "Cook's been saving a meat pie for you."

"No." Mary shook her head. She knew if she ate anything she would be violently ill. "No, I'm not hungry. Hand me my shawl, please. Thank you." She put it about her shoulders and hesitated at the door. "Please tell me when Miss Tavers is gone. I shall be in the bookroom."

She went slowly down the corridor to the cheery little bookroom, where the sunshine was streaming warmly in and a tiny fire was burning in the grate. She found one of the novels she had brought from the lending library and sat down to force her mind to concentrate on the perilous escapades of the heroine. It did not prove to be an easy task.

The clock had just struck three o'clock when Pitt quietly entered to set an arrangement of hothouse orchids upon the little table at her elbow. She started and almost dropped her book.

Pitt bowed. "A messenger just came with the flowers, miss. Here is the card." He handed it to her. "And

I must also inform you that Miss Tavers has made her departure."

Mary slowly took her attention away from the flowers. "I see. Thank you, Pitt."

He went out, and she ripped open the card. It was from Sir George Ellsford, begging her forgiveness for forcing her into an event so "unfortunately distressing for all concerned." He politely wished for her recovery and begged to remain her servant, etc. Mary put down the card with a wrench inside. How could she make a response to such a noble-hearted effort at forgiveness?

Pitt returned. "Forgive me, miss, but Lord Menton has called and is waiting in the hall. Are you receiving visitors today?"

Suddenly the exotic scent of the orchids was overpowering. How she would love to say no! But Mary knew with a sinking of her heart that Menton would not let himself be put off by the servants. It was all the more cruel that she must say the words: "Yes, Pitt. Please do show him up."

Then she sat rigidly waiting in her chair, gripping her book in both hands as something solid to cling to, and fighting off her struggling emotions. She had not thought he would come so soon.

Chapter Eleven

HE WALKED IN unannounced, startling her so that she jumped from her chair. Her heart thudded so strongly she feared it must be visible, and the old queasiness began to turn her stomach. He was here now, and her last moments of life in a sane, clean world were vanishing rapidly away.

He checked and frowned at her. "I hope you do not mean to faint again. I have had enough of such tactics, I assure you."

She struggled to gain control of her voice, determined not to betray the despair so close to smothering her. "I shan't faint! You . . . you merely startled me."

He sighed. "I seem to be rather adept at doing that."

She looked at him quickly, but could find no sign of mockery in his face. "I do not care for your jests, sir."

"No, you have told me so before." He lifted his thin dark brows at her. "Let's find a more original topic of conversation, shall we?"

"I wish you will have done with teasing me so!" She clenched her hands helplessly and stared at the fire. Must he prolong this so, play with her as a cat does a mouse? Why must he be so cruel?

He walked up behind her and forced her around, a frown marring his lean dark face. "Until yesterday I had begun to feel I had made a reasonable choice in you, but now you are back into one of your trembling fits. Is fear the only aspect of your personality?"

She gritted her teeth, wondering if this were not a nightmare. "No!"

"Then show me the rest of it." His hard voice made the words a command.

"Why should I?" She wrenched free of his grasp. "You've come to take me back to prison. There is no reason to show a smiling face for that."

The line between his brows deepened at once. "No, you—"

"You were quite right in not telling me your plans after all," she rushed on, heedless of him. "Since I won't be participating in them—"

"Take a damper!" he said impatiently. "I've never heard such raving fustian in my life."

The sharp words sliced through her fog of terror with alarming precision. She blinked at him. "What do you mean?"

"I might ask you the same question." He paused and glared sternly at her. "Will you not offer me some refreshment?"

Dazedly she rang the bell and requested the footman to fetch up a glass and some claret for his lordship. Her knees suddenly went weak, and she sat back down. She did not understand.

Menton crossed his arms and scowled at her. "Aren't you going to ask me to sit down? My word, girl, I hope this is not the best you know at playing hostess."

"I am sorry." She indicated a chair near the fire. He took one near hers.

James reappeared bearing a tray with two decanters and two glasses upon it. He set it down and bowed himself out. Menton rose to help himself.

"Ah." He took another sip. "If I'm not mistaken, this claret comes from my own stock. We've been provided with ratafia as well, from the looks of this." He held up the second decanter. "Shall you have some?"

"No." She shook her head. It had to be a dream; she knew herself fast losing grip on any sense of reality.

"You look to me as though you need it." He filled a glass and shoved it at her. "Drink it down."

She obeyed because his erect figure before her was

so commanding, swallowing part of the liquid in a quick gulp. It hit her empty stomach with a hard bounce, but surprisingly she began to feel a little more herself. Things steadied, and her wits began to turn once more.

She looked up at him. "So I am not to go back to . . ." She stopped, unable to say the dreaded word ". . . back *there?*"

"Certainly not," he said with irritation. "Where did you acquire such an ill-formed notion?"

Mary shook her head. "You told me not to fail, and I have. How could I expect otherwise?"

He snorted, and the drawl appeared for the first time this visit. "My dear ma'am, breaking a vase does not ostracize you from society." He studied his fingernails a moment. "Though I must admit having to be carried senseless from your first party is almost a sure guarantee that your name shall be bandied freely about town." He paused. "I think, however, that I can put a halt to most of that."

"Oh, I care nothing for that!" She pounded her fist in her lap. "I do not understand you at all. You told me I must make no wrong step, and now you say it does not matter." Suddenly realizing her outburst was becoming a bit shrill, she drew a shaky breath and put a hand to her forehead. "Oh, I am sorry. I'm all about in my head today, sitting here waiting to be taken back—"

"These are uncommonly attractive flowers," he said, aiming his quizzing glass at the orchids. "Did you select them yourself?"

"No, I . . ." With effort she momentarily squashed her vexation with his change of the subject. "They are from Sir George Ellsford. He . . . he wishes to apologize for causing me distress." All of her chagrin came rushing back upon her, and she jumped to her feet. "It is too bad of him to treat *me* as the injured party, when it is he who—"

"Return to your chair, please. You should not be taking on so while you are still not yourself." These words of concern were delivered in his usual imperious, supremely indifferent tone.

She whirled in fury at his hypocrisy. "You will not order me about in that way. I am not a schoolgirl!"

His bony face impassive, he lifted his quizzing glass at her but did not reply.

A little silence hung between them. Now that Mary's relief was swiftly washing away the last vestiges of her panic, she was gripped by active curiosity. Hesitating, she watched him sip at his claret, then at last pushed up her courage enough to speak, although she nearly feared to know the answer: "My lord, why have you come, then?" She swallowed down a dry lump in her throat. "I cannot think why—surely it is no idle visit?" He had probably come to give her another odious command, she thought.

He refilled his glass and reseated his long form in the chair beside her. "My mother has arrived in town, and I've come to take you to meet her. There is no harm in it, since you and I are supposedly previously acquainted through my sister."

Mary choked on the rest of her ratafia, coughing and spilling some of it onto her hand. He took the glass away from her at once and handed her his handkerchief, since she could not immediately find her own.

"What in heaven's name is wrong with you now?" he asked.

She could not immediately answer. His mother! screamed her thoughts. Fear, never far away, slipped back at once into gnawing at her stomach, and in a kind of horror her thoughts flashed back to that dreadful ball and the glimpse Mary had caught—as she slipped into the late earl's study—of the countess laughing with a circle of admirers. The countess would of course recognize her the minute she stepped across the threshold on Menton's arm.

Mary's breath caught desperately in her throat. She sat rigid, afraid even to glance at his lordship. What would he do when his mother denounced her as the thief who had been caught with her very hand in his father's desk? At first she had thought he knew the full details of her past, but since he had never made mention of it, she now believed otherwise. At all costs, then, she must prevent him from finding out, for she had not the least doubt that he would use the knowledge as yet another lever to force her obedience.

"Miss Clampton," he said sharply.

She jumped and cast about in her mind for something to explain such a reaction of guilt in her.

"I suppose you will think me a complete n-nodcock, but I . . . last night I met Lord Langfield," she began, not too coherently.

"My nephew. Yes." He nodded carelessly, stretching out his muscular legs in their skin-tight pantaloons and crossing his Hessians at the ankles. "And?"

"And I told him that I knew his mother. It was before I knew . . ." She looked up helplessly, twisting his handkerchief unconsciously between her fingers. "What if he tells her? She—"

"Louisa is a damned nuisance." He paced slowly, calmly, once about the room, his Hessians reflecting the bright light, his nostrils flared in thought. She watched him closely, hoping this problem would prove a sufficient diversion.

He kicked at the fire, sending sparks flying up into the chimney, and returned to his chair beside her. "We shall forget about Louisa for the present. I shall have to think up some story to feed her. Not the truth, certainly. Thomas can get her to blather out the closest of secrets. But she can wait. At the moment I desire to—"

"There is something else," Mary said, plucking his handkerchief to tatters in her agitation. "Please, I am so ignorant of these things. How must I make retribution to Sir George?"

His brows went up. "It is not expected of you to do anything more than formally apologize. I trust you have already seen to that?"

She shook her head in shame. "No, I did not arise until two o'clock. But surely I must try to do more than simply that. It . . . it was so dear to him."

Menton made no answer.

"Perhaps it could be replaced," she said. "Another vase that he might come to like almost as well?" Menton's brows drew together and she hastened on: "He . . . he was so very kind to me, letting me hold it when I should not, and I just cannot feel right in only writing him a letter! Is . . . is such a vase very expensive?"

Menton coolly named a sum that made her heart jump.

She sank down into her chair. "But that would buy so many things!"

"Yes, it would," he said with a hint of a smile. "Two fancy ball gowns for you. A riding hack for me." He picked an invisible speck of lint from his sleeve. "Wealthy men have their various little caprices."

Mary sat forward eagerly. "Rebeccah has told me I must have a new dress for every function. But that seems so extravagant. I could easily forgo two new gowns and wear what I already have. Some bows added, and they would not look exactly the same. Would that do?"

"No."

She frowned. "Then I can see no other solution."

"Good." He stood up in his languid way. "Shall we go now?" He rang the bell and instructed the servant who responded to fetch her hat.

But having hit upon the plan of persuading Menton to dawdle away the remainder of the afternoon in search of a vase, Mary refused to give up. She knew that it was probably foolish to provoke him, but if he did lose his temper it would be nothing in comparison to the scene awaiting them should she be made to meet his mother. She sent him what she hoped was an appealing glance and said: "You cannot truly expect me to be so heartless. Sir George was terribly kind to me—"

Menton looked bored. "Very well. I will agree that the fellow is kind." Then, surprisinig her with a smile of unexpected charm, he added: "And despite the fact that you have quite destroyed my new handkerchief, I cannot with all civility continue to refuse such a determined request. You may buy a cursed vase for Sir George."

She looked up in relief, hardly able to believe her ears. Now there was only one further point to win.

With her heart stilled in anxiety, she made herself frown.

"What is the matter now?" he asked in a voice of affected weariness.

She put her fist against her chin. "It has just occurred to me that I know nothing of choosing vases. I would probably buy something quite worthless. That would be an insufferable insult." She looked at Menton hopefully.

"Do you know, I begin to find you a most practical-minded female?" His eyes quizzing her, Menton took her arm. "I myself have some knowledge of this tiresome Chinese art. You must allow me to guide you in making your purchase. We can do it on the way."

"On the way?" Hardly knowing what she was doing for the numbness of defeat spreading through her, she picked up the hat Jenny had brought and put it on. "On the way to where?"

"To my house." He collected his hat from the table he'd tossed it onto. "I told you my mother has asked you to call."

"I . . . I suppose I was not paying attention," she said dully, her efforts crumbling to ashes about her. She bit her lip and wondered frantically if she should be brave and tell him the truth now. No, she could not do it. They were not at his house yet. Perhaps she would yet find a way to avoid going there.

Chapter Twelve

UNDER MENTON'S DIRECTION the vase was purchased speedily at a small shop filled to overflowing with every sort of intriguing object imaginable, and its fragile outlines were swathed in a careful bundle of wrapping paper. Now it rested on the curricle seat between them as they bowled through the congested streets at a smart pace. Quite without warning the day had become cloudy and now threatened a chill rain. Mary shivered from the quick nips of the breeze, but she took no heed of that. Lord Menton was now heading for his house in Curzon Street, and she had yet to think of a way to avoid going there. With increasing panic she gripped the seat and cudgeled her brain to think of some means of escape, but it seemed to have gone numb and was of no help to her at all.

Suddenly they were turning up Curzon Street, and her heart lurched within her. The doomed sense of her dilemma pressed down upon her until she longed to throw herself bodily from the curricle and dash away her troubles, along with herself, upon the pavement.

She swallowed, trying to force the strangling lump out of her throat. "My lord, there is something I must tell you—"

"Wait a moment." He pulled up the horses and jumped down, throwing the reins to a waiting groom. Then he put up his hand to help her down.

She stared at it, then at him. "But you should know—"

He snapped his fingers. "Come, come. We cannot be talking here in the street."

She sighed and placed her hand in his. Instantly he seemed almost to jerk her down into his arms. She caught her breath at his strength, but he only set her upon her feet politely and indicated that she precede him into the house. There was nothing to do but obey. Yes, there was. . . .

She turned to run, but already he was at her side, taking her elbow in his imperious way and steering her inside. She wanted to scream in vexation.

"Please, sir, I—"

But he had turned away to hand his shallow-crowned beaver, gloves, and caped greatcoat to the waiting footman. Mary bit her lip. Would he *never* listen? He must before they went any farther. There must be no humiliating scene enacted.

"Tell me, Andrew," said Menton in his careless way to the footman, "is the countess still about?"

"Yes, my lord. She is entertaining callers in the blue salon."

"Callers?" Menton's thin brows lifted. "Who?"

"Lady and Miss Monteforte, and a Mr. Monteforte too, I believe, my lord."

An unreadable expression flickered in Menton's face. "Ah, so much the better," he said in a voice that sounded pleased, and sent a glance toward Mary that she could not return. She began to tremble. This only made everything worse. How could she possibly . . . ?

"Clear away the cobwebs, Miss Clampton, and come along." He shook his head as the footman moved to precede them. "No, Andrew, there is no need for your services. You know I do not like to be announced."

He likes to surprise people, Mary thought bitterly, just to take his amusement from their reactions. But there was going to be a surprise for him, and he would not find it amusing. She jerked to a halt.

"I cannot meet your mother!" In her agitation the words came out much too loud.

He stopped and looked back at her with coldness at

once in his face. "You shall end this display of wretched manners at once, Miss Clampton."

"I do not mean to be rude," she said, flushing in shame. "I . . . you do not understand what I must—"

"No, I do not understand why you must enact a Cheltenham tragedy over the prospect of performing a very simple social function." He gripped her arm with his cold fingers.

"That is not the problem at all," she began in despair, trying not to shrink away. "You—"

"Oh! Pray, excuse me, sir!" Resplendent in a pink spangled waistcoat, Harton Monteforte halted abruptly in his progress of coming around the corner. "I was just taking a quick turn for some air. Salons get . . . uh . . . damnably stuffy when a pack of females get to chattering." He glanced at Mary from between the absurd height of his shirt points and colored slightly. "Beg pardon, ma'am."

She accepted the diversion thankfully, although deep within she knew it would not help her. "How is your ankle? I trust it is perfectly healed?"

"Yes." He eyed her coldly. "I thank you for your concern, although I do not recall making your acquaintance."

"Do not recall?" Mary stared at him in astonishment. "How could you—?"

"Excuse me, please." He bowed quickly at Menton and hurried on.

Mary stared after him in rising anger. "How dare he give me the cut direct!"

Menton shrugged in a broad manner. "Perhaps he does not recall you—"

"That is fustian," she said roundly, forgetting all else for the moment. "He was very glad for my assistance at the time. How very rude of him to—"

"Harton Monteforte came rude from the cradle. If it were not for his grandmother, he would not be tolerated." Menton sighed. "Now, what is this all important news that cannot wait?"

"I . . ." She drew a desperate breath, praying for courage. "I was the—"

"Hello, my lord!" sang out Arabella. "Did Harton

just pass this way? Grandmama has sent me to see if he has slipped out of the house." Then she saw Mary, and her young face brightened. "Miss Clampton! How wonderful to . . ." She stopped suddenly and lowered her eyes. "How wonderful to see you again," she said in a flat voice.

Mary stared at her, hurt. "Arabella, surely you are not going to give me the cold shoulder too?" she pleaded.

Arabella looked up; her blue eyes sparked suddenly with anger. "Did he do so? Oh, the wretch! I could quite strangle him for listening to Grandmama! I told her she was all about in her head to think such horrible . . . Oh!" She put a hand to her mouth and went pink. "But I don't care what anyone says. *I* shall stay your friend!"

"Your loyalty is commendable, Miss Monteforte," drawled Menton. "But what is the exact problem Miss Clampton has presented?"

"Oh, nothing." Arablla shook her head, shrinking back a little from him. "It is nothing! The veriest trifle!"

"You make a poor liar, Miss Monteforte," said Menton flatly. "I should like to know in what way Miss Clampton has displeased your grandmama."

The tone of his voice allowed for no more evasion. Arabella sent Mary a speaking glance of acute embarrassment.

"Grandmama was not pleased to find M-Miss Clampton promenading St. James's alone," she said in a very small voice. "And then Grandmama was told that Miss Tavers is a hurly-burly female notorious f-for making her living by sponsoring cits into the ton." Arabella's eyes met Mary's and dropped again. "I am sorry, but Grandmama does not find you quite the thing, and . . . and has told Harton and me to . . . to—"

"Avoid me at all times?" Mary's bitterness came out plainly in her voice. She had not thought the insult would hurt so much, but it did, terribly.

"Stay here, both of you." His nostrils flaring, Menton strode off toward the closed double doors of the blue salon and thrust them open. "Excuse me, ma'am," he said as he entered, "but I insist upon a word with you."

Arabella looked eagerly at Mary, who was wondering if she should not take her chance to flee. It would be easy to lose herself in the maze of London streets and be freed from his clutches forever. "Mary! Are you going to just stand there?" asked Arabella. "Come, let's follow him so we won't miss anything. He gives the most famous set-downs."

Giggling, she seized Mary's wrist and dragged her into the room despite Mary's protest. Menton was in a haughty stance before Lady Moneteforte's chair. The wilted dowager countess was reclining upon a sofa and waving her vinaigrette in a protest which the others ignored.

"Really, Aubrey," Lady Monteforte was saying in rigid tones, "I find no reason for such a display of temper. I confess myself astonished at this lack of manners in you."

"Then you will find yourself in my position, ma'am," he said in a voice like a whip. "I myself wonder at your own lack of them."

She drew herself up in her chair, formidable in her black sarcenet. "Pray, explain what you mean."

His dark blue eyes glittered at her equally formidable gray ones, and his nostrils flared once as he tightened his lips and lowered his head slightly. "Is it not you who has started a slanderous rumor concerning Miss Clampton?"

Mary caught her breath in surprise at this unexpected championship and dared wait to hear more.

Lady Monteforte's face flushed with anger, and her thin hands gripped her cane until the blue veins stood out plainly through the transparent withered skin. "I do *not* start rumors, Aubrey. Nor do I recall knowing this . . . this female to whom you refer."

Arabella stirred and would have spoken, but Mary had no wish to call attention to their presence, especially with the countess in the room, and seized her arm in warning.

"Certainly you know who she is," Menton was saying in his most top-lofty fashion. He locked his hands together at his back, his chin jutting hard atop the snowy folds of his cravat. "If you have instructed your grandchildren to give her the cold shoulder—"

"Oh, that." Lady Monteforte snorted and waved a dismissing hand. "I do not see how this concerns you."

"The lady—and she *is* a lady—is an acquaintance of mine." Menton went to the fireplace long enough to kick the fire back to life with one swift thrust of his boot heel, then returned to resume his stance before her. "I do not intend to have her slandered unjustly."

"Then perhaps you should know the facts," retorted Lady Monteforte, banging her cane on the floor in one decisive thump. "Certainly I know nothing against her personal reputation. But she cannot be considered of the highest ton if she is being sponsored by this Tavers woman, who may contrive to pass acceptance in the lower circles. In your set or mine she can only be looked upon with askance." Lady Monteforte turned her piercing gaze upon him. "In fact, I am surprised that you should know her."

"If *you* know her, I do not see why I should not." His jaw hardened. "Very well, ma'am. I will suggest to Miss Clampton that she select a new sponsor. But you, ma'am, must halt these notions of yours from spreading further."

"You are hardly a regulator of my conduct, Aubrey," snapped Lady Monteforte, gripping her cane.

The dowager countess half raised up. "Please, do stop this dreadful quarreling. I feel the headache coming on."

"If you would but stop quacking yourself, Olivia," said Lady Monteforte tartly, "you would not be forever susceptible to these spasms of yours. I have never had a fit or a spasm in my entire life. I cannot see what enjoyment you could possibly derive from them."

The dowager countess sank down with only a plaintive glance of appeal at her son, who ignored her completely.

"I suggest that you become better acquainted with Miss Clampton before you judge her so harshly," he said to Lady Monteforte.

She smiled sardonically. "Since the chit has been

standing inside the room for the past ten minutes without making the least push to defend herself, I—"

Menton barely stifled an oath as he swung around to glare at Mary, who stood petrified in her place. "I told you to stay where you were!"

"Don't shout at the poor child, Aubrey dear," reproached his mother from the depths of her sofa, to Mary's increasing alarm. "So embarrassing for her to be quarreled over."

Menton sent Mary a frown and beckoned for her to come forward. She obeyed reluctantly, struggling to hide her trembling and afraid to glance in the dowager's direction. Why had she been so foolish as to stay, when she should have fled?

"Now, ma'am," said Menton severely to her. He folded her cold arm in his, the material of his coat slightly rough against her skin, and positioned her before the old woman. "You have heard all that's been said concerning Miss Tavers. Is it true?"

Lady Monteforte's eyes pierced through Mary, who tried to keep her composure, though her heart was hammering so she feared everyone must be able to hear it. "She is already gone," said Mary with an anxious glance at Menton, unsure of how he would receive this news. "We quarreled shortly before you arrived, my lord, and she has left."

"Left?" His brows came together in a thunderous fashion over his bony nose, and his grip tightened on her arm. "For what reason?"

Mary flinched beneath the lash in his voice. And now that she was the center of attention, how long until the countess recognized her? "Because I embarrassed her last evening."

"What did you do?" askd Arabella, coming forward. "Oh, pray, Grandmama, do not be frowning at me. It is not an uncivil question."

"She dropped a vase of some value," said Menton. He was still frowning. "That cannot be the only reason. Have there been other quarrels?"

Mary hung her head. "Yes. But . . . but I am glad she is gone!" she said in defiance.

"Bravo!" declared Arabella. "I suspected she was

a selfish female the day she left you alone on St. James's and we were obliged to take you home."

"Arabella, *please,*" said Lady Monteforte, and in repressive accents dismissed her from the room.

Menton paced once about the room and came back to Mary. "You were to go to my brother's on the twelfth? With her gone, you of course shall not be able to attend. Damn!"

His mother sat straight up. "Aubrey!"

He frowned at her as though noticing her existence in the room for the first time. "Yes, Mama?"

"I beg you will not use that horrid language in our presence! You are not at a pugilist ring."

"Of course. I beg pardon." But he looked as though he had no conception of what she was talking of. He glanced round at all of them. "Excuse me, please. A . . . prior engagement," he said in his bleakest voice, and looked at Mary. "Forgive me. Rodney shall see you home." He bowed and strode out with an expression of muted fury in his hard face.

Mary stared after him in a panic at being abandoned here of all places. Her cheeks burned, and she knew not where to look with the two older women staring at her.

In a moment Rodney entered with the bundle containing the vase under one arm. Dull spots of crimson burned in his cheeks, but he managed a wan smile. "I am to escort you home, Miss Clampton. His lordship conveys his regrets."

"Of course." Thankful at this chance to escape, Mary made her curtsy to the two ladies, not meeting either's gaze. "I should like you to come to think better of me," she said impulsively then to Lady Monteforte, and turned nervously to the dowager. "I am so s—sorry we were not properly introduced—"

"That's quite all right, child." The pretty, faded dowager patted her cold hand. "Do you know, it is the oddest thing, but I am positive that we have met before, and so I shall tell Aubrey when I can recall exactly where. My dreadful memory—"

"Your memory is suffering only from a lack of use," snapped Lady Monteforte.

The dowager raised soulful blue eys. "No, how can you say so? It has never been good . . ."

Seeing that she had been momentarily dropped from the conversation, Mary felt her heart start beating again, and she all but ran from the room. But as she left the house and allowed Rodney to hand her into a waiting carriage with Menton's coat of arms emblazoned on the door in the most arrogant display of ostentation, she could not be relieved. How long did she have until the dowager countess remembered? How long must she wait in this anguish of suspense?

Chapter Thirteen

EVERYTHING WITHIN HER screamed out the need for solitude. She needed some moments alone to sort her chaotic thoughts and emotions back into order. But her hopes of being sent home alone in Lord Menton's carriage were dashed by Rodney's climbing dutifully in after her.

"Please, sir," she said at once, putting out her hand in protest. "I should prefer . . . really there is no need to trouble yourself in this way."

"It is his lordship's command," said Rodney in a slightly troubled voice, and ordered the coachman to drive on. He sent her a grave look. "I am most anxious to learn why my sister has put his lordship into such a taking. What has she done? I beg you will enlighten me."

For a moment Mary was checked by the fact that Rodney was Rebeccah's brother after all and hardly the person to unleash her pent-up spite and anger upon, but that reservation lasted but a moment. Mary drew herself a little more erect on the seat. "Yes, Mr. Tavers, I can tell you the problem." She jerked in a resentful breath. "Rebeccah decided I was not worth her effort and moved out of our house."

"She has gone?" He looked startled enough to almost arouse Mary's compassion. "But where?"

"She did not tell me her intended destination." The memory of Rebeccah's stinging words made Mary speak flatly.

"I shall have to find her at once." Rodney ran a hand through his shortly cropped brown hair and frowned. "Her temper is quick. She does not always allow her common sense to rule her. I did think it for the best to have her . . . but now his lordship is in a fury . . ." His voice trailed away, and he lapsed into a brown study.

Mary was likewise absorbed by her own troubled thoughts, and nothing more was spoken between them during the remainder of the ride to Bruton Street. Finally they arrived, and Rodney sprang to hand her out. Giving him an abrupt little nod, Mary hurried into the house with the vase clutched to her bosom. The door shutting behind her made her feel safe again. She loosed a tremulous sigh and managed to give Pitt instructions for the delivery of the vase.

His brows went up slightly, but he accepted the bundle with a bow. "Very good, miss."

Mary caught an impression of his disapproval, but she was in no mood to puzzle out its cause. She frowned. "Wait. I shall write a note to go with it."

"Yes, miss." Pitt paused, then cleared his throat. "Shall we be expecting a new companion for you soon, miss?"

So that was it! She shrugged. "I do not know, Pitt. Something must be contrived, I suppose. . . ." Allowing her voice to trail away, she dragged herself upstairs, her tension slowly draining away with every step. In its place a sort of general despondency settled over her, and it took her nearly a quarter of an hour to compose a note of apology to Sir George. But at last it was finished and sent downstairs via Jenny. Dusk was falling.

Going to her room to change, Mary braced herself up a little and made herself dress as neatly as though she were expecting guests, then went downstairs to dine alone.

She had scarcely swallowed the last bite of a tasty buttered crab when Pitt entered in his stiffest manner. "Excuse me, miss. A Lord Menton has called. Shall I inform him you are not at home to callers?" His outrage over the notion of a young lady entertaining a gentleman without proper chaperonship showed plainly in every line.

Mary had long ago thought herslf past the age of requiring a duenna, so that held no weight with her. Nevertheless, she had to consider whether her nerves could endure another encounter with him today. She had no desire to see him, but she was curious to know what he had done concerning Rebeccah.

She glanced up. "Thank you, Pitt. Please show him to the drawing room. I shall join him there in a moment."

Pitt bowed and stalked out. Mary looked at a side dish of broccoli that had particulary pleased her and decided on a final helping. Savoring the power of keeping no less an earl kicking his heels, she took her time and finally made her appearance in the drawing room when she deemed it uncivil to delay another moment. Menton was pacing before the fireplace.

She noted with interest that he was arrayed in splendid evening dress of black coat and satin knee breeches. Below his jet hair his eyes glinted a vivid blue, and a sapphire stud glittered from the white froth of lace at his throat. She decided that if his nose were not quite so aquiline and his mouth less sardonic, he could almost be termed a handsome man. She sighed and she raised her brows to him, wanting to give him a set-down.

"Was I so very long? I am sorry, but I was finishing my meal. What a pity you did not come in time to be invited to dinner."

He turned to her abruptly. "You are damnably poised this evening."

Her heart thudded a little faster, but she sent him what she hoped was a cool smile. "I shall accept that as a compliment, sir. Pray, take a seat."

She sat down and indicated a chair for him. He refused curtly.

"We have a problem with which to deal. You cannot live alone."

"No." She smiled into the distance and folded her hands together in her lap. "But that, I believe, is your problem."

His frown deepened. "Yes, it is. I blame Rodney, however, for foisting his sister upon us. I should have known better, but in the haste of the situation——"

"I am glad to be done with her," said Mary with all the coldness she could muster. "We did not suit. But this is hardly a matter that required a visit from you, my lord."

He leaned his shoulders against the mantel and frowned at her without reply.

She shrugged. "Please, do sit down. Would you like some refreshment?"

"No, thank you. I do not drink directly before dinner." His blue eyes glinted unpleasantly at her. "Nor do I maintain country hours in town. Yours is an unfashionable habit, ma'am."

"Perhaps." She looked at him directly, allowing uninterest to show. "But once again I must remark surprise that you could not write me a letter for this trivial——"

His brows snapped together. "Dammit, ma'am, it is not trivial!"

Her tight grip on her temper slipped a little. "If you have come here merely to insult and offend me, I——"

"I came here to take you to the opera, not to waste the entire evening shouting over Miss Tavers." He checked, and abruptly resumed his drawl. "Besides, she is not really worth the energy. I've been told there is a highly touted soprano performing tonight. I cannot recall her name—some ghastly Italian creation of some kind—but I have heard her before, and she is . . . ah . . . passable." He sent her an unreadable glance from beneath his brows. "I am told you enjoy the opera. I await your answer."

Mary had the strong suspicion that no such intention had been in his head until a moment ago, and his evasiveness did not in any way raise him back into her favor. She did not want to go to the opera or anywhere else with him. She wanted to be alone, and she wanted to be able to send him away.

"I am afraid I must decline, sir. Thank you all the same, but——"

"Do not hand me any fustian about being fatigued.

I know you did not rise today until the afternoon.
You are not going to fob me off with that excuse."

Any other man would be saying such a remark in a
flirtatious tone. She sighed inwardly. It was very de-
pressing for one's only attraction to be an ability to
steal that one did not truly have. She was tired of his
mysteries.

"I am not dressed for the opera," she said in final-
ity, and got to her feet. "If you will please excuse
me now . . ."

He pulled out his watch. "I shall give you a full
hour while I dine at my club. Come, Miss Clampton,
there is no point in delaying further. I particularly desire you to be seen in my company this evening." He
pulled a slim box from his pocket. "And you shall wear
this."

She stiffened. So that was his intention! She should
have guessed at once. "I refuse to be paraded around
as your latest cyprian!" The words were flung out
without thought; she did not care what she said as long
as she insulted him.

The brilliant flash of anger in his eyes should have
warned her, but before she could take heed, he seized
her wrist in a crushing grip and forced the box into
her hand. Crying out in pain, she struggled in vain to
jerk free. His grip tightened until she feared her bones
would crack. "You will cease to employ vulgar terms,
Miss Clampton," he said in a voice like steel. The danger in it made her shiver. He brought his face closer
to her averted one. "These jewels shall be considered
as your own, and certainly not as a gift from me."
Now his voice hardened until her heart thudded violently. "Furthermore, I wish this evening to be the first
occasion of my—shall we call it, captured?—interest. Do you understand?"

Her hand had gone numb. She stared into his glittering eyes and knew with a certainty that threw a
sudden chill over her rage that his mask of sangfroid
hid a dangerous man who was capable of bending any
will to his own. Defiance sparked desperately within
her breast. No, he was not her master in everything,
and he would not force her to accompany him any-

where! She threw the box in his face and twisted free to run.

He caught her before she could reach the door and jerked her roughly around. "You are becoming spoiled, Miss Clampton." His voice was still cold, still controlled.

She jerked in a ragged breath, glaring at him like a cornered animal. "I hate you!" she burst out. "I wish I had stayed in New—"

"So do I. But that is neither here nor there now, for I have no time to begin again." He picked up the box and held it out to her. "You will do as I say. You have no other choice. Now, get upstairs and make yourself presentable."

She eyed him furiously a moment, but she might as well have been glaring at stone. Recognizing momentary defeat, she snatched the box from his grasp, and picking up her skirts, hurried away.

"I shall show him, she thought, running up the stairs and slamming herself into her room. She rang the bell violently for Jenny and yanked the ribbon from her hair. Yes, she would show him that he was not quite the master of this situation. If he thought he could keep her dangling in ignorance forever, he was much mistaken. She flung the box onto the dressing table and kicked off her satin slippers.

Jenny hurried into the room and dropped a breathless curtsy. "You wanted me, miss?"

"Yes, Jenny," said Mary in a hard angry voice. "I am going out with his lordship. Is the new dress that came yesterday pressed?"

"Yes, miss. I did it this afternoon while you were out." Jenny began bustling around to lay out the toilet articles.

Mary leaned momentarily against the bedpost and smiled mirthlessly to herself. Thomas Keath might know something of this mysterious activity of his brother's, and it certainly would not hurt to ask. Perhaps if she did question Keath, Menton might discover it, and if he did, she hoped it would give him apoplexy. Then her problems would most certainly be solved.

She descended the stairs a little over an hour later

in a gown of burnt-orange silk that caught the highlights in her dark hair. The diamond necklace was cold against the base of her throat, especially so since her incensed blood still tumbled violently through her veins, spreading a flush throughout her body. Menton was several minutes late. When he at last did return, she lifted her chin at him, trying to sit as regally as possible in her chair.

"Well?" she asked, her voice a challenge for him to disapprove.

He bowed with languid grace. "Properly magnificent. You have my compliments."

She made no acknowledgment. For the moment her anger made her reckless enough to have no fear of him. Somehow she was going to show him that she was not a tool to be used as he pleased and then discarded; she would show him that she was a human being deserving of all the consideration he demanded for himself. And if he wanted to lavish money on her to please himself, she would wear his jewels and someday spit in his face.

That night the opera was filled to overflowing. Every box held its party, and most of the attention was being focused upon the royal box when Menton escorted Mary to his own. She allowed him to remove her cloak and gazed openly around her. The view of the stage was much superior to the seats she'd shared with Rebeccah, and she was a little surprised to find herself directly across from the royal box. Menton joined her side.

"Yes, my dear," he said softly into her ear. "Tonight, whenever the performance bores you, you may stare your fill at Prinny."

She sat down in silence, refusing to spare Menton a glance. Yesterday she would have been delighted by this treat, but she was in no mood now to be pleased. Tonight she could not be awed by the Prince of Wales. Tonight she saw a corpulent, dissipated man in the first stages of middle age. She suspected he must wear a corset, and could only eye his fawning companions with disgust.

There was a brief stir from some late arrivals; then the curtain rose and Mary turned her attention to the stage with relief. But it was difficult to concentrate on the performance with Menton beside her. Although he did not speak or wander in and out of the box, she was conscious of him shoving his hands in his pockets, and yawning, and silently tapping one foot to the music. She was furious with herself, but his was too powerful a personality to be ignored at any time. And when he unobtrusively leaned forward to direct his quizzing glass at a petite soprano pacing onstage, Mary had to clench her fists in her lap in an effort to bite back the rebuke that rose involuntarily to her lips. Why could he not be still?

At the first interval he loosed a grunt of satisfaction and suddenly rose to his feet. "Come along," he drawled, his eyes narrowed to bored unreadable slits. "His Highness is beckoning for us to join him."

Nervousness struck at the pit of her stomach, treacherously undermining all the poise she'd managed to maintain until now. Before she could stop herself she sent Menton an appealing glance.

"M-must we? He is royalty! I—"

"Would you refuse a royal command?" he asked in a mocking way. "Come, every woman wants to be noticed by Prinny. Count yourself fortunate; you're rising rapidly in the social circles."

She bit her lip to stop the retort against his mockery. No, she told herself, allowing him to lead her out. She would not—must not—permit him to bait her. Her tongue would only succeed in embarrassing her if she did.

She forced out her deepest curtsy for the prince, who greeted her with a smile she had to admit was charming. She wondered how Menton dared look so obviously bored.

His Highness, however, seemed to find nothing amiss. He bowed over her hand with a faint creak of his stays. "Ah, so you are Miss Clampton! I have been dying from curiosity to know who had charmed Menton into attending the opera. He does it so rarely, being no great lover of music, you know, that we must all of us hold it as a special event." He had retained his hold of her hand. Now he patted it and sent her a knowing smile. "But there! I could tell at once he is taken with you—and little wonder! Very nice, very nice." He leaned toward her with a confidential air. "And may I say you blush charmingly? Ah!"

Mary longed to stop the warmth stealing up her cheeks, and hardly knew where to look. Fortunately Menton turned his attention back to them and smiled in his cool way at the prince, who addressed a commonplace remark to him before bowing their dismissal. Menton bowed. Mary managed another curtsy and was relieved to be escorted away.

They were returning to their box when a voice suddenly called out, "Miss Clampton!"

Mary stopped and turned. She did not at once recognize the voice that had hailed her. Then she perceived Sir George squeezing his way through the crowd. He was red-faced and frowning. Her heart shrank. So she had insulted him after all by sending the vase. She should have been satisfied with making an apology and left bad enough alone. How could she endure his set-down here before half of society? Already people were staring and whispering. Her cheeks flamed with mortification, and she would have fled had Menton not held her arm tucked so firmly within his.

Sir George shoved past a slightly inebriated dandy who was trying to ogle the ladies with the wrong end of his quizzing glass, and planted himself before her with a triumphant snort. "I say, I thought you were going to get away before I could push through this dashed crush! Dreadfully close in here." He mopped his face with an oversized handkerchief and suddenly beamed at her. "My word, but your taste is exquisite, truly exquisite! I have been staring at that particular vase this past month trying to decide between it and a set of silk screens that dearest Kitty particularly favors. Ha, ha! Now we shall be able to have both, and there shall be no dust-up between us." He chuckled and pinched Mary's cheek. "Young lady, I am forever at your feet!"

Mary blushed to her hair. She found it hard to accept his obvious sincerity. "You . . . you aren't still angry with me?"

"Dear child!" He made a deprecating gesture. "I was never *angry*. A little sad, yes, for you broke a rather nice vase, but the one you've given in return passes all things! My dear, you must, simply must accompany me someday and give me your advice on some bowls I've been considering. I particularly wish to choose the right one, because it's to match the new wallpaper in Kitty's boudoir, you see."

Mary tried to hide her dismay. How could she? Her ignorance in such matters was complete. "But I didn't . . . it was not I who—"

"Miss Clampton is a great deal too modest concerning her accomplishments," said Menton suddenly. "By all means, coax her into advising you, Ellsford."

"I shall." Sir George looked at Mary, his expression reminding her of a dog's hopeful grin.

"If you insist, Sir George," she said reluctantly. "I shall try my best, but—"

"Splendid!" He laughed and bowed over her hand. "Then I may have permission to call some afternoon?"

"Please do," said Mary, and managed a faint smile for him.

Menton reassumed control of Mary's arm and led her back to their box. "Your first conquest, Miss Clampton," he murmured with a mocking gleam in his eyes. "Congratulations."

"It is not in the least amusing!" She sat down, not feeling the slightest interest in the performance. "What am I to do with him now, pray?"

"Choose something that has a clear, pleasing color, a shape which you personally admire, and a price which you find shocking." Menton affected a yawn. "Believe me, Miss Clampton, in that way you shall not go wrong."

Chapter Fourteen

THE FOLLOWING MORNING Mary lost no time in embarking upon her plan. She arose early and spent nearly an hour dressing. When she was at last satisfied that she was complete to a shade, she set off at a brisk walk with Jenny to Mr. Keath's house. She began to think about what she was doing, and a little thrill of nervousness ran through her. No matter, she told herself, putting up her chin. Keath could hardly eat her, and Menton need know nothing of it.

"I am sorry," the butler told her. "Mr. Keath will be away until Monday."

Monday—that was the date of his dinner party. Swallowing her annoyance, she thanked the man and turned away. It was a great deal too bad, she thought, and wondered how she was going to be able to contain her impatience for the next three days. One thing she did know, however: she was going to that dinner party, chaperon or not. At all costs she must talk to Keath.

When she returned to Bruton Street, she was surprised to find a letter waiting for her. Handing her hat and pelisse to Jenny, she went to the bookroom and stared at the plain white envelope. Her address was written in a neat open hand that was unknown to her. Curious, she ripped it open and pulled out the single sheet of hot-pressed stationery. It read:

                                    17 Curzon Street
                                    9 November, 1797
Miss Clampton,
   I have set about inquiries and find without further question that Miss Tavers is not whom I wish
to have charge of you. Instead you will remove
to Lady Monteforte's residence—preferably this
afternoon. She has expressed herself willing to
take you under wing.
   Also, you are to continue to claim friendship
with my sister.

                                    As ever,
                                    Menton

   She peered closely at the difficult scrawl at the end.
Yes, it was his name. Flinging the letter on the fire,
she gripped the mantel a moment. She did not at all
wish to give up this dear little house, and she certainly
did not want to be under the aegis of Lady Monteforte. How could he expect her to enter the home of
someone who disapproved of her so strongly? Did he
never consider anyone's feelings besides his own?
She heaved an angry sigh. When, when, *when* was she
going to be her own mistress?
   Going downstairs again, Mary was brought up short
by the sight of Arabella standing in the hall. Menton
momentarily slipping from her mind, Mary rushed forward to greet her youthful visitor with pleasure. "Arabella! How nice to see you!" They exchanged a quick
embrace, then laughingly Mary led her away to the
front parlor.
   Arabella's large blue eyes were glowing. "I am in
such transports that you are to come live with us that
I could not bear to wait another moment. I know that
it will be the most famous thing, for I like you excessively." She skipped about the room. "What fun we
shall have! I brought my abigail to help with your
packing so that you shall be able to come sooner."
   But Mary could scarcely summon up a reply. Her
lip started to tremble, and she stiffened it at once. She
would not be maudlin, no matter how unfair it all was.

But Arabella had seen, and the radiance suddenly faded from her young face.

"You don't wish to come," she said. "Why? Don't . . . don't you like us?"

The rather plaintive question wrenched at Mary. She put out her hand. "Of course I like you, but—"

"Oh, you have not forgiven Grandmama for thinking the worst of you." Arabella took her arm earnestly. "But she has quite seen how she was in the wrong!"

"Has she?" Mary looked directly into Arabella's guileless blue eyes with open disbelief.

They fell. "Well . . . yes! Grandmama thinks you are in all ways respectable, but . . . Oh, please do not misunderstand! You see, she is rather a Tartar, and she has not yet decided if she wants to be *fond* of you. But of course she does not mind taking you in for the season, since you have lost your chaperon. Please, do come live with us. It would be such great fun." Arabella suddenly drew in her breath. "You have not found someone else? Oh, surely not another *hired* companion! Grandmama has one, and she is so stupid I quite hate her!"

Mary frowned automatically in reproof. "Arabella!"

"Oh, yes, I know I should not say that, but Mary, you *must* come! I have been looking forward to it so much since Lord Menton called to persuade Grandmama—"

"Yes," interrupted Mary with a great deal of severity. "How did he do so?"

"That is easy." Arabella ran her fingers across the mantel. "Grandmama is his godmother and positively dotes on him. He's ever been able to twist her around to his side."

"I . . . I see," said Mary, since a reply seemed necessary. She gripped her hands together and stared at the wall with unseeing eyes. Oh, what a dreadful, annoying man he was! This was galling beyond measure. The very thought of approaching Lady Monteforte filled her with dread, and the idea of living beneath the fierce old woman's roof was unthinkable! A plague on Menton! Why must he delight in installing her into a marble palace where she should be terrified

every moment of her life lest she commit some sole-
cism? Why could he not allow her to stay here in Bruton Street and be comfortable?

Mary jerked shut her eyes with the pain of forcing
herself to face the facts which put her into such a
perpetual frenzy. The answer was always the same,
no matter how much she tried to circle away from it:
to get what she wanted, she must first do what he
wanted. Everything within her screamed protest
against the gall of his power over her. But with an inner drooping of spirits she made herself accept what
she must. Shuddering, she forced open her eyes, feeling
as though she had just run a long distance. She told
herself she must be thankful there would be Arabella
as a friend, and that the sooner she ceased trying to
hinder Menton, the sooner he would finish with her and
set her free.

". . . and, Mary," continued Arabella with eyes lit
with dreams, "just think of how glorious it would be
should you catch him."

Mary blinked in surprise, only now realizing what
Arabella was chattering about. "If I should what?"

Arabella blushed. "It is not quite so farfetched as
you might wish to imagine. Of course, you have only
just met him, but you've caught his eye immediately!
Oh, pray, do not scoff. He is two-and-thirty, quite old,
and he cannot remain a bachelor forever. I would
rather you catch him than someone else."

Mary barely suppressed a bitter smile. If Arabella
only knew the true reason behind Menton's interest. "I
am hardly chasing him," she said reprovingly.

Arabella made a face of exasperation. "But that is
the whole point I have been trying to make these last
minutes. Weren't you listening? You should set your
cap for him. It would not hurt, and oh!"—she clapped
her hands—"how famous it would be if he were to fall
in love with you!"

"Fudge!" said Mary with scorn, hoping to dampen
Arabella's chatter.

"No!" Arabella's eyes were dancing. "They say his
heart's never been touched. Now, *do* come home with
me, and we can set about fixing his interest."

"I suppose," said Mary with a sigh, having to smile for Arabella's sake, "you have convinced me to go with you." Already she began to have a sensation of stifling restriction.

Arabella hugged her. "Splendid! You shan't regret it, I promise you." She seized Mary's hand. "Come! Let's hurry and get you packed as soon as possible."

Mary arrived at the Monteforte residence with a still-radiant Arabella, a small mountain of luggage, and a very strong sense of nervous dread. A liveried footman led her and Arabella from the spacious hall to a salon on the first floor. There, two flunkies sprang to throw open the double doors. Arabella grasped Mary's hand and practically pulled her inside.

"Good afternoon, Grandmama!" she called out merrily, dropping Mary's hand to run and kiss Lady Monteforte's proffered cheek. Lady Monteforte sat in her chair like an ancient queen, all in black silk and Mechlin lace, her gray eyes very much alive as they swept over Mary, who was hanging back.

"You see, Grandmama, I have brought her." Arabella laughed, her cheeks all aglow. "She was a little reluctant to impose upon us, but I soon persuaded her out of that."

"Yes, my dear." Lady Monteforte patted Arabella's hand. "Thank you. Now, do run along while Miss Clampton and I grow better acquainted."

Mary dropped her eyes at once with a wrench of dismay. She had feared such an interview, but she had not thought it would come so soon. She swallowed and tried to encourage herself.

Arabella skipped out with a smile, and suddenly a tiny dried-up wisp of a woman whom Mary had not noticed before rose up from a cushion beside Lady Monteforte's chair with a large book clutched in her hands. Her features were unremarkable, and her eyes had a vacant cast.

"Shall I go also, ma'am?" she asked in a rapid, shrill voice. "For of course if you wish to have a proper chat, you cannot be needing my presence—though certainly if you should wish me to remain, I should never mind the least little bit, and then there is our chapter which we have not quite got finished, but I have marked the page quite carefully in my mind, and I know I shan't forget it—never fear—because ever since a girl I've been ever so clever about remembering figures, though when it comes to working with them, I always seem to wind up in the most frightful muddle and lose one of those horrid digit things (I believe they are called that), until I don't know what I am about and am obliged to call for someone's assistance, though of course—"

"This," cut in Lady Monteforte a little grimly, "is my companion Miss Pingleberry. May I make known Miss Clampton, who is going to be staying with us?"

Understanding perfectly now what Arabella had meant concerning Lady Monteforte's companion, Mary exchanged a curtsy with Miss Pingleberry, who said at once: "How do you do? We shall all of us enjoy having you, I am sure. I hope you do not think it forward of me to be welcoming you so warmly, but I am a third cousin twice removed of dear Lady Monteforte, and she has so graciously decided to call me companion in exchange for the trifling services I am able to perform, so you see that of course I am not official at all, but rather—"

"Yes, thank you, Chrysilla," said Lady Monteforte sharply. "Pray, do not forget that you've promised Cook to plan tonight's menu."

"Oh, dear!" Miss Pingleberry threw up her hands in a sudden flutter. "How kind of you to remind me. I shall have to hurry before I am considered quite tardy. . . ." She rushed out, scolding herself.

Mary stared after her with a smile that refused to be repressed. Then she returned her gaze to Lady Monteforte, reminding herself to be brave. "You are very kind, ma'am, to accept a stranger into your home."

"I am an old fool to have listened to Aubrey," snapped Lady Monteforte in apparent anger. She thumped her cane upon the floor. "But the announcement has been sent to the *Gazette,* so it is too late to have second thoughts now."

"The *Gazette?*" Mary blinked. "But I have not enough consequence to warrant such—"

"While your consequence may be slight, mine is not," said Lady Monteforte in acid tones, glaring at her. "Be sure that I should rather have you publicly announced as a part of my household than to be obliged to explain it everywhere I go."

The sharpness in her voice made Mary stiffen. "Perhaps I should not have come—"

"Enough! I've had plenty of browbeating from my grandson, thank you." Lady Monteforte fixed a stern eye upon her. "There is something havey-cavey about you, my girl, and I'll thank you not to feed me any fustian about being a friend of Louisa Langfield's. The rest of these idiots may swallow that without a murmur, but I know that Louisa has no feminine friends below forty."

Mary kept her eyes lowered to hide her resentment. It was proving as bad as she had feared. "What has Lord Menton told you about me?"

"Nothing." Lady Monteforte raised her brows. "Why should he? He is scarcely an acquaintance of yours, having been recommended toward you by Louisa."

"Well, then—"

"But I do not believe that tale either."

Mary threw up her head and let her annoyance show. "You are becoming most confusing, ma'am."

"Precisely. Now I hope you see the effect this Banbury story of yours produces. It does not hold together, girl." She stared at Mary very hard. "You will tell me exactly what you are about."

Mary swallowed, furious with Menton for leaving her always to carry on his improbable plan—though how he expected her to succeed when he would not tell her what that plan was . . . She felt like a blindfolded person expected to host a ball, and she was becoming very tired of it.

She shook her head. "I wish to enter the best circles of society."

Lady Monteforte leaned back in her chair with a snort. "You're very clever and very mysterious. What is your background?"

Mary glared at her. "Nothing to be ashamed of!"

"I did not imply otherwise," said Lady Monteforte coldly. "Tell me."

Mary sighed. "My father was the third son of a baronet, my mother the only child of a vicar. She died when I was a child. My father died almost two and a half years ago." Mary set her jaw tightly and glared at Lady Monteforte. "For the past ten years we lived in near-poverty because . . . because of my father's investment misfortunes. Now I at last have a little money to spend upon a season. Lord Menton was kind enough to give me permission to use his sister's name so I should not look completely green. I . . . Miss Tavers was employed on the basis of a good recommendation. I did not know that she . . ." Mary allowed her voice to trail off.

Silence stretched between them a moment. Then Lady Monteforte leaned forward, her withered face giving none of her thoughts away. "You are not the usual sort of miss. I think I shall believe you. Yes, I see that I've set your back up, but you may forget your notion of leaving. You shall stay. I wish to see what influence you may work over that madcap Arabella. I am past the age to properly keep ahead of all her hurly-burly ways. That is all for now." Lady Monteforte nodded sharply. "Dinner is promptly at nine. Tardiness is not permitted in this household."

Mary took a firm hand on her surging temper and told herself to be reasonable. Setting up Lady Monteforte's back in return would not help her. "I . . . thank you for allowing me to stay," she said, though it took all of her willpower to say it in a civil tone.

"You are welcome." Lady Monteforte rose with a sigh. "Also, please keep in mind that I will brook no misconduct of any sort. I wish to be very sure that your reputation remains above all reproach, or of course you shall be asked to go. There should be no cause for misunderstanding now between us."

"I understand perfectly well," said Mary through gritted teeth. So she was to remain on trial at all times. Apparently one brief mistake would see her thrown out in the street, Menton's influence or not. Mary's chin jutted. She would show this hateful old woman she was no cit! Sweeping Lady Monteforte a curtsy, she begged permission to go to her new room and went out with all of her determination aflame. She would show all of them.

Chapter Fifteen

THE WATCHTOWER chimed out one o'clock. The streets were dark and primarily deserted of carriages. Terrified of the night and of being without protection, Mary hastened along the street, not caring what kind of sight she presented. There was no one out at this hour, after all, to see her—save watchmen, a few foxed bloods, and footpads. Thoughts of the latter set her heart hammering faster. She broke into a run, feeling as though she were forcing a way through clutching mud. The distance seemed to grow longer, the streetlights dimmer and less frequent. Soon the blood was ramming again and again through her ears; every breath she jerked in was like a knife in her lungs. Then a shape, dark and sudden, flashed at her from the left. She screamed and threw herself sideways into a building. The cur snarled at her and trotted on up the street with its head lowered. Mary crumpled against the wall and nearly laughed in relief. She really must get hold of herself, she thought, and struggled to slow her panting.

Shivering, she pushed herself away from the building. She was freezing beneath her cloak, and the chill from the frozen cobblestones had long ago seeped through her slippers. How she wished she had hailed a hackney, but that had not been possible from Lady Monteforte's doorstep. The old women must never know of tonight's excursion. Glancing up, she saw the first few snowflakes spiraling down from a black sky.

Sudden exhilaration bubbled up within her. It was as though she were the only person in the world.

Then a carriage went by, its wheels clattering over the cobblestones. Mary jerked up her hood and hastened on until she came to Curzon Street. Her feet slowed of weariness, but she pushed herself onward. If she did not hurry she would be too late.

The sight of Menton's great house with all its windows dark sank her spirits. She hesitated at the steps. After all of this effort and personal risk to get here— to find everyone now in bed was too much. She gritted her teeth and marched up the steps, then stood facing the door. Did she dare rouse the house? The servants would certainly think it very odd, but she cared nothing for that. If they did try to turn her away, she would make such a fuss Menton could not help but be summoned.

Drawing a deep breath, she grasped the metal, wincing as the cold surface burned her fingers, and raised the heavy knocker. To her surprise, however, the door gave slightly before her touch. She frowned at it. He must still be out, she thought, and the servants had left the door unlatched for his return. There could be no other explanation. She nodded to herself and lowered the knocker silently. She would go in and wait for him.

It took but a moment to slip inside. A single guttering candle on a side table lit the hall. She stopped, her heart thumping. Heavens, if the butler were still up and encounterd her . . . Weakness hit her knees, and she slid onto the one chair there beside her. No, she told herself firmly, the candle was well guttered; it had been left here so that Menton would not be obliged to enter into the dark. That was all. She need not fly into a pelter over every little thing.

The gloom and silence of the house were oppressive. Somewhere the faint ticking of a clock could be heard like a menacing whisper. She shivered in her cloak, disliking this house as much as it seemed to dislike her. Almost she was tempted to go, but she had to talk with him; it could not wait another day. Wearily she rubbed her hands together, wishing the hall were not so drafty. As though her movement conjured him up, Menton suddenly appeared out of the gloom. Mary jerked to her feet with a little cry. She stared at him, and all her sense of capability sank away.

He checked a moment, a swift expression of concern crossing his face. "What has happened?"

She thought she'd never heard a more irrational question. He should have demanded what she was doing here. She jerked her cloak more closely about her. "Nothing has happened," she said, struggling to maintain her sangfroid. "I came to have a word with you, that is all."

"Gad, of all the unearthly hours . . ." In two rapid strides that frightened her, he grasped her arm to hustle her toward the door. "You will get in your carriage and go home at once, where you belong." He wrenched open the door and stopped as though the sight of the empty street astonished him.

She tried to pull free of his crushing grip, and he whirled on her.

"Where is your carriage, ma'am?" he asked with a blaze of anger.

"I . . ." She stared at him, and the words caught in her dry throat. "I don't—"

"Do you mean you dismissed it?" His face went tight. "Of all the audacity—"

"No, no." She eyed him in exasperation. "Why do you never understand me? I had no carriage *to* dismiss!"

He grabbed her by the shoulders and shook her until she thought her teeth would all shatter. "Are you saying that you *walked* here?" he demanded.

She nodded, and was pleased that her head continued to remain attached to her neck.

"Good God." He yanked her back inside and slammed the door.

"The servants . . ." she ventured, wincing at the noise.

"Hang the servants. Why the devil should you care about them? Come in here to the library."

He dragged her away to the large room with its musty-bookish smell and lit several candles. He was still wearing his greatcoat, she noted, and his hat and stick were lying on a pedestal table. He must have arrived just before she had. She eyed him nervously.

"You may as well stop looking at me like that," he said. "You are the most idiotic female it has ever been my misfortune to meet, but I am not going to murder you."

She could find no reply; he did not reassure her at all.

"Dash it, ma'am, you say you have to talk to me—why the devil are you silent?"

She clenched her fists. "I . . . I cannot speak as long as you shout at me so!" She bit her lip to stop its trembling, and fought tears. To endure so much to get here and then be faced with yet another of his violent moods was more than she could stand.

He made a gesture of distaste and turned away. "Why can you not ever face me in a rational way?"

She needed her handkerchief, but somehow she had come out without it. A little gulp escaped her; she choked down another in fury. She would *not* cry! "I am sorry, but I do not have the temperament of . . . of a board!" she said, angry that her voice shook so. "If you would but allow me a moment to compose myself—"

"I am too tired to wish to deal with a display of hysterics." He began divesting himself of his greatcoat. "You are keeping me from my bed, and for no apparent reason."

Everything within her churned overwhelmingly. She rushed forward and slapped him hard enough to make her hand sting. She clenched it into a fist. "I hate you! I hate you!" She pounded blindly at his chest, longing for the strength to strangle him. "You have no right to treat me in this callous way!"

He caught her wrists and wrenched her around. "That is enough, my girl! I may treat you any way I please, and you know it as well as I."

His brows were drawn, and he was set about the mouth. She caught her breath and jerked her eyes away from his. He forced her chin up, his eyes glinting.

"You may think," he said, "that throwing this tantrum will keep you from going to Lady Monteforte's home, but I assure that it will not—"

"Oh, have done!" She wrenched free from his grasp and rubbed her aching wrists. "I did not come here because of that. I was willing enough to go to her home."

"Were you?" He cocked his dark head with a faint derisive smile.

She struggled to hold back tears of frustration. "I beg you to stop mocking me and listen. Please, for once listen!"

He leaned against the back of an armchair and crossed his arms, but his face was still set like stone against her. "Very well. I am listening."

His tone betrayed his disgust with her. Very well, she thought, there was no point in trying to keep on the good side of his humor. She did not think she had really ever been there. With lifted chin she faced him squarely, determining to give him back full measure, and be hanged to him. "Obviously you have gone to a great deal of trouble for whatever scheme you are planning—"

"Yes, I have," he broke in fiercely, "and the devil take you if you try to spoil things now."

"It's *you* who are doing the spoiling. You refuse to tell me anything of what you are about. You say you do not trust me." She clenched her fists. "That's all very well, but—"

"You may be very sure I do not trust you." His eyes lifted to shoot blue fire at her. "How many little visits have you paid my brother so far?"

"What?" She took an involuntary half-step backward. What was he talking about? "I do not understand you."

"I think you understand very well." He drew a deep breath, and she saw the cloth of his coat tighten across his broad shoulders. "I am no fool, Miss Clampton, and—"

"You have been spying upon me!" Mary was suddenly almost nauseated with rage. She brought a fist up to her small heaving bosom. "How dare you! You have no right to—"

"Yes, I do." He stood away from the chair, the mask of urbanity slipping just enough to show the dangerous side of him she feared. "But I have not had you spied upon. I now know the folly of that." He seized her arm and turned her to face him. "How many times have you gone to see my brother?"

An ugly thought came to her mind; she pulled free of his grasp. "Can you be jealous, my lord?" She forced out a laugh, then choked on it in self-disgust.

He stared at her as though he was looking at a monster. "Is it true?"

What did he think she was? "No! No, you abominable man, I have not been visiting your brother! Why should I? I hardly know the man."

"Nevertheless you have gone."

"Yes, yesterday morning!" He made her feel guilty for doing something that had been of no harm. She wished she were a man so she could call him out for the insult, and she longed to see him at the wrong end of a smoking pistol. "I went to his door, but he was not at home."

"Yes, he's gone to Brighton."

She blinked, and fresh indignation rose within her. "If you know that, then why do you accuse me of—?"

"Because you were seen on his doorstep, Miss Clampton! And because having been seen there once, there is no reason for me to doubt there have been previous times when—"

"There have been none!" She gestured emphatically. "I went to see if he might not be in your confidence. Since you will tell me nothing of what I am to do, I thought perhaps he could—"

"Thomas is not in my confidence." Menton's tone sent a chill through her. "He is my deadliest enemy."

Chapter Sixteen

"ENEMY?" Suddenly very drained, she sat down on the nearest chair. "So it is against him that you are . . ."

"Yes, Miss Clampton." Menton crossed his arms and assumed his sternest expression. "Now, how much have you told him?"

"Oh, what fustian!" She jumped to her feet. "What an insufferably thick brain you have! *What* could I betray to your brother? You have told me nothing except that I am to steal something, and that is not what I wish to announce to the world. Be reasonable and stop accusing me of being a traitor to you. I came here tonight to find out how I may not be one, and you set at me with this!"

She walked across the room and kicked at the unlit log in the grate. Chill air continued to cling to her cloak. She shivered violently and rubbed her hands up and down her bare arms. Was he such a pinchpenny he could not stand even a small fire to be built?

"Then perhaps I have wronged you," said Menton slowly, his brow knitted.

"You have."

"I apologize. When my valet saw you on his way home from an errand and told me . . ." Menton paused. "Well, that is enough on the subject. Come, it is time you were getting home."

She turned back to face him, gripping her cloak tight to her throat. Weariness swam through her sud-

denly, and it was tempting to give in and allow him to
take her back to Lady Monteforte's. But, no, she
would not give in yet. She would not go until she
found out what she had come to find out. She straightened her shoulders. "I am not yet ready to go, my
lord. I came here with many questions, and you have
answered only one."

He looked at her with almost a smile. "Have I?"

Mary decided he'd led her off the subject far
enough. "You must tell me more of what you are planning. I cannot keep up my part much longer. It began
with my blunder before Lord Langfield—"

"That's all right. Louisa has written to my mother to
say she's not coming to London until spring. So we
are all right on that head."

Mary shook her head. "No, we are not."

He looked at her sharply. "What is that supposed to
mean?"

"Shouting at me will not help." She met his eyes
defiantly, though their expression made her shrink a
little inside. "Lady Monteforte says I cannot possibly
be a friend of your sister's. She kept at me so until I
had to admit she was right. I said that . . . that . . ."

"Go on," he said in a dangerously quiet voice, the
previous hint of laughter gone from him as rapidly as
it had come. His eyes never left her face.

She glanced away uncomfortably. Why did she suddenly feel as though she had betrayed him? "It is most
difficult when you stare at me so."

"What did you tell her?" he asked sharply.

"I told her that you had given me permission to say
that I knew your sister so that I should not appear
completely green."

He winced. "My God, what a tale."

"But it is a true one," she said stoutly to cover her
inner dismay.

He turned away from her and began to pace. "This
has torn it completely. I wonder she has allowed you
to remain under her roof."

"Oh, she has a good reason for doing so," said Mary
in a voice that sounded very hard to her own ears. "I
am to keep Arabella out of mischief."

He did not seem to be paying any heed. "If only you had fobbed her off."

"Lady Monteforte is not someone who can be fobbed off." Mary thought herself done an injustice. Why did he always blame her? "You should know her that well. And she said she believed me."

He stopped his pacing and half-turned. "Did she?"

"Yes, but surely now you see that this cannot go on. I have not a good faculty for telling lies, and who knows what thing she will ask me next?"

He nodded. "She will ask about your family background."

"She already has."

His startlement was plain. A frown creased his forehead. "What did you reply?"

She caught the faintest note of anxiety in his voice and was astonished at it. She had not thought worry could pierce his sangfroid—anger, yes, but not worry.

"I told her the truth," she said, eyeing him closely.

"The devil you did!" He caught up a porcelain figurine from one of the bookshelves and fiddled with it. "And that satisfied her?"

A little glow of smugness spread through Mary. "It did," she said. "It is not as though I am of low birth."

"No," he agreed, almost beneath his breath. His eyes glowered into space.

She sighed. "Now, sir, if you please. May I know what you have in store for me?"

"I suppose it is time you did know." His jaw tightened, and he cast a measuring glance at her. "My brother is an undersecretary to the Minister of Defense. He has access to many important strategy outlines against the French. I shall see that you gain entry to his personal effects—by aboveboard or clandestine means, whatever is necessary—and it shall be your task to remove as many of these papers from his possession as possible. Later I will instruct you more fully."

A sudden void she did not understand opened abruptly within her. A traitor! So he was a supporter of the revolutionaries, perhaps even a friend of General Bonaparte. What kind of man could play the part of an English gentleman while he helped the enemies of his own nation? No wonder he had feared she was in cohorts with Keath. She began to shake and had to lean against the heavy mahogany desk for support. "No." She shook her head violently. "No, I won't do it. This is madness! You don't need me; you need to hire a professional housebreaker."

His head was slightly lowered, but his eyes watched her intently, like a cat's. "I prefer to use you."

"Why?" she asked flatly.

"Because you are more easily bent to my purposes," he replied. "And Thomas shall relax his vigilance against me when he sees that my *new bride* has mellowed me. Pray, cease these agitations. You have no choice."

"I do." She bit her lip, wishing he were not between her and the door. If only somehow she could escape from the house, he would never find her among the streets. She would be able to get away and manage somehow. Suddenly even the idea of gaining employment as a maid did not seem repugnant as an alternative to this.

"If you are thinking of running away, I do not advise it," said Menton in a voice that pierced straight through her. "You would not last long on your own with no money and no means of getting any." His teeth flashed in a mirthless smile. "Besides, if you dare try, I shall put you back in Newgate."

She gasped, utterly confounded. "But how can you be so cruel?"

His cold eyes flicked over her. "What good will all these sudden scruples achieve for you? A dank cell with rats? Do you want that? Or do you want to keep your feather bed and warm fire?"

She shook her head, unable to believe he would really carry out this threat. "You would not dare."

An awful expression flashed in his face, and she knew at once with a quake of terror that she had at last gone too far. He came forward. She tried to dodge around the desk, but he was quicker and caught her by both arms. He pressed her back against the desk.

"It is very easy to show you that I shall dare." What

frightened her most was his relentless cold voice that remained calm—despite the white fury in his face. "I have only to order my carriage put to," he said. "That takes a very few minutes, even for a sleepy stableboy. And it is but a short distance to Newgate."

"No!" She tried to kick him, but her skirts muffled the blow.

"Come along, Miss Clampton. It will be a nuisance to find a more willing replacement, but not so very difficult, I imagine."

She could not bear it. She could not decide. Everything within her screamed against prison, but she could not do what he demanded, either. The risk was too great. She could think of nothing save she must get free of this monster. With desperate strength she suddenly wrenched half-free from his hold and seized a silver letter opener from the litter of things on top of the desk.

Menton's eyes widened slightly. "You little—"

She struck at him blindly, afraid of what she might do, yet frantic to get free. He grabbed her wrist in a crushing grip that numbed her hand. She fought to keep her fingers tightly around the knife, but he used his other hand to try to twist it away. She hung onto it, striking at him with her other fist. He swore and jerked with a great wrench that seemed to separate her hand from her wrist, tearing the knife from her grasp with force enough to send him back a step.

Hot tears of frustration began streaming down her cheeks, and she clenched her fists. Sudden pain lanced her palm. She stared down at it in surprise, to see blood dripping rapidly onto the priceless carpet. Things spun. She blinked the room back into focus and was astonished to find herself kneeling.

"Here, don't go off into a swoon." Menton was crouching at her side. He yanked out his handkerchief and quickly swathed her hand. In a moment red seeped through the delicate linen.

She tried to push him away. "Take it off. You're ruining it."

"Damn the handkerchief," he said.

Strong arms scooped her up and deposited her in a

chair. She glanced away from her hand and did not feel quite so dizzy. But it throbbed, and her stomach turned queasily. There was a strange fuzzy sensation beneath her skin, too.

Then Menton's face was before her again. "Has the bleeding slowed?" He seized her hand, though she tried to shrink away. "Some." He strode over to a side table and fetched back a glass of an amber liquid. "Drink." He shoved it at her.

She turned her face away. "What is it?"

"Brandy. You need it. Drink it before I make you."

Slowly, resentfully, she took the glass and sipped some of the fiery liquid. It set her insides on fire, but at least her hand did not seem to hurt quite so much, and the fuzzy sensation faded. She gave the almost-full glass back to him. "I don't want any more."

"All right." He seized her hand and poured part of the brandy onto the wound.

She jerked and cried out. It burned as though he'd set a white-hot poker to her palm. Then his arm was around her, and she could not help but cling to his broad chest for a few moments. As soon as the pain abated, however, she jerked back and sat angrily trying to rub away her tears.

He straightened slowly. "Thank God. I thought at first that I'd gotten your wrist. Do you feel better?"

She huddled in the chair, refusing to look at anything but the bloodstains upon the carpet. "Why should you care?"

"I do not like to see you suffer."

She managed a weak but scornful laugh. "I suppose I shan't suffer in prison?"

"Yes, you shall," he said in a regretful but firm voice.

Mary glanced up at his set face and knew then with a sickening thud of her heart that she had gained nothing.

"Good Lord," Menton said after a long moment of silence. "You're getting onto the carpet again."

She caught at the diversion gratefully. "I suppose I have ruined it."

"Yes, rather." His eyes met hers, then quickly glanced away again. With a sudden movement he jerked off the exquisite arrangement of his cravat and began wrapping it about her hand.

She looked at him in astonishment. "Have you gone mad? You cannot use your cravat. It will be ruined."

In silence he continued to bandage her hand. Suspicion rose up within her. "You are being extremely anxious for my well-being, sir. Isn't that a little hypocritical?"

His mouth set into a thin line. "Have the courtesy, ma'am, to shut up. I assure you it is not every female I would waste a good neckcloth upon."

She gasped with indignation. "I suppose you do not like for me to ruin all your floors."

"Precisely."

"Then you should have considered that before you stabbed me!" She wanted another argument, anything to delay their departure.

But he merely raised an eyebrow coolly and said: "It was you who introduced the weapon. If you feel more recovered, shall we go?"

Hideous man—he'd thrown the threat right back in her teeth. She glared at him while he crossed the room to collect his hat and gloves. How self-possessed he was! He knew she'd never do anything that would return her to prison; it was all a question of waiting until she gave in. Well, she would not. She was not going to be hanged for treason just because he'd forced her into doing his dirty work. But it was as though the bloodletting had spilled all the determination from her. She could not face prison again. The very thought of rotting away the rest of her existence there overwhelmed her with horror. Wasn't taking the risk of being caught at treason worth it if she was not caught?

She straightened in her chair. "As usual, my lord, you make it impossible for me to refuse. I will help you"—she drew a deep breath—"with your treason."

He turned around sharply, and she was surprised to see anger instead of satisfaction in his face.

"That is all very well to say, Miss Clampton," he

snapped. "But it is also very easy to say. How do I know you will keep your word? I've had to force your every move up to now. Quite frankly, I am growing tired of having to keep a close watch on you, just to—"

"All right!" She shoved her good hand over her forehead. What did it take to satisfy this man? "All right." She struggled to keep her voice calm; it seemed to help her think better. "I've tried to get out of this at every turn, hoping you would be merciful. I see now I cannot expect that. So I will help you, but you must keep your end of the agreement."

"You may be sure I shall," he said harshly. He stared hard at her. "Are we perfectly agreed? I do not want this question to arise again."

She almost choked, but she forced herself to answer. "Yes, we are agreed."

"Good." He paused. "Let me warn you now that there will be no more leniency on my part, should you make the slightest attempt to back out in the future."

She hid her clenched fist beneath the folds of her skirts. Her illusions concerning him were now stripped away; it made her ill to think she had believed him to be a gentleman. He was a blackguard and a traitor. She wondered how much French money had been used to pay for his clothes, his gambling, his . . . his mistresses. Worse, he was forcing her to participate in his treachery. She would never forgive him for this. Someday, she vowed, someday she would . . .

"Are you able to stand?"

He seemed to tower over her. She started to shake her head, then abruptly decided she could not bear for him to carry her. "Yes, I am quite all right . . . now." Awkwardly she pushed herself to her feet. Everything wavered a little.

She must have swayed, for he seized her elbow. "It's all right," he said. "We shall go slowly. You are looking damnably pale. Perhaps I had better fetch a doctor—"

"No!" She drew in a ragged breath and forced the dizziness away. "That would only bring on too many questions."

"The devil with questions! If you are too badly hurt—"

"I am not." She shook her head and pulled away from his grasp. She could not stand his touch. "No, please, just take me back to Lady Monteforte's. She must never know I have been out."

"That would not do," he agreed in a thoughtful tone. "But how shall you explain—?"

"I shall invent an accident. That won't be as hard as your task of explaining the blood and brandy on the carpet." She eyed him, but he seemed not at all put out of countenance.

He shrugged. "I have no explaining to do. It shall be the servants who must explain to me."

She resented his self-assurance. "That is cruel."

He smiled grimly, his eyes looking past her. "By now you should have realized that I am not a pleasant person."

He opened the heavy door and led her out of the library, down the hall, and outside around to the stables. He pushed her into a shadow. "Put up the hood of your cloak and say nothing. I do not want you recognized."

She obeyed wearily and waited in the falling snow while he roused a groom and had a team harnessed to his carriage. The yawning coachman watched him hand her in with no visible sign of curiosity. She supposed, with a good deal of pique, that the man was used to these small-hour excursions of his master's. She settled into her corner and neither moved nor spoke during the brief journey to Lady Monteforte's.

Menton ordered a halt perhaps a block away. "We do not want to arouse anyone by driving up to the doorstep."

"No," agreed Mary. She wished only for some sleep. "I can go the remainder of the way without any problem."

But he insisted on coming with her.

"This is unnecessary," she told him, though now at least she was spared the worry of being set upon by footpads.

He shook his head at her. "How shall you get back in?"

"The same way I slipped out." She stopped before the tradesman's door and nodded for him to go.

He stared at her a long moment as though he would speak, then finally tipped his hat and strode away.

Chapter Seventeen

MARY'S ROOM WAS just as she had left it; elegantly furnished and drafty. The fire had burned down to red coals. She put away her cloak and hung up her crumpled dress. She examined it carefully and was relieved to find no blood upon it. Quickly she got into her nightgown and unwound the cravat and handkerchief from her hand. Now that the bleeding had stopped, the wound did not look quite so horrifying. She wrapped most of her own handkerchiefs around it and threw out the blood-soaked bandages. Then she picked up the almost empty water pitcher from off her dressing table and set it down on the hearth. She smashed it with the poker, then carefully shoved all the bits into a little pile.

She returned to the dressing table and stared at the shredded handkerchief Menton had lent her the other day. How absurd of her to have kept it this long; it should have been thrown out at once. She picked it up gingerly, hating to touch anything of his. The precisely embroidered coat of arms around the initial M caught her eye. She thought him odiously conceited to have his rank announced on even his linen. But it didn't matter. She shook her head to clear him from her thoughts and threw the handkerchief on the coals.

In the morning when Jenny awakened her, Mary was obliged to try to shake off a strong sense of unreality that threatened to nearly smother her. Dragging herself out of bed and shivering in the cold room, she gave Jenny a lethargic explanation of how she had broken the pitcher and thus cut her hand, and remained sunk in her own gloomy thoughts while the maid assisted her in donning the walking dress of pink sarcenet. With a last adjuration to Jenny not to fuss over her, she headed for the breakfast parlor with the miserable thought that soon she would be joined in holy wedlock to the most treacherous blackguard in all England, and that she was too great a coward to take the necessary step to stop it.

She was halfway down the stairs when a strange sensation struck her. It started with her eyes: suddenly they seemed all fuzzy. She stopped and rubbed at them. That seemed to help, but then her knees went rubbery. She was obliged to seize the polished oak banister, and she clung to it in sudden fear that if she tried to go down even one more step, she would fall. Panic snatched at her throat. She tried to call out for help, but the words tangled around her tongue and fled before the dizziness coming upon her. She shook her head, deciding she must be light-headed from lack of food. But she could not get down to the breakfast room to remedy the matter—she could not even get to the next step. It was maddening; she could not stay here like a ninnyhammer forever.

She bit her lip and forced herself to take that step, her brow knit in concentration. It was a mistake. Hot, then cold prickled rapidly all over her body. She was almost nauseous, and clung to the banister tighter than ever. This was silly to be so weak!

"Miss Clampton? Is something the matter?"

It was a young fresh voice she thought she remembered but could not recognize. She forced herself to turn her head so she could look down. Young Lord Langfield, resplendent in a green hussars uniform laced with silver braid, stood peering up at her from the foot of the stairs. He twisted his riding crop between his hands and frowned at her.

"Are you ill, Miss Clampton? You're looking rather pale."

Irritation burned up within her. Why did he do nothing but stand down there and ask doltish questions? Surely he could see that she needed help. Something light, like a strand of hair, tickled across her forehead. She tried to rub it away, but all of her hair seemed to be in place.

His frown became more pronounced. He took one step up, then stopped. "Miss——"

"Yes!" Her own voice burst too loudly upon her ears. She tried to put up a hand to her temple to stop the ringing there, but it was like reaching through fog. Then, as though she had suddenly stepped away from her body, she heard her voice say with astonishing firmness and clarity: "Help me. I am going to faint."

"Good Lord! Hang on!"

Dimly she heard rapid clomps, which she took to be the sound of his boots running up to her. Then strong hands gripped her arms. She shuddered; their grip was too much like Menton's. Abruptly the mist cleared and she found herself staring into his troubled eyes. How silly of her to compare him to his uncle. This boy was no traitor; one could see straight to his clean heart through his guileless eyes. Menton's eyes—how beautifully vivid they were—reminded her always of closed shutters, but he was black inside, all black and rotted.

She shook her head and drew back a little. "Thank you. I . . . I am better now."

"Well, you are looking burnt to the socket," he said in a tone she was sure he meant to be bracing. "Just lean on me and I'll help you on down—unless you'd prefer to return to your room?"

"No." She sighed. Her voice sounded absurdly quavery, but she was all cold and somehow crystal inside, as though learning the truth about Menton had stripped bare something vulnerable within her and left it all ready to be shattered. She shook her head again; she did not want to think about him. It hurt her, and she did not want to wonder why. "I think I only need my breakfast," she said, holding herself up rigidly between the banister and Lord Langfield's steadying arm. She tried to laugh. "You must think me so silly . . ."

He was attempting to assure her otherwise when Arabella, radiant in a riding habit of peacock blue,

ran down the stairs behind them. "Charlie! Mary!
Good morning . . ." She faltered and tried to peer at
Mary over Langfield's arm. "Whatever is the matter?
Mary?"

Already Mary was weary of explaining. She thought
of all those yet to be told and mentally snarled at
Menton. It was all his fault that her hand was aching
and her head was pounding. He had wounded her and
caused her to be now in this horrible invalidic condi-
tion. And indeed, scarcely had she reached the foot of
the stairs and finished her little story concerning her
hand than she was forcefully borne off to the morning
room by Arabella and Langfield, who pushed her protesting onto a day sofa and then proceeded to discuss
whether a doctor ought to be sent for.

"Certainly not," said Mary, struggling to get to a sitting position.

Arabella pushed her down again with more determination than solicitude and stuffed another cushion
beneath her. "Yes, don't you think we should, Charlie?" She turned her huge blue eyes upon him with
such attention that it was obvious Langfield's breathing became impaired and he had to struggle to keep
his mind upon her question.

"By all means a doctor should be sent for," he said
manfully, and drew in another deep breath. "Mean to
say . . . might get infected or something, and that can
be nasty."

"Nonsense," said Mary, but she was obliged to
abandon her argument, since she could think of no
way to tell them that brandy had already been applied
against infection.

The doctor was sent for, and Arabella and Langfield delayed their morning ride to remain with Mary
for the quarter of an hour it took the man to arrive.
But as they spent the greater portion of the time with
their heads together over at the bow window, Mary
thought they might as well have gone on for all the
company they were providing. She also thought some
breakfast would do her far more good than any doctor,
but perhaps once he was finished she would be able to

escape to her room and let the quiet relieve her headache.

But it was not to be. The doctor bustled in and without further delay shooed Arabella and Langfield from the room. Then he just as firmly shut the doors in the faces of the gathering servants and returned to Mary while rolling up his shirt sleeves.

His eyes twinkling at her through his spectacles, he seized her hand and ripped off her crude bandaging. She could not bear to see the wound; she swallowed down the nervousness bubbling up from her stomach and kept her gaze averted. Surprisingly, however, his stubby hands were deft and gentle.

"Rather a serious cut for a young lady to receive," he said at last, "but it's very clean." Pursuing his lips, he plunged a hand into his bulging bag as though in pursuit of something that might elude him. An apologetic look crossed his face. "I'm going to stitch it up for you. Now, don't have the vapors on me, mind!"

Mary, who wanted very much to have them, instantly braced up. Certainly she would not show her cowardice. "Will it b-be very painful?'

"Oh, a little. But I shall give you some laudanum in water afterward so that you can have some rest. Now, hold out that hand for me so I can be quick and get back to my breakfast.'

Several minutes later he bandaged his handiwork, ordered three days of absolute rest, and promised to call again the following afternoon. Mary watched him with slitted eyes. Her hand seemed to be swelling, and certainly pained her far more. Her temples still pounded, and her stomach heaved with a hideous combination of nausea and starvation.

"Oh, my goodness! Dear, dear me. You poor thing . . ." Miss Pingleberry pattered into the room and at once took Mary's good hand. She patted it and beamed. "I simply *adore* nursing people, for it makes me feel as though I have something worthwhile to do, though of course *dearest* Honoria keeps me quite busy —but you mustn't think that I am oppressed with work, for I am not! So now you see how determined I am to make you perfectly comfortable and well again."

By the afternoon Mary still had not managed to fob her off. Miss Pingleberry had just stepped out to confer with the cook concerning the menu for that evening, and Mary had gratefully opened a book of poetry when Lord Menton was announced. She looked up in surprise and annoyance; she had not expected to see him again so soon, and she was not sure she wanted to see him at all. That dreadful Pingleberry woman had given her no opportunity all day to collect her thoughts, and she desperately needed to do so before she dealt with him again.

She snapped shut her book and darkly watched him cross the room toward her. His black locks were brushed à la Brutus, and his top boots shone with equal luster. Buckskins sheathed his powerful legs, and he wore several whip points thrust through a buttonhole in his coat. How can someone so magnificent, she thought, be so horrible? His blue eyes caught her unfriendly gaze, and he frowned. He did not speak, nor did she. Then he shifted his eyes away from hers. She followed his gaze to Miss Pingleberry's knitting, then to a large volume with the daunting title of *An Amateur's Guide to Botanical Studies*, and finally to the bottle of laudanum drops.

His lips tightened, and his gaze swung back to hers. "You are injured more seriously than I had thought." He made it almost an accusation.

She shook her head, yet allowed her frustration to come boiling out. "Oh, it is nothing. I am a little weak, and what must they do but fetch a doctor, who was not satisfied until he stitched on me in the most odious fashion . . ." She broke off, surprised by the swift look of concern that flashed across his harsh features. He stepped to her side and lifted up her chin to carefully search her face, until she grew flushed and jerked free. "Why must you stare, sir?" She tried for a light tone, but her voice sounded brittle.

He clenched his hand into a fist and stared at it. "You are looking so worn down—"

"It is only that tiresome woman!" Mary pitched her

book aside. "She has fussed over me the whole day."

He frowned in puzzlement. "What woman?"

"Why, it is Lord Menton!" Miss Pingleberry, bearing a tray, bustled into the room and bobbed him a curtsy. "So good to see you, and so kind of you to come and visit our invalid—would you mind, dear sir, to place that little table over here by the sofa?"

Menton obeyed with a grave countenance; Miss Pingleberry set down her tray and took up a cloth with a sigh of pleasure.

"How pleasant this all is," she said. "Now, Miss Clampton, I am quite persuaded that you have the headache, and after you swallow your drops, I shall bathe your temples with this lavender water; but of course, should his lordship care to read to us, I am sure we would both greatly appreciate the soothing effect of his lordship's fine voice." Quickly she picked up the botanical tome and showed him a passage. "Here you are, my lord. We were just about to begin the description of willow leaves. I do so love willows—they are such curious things, with all their whispering whenever the wind blows."

Despite herself, Mary sent Menton a glance of appeal, and to her great relief he responded by slamming shut the book and tossing it aside. He stepped between Miss Pingleberry and Mary.

"I have come to take Miss Clampton for a ride around the park," he said. "There is a touch of more snow in the air, but being out shall do her good, I think."

Miss Pingleberry spluttered a moment, then waved her lavender water dramatically. "She will catch her death of cold."

"Nonsense." Menton helped Mary off the sofa. "Please have her pelisse sent down at once; my tiger can't be walking my cattle all day in this weather."

From the expression on her long face, Miss Pingleberry clearly wanted to argue; but she gave ground before Menton's greater authority and dispatched a servant for the requested wraps. Mary watched this interchange absently; for the immediate moment she was more concerned with herself. But although weak and listless, she seemed free from the morning's giddiness and was eager to put up with even his company to be free of this excessive fussing over her.

While Miss Pingleberry was occupied with the servant, Menton inclined his head toward Mary. "Do you not feel up to this venture?" he asked in a low voice. "I do not wish to be forcing you outside."

Hypocrite! her thoughts screamed. He knew no other way to handle people save by using the force of either his personality or his position. But she had to escape Miss Pingleberry. "I wish to go out," she said, also softly. "She would have me on my deathbed if she could."

He smiled but made no reply. As soon as Mary had on her pelisse and hat, he whisked her outside and put her up into his curricle as though she were fragile. His blood chestnuts were fretting, and pranced off the instant his tiger released their heads. For a moment Menton was silent as he guided them through the heavy afternoon traffic, driving the horses well up to their bits at a spanking trot. The cold air set Mary's cheeks tingling.

She sat up straighter, taking great interest in his deft handling of both reins and whip, the latter being wielded with such precision he was able to flick the ear of his left horse without once startling the other one. "How I wish I knew how to drive," she said suddenly.

"Then someday I must teach you."

At once everything was wrong again. Mary bit her lip and gazed at his profile unhappily. Why had she spoken so impulsively? Although she had been in earnest, she knew he was not, despite his prompt reply. Then he suddenly met her eyes before she could avert them. "Shall we discuss driving further or change the subject?" he asked.

She looked down; the snow in the street was dirty mush. "I'd rather we just be silent."

"As you wish." And without another word he drove them through the park, stopping only once in response to her quick touch of his arm. They sat a moment, watching a group of red-cheeked children play ball with their dog, while the horses stamped and champed at the bit. Then a governess called the children to order again, and Menton drove on.

Suddenly Mary's stomach growled. She held her breath in embarrassment, hoping he'd not heard. But her stomach rumbled again in a fashion most unbecoming for a lady, and Menton gazed at her with his brows lifted. She returned his stare in defiance, hoping she was not blushing and afraid from the warmth in her cheeks that she was. "I am sorry," she said, "but all they will feed me is broth and toast soaked in hot milk."

"Good God." He shuddered. "That female's idea, I suppose."

"Yes," said Mary, "I have been ravenous all day, but she says I mayn't have any real food until I drink that horrid laudanum she is so set on pouring down me."

"Then you are not taking your medicine?"

"Medicine, fiddle! The doctor left the beastly stuff behind if I wanted it to sleep, but that *woman* cannot get it through her . . . her head that I do not *have* to take it!"

"No need to fly up into the boughs," he said mildly. "*I'm* not forcing it down you." He paused. "It's rather surprising that Lady Monteforte is allowing Miss . . . er . . . Pitterbrain to—"

Mary choked on an involuntary chuckle. "It's *Pingleberry.*"

"Whatever." He was unperturbed. "Why my godmother is allowing her free tyrannical rein, I do not understand."

"Lady Monteforte has spent the day shopping with Arabella," said Mary. "I had planned to go shopping too, but since you've stabbed me—"

"I'd rather hear what story you told them," he cut in sharply.

Holding back her annoyance, she told him, and was rewarded with a nod of approval.

"I am glad you are needle-witted." Quite abruptly he pulled up before a Bond Street pastry shop.

Mary sniffed the heavenly smells wafting out and

nearly melted inside from delight. That delight changed to apprehension, however, when he shoved the reins into her good hand.

"Hold 'em. I shan't be a moment."

"But, wait . . ." She broke off in exasperation, for he was already striding into the shop. Not daring to move lest she signal some undesirable command to the horses, she gripped the reins so tightly her hand began to perspire inside her glove and her fingers grew numb. One of the horses stamped and tossed its head up and down; the other shifted its hindquarters about restlessly. The curricle rolled back a couple of inches. Panic petrified her, and she gripped the reins more tightly than ever. He knew very well she had no notion of how to handle his blood cattle—he must have done this deliberately to cause her discomfiture. But her flaring of anger did nothing to allay her terror.

One of the horses snorted, and she jumped. In doing so, she seemed to have tightened the reins, for they each backed up a step. Never in her life had she felt more helpless as the curricle rolled back a little more and stopped. How long, she wondered, until the horses discover no one is in control and decide to bolt? She was tempted to throw away the reins and scramble down to safety, but her visualization of Menton's probable fury was almost as dreadful as what she was experiencing now. He had promised not to be long. Surely he was not so dim-witted as to leave his prize horses in her care for more than an instant. He should have brought his tiger, she thought angrily. Drat it all, that was what the urchin was paid for.

Then another curricle pulled up alongside, and Mr. Keath made a polite bow. He pretended surprise. "Why, Miss Clampton, how long have you been privileged to drive my brother's cattle? I do not recall his ever allowing a female to handle them before—especially his blood chestnuts."

There was something in the tone of his voice that she did not like, but she suddenly determined that she must warn him of his brother's treachery.

"Mr. Keath," she began a little breathlessly, glancing over her shoulder to see if Menton was coming out yet, "there is something I must say to—"

"Oh?" Keath's straight golden brows frowned over his perfect nose, and he leaned toward her with an intentness that suddenly, irrationally alarmed her.

She could not understand why she should feel this way, but the sudden thought that if she betrayed Menton she betrayed herself flashed into her mind. Now she had no idea of what to say. It was incredible that she was again on the brink of falling into a trap of her own devising. Would she never learn?

"Yes, Miss Clampton?" said Keath with a touch of impatience.

Somehow she forced an apologetic smile. "I . . . well, I am afraid I shan't be attending your party. I have hurt my hand and cannot be making all of my engagements for the next few days."

For the merest instant his pale blue eyes were blank. They were the flaw in his perfect face, she decided. There was something a little too cold and hard about them—though Menton's were likewise cold and hard. But Menton's had the brilliancy of blue fire. Keath's were like dead stone. She shivered.

"Ah." Keath abruptly nodded. "I have just returned to town, and it had slipped my mind. Did you not receive my notice?"

"No. What was it about?"

Discomfort crossed his face so quickly she wondered if perhaps she'd imagined it.

"I . . . er . . . was forced to cancel my dinner party due to a trip I must be making on that date."

"Oh?" She was puzzled. "Even when you have just returned? You must travel a great deal."

"Yes, I do," he said bitterly. "We who must work for our living are not allowed the luxury of coming and going as we please." His eyes looked beyond her as he spoke, and she knew Menton had reappeared from the shop. The suaveness of his features was replaced by a wariness that was reflected in his voice when he greeted Menton.

"Ah, hello, Thomas." The cool, bored drawl was strong in Menton's voice. He climbed up onto the curricle seat and exchanged the pastries for the reins. Mary was happy to relinquish them and thought that nothing had ever so exhausted her in all her life.

Keath's eyes shifted away from Menton's. "I was just informing Miss Clampton that I'm not having that dinner party I invited her to some time back."

"Oh?" Speculation hinted through in Menton's voice. "Well, that is all right with her, I am sure."

Mary was not very certain of the nicety of that remark, and hastened to add a more civil comment.

"Thank you." Keath's face cleared and he bowed to her. "Now that we have that matter cleared away, Miss Clampton, I beg to be excused—"

"Oh, Thomas, wait a moment," said Menton.

Mary saw Keath tense himself. "Yes, Aubrey? What the dev—what do you want?"

"Just to let you know Mama expects you to show at her ball next week. She's in a dither that you will forget or else be off on some of your business."

Keath's face hardened. "I had not thought you would let me in Menton House."

Menton's smile had a malicious cast to it that Mary distrusted. "Why, Thomas," he said, "of course I want you there. Can't have you miss our annual winter ball. Besides, I'd rather have you there for all the chits to swoon over than present myself as the victim."

Keath scowled and picked up his whip. "You're too damned arrogant." Without another word he swept on.

Menton likewise pulled out into the traffic, but at a much slower pace. The exquisite aroma of the hot pastries wafted up between them, but Mary forced herself to ignore them.

"Well?" she finally asked. "When are you going to accuse me of conspiring with Mr. Keath?"

He kept his eyes ahead, but the set of his mouth was complacent. "I am not going to accuse you at all. Eat up. You must get your strength back as soon as possible, so that you may attend Mama's ball." Then he glanced at her with his eyes hooded and flicked her cheek with his forefinger. "One request: if you come, be as stunning as possible."

No command or hint of arrogance was in his tone.

She was puzzled, but obediently she promised to do her best. But as she unwrapped and bit into her pastries, Menton began to hum to himself softly, causing the left horse's ears to flick back again and again. Mary thought of him and his brother. Menton was strong, Keath weak. What a pity the stronger was the bad one, and the weaker the good one. She suddenly wished it were the other way.

"What?" said Mary, suddenly conscious that she had not been listening.

"I asked," repeated Menton, "if I might have that last cream puff."

"Please do," mumbled Mary. "I am quite stuffed." Her stomach now satisfied, she found herself incredibly tired. Her eyelids were so very heavy they just would not stay open, no matter how many times she raised them. She yawned and sighed. It was impossible not to lean just a little on his solid shoulder; after all, it was *there*. She yawned. "Thank you for the pastries. I feel much better now."

"Good. Sleepy?"

"Umm."

"I've worn you out, then." Satisfaction was in his voice.

She came a little alert. "Why, did you plan to?"

"Certainly." His team started to shy at a cart, and he barked out a stern reprimand. "You need rest, not that stupid female's ministrations. If you won't let her quack you with that confounded drug—which, by the way, I think very wise of you—the only thing to do was to get you outside to some fresh air and tire you out. Now you'll sleep despite . . . er . . ."

"Miss Pingleberry," said Mary through a warm fog.

"Yes, a frightful woman."

"You really should try to remember her name—courtesy." Her eyes closed for a blessed moment, then jerked open again.

"Courtesy or not, it is still . . . Ah, here we are. Just go ahead and sleep. . . ."

There were some sounds she did not bother to identify; then strong arms—which she found very comfortable—lifted her down. The clean, starched smell of his cravat came to her nose, and she sighed happily. Even her hand had stopped throbbing. Dimly she took note of a murmured conversation between Menton and the butler, Grindle, and of being carried upstairs by those same strong arms over the protests of someone shrill. Mary eased one eye open, glimpsed an excited Miss Pingleberry, and hastily let it fall shut again. She was safe from the creature as long as Menton's arms held her. Shameless baggage, she told herself, but his chest was such a comfortable place to rest her head. . . .

Chapter Eighteen

IT SEEMED THAT Lady Monteforte had chosen the rawest, most stormy night to have her rout. Huddled in her dressing gown, Mary stood gazing blindly out the window while the wind gusted and rattled the panes. Its wail through the chimney made her shiver, and she turned away with a restless shrug of her shoulders. A fire snapped on the hearth, but it did not cheer her. She was too nervous to be cheered.

Jenny came forward with the new wine velvet gown that had been bought from Lady Monteforte's dressmaker, Madame d'Eutere, and Mary's spirits bounced up a little. The dress was cut low over the bosom and fell in straight full folds from the high waist to her white satin slippers. She knew it set her off, and swallowed down a violent little thrill of excitement. Perhaps . . . perhaps despite everything, someone would find her pretty tonight. Perhaps she would capture some dashing blade's heart, and he would sweep her off in a whirlwind romance to marriage while Menton gnashed his teeth helplessly at the destruction of his plans. She hesitated a moment at her dressing table, then drew out the diamond necklace from its case and had Jenny fasten it for her. As always, the heavy feel of the stones chilled her. Quickly she patted a dark curl into place and pulled on her long white gloves. With them on, the bandage on her hand was no more than a vague lump. She drew a deep breath and firmly took control of her quivering knees. She looked her best, and there would be no broken vases to spoil *this* party; she might as well cease being afraid.

Resplendent all in pink, Arabella met her at the foot of the stairs with a frown. "Mary, do hurry and come. Grandmama wishes you at her side to be introduced while she greets everyone." She seized Mary's arm and drew her along at a pace Mary found more than a little embarrassing. "I cannot understand why you should be tardy tonight," she went on with a shake of the head. "You are ever on time. Grandmama is a little vexed, I warn you."

Mary tried to pull up with a retort, but Arabella dragged her on unheedingly right to Lady Monteforte's side. "Here she is, Grandmama. I caught her the moment she came down."

Lady Monteforte turned away from the gentleman who was kissing her hand and withered both Mary and Arabella with a single collective glance. Then she cut off the man's gallant sentence with, "Do be quiet a moment, Gilly, and let me make you known to these two hoydens regrettably beneath my roof. Mr. Gilbreath, my granddaughter, Arabella. And this," she added with more politeness than pleasure, "is Miss Clampton. She is spending the season with me."

Now those mischievous green eyes were turned full upon Mary. She saw them widen slightly and a twitch of a smile touch his lips before he swept a low bow over her hand. He squeezed it lightly as he kissed it, and she could not stop herself from jerking back with a wince.

He glanced up with a quick frown of puzzlement. "Forgive me."

"Oh, it is nothing," she said in an embarrassed rush. Now he would think her a prude. "It was silly of me to jump, but I have cut my hand and it is still a bit tender."

"Ah." To her relief he accepted that. Then his eyes crinkled at her. "Come, let's go off and look over the refreshments, shall we?"

"Not now, Gilly," said Lady Monteforte with a reproving frown. "Do take yourself off and mingle about until we are finished here."

He laughed, showing even teeth as white as his starched cravat, and obeyed. For the longest time Mary concentrated so upon all the people she was introduced to that she had no time to think any further of him, and she did not at all expect him to regain her side when Lady Monteforte finally released her. Nevertheless, he appeared at her elbow almost the instant she walked away from the door, and awarded her a glass of punch.

"Thirsty?" he asked, his eyes laughing for a reason she could not guess.

She nodded and accepted the glass. "Thank you, Mr. Gilbreath. I—"

"Call me Gilly. It is much more comfortable." Taking her hand, this time carefully her left one, he led her across the room to an empty sofa and bade her sit down.

Mary did so warily. He saw her expression and laughed.

"Here," he said. "You must tell me how it happens that I have never seen you before—after all, you are hardly a milk-and-water miss taking her first crack at the ton."

"Oh, but I am," said Mary. She had placed him now as an accomplished flirt—something of a rake perhaps—and relaxed a little. It might be fun to banter with him. "Tell me, Mr. Gilbreath, are you held to be something of a wit?"

He bowed. "My only virtue, I'm happy to say. The drolleries I spout are my guarantee of an invitation to all the best parties. I, the jester of the ton . . ." The roguish gleam in his eyes became more pronounced, then he sobered. "But seriously, Miss Clampton, how come you to be missing town gaiety until now?"

Instantly flustered, Mary began a muddled explanation.

"Brighton?" He picked it out of her jumbled sentences. "Rebeccah Tavers was there just prior to the opening of the season. Are you acquainted with her, by any chance?"

Despite herself, Mary stiffened. "Yes, I know her well."

"And loathe her soul." He nodded, then grinned. "But there's no real harm in Becky, just venom. If she was not so besotted on that Keath scoundrel, she'd be a good deal happier. Unsteady lot, all the Keath family—save the earl. Menton's the best whipster in town, you know. A top sawyer in every way. I'll bet on his blood chestnuts anytime—provided he'll lend me the blunt to do it!" Gilbreath winked and chuckled. "Know him?"

The mention of Menton had brought an unexplainable tightness to Mary's throat, but she was spared having to answer by the sudden appearance of Lady Jersey before them.

"Gilly!" With her rich laugh she held out both hands to him, and he promptly jumped up to bow over them.

"Hullo, Sally. Haven't seen you in an age."

"That's your fault," she said, and rapped his knuckles playfully with her fan. "Silly man, why must you go to Paris with the war on?" Without waiting for him to answer, her brilliant gaze found Mary's. "Ah, yes, I recall you now." Lady Jersey opened her fan and flicked it about restlessly, while Mary's breath seemed to catch nervously in her throat. "You were the spectacle of the evening not so long ago." Mary glanced up in anger, but Lady Jersey smiled and laid her gloved hand on Mary's arm. "I was excessively diverted. Oh, yes, you may color up, but let me say that you had exquisite taste in replacing that hideous vase of Sir George's. I have always loathed it, so be sure you have all our thanks for disposing of it." She chuckled and pinched Mary's cheek. "I've been wanting to speak to you on that head, but I seem to have lost your direction."

Mary quickly waded through her astonishment to find her tongue. "I am staying with Lady Monteforte for the remainder of the season."

Lady Jersey's shaped brows lifted, then she glanced at Gilbreath's quizzical face and her brows came down in a slight frown. "Do stop standing about with that imbecilic smile on your face, Gilly! Run along and fetch us some punch." She waved her fan. "These rooms are overheated almost as badly as Carlton House. I am persuaded Honoria's butler must be cold-natured."

Gilbreath took himself off with a grin, and Lady Jersey shrugged after him. "An odious man."

Mary smiled, beginning to find her not such an ogre after all. "You are very kind not to be angry at my clumsiness," she began, but Lady Jersey halted her with a flutter of her fan.

"Fudge, my dear. You amused me, and so I like you. Be sure I shall send you vouchers! Almack's needs to be livened up. The chits this year are the dullest creatures . . ." She strolled away, her shawl trailing deliberately from one shoulder.

Delighted by the unexpected favor, Mary watched her cross the room, then spied another patroness of Almack's named Countess Lieven just rising from one of the settees, and forced herself to move off in that direction. Lady Jersey's show of friendliness had given her courage. If she must have vouchers from *two* patronesses, then she would obtain them—even though this Russian woman looked terribly high in the instep. Still, she must gain entry to Almack's if she expected to avoid Menton's anger.

"And what are you frowning about?" inquired a merry voice at her elbow.

She whirled to gaze too fully into Gilbreath's twinkling green eyes. "Oh, Gil . . . I mean, Mr. Gilbreath!"

He sighed and handed her some punch. Mary set the glass down upon a marble-topped pedestal table and took his arm. "Do you know Countess Lieven?"

He blanched, and the twinkle all but faded from his eyes. "Lord, yes—a regular she-dragon. You don't want to meet *her!*"

"Yes, I do," said Mary, ignoring the temptation to agree with him. "Do you know her well enough to start up a conversation?"

A shrewd expression crossed his features. Mary heated a little beneath his gaze, but stood her ground and met him stare for stare.

Then he shook his head with eyes uplifted. "You females," he said in mock pity. "Always scheming to get into those cursed assembly rooms. Flattest place in town. You don't want to go there."

"Yes, I most certainly do," she said primly.

"All right." He sighed. "I resign myself to it. But only if you will go driving with me in the park to-morrow afternoon. Ah, no," he said as Mary started to speak. "It has to be tomorrow—no putting me off for a vague sometime."

Mary eyed him in some annoyance, not liking his tactics. But she wanted those vouchers. And if meeting this countess would help get them, then she must not squirm off from a mere drive in the park.

"Very well," she said at last. "I agree to it—but only if the day is fine."

"I promise it," he said, and led her away.

Countess Lieven was higher in the instep than Mary had feared. She stared down her aristocratic nose while Gilbreath made her aware of Mary's existence and then took himself off. "Yes," she said suddenly in a frosty voice that made Mary think of ice and whips. "I met you, Miss Clampton, at the door with Lady Monteforte. Do you speak French?"

Daunted by those formidably high cheekbones, Mary frowned. "A little, my lady. Not very well."

"A pity." The Russian countess shrugged and started to turn away.

Mary realized that if she did not forget caution, she was going to get nowhere immediately. She drew a deep breath and plunged. "My lady, please do not think too ill of me, but I desired to meet you tonight to . . . to . . ."

"Obtain vouchers? It is obvious." Countess Lieven's face remained cold, and Mary's hope sank.

"Yes, I am sorry. You must feel terribly cynical about ladies making up to you only to get into Almack's."

"I do." Something cold flickered in the countess's eyes. "But there is likewise enjoyment in banning cits from the assembly room."

"Miss Clampton ain't a cit, if that's what you're say-ing," piped up Langfield as he passed them with a plate of refreshments. "She gave Ellsford that Chinese thing you admired so much the other evening." He nodded at Mary, who frowned at him in puzzlement as to where he had suddenly sprung from. "Hello. Must say you're looking bang up to the mark tonight. Red suits you rather well. Too bad Uncle Aubrey isn't here." He winked and moved on.

Mary watched him weave his way through the crowd before glancing up to catch the countess with a look of surprised speculation on her face. It vanished instantly, and the countess nodded. "I must get to know you better, Miss Clampton. It seems there may be more to you than I surmised. By all means you may enter Almack's. Excuse me." She turned abruptly away.

Beside herself with delight, Mary hastened off through the crowd to finally find Langfield and Arabella sharing their plate of refreshments with Harton Mary blinked at his bright yellow breeches and green striped waistcoat, but just managed to retain the laugh that threatened to escape her.

"Oh, Charlie, *thank you*," she said, and then her laughter did escape her. Her cheeks flushed a little and her eyes sparkled gold flecks. "Countess Lieven was about to give me a horrid set-down when you came by at just the right moment."

Arabella stared up at her, then suddenly clapped her hands. "Mary! Never say she promised you vouchers?"

Mary nodded and was almost willing to hug Harton, though he would be terribly furious if she did so and crumpled his shirt points. Excitement and triumph bubbled through her, making her want to spin about the room with joy. At last she had gained the hardest-to-overcome hurdle in society.

Langfield looked much struck. "By Jove," he said suddenly. "She's finally called me Charlie."

Chapter Nineteen

JUST AS GILBREATH had promised, the following afternoon was flooded with brilliant sunshine. The air was
of that still, crisp coldness that makes one glory in
winter. And when he set Mary down on Lady Monteforte's doorstep an hour later without mishap and
wished her a pleasant day before driving off in fair
style, she was left in the mood that on the whole it had
been a very agreeable outing. She decided she would
not mind in the least sharing his company again.

Passing upstairs to her room, she had scarcely removed her pelisse when Arabella peeped in with a
frown on her pretty face. "Mary? Something odd happened here while you were out." She crossed the room
to Mary's side and said seriously:"I hardly know
what to think about it. There was a dreadful man that
came to the door. He had a sort of a crippled back,
and he was dressed in clothes of the vilest kind."
Arabella wrinkled her nose. "Grindle would have
sent the rascal off at once, but he asked for you by
name. The greatest piece of impudence! Since he refused to say what he wanted with you, I had Grindle
dispose of him at once. Be sure he was up to no good,
for I cannot think how you could possibly know such a
low person."

"No. You are right," said Mary in an almost inau-
dible voice. Her contentment with the day had vanished. Could it—no, she dared not think it! But could
it not possibly be her jailer? Suddenly cold fear

gripped her all within, making her shiver. If it had been him, she could not understand what he was about, but there could be no doubt that it must mean ill for her somehow. She did not like this at all.

Arabella hugged her. "Stop looking like that, Mary! There is nothing to be frightened of; you are safe with us. Perhaps he only heard your name read from the *Gazette* and thought to beg for your charity."

"Yes, perhaps," said Mary. Instantly she rejected the thought of applying to Menton. He might set about inquiries which would only dredge up that part of her past he must never know. All she could do was try to forget the incident. "Well, never mind," she said in forced briskness, assuming a bravado she did not at all feel. "I daresay it is all nothing. Let's put it out of mind, shall we?"

Arabella dutifully agreed, but for Mary it was impossible to follow her own suggestion—until the subsequent arrival of her vouchers served to drive all other considerations from her mind. Admittance to Almack's at last! A little thrill of relief ran through her excitement. Now that she had succeeded in gaining the admittance Menton said she must have, perhaps he would be less harsh with her. Lady Monteforte did not approve of young ladies exchanging correspondence with gentlemen, so she could not tell him her news. But perhaps it would be better not to go boasting to him. Let him look in at Almack's this Wednesday and find her there; the expression on his face must surely be well worth seeing. She smiled to herself. If he did come, then her satisfaction would be complete. He must be made to see that she did not deserve to be returned to prison for any reason.

Counting the days to Wednesday in a veritable fever of impatience, she at last stepped through the portals of Almack's under the sponsorship of Lady Monteforte. Menton was not there when she arrived, but Lord Langfield was. He came over at once while she was still trying to reconcile her expectations of magnificent grandeur with the large, rather sparsely ornamented ballroom. Through the doorway to one side she could glimpse the famous cardroom where dowagers played for penny stakes, but it did not appear in the least ostentatious either. She glanced all around and decided the people present were the assembly room's splendor, though she could not precisely see what drew them all here.

"Hello," said Langfield, coming up to her. A frown darkened his youthful face. "I did not see Miss Monteforte arrive with you. Is she ill?"

Mary shook her head with a sigh. "No. She was impudent at dinner, and her grandmama would not permit her to come." She frowned, not liking to remember that rather frightful scene between two strong Monteforte tempers. "I am sorry. Were you to meet her here?"

"Yes, I'd hoped to." He scowled in Lady Monteforte's direction. "Outmaneuvered me, by Jove! She must have seen us too much together and thought she'd put a spoke in our plans."

Mary raised her brows. "Why should she object—?"

"Oh, Lord, that's obvious," he said with a frown. "I ain't wealthy, you know. No more than an easy competence, though Uncle Aubrey says I can get my lands to provide more if I whip 'em into shape. But Arabella's been raised to live all crack up to the style, so I daresay her grandmama thinks I'm not the right sort for her." He looked gloomy.

Mary pressed his arm in sympathy. "I understand. How I hate all this emphasis on marrying just for title and money! It makes so many people unhappy."

"Yes, don't it?" Abruptly he grinned at her, much of his disappointment sliding behind his amiable disposition and good manners. "I'm a frightful wretch to bore you so with my problems. Dance?"

"Yes, please." She could scarcely keep her voice casual for the thrill of excitement that ran through her.

Sending up thanks that she was not doomed to be a wallflower, she allowed him to lead her out to the country set that was forming. It was her very first dance in society, and for a moment it seemed too much a dream to be true. The swirl of the ladies' dresses, the bright coats of the gentlemen, and the brilliance of the hundreds of candles all combined with the strains of the orchestra to set her in heaven. She laughed in sheer pleasure as she passed back up the line to Langfield and caught his glance of admiration.

Very conscious of Lady Monteforte's watchful eye, Mary refused to dance more than twice with Langfield. But she found herself with no lack of partners, as all of his cronies came up sooner or later to solicit her hand for each dance. She saw several amused glances cast her way by the matrons, but she did not care if her partners were nearly all of the military. Officers were very much the vogue, she knew. Besides, she much preferred their company to the throng of fortune hunters and simpering dandies swarming some of the other damsels.

Then there was a visible stir. Ladies stopped chattering and fluttering their fans, and gentlemen turned with lifted quizzing glasses. Mary looked toward the door in curiosity. With a languid step Menton sauntered in, attired in white satin knee breeches and a long-tailed cutaway coat of royal blue.

He paused and glanced about with cool assurance, then strolled directly to Princess Esterhazy's side. Mary was close enough to hear them converse briefly in French, laugh, and take their places on the floor. Menton glanced her way, and she smiled; but though she was positive he saw her, he turned away without the least show of recognition. It was like a slap to the face; because he had ordered it, she had never suspected he would greet her successful entry to society's ranks with such galling indifference. She whirled around to put her back to the dancing couples, her fists trembling in fury.

Langfield arrived with her lemonade and hesitated in surprise. "What is the matter? Some fellow being rude to you?"

"Only your uncle." She snatched her lemonade from his hand and gulped it down. It did not put out the fire within her. "He gave me the cut direct." She did not care that her voice betrayed her rage.

Langfield shrugged. "Oh, well, perhaps Uncle Thomas was in a bad humor and did not recognize you. He gets dashedly shortsighted when he is angry, you know."

"No, I do not know." She shoved her empty glass back at him. "And it is not Mr. Keath that I am speaking of!"

"Aubrey?" Langfield blinked, then glanced out at the dance floor and nodded. "So he put in an appearance. Good! Oh, I say, don't be flying into such a pet. Daresay you only thought he saw you."

"When he was looking directly at me, I cannot see how I am mistaken." Mary made no effort to calm her rage. She'd gotten vouchers and made every effort to look her best, and still he refused to award her the least approval. "The wretch."

Langfield bent his head forward. "Sorry. Didn't catch that."

"Nothing." She searched for a way to fasten her mind on something else, for she could not stand here forever in this strangled way. "Let's find a place to sit down for a few minutes."

His frown deepened, but obediently he led her to an empty sofa in full sight of the room. She sat and glared at the twirling couples. When that dance ended, Menton took his leave of the graceful princess and effortlessly separated the Beauty, Miss Lucy Thraude, from her mob of protesting admirers. Mary watched the blushing, timid girl take her place with him for a country dance and found her type of fair looks insipid.

"I say," said Langfield after a few minutes of this. "You've gone dashedly sphinxlike."

Mary came to herself with a start and realized she was fast making a cake of herself. Trying to return her distracted attention to Langfield, she saw Menton take an obviously charming leave of Miss Thraude, and pause to flirt with Lady Jersey, who laughed and tapped his cheek with her fan. In the next moment he was gone—as quickly and as arrogantly as he had come. Mary drew in a breath of sheer frustration.

"Excuse me, Charlie." She jumped up in the middle of his sentence and went to Lady Monteforte's side with the request that they might go. After making a derisive comment about silly chits who allowed too much excitement to give them the headache, Lady Monteforte agreed.

The carriage ride home was almost unbearable, for she had to bottle up her mortification and rage and sit quietly in her corner so that Lady Monteforte would not guess that anything was amiss. What an utter pudding brain she was, to be sure. As though she need care a jot for whether he found her attractive. Self-scorn burned through her, and if her hand had not yet been too stiff and sore, she would have clenched it into a fist beneath her cloak. She hated him, but she hated herself more for losing sight of the fact that he was a traitor, a confessed blackguard who was despisable and not to be trusted despite his charm and fine looks.

But he should have at least acknowledged her presence tonight. It was no easy thing to gain access to Almack's assembly rooms. He should have had the grace to approve of her success. But instead he had pretended not to know her. She had been passed over as though she were a . . . a *mawworm,* and that was not to be borne! A mere nod would have been sufficient on his part; he was far too steeped in his own conceit.

She tossed and turned all night, too aroused to sleep well, and in the morning arose in a vile mood. Wandering aimlessly throughout the silent house, she at last entered the library, nodded a greeting to Miss Pingleberry, who was installed there with her tatting, and stalked over to glare out the window.

Not even the arrival of a nosegay in a filigree holder from Langfield and a profusion of cards from the other gentlemen she had met last night could lift her into a better humor. Leaving Miss Pingleberry to exclaim over them, she returned to the window and tried to distract herself by thinking of the doctor's impending arrival. A little qualm of nervousness shook her; then she decided that the taking out of the stitches could surely be no horrifying ordeal. Her mind slid quickly on to thoughts of tomorrow, and a furious resolve hardened within her. Tomorrow was Menton's ball. She was going to attend it free of bandages and nasty stitches, and she was going to look as stunning as was in her power. Tomorrow Menton would not be able to ignore her.

But her militant thoughts were cut short as she gazed down on the street and saw an affronted Grindle and the footman hustling a hunchbacked man in a foul-looking coat down the front steps. They shoved him roughly out into the street. He stumbled, then recovered his balance and turned to hurl back a curse with a raised fist. Now Mary was able to see his greasy, pocked face plainly, but it only served to confirm the identity which she had recognized instantly. It was the jailer from Newgate! She jerked back from the window in sudden uncontrollable horror and gripped the marble-topped table behind her. Overwhelming fear iced over her veins, and she could not stop her trembling. The sight of him had brought back all those hideous, terrifying memories she could not bear. For one appalling moment she could even hear the grating squeaks of rats in her mind; then she took a better hold of herself and forced away the horror by trying to make herself think.

Why had he sought her out? For blackmail? The answer could be nothing else. Dread crept over her, and she shivered violently, afraid to wonder how he had discovered her whereabouts. Menton must be told, of course. And she did not doubt that he would be furious. He would be sure to find some excuse to blame this upon her. She shivered again.

Engrossed once more in her needlework, Miss Pingleberry had apparently failed to notice that anything was amiss. But now she did look up, and concern instantly appeared in her indistinct features.

"Why, Miss Clampton, come over nearer to the fire. You look cold."

"I am cold," said Mary, though she knew the fire could not thaw away the black fear spreading all through her. "Terribly cold. Let's ring for a servant to build up the fire."

Chapter Twenty

FRIDAY EVENING Mary arrived at Menton House muffled from chin to toe in her dark cloak, and she had the supreme satisfaction of being the focal point of every eye present when she removed it and passed into the ballroom. The cloth-of-gold fabric of her gown glittered in the light of perhaps a thousand candles and set her as a star come to earth among the pastel hues of the other ladies. Though the fabric was out of fashion, the styling was at the top of it. Soft dark sable trimmed the daring V which rose from her small bosom to her shoulders. It was the only bit of ornamentation—for she had not dared to wear any jewelry—to relieve the narrow-cut gown with its long tight-fitting sleeves that ended in a point at the top of each hand and its elegantly tailored demitrain. Despite the shock she had sustained yesterday from seeing the jailer, she was still determined that tonight Menton would not be able to ignore her.

Everyone continued to stare at her—the ladies with widened eyes and the gentlemen with opened mouths —until Mary suddenly feared that she had been too forward, too daring. She was aware of the thin line between leading fashion and stepping completely beyond it. It seemed now that the latter had happened. Her eagerness had made her a fool. Bitterness welled up within her, and she had to blink quickly to hold back tears. She lifted her chin to affect unconcern. Somehow she would have to endure the evening.

Then above the near-silence came a voice clear and awed: "By Jove, Menton, I must meet this goddess!"

The laughter and gaiety began again, and Mary found herself able to breathe once more in a little disbelief that her fears were not to be realized after all.

Lady Monteforte patted a small fold of her puce satin skirt smooth and steered Arabella off in the direction of a slightly overweight young man who was surveying the damsels with his quizzing glass. Mary was left standing to one side with the rueful thought that despite her grand entrance she was still all too likely to spend the evening as a wallflower. Then she became aware that dancing or not, almost every gentleman was ogling her. Suddenly she was uncomfortable and began to edge toward a corner.

"Ah! Here she is," said a loud cheery voice suddenly near her. "Damnable crush here, Menton. Thought she'd been swept away. . . . Well? Don't just stand there, man! Introduce us."

The Prince of Wales came to a halt and leered at her. Turning to face him and an impassive Menton, Mary could not keep her eyes from flying to Menton's face in search of his reaction. There seemed to be none. The bone of his cheeks and temples appeared more prominent than she last remembered, and his mouth was a little drawn. She wondered what could have wearied him so. The business of a traitor, she thought angrily, and a tiny but sharp pang wrenched her insides. That was when she suddenly wished they could have met under entirely different circumstances, with no dark pasts, no threats, and no fear.

"Sir," said Menton, his drawl marked and his lids dropped to mask glittering blue eyes, "I have already made you known to Miss Clampton."

The prince swung his pear-shaped head around. "Oh? Devil take you, Menton. Trying to embarrass me, eh?"

"No, sir." Menton was using his stiffest manner, but she could not be sure whether it was because of her or the prince. "But surely you do not wish to discomfit

Miss Clampton by ignoring the introduction to her at the opera not too many days—"

"The opera! Ah, certainly, certainly." The prince beamed at Mary and bowed with enough enthusiasm to make his corset creak. "You must think me an abominable slow-top, Miss Clampton, but I see what it is now. You have changed your hair."

Mary made her curtsy, obliged to accept the thin excuse. "Yes, your Highness," she said, and wished he would not stare at her quite so . . . so . . .

"Ah." He rubbed his hands together briskly. "Be sure I shan't forget you again. They're forming one of those charming little country dances. Simplicity, that is what I prefer—none of these cursed French minuets." He extended his arm to her. "Would you honor me, ma'am?"

Involuntarily she glanced at Menton, but he merely lifted one dark brow with an amused twitch of his lips. So now he intended to amuse himself tonight at her expense. She was instantly on her mettle and returned her gaze to the prince. "It is you who honor me, sir."

He laughed. "Prettily said. You may take yourself off, Menton; we have no further need of you." Menton bowed coolly, and the prince smiled at Mary. "Come along, my dear."

But the remembrance of Menton's mocking eyes followed her out onto the floor and managed to undermine her sense of accomplishment at having attracted his Highness to her side so early in the evening. She tightened her lips as the dance began. His lordship might be jaded with the privilege of rubbing shoulders with a royal personage, but she was not, and he had no right to deny her every attempt at satisfaction. Her annoyance growing, she had no doubt that even her appearance tonight was a matter of complete indifference to him now that she had obeyed his orders to look her best.

The prince was a surprisingly nimble dancer despite his corpulence. She tried to look past the heavy lines of dissipation that marred his countenance for the handsomeness he had once been reputed to have.

Then the dance was over, and he was bowing over her hand again.

"Thank you, thank you, for dancing with a bluff old fellow." He stopped suddenly and cocked his large head as though listening to something no one else could hear.

"Is something the matter, sir?" she asked politely, wondering how long he was going to retain her hand in his pudgy grasp.

"Eh?" His protuberant eyes with their washed-out shade of blue swung back to her. "Why, yes, I thought I was getting a touch of a cold this morning; now I am sure of it. Blast Menton and his drafty rooms . . . I had better take my leave at once or I shall be obliged to have myself cupped first thing tomorrow."

Mary eyed him in disbelief. "Cupped?" she blurted out. "For a cold?"

"Why, certainly. I strongly believe that too much blood in the body is a great hindrance to one's health. Good evening, Miss Clampton. I hope you mayn't catch my cold."

He hurried off, and Menton appeared at her side in his sudden, silent way, startling her.

"Well?" he asked with a hint of amusement or mockery—she could not be sure which. "Have my drafts chased Prinny away so soon?"

"Yes." Mary frowned up at him, still annoyed. "I hope you have not fallen into disfavor because of it."

"Do you?" He laughed. "No. Be assured I have not. No one except Prinny himself has rooms hot enough to suit him." He smiled down at her in a way that made her heart suddenly pound faster, and took her arm in his. "Your bandage is off." He turned up her palm and traced the thin pink scar with a gentle finger. His jaw tightened. "A scar. I am so sorry."

There was a note in his voice she had never heard before. Suddenly, though she knew not why, it was apology enough. She quickly laid her hand on his arm. "Please. Do not reproach yourself. It was my fault. I should not have lost control of myself."

"No, you should not have."

She stiffened, but his soft laugh immediately chased away her returning anger.

"My dearest firebrand," he said with laughter still in his voice. The light in his eyes was softer now, and more friendly. "I promise I am only teasing you. This will seal the end of an unfortunate quarrel." Before she could move, he bent his head and kissed the scar.

It was as though he had put a white-hot brand to her. A quiver ran all through her body, and a hot-cold flame sparked to fierce life in the depths of her heart. She pulled away her hand desperately in a shaken effort to regain her composure, afraid to examine her response.

He seemed to have noticed nothing. The earlier sternness was gone from the hard lines of his face. He seemed relaxed now that the Prince of Wales had gone. "Now, come and make your regards to my mother before all the bucks swarm you. Prinny ever succeeds in rearranging convention."

"But he was very kind in dancing with me," said Mary, struggling to return herself to the chore of mundane conversation. For the briefest instant she dared wonder what she might have done had he kissed her lips instead, then hastily shoved the thought away.

Menton was silent a moment. "Er . . . yes. I trust he is not going to call?" he asked, steering her around a small group gathered about the statesman Charles Fox.

She frowned, not understanding him. Was he afraid that she would betray him to the prince? "He made no mention of it. Should he not?"

"No," said Menton in a dry voice. "I prefer that you not be subjected to the embarrassment of trying to fend off his amorous advances."

Mary blinked, his words effectively dashing the rising irritation out of her. "Oh. I had not thought him to be that sort."

The smile whipped across Menton's face again, sending a fresh thrill through her that she could not suppress. "Yes, my innocent," he said, "he is *that sort*. . . . Ah, here she is, Mama."

Mary had wrestled all week with the problem of

Lady Menton, and she had at last decided that a brief greeting at the beginning of the evening and a simple leave-taking at the end—with no contact the rest of the time if civilly possible—would be the best she could manage. It would have to do, and if Lady Menton ever did remember her . . . well, she would just have to deal with that crisis when it occurred. She was worn out with worrying about it, and tonight she was just reckless enough not to really care.

Lady Menton greeted her with an effusion of charm, congratulating her on being singled out by his Highness, lamenting his early departure, and exclaiming herself to be in raptures over Mary's dress. "Do you not agree that it is exquisite, Aubrey?" she asked, gazing up at her tall son with one willowy hand on his arm.

"I think Miss Clampton looks magnificent."

He stated it matter-of-factly, with no trace of mockery. Surprised by this admission, Mary believed him serious, but even as her heart sang with triumph, there came again that little pang within her to undermine her momentary happiness. How could he—with wealth, position, and such high regard in society—have sold out to the French? What had forced him to it? Bitterness welled up within her for a moment. She could not understand people who could accept or denounce a person on the basis of the clothes on his back, or betray their country on the sudden whim for a bit of a lark.

The dowager countess nodded. "Yes, she is magnificent. How good you are with words, Aubrey! She should be painted in that dress."

"She shall be," said Menton.

Before Mary could puzzle over this statement, he was leading her away again. She was glad to go, for although Lady Menton was obviously distracted by her duties as hostess past the point of thinking about her at all, Mary was still uncomfortable in her presence and eager to be gone from it.

"Now we shall dance," said Menton abruptly, still retaining her hand in his large strong one.

She stopped in immediate panic, all of her enjoyment of the evening melting away. "Now?" She swallowed with difficulty. "But that is a minuet! I cannot . . . I have never danced the minuet in public. You—"

"Nevertheless, you shall do so now," he said, instantly impatient. "Come. I particularly favor minuets."

Without further discussion he forced her out onto the floor. Somehow she stumbled through all the steps in an awkward manner she thought appalling. Her musical ear was good, but now her distress was such that she could not seem to grasp the rhythm of the music at all. And she was seething so that she could scarcely concentrate on what she was doing anyway. Any gentleman with the *least* amount of civility would not have forced her to dance when she was unwilling. Menton was an odious, heartless beast. Nor did the other dancers' smooth grace through the intricate steps soothe her anger. She faltered, and hot tears of fury sprang to her eyes. At that moment she was ready to flee, but Menton's hand grasped hers and led her into the second part so swiftly she had no choice but to continue.

Finally the music ended, and she was allowed to escape her torture. She began to tremble, hating him and longing to run from the room.

Menton glanced down at her. "You will improve once you overcome this crippling tendency to fall into a distempered freak every time you are presented with a difficulty. Would you care for some punch or ratafia?" She made no answer, and he frowned. "Steady up, girl. It was not such an ordeal as you wish to believe." His voice was cold and unfriendly again. The few minutes of accord between them were lost.

"Thank you," she said acidly, lifting her chin. "I am thrilled beyond measure to know that." So much for romantic dreams, she thought, and decided she was a fool to have let herself be deceived by his occasional flashes of charm.

When she had her punch, she did feel better, though she was still out of temper with him. Distempered freak indeed. She snorted to herself, then remembered that she had made up her mind to tell him about the jailer. It might as well be now, when things were back to their normal, cold level between them. She put her hand on his forearm to gain back his attention, telling herself it was of no consequence to her if he was watching Lucy Thraude again. "My lord, there is something disturbing that has happened."

"What is that?" he asked, surveying the company with his quizzing glass.

Mary made certain no one within earshot was paying attention. "One of the jailers—"

"Good Lord!"

Mary whirled to see what had forced his exclamation, and almost echoed him. A somewhat inebriated Thomas Keath was strolling unsteadily in with Rebeccah Tavers upon his arm. She simpered around at the company slowly turning to stare.

Mary glanced away in disgust. How could Rebeccah make such a cake of herself?

Menton cursed beneath his breath. "Roaring drunk, blast his eyes! And to lead that Tavers female in like his doxy. I ought to take him outside and horsewhip him in the street."

Mary looked up at him swiftly and did not trust the flaring of his nostrils or the set of his mouth. Suddenly this animosity between the brothers frightened her. She quickly placed her hand on his arm, but he wrenched away without a word and strode off toward his brother.

In an agony of anticipation Mary watched him push his way through the crowded room. She could not believe he would create such a scandalous scene by carrying out this threat of whipping Keath, but at the same time he looked angry enough to do just that. She told herself she did not care what he did, but she did care, and her heart ached from the turmoil within it. Then an elderly gentleman solicited her hand for a cotillion that was forming, and she was swept away from any chance of observing Menton. Presently Keath and Miss Thraude took their places in the set. Mary released a tense little breath. She should have realized at once that Menton would not enact a scene, no matter how furious he might be.

When the dance ended, she strolled off in search of refreshment with Gilbreath, who laughingly admitted that he had been allowed through the door on no more basis than a sovereign in the porter's fist and the fact that the dowager countess sometimes found him amusing.

Mary drew in a surprised breath. "I wonder at your temerity, sir. Lord Menton is in short temper tonight, and if he should take exception to your presence . . ."

Gilbreath's impish eyes twinkled, and he shrugged. "I've been thrown out by my collar before, dear ma'am. But it is good of you to be concerned."

"Gilly!" Without warning Rebeccah came up in a dress of an órange shade which did not suit her. She held out her hands to him. "It has been an *age*. I am so surprised to see you."

A little to her surprise, Mary quickly perceived that Gilbreath had for all purposes forgotten her existence. Of course, she thought with sudden interest. He and Rebeccah were two adventurers with nothing but their wits keeping them on the fringes of polite society. It could be nothing but natural that they be so well-suited for each other. But Rebeccah looked bored behind her coquettish smile, and Mary sent her an angry glance, pitying Gilbreath for having fallen into the coils of such a shallow female. But Mary knew this was none of her business. Shaking her head, she moved away to find the glass of lemonade that Gilbreath had failed to procure for her.

But before she got it, Keath materialized at her side. "Miss Clampton, I have been looking for you." He took her arm. "Let us go to the library and talk."

She drew back at once. "No, thank you." He was not "roaring drunk"—as Menton had claimed—but the flush in his normally pale cheeks and a cloudiness in his light blue eyes proclaimed to all that he was a little on the go. And she had no intention of going off for an uncomfortable coze with him. "I . . . I am claimed for the next dance, so you see that I—"

"Perhaps this will change your mind." He pulled a

handkerchief from his pocket and held it out to her.

It was a grimy, tattered thing; at first she hesitated to touch it. She did not see why she should. Then she saw the embroidered crest and initial in one corner and gasped.

"You recognize it. Excellent." Keath's thin lips stretched into a mirthless smile. "And you know where it came from, too, don't you?"

She was cornered. Fighting down panic, she lifted her chin. "No, why should I?" she tried to say calmly. "I am afraid I am not very good at your game, Mr. Keath. Please excuse me."

"No." He blocked her path. "This is not a game, Miss Clampton. You have already given yourself away. I wish to know more—a great deal more. We will go to the library."

She went with him, her hands clenched into fists at her sides, her mind in a turmoil. What should she do? Did she dare betray Menton? She must; she could not allow him to continue his treachery. But what if he found out? Her knees weakened at the thought of it. She glanced at Keath's perfect profile and was dismayed. The man aroused no feeling of trust and confidence in her. No, she must not be foolish enough to depend upon Keath for protection. But what else could she do? Mary rubbed her forehead anxiously.

"In here." Keath allowed her to precede him into the library, then shut the door after him.

She was interested to note that the carpet had been removed and several small area rugs had taken its place. But quickly she shut the memory of that night out of her mind. She could not afford to think about it now.

Keath rubbed his hands together briskly, then drew out the handkerchief again from his pocket and tossed it upon a small carved table between them. She shivered; the servants had allowed the fire to burn itself out.

"Please get on with this, Mr. Keath," she said with sharpness born of fear. "I am cold and do not like to be missing so much of the gaiety."

He bowed sardonically and pointed at the dirty

handkerchief. Mary thought it looked as though it had been dragged through everything from mud to candle tallow to coal dust. "This article, Miss Clampton, bears the arms of my brother. There is no question of his ownership; his handkerchiefs are one of his trademarks."

He paused and glanced at her, but Mary refused to commit herself yet. "How very interesting," she said coldly. "Do go on."

He frowned and ceased staring at her. "This article was left—so very carelessly by my brother—in *your prison cell.*"

Knives seemed to slice up Mary's stomach. Instantly there flashed into her mind a picture of Menton spreading his handkerchief over her stool before sitting upon it. How horribly, dreadfully careless of him to have left it there! But even as she bottled up her vexation, she understood why. The handkerchief had been soiled by its contact with her filthy cell; being a gentleman, and having his mind so occupied, Menton must have unconsciously discarded it.

Glee bubbled up within her. At last he had made a mistake. This could easily put a stop to his black plans. But at the same time there flashed into her whole being the memory of his kiss tonight, his warm smile, his sardonic one, the wonderfully clean smell of him. At that moment she thought no one in the history of the world had ever ached so much inside. She could not betray him, no matter how evil he was or how cruel he sometimes treated her. She knew that his every word and move concerning her this evening had been a falsity. He felt nothing for her; she knew that. She was only his tool, and she had made the stupid mistake of falling in love with him.

Fighting back tears, she whirled away, but Keath sprang to block her path. "You make no reply," he said with all the eagerness of a wolf with a rabbit trapped between its front paws.

Her mind was made up now. She faced him with outward calm. "I fear for your reason, sir."

Again he frowned, as though puzzled by her type of

answer. "You will not fob me off, wench. I want to know what he is up to with you."

"I beg your pardon?" She summoned up a show of mounting irritation, knowing that she must act a better performance than any player at Drury Lane. "You are foxed, aren't you?"

"No, I am not foxed!" he shouted. "You are cool-headed enough, but it won't help you. I have been talking with your jailer and—"

"I refuse to be subjected to this further!" snapped Mary, struggling not to tremble. "Allow me to leave this room at once."

He seized her arm and swung her around roughly. "You cannot deny that you have been an inmate of Newgate Prison!"

She eyed him for what she hoped was a convincing length of time, then laughed scornfully. "Certainly I deny it. You are drunk. Or mad."

"And this? What about this?" He drew out a copy of the prison records and stuffed it at her.

She saw her name among those listed upon it and remembered precisely the time she had watched the jailer write it in. Then she nearly laughed aloud and sent a thank-you to heaven. Her fear melted away.

She shoved the paper back at him. "What is this supposed to show to me?"

He almost snarled. "Your name is written there."

She lifted her brows. "I did not see it."

"Here." He jabbed a forefinger at her name.

She smiled and shook her head. "My surname is not spelled with an *e*."

He looked plainly startled; she could almost see his thoughts turning. He turned away and drummed his fingers on the table. Then he jerked back. "It is a mistake of handwriting then, for there is no question that my brother authored your release. I want to know why."

"And I want to know why you have placed me in this fantasy of yours." She must be careful; her voice was starting to betray strain. Why couldn't he have been put off by the error with the name? Why must he come at her from a different angle? "Do I appear to you as an escaped prisoner?"

He shook his head. "You are a clever woman. You have learned your part well. My brother must be paying you a great deal."

She turned the fiercest glare she could muster on him. "I need not reply to that insult, sir. You require an adjustment of your manners."

He sucked in a harsh breath. "I know—"

"On what authority?" she demanded, eyeing him squarely.

"The jailer—"

"Jailer? What jailer? I do not understand."

"He came to me to sell me this information—"

"Come, Mr. Keath," she said with a smile. "That is hardly believable, is it? I think you have been tricked out of your money. If this man had the information you claim, he would have been smarter to try to blackmail me—or even Lord Menton."

"He told me he could not get in touch with either of you." Keath looked a little bewildered, as though he had not expected to be on the defensive.

She laughed, so very thankful she had never had to encounter the jailer. And Menton had been gone from town this week. She wished, however, that the scheming little wretch had caught Menton at home. Menton would have dealt with him speedily and in a manner she suspected she would have found great satisfaction in.

"How," she asked, "could he fail to reach me if he chose to? I repeat that you have been hoaxed."

He swore. "Impossible! I know he is up to no good."

"Certainly he is up to no good—especially since he has taken your money."

"No, no. I am referring to my cursed brother." Keath raised a frustrated fist and let it fall again. "Damn! I—"

"Please excuse me," Mary said. "I am weary of this most fruitless conversation."

"No! Wait!" He took a step toward her, but she shook her head.

"I shall endure you no longer, Mr. Keath. Perhaps

when you are more sober I shall be persuaded to listen to your apologies. Good evening." She gathered up her skirts and hurried out as fast as she dared.

Somehow she maintained her composure throughout the rest of the evening, but once she was alone in bed in the darkness of her room, she allowed all the emotions pent up within her to escape through tears. At last she had admitted to herself what she felt for Menton, and now she was irrevocably on his side. If he was found out, her head would fall with his. But her victory over Keath this evening had given her the confidence that they would not fail. It was hard to believe that suddenly she was willing to surrender all her revulsion against treachery merely on the basis of emotion.

If only he returned it. If only he felt even a modicum of attraction for her. But he did not. And when this business was all over—whenever he no longer had any use for her—he would send her away and she would never be able to see him again.

Mary pushed away her soggy pillow and lay staring into the darkness, wiping away the endless tears with a corner of the bedclothes. She had no idea of where she was going to find the strength to endure the pain that was tearing her apart inside. She only knew that she must.

Chapter Twenty-one

THE FOLLOWING DAY, after a luncheon of cold duck and syllabub pie, Mary set out for the lending library with Jenny. It was extremely cold and the streets were lined with filthy slush that had frozen hard again, but Mary took no heed of either. She walked briskly in hopes of clearing her mind and spent a pleasant half-hour among the bookshelves. At last she selected one of Scott's volumes and gave it to Jenny to carry before setting out for home, wishing she truly did have a place to call her home.

"Hullo!" With a clatter of hooves on the frozen pavement, Gilbreath reined up beside her in his blue tilbury. He grinned and tipped his shaggy beaver hat. "You're looking delightfully chilled, Miss Clampton. Allow me to drive you and your maid home."

Mary hesitated, but her own feet were cold and Jenny's nose was bright red. Giving in, she allowed herself to be settled between Jenny's slight frame and his broad shoulders. They drove off in silence for several minutes; then he glanced at Mary.

"I've been particularly wanting a word with you, Miss Clampton. But first tell me something: are you an heiress? You're always dressed in full rig, everything of the best, but no one can tell me the answer." His eyes crinkled charmingly. "Am I being too forward? Please don't reprove my curiosity."

She colored up, and he brightened. "It is true, then? You have at least ten thousand a year?"

Mary eyed him in startlement. Did she look that affluent? Abruptly impatient with Menton's instructions, she shook her head. "No, Mr. Gilbreath. I am not an heiress in the slightest way."

"Oh." He seemed a little deflated. "Any excellent expectations?"

"Very minor ones." She thought she guessed where his questioning was leading to and smiled. "Why? Are your pockets to let?"

"Oh, tra-la. Nothing to speak of." He gestured airily, then eyed her with his head cocked. "Do you know that you are an unusual sort of lady, a . . . a cut above the average?" He sucked in a deep breath. "Will you marry me, Miss Clampton?"

Her heart jumped and she glanced at him swiftly to see if he were quizzing her. He was not. There was a serious if somewhat apprehensive expression on his face. Jenny stirred on her other side but stayed silent. Mary barely kept herself from laughing outright and decided to prolong the moment.

"Why, Mr. Gilbreath," she said sunnily, feigning surprise. "What a terribly public place for such a question. You have put me to the blush!"

Her acting was not good enough; he caught on at once and grinned in visible relief.

"Whew." He tugged at his cravat. "You had me dashed worried for a moment. Thought you were going to cry and accept my offer. Terribly unpredictable sort, you."

Mary laughed. "It would have been your own fault had I accepted. What made you try such a harebrained thing? You just learned how poor I am."

"Not poor. Couldn't be with those rigs you step out in. But I daresay you're like me—one step ahead of the creditors, eh?"

Jenny leaned forward to protest, but Mary nudged her to silence with an elbow.

"Just felt dashed fond of you," he said suddenly, staring at the backs of his team. "I know it's damnably silly of me to go around feeling fond of people. The last time, I lost five hundred pounds—cold." He laughed shakily. "But I think we should have suited tolerably well. At least you understand my jokes. Nothing more appalling than to go out of one's way to be as witty as possible and meet total lack of comprehension in a damsel's eyes." He shuddered. "Enough to make one go over to the French. Smart lot, the frogs."

Mary involuntarily winced, but he seemed not to notice.

"I suppose it's for the best, though," he said. "I mean, don't feel that I shouldn't be pleased to have you as a wife, but I have to marry an heiress to keep my head afloat, and in any case there's—"

"I know," said Mary, wishing she could slap some sense into Rebeccah. "She is an idiot."

He looked startled. "You know who—?"

"Yes. I do know." They were slowing to a stop before Lady Monteforte's steps. Mary gazed up at him in sympathy and suddenly put her gloved hand to his cheek. "I am so sorry," she said, the words seeming inadequate. Tears threatened her, and she was forced to thank him hurriedly and rush inside.

Grindle was waiting for her in the hall. "You have a gentleman caller waiting in the library, miss."

"Do I?" Mary raised her brows, unable to guess who it was. It might be any of several, she thought with a little rush of pleasure, and hoped it was not Sir George, for she was not at all in the mood to deal with his odious Chinese bowls. "Has he been waiting long?"

"No more than a quarter of an hour, miss."

That was long enough to set anyone in the fidgets Mary hurried upstairs to the library, stripping off her hat and gloves as she went. Pushing open the door, she stopped on the threshold to stare in a good deal of astonishment at the profusion of red roses in a large basket and a gaily wrapped gift set on a marble-topped table.

She tore her eyes away to look with rising delight at the tall broad-shouldered figure turning away from the mantel toward her. "For me? Why, Lord Menton, thank . . ." She faltered at the black expression on his face.

He raised an imperious hand and beckoned. "Get inside and shut the door. I came to celebrate the recovery of your hand, but I just saw your method of arrival." He nodded at the window and scowled even more fiercely. "It does not please me to discover that I've been kicking my heels here half the afternoon while you have been flirting with a gazetted fortune-hunter in an open carriage for the amusement of all London!"

It took Mary a full moment to register what he was saying. Then she stepped forward hastily. "You take a good deal upon yourself, sir! How dare you give me a scold for—"

"—acting like a green girl?" He snorted. "In a woman your age it is inexcusable."

"*What* is inexcusable?" She drew herself up and was angered further by the lack of difference her action made in the discrepancy between their heights. "I was walking back from the lending library when Mr. Gilbreath was kind enough to offer me and my abigail a ride. As I did not care to return thoroughly frozen, I accepted." She threw down her hat and gloves upon the settee and glared at him. "And precisely what is inexcusable in that?"

"Nothing, if *that* were all." His jaw tightened, and he met her glare for glare. Then carefully he placed his fist among the Dresden figurines lining the mantel. "When I looked out and saw such a tender scene being enacted upon the front steps—"

She was furious with him for making her feel guilty. "You know nothing about what was . . . I was not—"

Menton snorted. "I know that scoundrel well enough to guess what *he* was about, although you did not seem too averse to his attentions."

"His attentions . . ." She gasped. "Pray, why should I have been averse to them? I naturally expect some attention paid to me while I am receiving an offer of marriage."

"Marriage!" Menton took a hasty step forward and inadvertently swept off one of the figurines. It shattered into a thousand pieces at his unheeding feet. He scowled. "Let me tell you, my girl, that he is only after any money he thinks you have."

"No, he most certainly is not." Totally furious with him now, Mary shoved him to one side and kicked all the little pieces into the fire. "You have made a fine mess; I hope Lady Monteforte is not particularly fond of that swan."

"I do not particularly care whether she is or not," he said with a roughness that almost frightened her. But Mary raised her chin. He had no right to be flying into the boughs over such a trifle, and she would not let him intimidate her today. "Perhaps," Menton continued, pacing around the room and punctuating his words with punches of his fist, "perhaps you have been taken in. I know how charming he is. Such easy manners, such a ready address. Bah!" Menton stopped and swung around to face her. "He is a coxcomb, a . . . a fortune-hunter, and I tell you he is after money. With me providing the blunt for all the gewgaws and lace you want, it is no surprise he thinks you an heiress."

Disgusted past patience, Mary made a silencing gesture. "Pray, hush. You have gone on in this vein long enough. I have told you, sir, that Mr. Gilbreath is *not* after money from me. He knows I am no heiress because I told him so. Only then did he make his offer." He started to speak, and she raised a hand. "Do not interrupt me! I consider it a very honorable proposal."

Menton's nostrils pinched white and flared. "So you accepted it," he said flatly, jutting out his chin with an expression that boded no good for her.

"Of course I did not accept it!" Now she did the pacing. "Of all the harebrained notions . . . I daresay that is why you are so furious." She stopped and crossed her arms. "I may be green, sir, but I am not a flat. I have been very well aware of what Mr. Gilbreath is, but I am not ignorant of the fact that he has treated me with the utmost courtesy."

"See how fast he drops you." Menton's eyes glinted.

"I imagine he will, with you always glaring about over my shoulder," she snapped. "Oh, I am so out of patience with you!" She flung herself in a chair and turned her head away. "Please leave. And take your flowers with you. I have never seen anyone more churlish!"

"Churlish! I?" He sounded distinctly startled.

She whirled round in her chair and slapped the upholstered arm. "Yes, *you!* Flying into a passion over such a trifle—"

"I have a right to be in a passion if I choose!" he shouted. "How do you expect me to possibly keep my temper when you are allowing that coxcomb—that puppy—to make up to you at every turn? You were furious at dancing with me, yet you could not wait to step onto the floor with him. You went out driving unaccompanied with him upon having scarcely made his acquaintance—yes, I know all about that! He is at your side at every gathering." Menton strode to the mantel and pounded his fist there so that all the remaining figurines jumped. "And you call all that a trifle? Today he has offered for you! How long has your acquaintance been? Not even a full week!" Menton pounded the mantel again and pushed himself away. "Dammit, I won't have the fellow hanging about! Do you hear?"

"Yes, I hear," said Mary dryly, a little surprised that he had lost his sangfroid so completely. "And I daresay everyone else in the house can likewise. But be reasonable. He is at all the functions I attend. How can I—?"

"You do not have to encourage him." Menton towered over her chair, his nostrils still flaring rapidly.

In response she widened her eyes at him. "Then are flirtation and encouragement the same thing? For I only meant to fiirt."

He nodded curtly. "Certainly they are the same."

Mary tightened up her lips in satisfaction that he'd taken the bait. "Then the morals of everyone—yourself included—are in a shocking state of repair."

He choked. "Blast your tongue! That is not at all what I meant. And my morals are not for duscussion!"

She stiffened, longing to plant a fist in his eye. "No," she said acidly, "I am sure they are not."

He seized her arm and jerked her out of her chair. "You are getting beyond your place, my wench."

She tried to draw out of his painful grip and failed. "I am not a wench! I am not yours! And you do not own *all* of me!"

"We shall see about that." He crushed her in a searing kiss.

She had scarcely time to register her fury—or her beginnings of a response—before he released her and stared down with an arrogant smile on his lips.

Enraged beyond measure, she slapped him full across the face and jerked back out of his hold. "Don't you ever touch me in that manner again!" She ran to seize the basket of roses, and heaved them onto the fire, where they blackened and curled immediately. "You have bought my loyalty, sir, but you have nothing else. Do you understand? Nothing!" She picked up her skirts and ran out past him to her room, where she slammed and bolted the door and spent the next several minutes rubbing and rubbing at her lips to erase the fire that his had left still raging there.

Chapter Twenty-two

THE FOLLOWING DAY brought a curt missive in his own difficult hand, asking—though it read suspiciously close to a command—her to accompany him and his mother on an afternoon excursion into the country. Mary tore up the letter in fresh anger and went ice skating on the Thames with a cheerful party of Arabella's friends without bothering to reply.

She noticed that although as energetic as ever, Arabella seemed not herself, and when Arabella came peeping into her room that evening as she was dressing for dinner, Mary was quick to dismiss Jenny and invite her in.

Arabella entered slowly, looking as though she had been weeping a little. "Dearest Mary, may I ask for your help? I . . . I have no one else to turn to."

Mary gave her a warm embrace. "Why, certainly you may! I thought I had noticed something was troubling you."

To her surprise and dismay, Arabella burst into tears. This went on for some time, but at last Mary was able to coax her to stop crying. Arabella accepted a handkerchief and stood sniffing woefully.

"I do not *ever* cry," she said fiercely as a great teardrop rolled off the tip of her upturned nose. "But you do not know what Grandmama is about, Mary. S-she means to marry me off to that . . . that horrible Sir Oswald!"

Mary blinked in puzzlement. "Who on earth is he?"

Arabella twisted her handkerchief around and around in her hands. "He is the most odious creature —so puffed up in his own conceit there is no bearing him! Oh, you should hate to meet him, though you are going to. He is fat, and prosy, and stupid! I loathe him more than anyone in the world! Grandmama has invited him to dinner, and I just know that afterward he will . . . he will . . ." She broke off to blow her nose.

"Does Charlie know about this?" asked Mary, sitting down on the edge of the bed.

"No," said Arabella with a great sniff. "He has gone to visit his estates. Oh, Mary, what am I to do? I love Grandmama dearly, but she just will not see that I would rather die than accept that fish's suit!" The large blue eyes began to spark behind the tears. "I do not want to disobey her wishes, but I must! It is Charlie that I love. Oh, dearest Mary, please tell me I am not wrong."

"No, of course you are not wrong," said Mary, pressing her hand in reassurance. "If this suitor fills you with the utmost repugnance, it cannot be right to—"

"I knew you would agree!" Arabella gave her a swift hug. "Thank you! I can be brave if I know that you are on my side."

She rushed out to finish getting ready. Curious to view the suitor, Mary completed her own toilet and five minutes later went downstairs to the dining room. Scarcely was she introduced to Sir Oswald Hart before she realized with relief that she had been right to encourage Arabella to rebellion. Sir Oswald was a stout young man with brown hair of a limp nature which resisted all of his efforts to arrange it in a Windswept, preferring instead to drape about his ears and forehead in long, languid strands. A bovine complacency shone in his limpid eyes. Mary decided his shirt points were even higher than those sported by Harton, who was staring dolefully at them through his quizzing glass. Sir Oswald made a great show of bowing over Mary's hand, but his own grip was warm and damp. She retrieved hers as soon as possible and barely resisted the urge to wipe it on her handkerchief.

The five-course dinner seemed interminable—especially with Sir Oswald's droning monologue on the merits of keeping singing canaries in one's parlor—but at last the dishes were cleared away, port was set out for the gentlemen, and the ladies rose to depart the room.

"Arabella is going to be practicing her music," announced Lady Monteforte as though to no one in particular.

Harton looked up. "Lord, Grandmama, who wants to endure that at this hour of day? Enough to give one indigestion."

Sir Oswald straightened his shoulders. "I find music of all sorts most soothing. Do you know, dear sir, that gout and dyspepsia are two of the most common afflictions . . ."

Lady Monteforte swept all of her ladies out of the room at that point, and so Mary was unable to hear Harton's reply. Arabella trudged off to the music room, though "I had rather hide somewhere," she whispered to Mary, who nodded in sympathy.

In about two minutes Harton and Sir Oswald entered. Harton looked at his grandmother and shook his head. "Dashed fellow wants to play cards. Scarcely let me get my port down."

A few sulky notes banged out from the distant pianoforte, and Sir Oswald glanced up. "Ah! Do I hear the sweet strains of music?" He caught Lady Monteforte's eye. "Do I have your permission, ma'am, to go and lend what encouragement that lies in my possession to the fair Miss Monteforte?"

Harton stepped hastily back from the cabinet where he was digging out a deck of cards from beneath a backgammon set. "What the devil does the idiot want to go off alone in there with my cousin for?"

"Be quiet, Harton," said Lady Monteforte with a pronounced snap, and turned a smile upon Sir Oswald. "Of course you may go, Sir Oswald. The music room is just through that door and off to one side."

Sir Oswald departed with ponderous eagerness. Harton frowned from him to Lady Monteforte. "Something dashedly smoky here, Grandmama. You don't want that nodcock dangling after Arabella, do you?" He stared at her complacent face, then blinked. "You set the whole business up!! I thought there was something havey-cavey about all this. Well, I don't like it, let me tell you. Don't care for the fellow above half. Langfield's more her style, you know. Ought to be making your push in that direction instead of—"

There was a sudden slam of a pianoforte lid from the music room and a masculine howl of pain. In a moment Arabella appeared breathlessly in the doorway with a militant spark in her eyes.

"That . . . that fish tried to kiss me, Grandmama," she declared. "If that is your notion and his of a proper marriage proposal, it is not mine." The spark in her eyes flared. "I shut his fingers in the pianoforte. I hope I broke them all!"

Chapter Twenty-three

MARY WAS HUMMING to herself as she arranged a bowl of hothouse flowers on the hall side table when Menton came calling to drop off his card. Startled, she turned and met his gaze over the shoulder of Grindle, who attempted to step unobtrusively to one side.

"Do come in," she said with a ready smile, unexpectedly glad to see him.

He looked a trifle disconcerted. "Am I so quickly back in your good graces?"

"Yes, I forgive you." She put the last bloom in its place. "I am in such a mood today I cannot be out of temper with anyone."

"And what has caused such a miraculous mood?" he asked, the frown clearing from his face.

She tried to hold back her laughter and gurgled instead. "Come inside and I will tell you."

Obediently he stepped inside, handing his hat and stick to Grindle, who dropped the latter and turned fiery red in trying to recover it.

"Do not remark it." Mary laid her hand upon Menton's arm and drew him into the morning room. "This household has been all at sixes and sevens since the excitement of last night."

"But what is this that has happened?" he asked, almost smiling at her. "You have set my curiosity alight."

Mary smiled mischievously and sat down upon the sofa near the fire. "Arabella received an offer of marriage last night. Rather a bungled one, I might add."

"Good Lord!" Menton frowned. "I told that boy to have patience. If he can't keep a better damper—"

"Oh, not from Charlie. Are you acquainted with Sir Oswald Hart? No?" She could not help it; she began laughing again. "What a . . . a pity," she said unsteadily. "You are missing *such* a source of entertainment." She told him of the past night's events. "Poor Sir Oswald," she finished with a fresh fit of giggles. "I am sure his fingers hurt dreadfully, and there was Harton shouting at the top of his lungs, demanding a meeting with pistols, until Sir Oswald was quite terrified that he really meant it. And Miss Pingleberry had a spasm right in the center of the floor."

Menton laughed with her, showing his strong white teeth. "And what of Aunt Honoria?"

"Arabella has been banished to her room for the day, and Lady Monteforte is keeping to hers likewise, with the declaration that her hair will be forever grayed in mortification."

"Grayed in age is more to it," he said with a shug. "My godmother is a fool if she expects to make this match."

"I do not expect her to make it." Mary lowered her gaze in sudden guilt. "I am afraid I helped fan the rebellion."

"Bravo!" He applauded, with the faint mocking smile back in place on his lips. She was sorry to see it appear. "And what is your next planned tactic?"

"I have none," she said frankly. "But if you would . . ."

His raised brows checked her, and he shook his head. "Ah, no, not I. You shan't mix me up in this imbroglio."

"But you cannot be so shabby as to refuse to help your nephew!"

"It is not me who wants to see him married and setting up his nursery before he is of age."

In annoyance Mary watched the stubbornness coming into his face. Why must he delight in throwing a spoke into every plan? She had counted on his willingness to help Charlie. "But you have influence with

Lady Monteforte," she said pleadingly. "Would it be so very difficult for you to convince her that Charlie is not such a terribly poor match?"

"Somewhat difficult," he said dryly, crossing his arms. "Since it was I who convinced her of my nephew's unsuitability."

"You!" Mary stared up at him, for a moment conscious only of a strong desire to shake him. She stood up with a gesture of defeat. "That is it, then. I have no more ideas."

"Excellent. I am weary of this topic." He looked at her inquiringly. "May I switch to another?"

"Very well," she said grudgingly.

"If I am forgiven for losing my temper the other afternoon," he said, drawing out the small wrapped gift from his pocket, "may I present this to you now?"

She took it readily. "I wondered where that had gotten off to, for I could not find it anywhere later "

He smiled ruefully. "Yes, I decided to take it with me, lest your temper induce you to . . . er . . . fling it also on the fire."

"Oh." She looked up guiltily, wishing he had not reminded her. "I have been giving myself a scold ever since. They were such beautiful roses." She drew in a hasty breath. "But if you had not angered me so by that display—"

"Pray, let us drop that before you go into a new fury," he broke in, still smiling at her. "Aren't you going to open my gift?"

"What? Oh, yes! Of course I am going to." His eyes were watching her too closely; she looked away in some embarrassment. "But why . . . what is the occasion? My birthday is not until January, and it is some weeks before Christmas yet."

"I told you before," he said gently. "There should be some celebration now that your hand is well."

She swallowed and began ripping paper to cover her confusion. "I . . . I hope this is something I may accept. It is very kind of you to . . ." She opened the box with excited, fumbling fingers and stared in at the fan lying in a mass of silver paper.

"Well?" he said impatiently after a long silence.

"Does it not meet with your approval? You do not like it?"

"Oh, yes," she whispered "I like it very much!" She lifted it carefully out and spread it open with both hands.

Menton seized her wrist. "No, my dearest. You must learn to snap it open with a flick of the wrist. Like so." He took it from her and snapped it out in demonstration.

Even as her mind wondered how he was so expert at a woman's trick, her hand flew out in protest. "Do not be so vigorous! You will break it!"

"Hardly." He chuckled in a soft way that sent tingles across her back. "Chicken skin is not so fragile as that." Lifting it, he traced the handpainted design of delicate lavender with one forefinger "Is the color acceptable? I do not know your favorite shade—"

"It is yellow." Mary warmed to so much of his exclusive attention. "But I think this one is beautiful. Thank you so much!" She met his blue eyes a little shyly. "I have never had a fan—such a trifliing object in most women's wardrobes, but I shall keep mine for special occasions."

His eyes swung away, and he coughed into his handkerchief. She frowned at it, flinching away from the thought of her encounter with Keath. No, she could say nothing about it to Menton. He had made a mistake, but perhaps no harm was going to come of it

"What are you thinking about with such energy?" he asked, sitting down in a chair near her and neatly folding away his handkerchief into his pocket.

She looked up hastily and searched for something to tell him. "Only that . . . that I shall have to get a dress made up to match." She knit her brow. "I think lavender is a pretty color, but my dressmaker has forbidden pastel shades for me."

"Nonsense," he said at once. "Order a gown immediately." Bringing out his quizzing glass, he aimed it at the gleaming toe of one of his Hessians, nodded in satisfaction, and stood up. "It is time I was on my way. Practice using your fan. I shall be by to inspect your progress."

She stood up also. "Thank you again, sir. I am glad we are on good terms once more."

He bowed over her hand. "So am I. May I send you more roses?"

She smiled in a little shame. "Yes, please. I promise not to burn them."

By that afternoon two enormous bouquets had arrived for her—one of pink roses, the other of yellow. Mary was both delighted and a little skeptical of so much attention. He was an accomplished flirt. Everyone said so; she had no reason not to believe it. She knew he was only going to all this trouble for appearances; people must believe she was being courted. But she was troubled as she and Miss Pingleberry arranged the flowers. Why was he so insistent on marriage? It made so little sense for him to shackle himself to her forever. He did not want her as his wife or the mother of his heir, but did he plan to set her far away and marry again? Surely he would not trust her to stay away. Her insides twisted He would always see in her the potential for blackmail. Perhaps he meant to have the marriage annulled, but that would mean scandal. She did not understand any of this, and determined to persuade him out of such a permanent step at the first opportunity.

That opportunity came the next day while he was driving her to the milliner's. He asked about Arabella.

Mary came instantly alert but tried to remain casual. "She has not been locked into her room for the next six weeks. Fortunately her grandmother has no such gothic notions."

He smiled, and hope perked up within her. As long as he stayed in a pleased mood, it would be much easier to catch him off his guard.

"Have they come to actual dagger-drawing yet?" he asked.

"No, not yet." Mary returned his smile. "But the glares are quite fierce, I assure you." She sighed. Now was the time to change the subject. She must do it before she totally succumbed to cowardice and kept silent. "My lord?"

"Yes?" They were weaving their way through a

particularly snarled corner; Menton's eyes were on his driving, and the driver of every other carriage in the vicinity was shouting or hurling curses.

She waited until they were around the corner and into more sedate traffic. "Must you marry me?" She stopped, appalled at herself. She had not meant to blurt it out in such a manner. Quickly she laid a hand on his forearm. "Wait. I am sorry. I did not mean to phrase it so."

"You know I prefer plain speaking." But his voice was tight and hard; his lips were thinned.

She bit her lip to surmount her dismay, and tried to recover her blunder. "No, I mean . . . Can we not accomplish . . . would it not be possible if we were only betrothed?"

"No," he said curtly, brushing the wheels of a gig with chipped paint, heedless of the driver's warning shout. "So you do not prefer to be my bride."

"No," she said just as curtly, knowing that she could not bear a union of any sort as long as he did not love her. She strove to keep her voice as cold and as businesslike as his. "And that is no insult I hand you, for ours is a different situation than that of other people."

"How very true." The muffled quality of his voice betrayed his checked fury.

But she dared not stop now. She must flounder on with what must not be left unsaid. "You see, I do not understand your reasoning. Neither of us wants the other as . . . as a mate. But marriage is irreversible, and . . . and I believe it should be." She raised her chin in defiance. He made no answer, so she went on: "And how you shall . . . what sort of explanation shall be made afterward, I do not—"

"Then I shall explain it to you, Miss Clampton," he broke in abruptly. He was very white about the mouth. She wondered how he could still maintain such excellent light contact with his horses' mouths and be in such a rage "We must be wed. You seem to think a mere betrothal would suit the purpose. Let me assure you it will not. Thomas will accept without suspicion many actions in a sister-in-law that he would not otherwise. Furthermore, you must always be on hand. I cannot use you as long as you are beneath the eye of Lady Monteforte. Once we are finished, you shall be paid in accordance with our agreement and sent abroad. There will be a quiet annulment, and perhaps an announcement of a shipwreck. Since you should never be returning to England—which shall think you dead—there will be no difficulty in establishing my nursery at a later date."

Her heart shrank in upon itself, and she stared blindly down at the backs of her clenched hands. "You should have wed long ago, sir," she said barely above a whisper, unable to suppress her bitterness. "Then you should not be obliged to go to the effort of replacing me."

"Since we are being frank, ma'am," he said in a voice that slashed through her raw feelings, "allow me to express my sentiments on that for the last time. If Thomas should be able to prove that I have any government papers in my possession, my head will fall. Not for anything in the world would I subject the woman who shall have the honor of giving me heirs to such a devastating scandal. Therefore, I shall make use of you."

An iron band seemed to be constricting round her throat, but she managed the resentful words: "How beastly you are!"

"You shall accept the annulment," he said, as unyielding as granite. "You will invent a new past and make a new life for yourself. I believe India would hold excellent opportunitites for you. Or Spain, once the war is ended." He stared down at her, and a muscle leaped in his set jaw. "If you do not accept it in your heart, and choose to be an idiot, that is entirely your affair. I shall not even mind if you change your faith and enter a convent. But we shall be wed by Christmas!"

Chapter Twenty-four

SNOW WAS FALLING HEAVILY, but the assembly rooms at Almack's were crowded. Mary was plagued with the jitters, which made her unable to sit still for more than a second. She had cried herself dry of tears; now the resignation that had finally smothered her in prison was slowly settling over her again. She feared it and tried everything to shake it off, but there was nothing to be done. Menton was going to have his way in everything, and she had no choice but to let him.

Her nerves were not in the least soothed by being in charge of Arabella this evening. Lady Monteforte had taken one look at the snow piling over the ground and had refused to set foot outside. Miss Pingleberry had declared herself undaunted by the weather and volunteered for the chore of chaperon. There she was now, chatting merrily to some deaf old general near the refreshment table, but it was Mary who was having to keep half of her attention on her own activities and half on Arabella's.

Then Menton arrived one minute before eleven, striking to the eye in black coat and breeches and white smallclothes. He joined her side at once, his face blue with cold His greeting contained neither the warmth he had been showing her of late nor the traces of his most recent anger. Her spirits drooped further.

He frowned faintly at the dancing. "I made

a special effort to return to London in time to see you here tonight."

She looked at him in surprise. "You have been gone from town in this weather? No wonder you look so bluish."

The stern expression stayed firmly on his face. "It came to me that perhaps I should apologize. I am too curt with you too often. Please forgive me."

"Of c-course." The unexpectedness of this apology confused her so, she hardly knew where to look. Her eyes settled across the room, where a rake was engaged in persuading Arabella for a third dance. "Oh!" she gasped in vexation. "The little fool is standing up with him again."

She started to hurry off to put a stop to it, but Menton seized her arm. "Let her," he said.

Mary shook her head. "No, no. It will reach Lady Monteforte's ears, and then we shall all be in disgrace."

"Please. I am not staying," he said.

That caught her attention. She frowned. "But you have only just arrived."

"I know," he said with a touch of impatience. "But I came here only to see you . . . and to give you this." He pulled an envelope from his pocket and slipped it to her. "Keep it safe. If you do not hear from myself or Rodney by tomorrow afternoon, burn it."

There were a thousand questions in her mind, but all she could say was, "Yes, I shall do so," and slip it quickly into her reticule. It was not hard to sense something dangerous was afoot. She gripped his arm in sudden fear. "What are you going to do?"

He smiled mirthlessly. "Play a midnight game in the snow. A game called interception."

She shivered. A sense of wildness swept over her. "May I come with you?" she asked, not understanding why she wanted to go with him so desperately. *"Please!"*

"No." He bent his head and kissed her hand. "I have given you something to do, and it is very important. Were that paper to enter the wrong hands, it would likely be all over for me." He smiled. "Yes, a pretty trap I would fall into. You see how I trust you now. Do not fail me."

The smile faded from his face, leaving a pleading in his eyes that she could not refuse. She looked away to quickly blink back tears. "Thank you for that trust. I shall keep it until tomorrow for you."

He bowed. *"Au revoir."*

His departure sent a good many side glances and raised brows in her direction. In an attempt to collect herself, she headed off toward Arabella to deliver a scold, but she was forestalled by Rebeccah, who smiled at her archly.

"Why, you sly creature," she said warmly, as though they had never quarreled. "I believe you have quite succeeded in turning Lord Menton's head permanently." She tapped Mary's arm with her fan and nodded with a smirk that was quite disgusting. Mary wished she would go on. "Dropping by only to put a word in your ear and . . . goodness, even a love note."

Mary burned in embarrassment and resisted the urge to grip her reticule with both hands. Did Rebeccah never miss anything?

Rebeccah seemed to expect her not to answer. "But are you here without escort? Thomas is gambling tonight, so I have come with Gilly—such a droll thing to do, don't you think? But he is amusing once in a while."

Mary frowned. "You are too harsh with him. I think he has a *tendre* for you."

"Then the greater fool he." Rebeccah shrugged. "I have made my choice." She smiled brightly to mask her apparent pique and walked away without another word.

Mary went on and reached Arabella in time to rescue her from a highly frustrated Sir Oswald. "Arabella!" she said severely as soon as they were to one side behind a great potted fern. "Are you about in your head? Why are you misbehaving so?"

Arabella looked sulky. "I would have been obliged to dance with Sir Oswald otherwise, and that I will not do!"

Mary gave her a little shake. "Use a little sense! Antagonizing your grandmother further will not help you."

"Pooh. If you are going to be so poor-spirited," retorted Arabella, tossing her curls, "why don't we simply go home?"

"I think that we should," said Mary swiftly, wondering if Menton was already in a change of clothing and riding hell for leather somewhere through the outskirts of London. "Now, please behave while I gather up the others."

It took a full half-hour to pry Miss Pingleberry from the cardroom, but she arose from the table at last, cheerfully bemoaning her losses. Harton, however, needed no persuasion to leave early. He glanced at his large turnip-shaped watch and declared there would be plenty of time now for him to look in at Brooks's.

Outside among the great confusion of waiting and departing carriages were large piles of rutted snow. Snatching up her skirts so as not to get them wet, and scrambling to get over the snow and into the carriage, Mary dropped both her new fan and reticule. She jumped back out of the carriage with a cry of dismay, but Gilbreath was there suddenly before her to pick up her things. He handed over her fan and began carefully brushing the snow off her beaded reticule.

Harton stuck his head out the carriage window. "Do hurry up! It is freezing cold out here."

"Yes, all right," called Mary, and turned back to Gilbreath.

He handed her the reticule with a bow. "I do not think it is much hurt," he said with his ready smile.

"No." She clutched it close to her in overwhelming relief. Of all times to drop it! It might have been lost —and its precious contents with it—forever. "Thank you so very much."

"Come on!" called Harton again.

"Yes, Harton, I am doing so." She was glad of Gilbreath's assistance into the carriage, for she was trembling so in relief and mortification, she doubted she

could do much under her own power. She glanced
back and saw Rebeccah waiting impatiently by the entrance. "Thank you again, Mr. Gilbreath. I am in
your debt."

"No, no, Miss Clampton." He put up the steps and
shut the door with a pronounced gleam in his eyes.
"It is I who am in yours."

Upon their arrival home, Mary did not delay, but
instead hurried directly to her room with the intention
of putting the letter in a safer place beneath her mat-
tress. But though she dug and dug all the way to the
bottom of her reticule and at last dumped out all the
contents upon her bed, it was nowhere to be found.
She jumped off the bed and hunted all about the floor
in a frenzy, but even as she did so there grew within
her the certainty that the letter must have slipped
out unnoticed somewhere in the street at Almack's.

Panic strangled her. She must find it without delay.
Snatching up her cloak, she flung it about her shoulders and rushed madly out—to collide with Harton at
the head of the stairs.

"Have a care, won't you?" he snapped, stepping
back.

She took no heed of him. "You've left the carriage
at the door, haven't you? Good." She picked up her
skirts and hastened recklessly down the stairs.

He bolted after her. "Hold up! Dash it, you can't
have my carriage . . ."

Mary kept going in desperation, and he followed
her all the way to the carriage door before catching up
with her. He seized her arm and jerked her back. "I'd
like to know what you think you're about. If
you're . . ."

Without listening, she climbed into the carriage and
pulled him in with her. "Almack's, coachman! Hurry!"

Harton righted himself hurriedly upon the seat as
the carriage started up with a lurch. He snatched at his
hat to keep it from tumbling off his head. "Are you
mad? I'm going to my club!" He pulled down the window and stuck out his head, but Mary yanked him
back and shut it before he had a chance to order a
halt. The carriage rounded a sharp corner too quickly,

and they were both flung roughly about. Harton righted himself with a curse. "This *is* madness. Let me out at once!"

"No!" said Mary in an agony of apprehension. "I have lost a . . . a letter on the steps of Almack's, and we must get back there before someone picks it up." She pounded the seat with her fist, unable to keep still. "Why doesn't the coachman hurry?"

"Dashed well about to kill us now," said Harton, exclaiming as one back wheel bounced over the curb. "Damme if you don't get worse starts in your head than Arabella!"

The carriage jerked to an abrupt halt. Mary looked up. "Good! We are here. Get out and help me look— quickly!" She thrust herself out and began to run frantically back and forth through the dirty snow and slush. Harton caught at her arm, and she looked at him imploringly. *"Please* help me!"

"All right. All right!" He sighed fiercely. "I shall go up and ask the porter if anything has been turned in."

While he was thus engaged, Mary searched the street some more, shivering and almost crying with cold and despair. The letter was not here either. She turned eagerly to Harton, who was coming back down the steps.

"Well? Did he know of it?"

Harton shook his head. "A lady's glove has been turned in, but nothing else." His foot hit a slick spot, and he almost slipped. "Blast this weather! Get back into the carriage at once."

Mary shook her head. "If I can search about just once more—"

"No!" He shoved her into the carriage. "You've already made a great cake of yourself. The thing ain't to be found, and that's all there is to it." He tossed the rug at her. "Here, huddle under that. Dashed fool thing to do. Now you're jolly well bedraggled."

He went on scolding her, but Mary stopped listening. Menton had put his trust in her, and she had failed him miserably, perhaps disastrously. Like an idiot she had left his envelope lying in the street for some honest person to scoop up. Now his treachery was discovered. *Were this paper to enter the wrong hands, it would be all over for me.* His words pounded over and over in her mind. Hot tears slipped over her numb cheeks. He would be trapped and captured in shame and disgrace. He might even be killed. That thought was unbearable; she turned her face to the corner of the seat and began to weep uncontrollably against the velvet squabs.

Harton squirmed uncomfortably. "Er . . . here, dash it. No need to carry on forever like an infernal water-pot."

"Leave me alone," said Mary through her tears.

"I say, I jolly well won't! Look at you, maudling all over the squabs. Daresay the velvet shall have to be cleaned." He paused a moment, but her tears did not abate, and she did not want them to. "Don't you have a handkerchief to—?"

Mary reared up fiercely. "No, I do not! And I wish you would hush!"

"How can I?" he shot back just as fiercely. "With you blubbering all over the place, can't very well just sit and hold my peace. Oh, here." He handed over an enormous green handkerchief.

"Thank you." She took it and quickly blew her nose, but almost at once began crying again.

"Look here"—his tone gentled a trifle—"I daresay it was not all that important. Certainly not worth—"

"Oh, it was. It was." Mary tried to breathe and swallow away tears at the same time, and almost choked herself. "You don't understand. The letter did not belong to me! It . . . it was only left in my safe-keeping, and now I have lost it."

Harton snorted. "If it's gone, it's gone. Do stop crying! I daresay it wasn't you that lost it after all. That card-turner Gilbreath was hanging all about close enough."

"You aren't accusing him of taking it, are you?" Mary blinked in disbelief. "What reason could he have?"

"The man's too sharp by half," said Harton. "There ain't a gentleman in town that would trust Gilbreath with his last shilling, unless he's a flat."

Mary jerked erect, almost losing her balance as the carriage swayed around a corner. "You are lying! How dare you slander him so behind his back!"

Harton glared back at her. "It is the truth I am telling you, be sure of that. It would not surprise me if his fingers are a bit sticky once in a while."

"Oh, pray hush," said Mary, putting a hand to her pounding temple. She must not listen to Harton. But despite all her desire to disbelieve him, he did have a ring of truth about him. Various comments of Gilbreath's came to her mind like unwanted little pricks of spite. Perhaps it was true. Indeed it seemed very odd that the letter had not turned up somewhere. And Gilbreath had been most assiduous in helping her.

She gave her head a little shake. No, whatever Harton might say, she would not believe it. Gilbreath was something of a rogue, and he might frequently find himself in dun territory, but he would not steal from her. There was no reason for him to take the letter: for all anyone who had observed Menton slipping it to her might know, it was no more than a love note. And no one had any need to steal such a thing.

Leaning forward, she said, "Say what you like, I count him as my friend, and I refuse to believe such a charge against him."

"Menton disapproves of him, too," said Harton with a slyness that infuriated her.

"And what, pray, is that supposed to mean to me?" she demanded hotly.

"Nothing, I daresay," he retorted with equal spirit. "Save that Gilbreath's all but in the dowager's pocket. He's ever charming her out of blunt."

Mary sat back with tightened lips. "And next, I suppose, you shall be telling me what good friends Keath and Gilbreath are and how they delight in baiting Lord Menton's temper." She tossed her head. "What rubbish."

Harton eyed her coldly. "Are you so sure?"

Quite suddenly, the tone of his voice gave her pause, and she was no longer able to be quite so certain. She had spoken the words in sarcasm, but could he actually be implying that such a thing were true?

Or perhaps that Gilbreath and Keath were united against Menton for a deadlier reason? She drew a breath sharp enough to hurt. "Harton . . ."

But the carriage was pulling to a halt.

"It's jolly well about time we arrived." He pushed open the door and beckoned for a sleepy footman to assist her out.

She tried to turn back. "But, Harton, wait."

"Can't. Wasted too much of my time on your behalf as it is." He slammed the door. "Get on, coachman!"

And Mary was left standing on the steps with even more questions and more fear whirling up a torment within her.

She went directly to bed, but sleep eluded her fretting mind for what seemed like ages, while she tossed about and wept a little more and occasionally got up to stare blindly out her window. When she did at last fall asleep from exhaustion, it was to dream wildly of Menton bound by a rope around his neck with black water lapping higher and higher about his chin while Gilbreath laughed in her ear and made her dance and dance and dance. . . .

Chapter Twenty-five

SHE AROSE LATE the next day, listless and exhausted. Putting on a walking dress of rich brown serge, she went downstairs to try to eat something, but the food seemed tasteless enough to make her give it up in discouragement. Inside she was both raw and tight, as though her nerves, which had been stretched to the breaking point too many times, were upon their final test of endurance.

She remembered the last time she had felt like this —the horrible waiting for Menton to take her back to prison. How green and simpleminded she had been then. She was wiser now, she thought, and this pain of waiting for the unknown to happen to him was quieter than when she had feared for her own self, quieter but somehow harder to endure.

Arabella sat down beside her once with a troubled frown. "What is wrong, Mary? You look so sad."

The loving concern in her voice was just enough to melt all of Mary's resolve to hold everything silent within her. Her lips trembled; she started to speak, but at the last moment the memory of that odd pleading look in Menton's vibrant eyes checked her. No, she knew nothing for certain yet. She would wait a little longer, as she had promised, before she let fear completely overtake her.

So she straightened her shoulders a little and tried to smile. It would not be believable to say that nothing was wrong. "Why, only a little case of low spirits, Arabella. The weather is so dreary today."

"Yes, isn't it dreadful?" Arabella peeped out the window. "I think I shall practice my sketching."

Mary hardly noticed her skipping out to fetch a sketchbook; her thoughts were on Menton, perhaps lying now out in some snow-covered ditch. Going to the window, she stared out at the fluffy snowflakes drifting down, until the drafts seeping in around the panes chilled her into seeking out the warmth of the fire once again. Would this dreadful waiting never end?

She was dozing before the fire when the click of the door and the hasty stride of booted feet awakened her. Pulling her neck erect from its cramped position, she opened her eyes to see Menton coming purposely toward her with no apparent hurt other than a bit of sticking plaster on his temple.

She jumped to her feet. "Thank God!"

His jaw jutted, and he extended his hand. "I believe you have—"

She gave him no time to finish. She flung herself at his knees with her tears spilling freely. "Oh, please!" she cried. "I did not mean to lose it! I searched everywhere, but to no avail. Oh, I am so terribly sorry! I have been in the most fearful quake since last night, dreading to hear ill news. . . . But at least you are safe!"

"Yes, I am safe," he said in a voice like iron, and jerked her to her feet. "But Rodney is severely wounded."

"Rodney?" She thought of the quiet, unassuming young man—so very unlike his sister. "Will he—?"

"He will recover, yes, despite your efforts."

Her eyes widened. "No," she whispered, shaking her head. "No, I swear I meant—"

He seized her chin and forced her eyes to meet his burning ones. "Listen well, you little—"

"Oh. Excuse me. Thought the room was empty." Harton sauntered in as though unaware of Menton's hasty release of her. He swung up his quizzing glass and frowned. "By Jove, looks as though something's been rather bashing you about."

"Not really," said Menton, reassuming his languid drawl. "I merely overturned my curricle in the snow last night—lost the road."

"Good Lord! That's rather nasty." A look of horror crossed Harton's face. "You didn't hurt those blood chestnuts?"

Menton shook his head. "No harm done."

Mary unobtrusively drew her handkerchief from her pocket and turned to wipe away her tears.

"Oh, burn it," said Harton in disgust. "She's sniveling again. Look here, my lord, I wish you'd make a push to raise her spirits. Had the devil of a time with her last night."

"Really," said Menton in his most uninterested voice.

"No, I ain't handing you any Banbury tale," said Harton. "Dropped her cursed reticule while getting into the carriage. Waited until we were home before flying into strong hysterics over some letter she'd lost—"

Mary made an inarticulate sound, and he glanced at her. "You dashed well did so. Have a seat, my lord. Can you believe she dragged me all the way back to Almack's to search the street? I felt a regular fool." Harton glanced in the wall mirror across the room and gave his cravat a quick twitch.

Menton, who had refused to sit down, positioned himself near the fire. "I don't suppose the letter was found."

"No, and it's my opinion that card-turner Gilbreath lifted it. Told her so, but she'd have none of it."

"Gilbreath!" Some of Menton's drawl vanished. A line appeared between his dark brows. "Explain."

"He was a little too handy to pick up her things when she dropped them." Harton shrugged and sent her a smug glance as though to say: You see? Menton believes me. "Of course, that's only my opinion. Don't know why he'd be doing such a smoky thing, but he sharped me out of a tidy sum once, and I don't

care for the fellow." He paused and crossed to the
brandy cabinet to pour himself a liberal portion.

Mary looked at Menton in tremulous hope. "I am
so terribly sorry." she said scarcely above a whisper.
Her heart thudded at his unchanging scowl. "Indeed,
I would have searched for it longer, but Harton
would not let me. Surely it can still be found in the
street beneath the snow—"

"No." He said it with curt force, like a blow to her
cheek. "There was a trap, though fortunately we escaped it. I wanted to test you, and now I have my answer." He expelled a harsh breath; his eyes did not
even trouble to meet hers. "You and Gilbreath, thick
as thieves." Now his voice was bitter. "How true the
pun can be. I might have guessed—"

"But you are wrong. Wrong!" Mary ran to grip his
coat, forgetting everything—even Harton's presence
—in her desperation to convince him. "Do you think
I gave him your letter?"

Now his eyes did meet hers, and there was such an
expression in them she wished they had not. Slowly,
deliberately he removed his coat from her clutching
hands and smoothed his lapels. He said, "Yes, Miss
Clampton, I think that is precisely what you did."

He turned on his heel and strode out. Though she
rushed to stop him, he brushed her off as though she
were some urchin begging for pence.

"But why?" she called after him in the hall, crying
without noise or tears. "Why would I do such a
thing?"

In the act of accepting his hat, he at last did glance
her way. "There is no need to answer your question.
I believe we both know the why of your regrettable
actions." He ran a finger over the tightly curled brim
of his hat, then shot a withering glance at Grindle,
who retired with some haste from the area. "Tomorrow morning you shall call at my residence—nine
o'clock precisely, if you please." His voice held that
exceptional quality of hardness which had frightened
her so that night at Newgate. "At that time we shall
terminate our contract."

She jerked in her breath, almost choking upon it as

everything whirled about her. Shakenly she clutched at the side table near her, for she was certain she could not stand on her own. "What does this . . . ?" She stopped, and a strange, hard calm overcame her. She straightened her shoulders. "Do I return to jail?"

His bitter smile sent a chill through her. "You little fool. Why couldn't you see that I would never return you there?" He half-shut his eyes so that she could not read their expression. "Enough of this affair. I am wearied of it. Tomorrow I shall give you a sum which will support you until you find work."

It was what she had longed for since their first encounter, yet she could not understand why his every word was another nail hammered into her flesh. In stunned silence she watched him walk out the door; then at last her limbs jerked free of their momentary paralysis, and she ran to look outside in time to see him falter to a halt in the act of getting into his curricle, and cover his eyes a moment with his hand. Then he was lashing his team away in such a furious bound of speed that his tiger barely had time to swing on behind. Mary wiped one lone tear from her cheek and closed the door. She folded up her cambric handkerchief and shoved it into her pocket while she slowly wandered back down the hall.

Harton was still at the brandy cabinet, standing rock steady with the decanter in one hand and a half-empty glass in the other. He frowned at her entrance. "What, has he gone already?"

Dully she looked at him. "Yes, he is gone," she said in a small voice.

Harton shrugged. "Daresay your vapors chased him off. Sounded all about in his head anyway. Must have been quite a knock about in the ditch."

She could not answer for the resentment flooding through her. Harton's chatter had served only to connect her unfavorably with Gilbreath's name. Fury, like a dash of freezing water, stiffened her suddenly. She clenched her fists. No, she would not stand aside tamely and let herself be wronged in this way! She would prove her innocence, even if she had to strangle a confession out of Gilbreath.

At once she fetched her pelisse and hurried outside into the dreary weather. Carriages were almost nowhere to be seen, and pedestrians were likewise sparse. At first Mary had hopes of hailing a hackney, but it did not take too much of the snow swirling into her eyes to make her give up on finding one and trudge along at the best pace she could manage. The cold seeped quicly into her stout half-boots, and her skirts dragged the snow, tangling her feet and slowing her considerably.

Because she did not know the location of Gilbreath's lodgings, she turned toward Keath's instead, not daring to let herself think about the evils of putting herself into an encounter with him again. Preferably Keath would be in his office today, and she would only have to pry Gilbreath's direction from the servants. She clung to that hope for encouragement against turning back.

Keath did not live too far away, though it was farther than she liked to go in this grim weather. His small, rather cramped house stood in a section of small houses—all leased by their inhabitants. This time the servant allowed her in and showed her into a small parlor furnished in an opulent if slightly shabby style. Mary entered the warmth of the room with caution despite her frozen fingers and toes. To her surprise, Lady Menton was pacing back and forth before the hearth in visible agitation.

A petite woman with a good figure and fair, delicate features once pretty but now a little faded, she glanced up at Mary's entrance and at once sank into a chair with a languishing sigh. "Oh, dear," she said in faint tones. "I was so hoping that would be Thomas."

Mary walked in to be closer to the meager fire. "Mr. Keath is out, then?" she asked, looking at the dowager with caution. "The servant would not give me a direct answer."

"Yes, yes, I have been waiting an age. I fear he will be gone forever." She waved a vague hand. "My smelling salts . . . on the mantel."

Mary handed them to her. "My lady," she said eagerly. This was her chance to avoid seeing Keath al-

together! "Please, could you . . . would you be kind
enough to tell me where Mr. Gilbreath's lodgings are
to be found? It is an urgent matter, and I have no way
to get in touch with him."

The dowager's head jerked up. She seemed about
to comply; then a startled expression crossed her features and she jumped to her feet. *"You!"* She almost
screamed it. "Now I remember who you are!" She
stared hard at Mary with widened eyes. "You . . . you
have come back for your revenge upon us, haven't
you?" Her features twisted in a sort of panic-stricken
anger. "Oh, you odious hussy, I shall expose you at
once to—"

"No! That you will not!" Mary sprang to seize her
shoulders in fierce desperation. "If you dare reveal me
to *anyone I* shall—"

"Do not threaten me! I shan't let you continue,"
said Lady Menton with unexpected bravery. "Somehow you must be stopped. You have fooled my son to
the point of being ready to offer for you, but I will not
have him deceived so!"

"You may put up all the resistance to him that you
please," said Mary, glaring at her. "But you will not
speak to him of my identity!" She took a step toward
the dowager, who shrank deep into the cushions of the
chair.

"Very well!" The dowager raised a hand as though
to ward her off, and shuddered. "Just go. I cannot
bear to be in your presence."

The bonds on the old hurt snapped. Mary drew
herself up, clenching her fists. *"You* cannot bear to be
in my presence! Well, I am not quite so lowborn as
you would wish me to be. Do you remember my father, Andrew Clampton?"

The dowager shook her head in immediate scorn.
"Why should *I* know any of your connections . . . ?"
She broke off, suddenly white. "Of course," she whispered. "Andrew Clampton. I remember now. He was
that perfectly horrid man always embarrassing my
husband."

"Your husband stole his money by persuading him

into that dreadful investment scheme which proved an utter fraud!" flashed Mary.

"Fraud!" The dowager shoved herself to her feet. "It was no such thing. You will leave this house at once." She stamped her foot. "Go!"

"Certainly," said Mary harshly. She backed away a step. "If you will tell me the name of Mr. Gilbreath's street . . ."

"No," said the dowager in excessive hauteur. "I shan't. Good day."

As Mary stumbled homeward in the heavy snow, her anger fanned itself hotter with every step. She found herself no longer in the least dismayed if that abominable woman spilled the whole to her odious son. In fact, Mary rather hoped she would do so. That would certainly set Menton down to no small degree. He would be shocked and infuriated to find that he had been nursing a viper in his bosom, that Mary's career of thievery had begun and ended in his father's study. Yes, he would be infuriated by this deception practiced upon him, but he would be powerless to act against her anymore. She laughed to herself in a kind of savage relief. Tomorrow she would be released— at last able to be her own person. And it would not in the least matter what Lady Menton said or what Menton thought of her. She was finished with all of this, and she was glad of it.

A sudden ripple of throaty laughter caught her attention. She glanced up to watch a curricle drawn by two proud-crested horses speed smartly down the street. The woman on the seat was richly dressed but obviously a fair cyprian. She leaned heavily on the broad-shouldered gentleman's arm and laughed again. And quite suddenly Mary was far too conscious of standing forlornly on the snowy walk, alone with no one to care about her, and most wretchedly once again outside the glittering world he had allowed her to taste.

Chapter Twenty-six

MARY WAS DEFIANTLY a bit late in reaching Curzon Street the following morning, but when the footman showed her to the library, Menton greeted her coldly without any remark concerning her tardiness. The crooked bit of sticking plaster on his forehead lent him a rakish appearance that did nothing to dispel the grim air hanging about him.

"Let us not delay over this matter," he said, walking toward the large mahogany desk in the center of the room.

Numb with helplessness, she seated herself and wondered why it should seem so awful to be finally receiving her freedom.

The door opened, and Tyler entered with a discreet cough for attention. Menton looked up with some impatience. "What is it?"

"A letter was just brought round by hand for you, my lord." Tyler extended his salver, and Menton took the letter with complete uninterest. Tyler stood his ground a moment, then inquired: "Shall I have the lad wait for an answer?"

Menton glanced at the letter more closely, and his features hardened to bleakness. "No," he said curtly. "Give him a shilling and send him off. My brother will need no answer from me."

Tyler departed with his salver correctly under one arm, and Menton glanced perfunctorily at Mary. "Ex-

cuse me." He made it sound like an order rather than a request, and ripped open the message.

That it was of a galling nature Mary could easily tell by observing Menton's face as he read. It paled with anger at the opening line and began to look so tight with controlled rage, she thought his jaw muscles must soon snap. Then abruptly everything seemed to drain out of his face. His eyes stopped as though fixed upon a certain sentence, then they rescanned the last quarter of the page. After a moment he slowly folded the paper as though he did not see it and circled the desk to stand staring out the narrow window overlooking the street.

Mary stirred restlessly, and his head swung to face her. "So I have wronged you again," he said quietly.

She stared back at a loss, not knowing what to say. To agree would only set up his back again, and she was wary of coming out on the worst end of yet another argument.

"Tell me the truth, little Mary," he said.

That was enough. She clenched her fists. "No, I shall not tell you the truth! Every time I do so, you only call me a bare-faced liar and seek to give me punishment. I have told you all that I shall."

Did he flinch, or was she only imagining it? He glanced down at the letter in his hands and frowned at it. "Was there anyone who observed my giving you the paper at Almack's?"

Mary held back the scornful urge to laugh. "I daresay the entire company observed it."

"But Thomas was not there." He seemed almost to be reassuring himself.

"No," said Mary. "Rebeccah mentioned that he was gambling at his club."

Menton looked up sharply. "Rebeccah? She was there?"

"Yes." Mary raised her chin defiantly. "With Gilbreath."

He muttered something. "The slut. I suppose she missed nothing."

"Directly upon your departure, she approached me

about it," said Mary woodenly. She hoped he would let her go soon.

"You say that you dropped the letter while getting into your carriage?" His voice grew sharper by rapid degrees, but it was not from anger, she sensed.

She nodded. "It was in my reticule. Mr. Gilbreath was on hand to pick it up for me. He took quite a long time in brushing off the snow, but I do not see how he could have stolen it, as Harton claims. Are he and your brother friends?"

Menton frowned at that last question, but instead he said: "From the . . . ah . . . unflattering comment concerning your loyalty to me made here by my brother"—he tapped the paper in his hands—"I am inclined to believe that you have not been lying to me."

Mary's heart jumped, but she refused to allow all of her skepticism to be swept away so easily. "How nice," she said tartly. "You fill me with gratitude, sir."

To her surprise, he did not take up the cudgels but instead shook his head. "Has my brother tried to sound you out?"

"Not really," she said warily, unwilling to mention Keath's confrontation with her. "He has been easy to fob off."

"I see."

She stared at him in bewilderment, unable to fathom him at all. His behavior—or rather mood—was certainly very odd today. She began to think he was deliberately avoiding another argument, and did not know what to make of that either.

"I was extremely unwilling to think yesterday," he said, still in that unusually quiet tone. "I could not get past the belief that you were in my brother's employ in hopes of escaping our contract. I see now that I was mistaken. Thomas has let slip that much here in this note with his gloating over me and his haranguing of you." Menton sighed. "The other night was indeed a failure, but I shall terminate that blackguard's French career yet. Neither of us can yet prove out the other's activities, but his day of reckoning will not be too far now in the future!"

Mary's breath seemed to have been snatched away. "I do not understand what you are saying. Your brother—"

"—is using his position in the government to sell papers to the French." Menton's jaw jutted. "And I am attempting to stop him."

Everything jumbled up within her so, at first she was unable to speak at all. Relief was foremost of her emotions. It flooded over her in a great wave: he was not a traitor! Keath was the one! The realization of what a fool she had been struck her like an actual blow. Had she not been so quick to make that wrong assumption, she could have spared herself a good deal of misery these past weeks. And with all of her whining and hanging back, it was no wonder she had given him such a disgust of her. She looked up to meet his eyes and became conscious by his somewhat uncertain expression that she had been silent too long. Desperately she wanted to spill out everything to him, especially all of her joy that he was not the evil creature she had thought him.

She opened her mouth and said: "Why in this manner? Why do you not go to Bow Street?"

An invisible wall crashed down around her, and her appalled heart plummeted to the pit of her stomach. Why had she said that? Now everything was back on its normal uncommunicative plane. She had lost her one opportunity to tell him . . . No. She saw the customary closed expression returning to his face and realized painfully that it was for the best that she had not spoken out and embarrassed them both. Nothing between them was really changed, except now she knew that she had been right in remaining loyal to him.

Menton rubbed his jaw and tossed Keath's letter on his desk. "I do not call in the Runners because I do not want scandal to touch the Keath name. He is my brother, though he should be run out of the country. No, Miss Clampton." His mouth set firmly. "I prefer to handle this deplorable affair in my own manner. Though perhaps I have been wrong in forcing you to participate . . . I suppose, ma'am, that an apology is in order. I have treated you badly. Now I shall allow you a choice of continuing our agreement or going your own way."

Mary eyed him with angry distrust. Yesterday he had blown up in her face and all but called her a slut. She frowned unseeingly at the bookshelves, struggling to keep grasp of all that was happening. Could a brief note from Keath have truly changed him so promptly back into regarding her with favor? It was wonderful, yes, that Menton was not the traitor he had perhaps unwittingly led her to believe, but certainly he was trying to stop his brother in an underhanded way, and his reasons for employing her were hardly admirable. Quick resentment surged up within her, but she stifled it, trying to make a reasonable decision over this tangle. She knew she should take her chance to go. It was the wisest course.

She looked up to catch him with a—could it actually be gentle?—smile on his face, and her resolution drained away. "I shall finish our agreement," she said, and was at once appalled at herself for saying exactly the opposite of what she had decided to say.

To her annoyance, he looked distinctly pleased. Now she had given him the future use of her services, which were nonexistent. That would serve him a fine turn. It didn't matter that she had again agreed to participate in this deadly business of his. She wanted more than just a sum to support her until she found work. Nor did she want to be someone's drudge for the rest of her life. Be hanged to the consequences; she would stick this out until he paid her fully what was owed her. And this way it was best that he did not love her.

She swallowed down the lump that last thought brought to her throat and straightened her shoulders. "I should prefer to return to Lady Monteforte's now."

"Certainly." His sangfroid was regained, and yet the ease of manner which had never failed to warm her in the past continued to linger about him. "Have you breakfasted?"

"Yes. Thank you." She was impatient to be gone now.

He glanced at his watch with an absent frown, then snapped it shut. "I shall call upon you this afternoon—if that is convenient. I think you understand the reason."

"Yes." Her heart thundered out of control, and the palms of her hands went all damp. "I shall await you, sir," she said with rather a dry gasp. *So soon!* Suddenly events were moving too quickly for her.

He took her hand and kissed her knuckles lightly. "Until this afternoon, Miss Clampton. Do try to stay out of trouble until then. My footman shall escort you and your maid home."

She murmured something incoherent and fled.

From the moment they arose from luncheon, she was unable to completely suppress her agitation. Never, she thought in vexation, had she been rendered more nervous, and she tried to overcome it by taking over Miss Pingleberry's daily chore of reading a book chapter to Lady Monteforte. The novel was penned by an anonymous hand, and it was obviously based on the exploits of actual members of the ton. Its satiric wit was greatly appealing to Lady Monteforte. She had not the least difficulty in guessing the true identity of the characters, and alternately hooted with laughter or thumped her cane at each sally. This proved satisfactory for the better portion of an hour in entertaining them all—except Arabella, who was still indulging in a fit of the sulks caused by a morning call from the still-determined Sir Oswald, and Harton, who was more engrossed with the degree of polish upon his boots than with literature.

Mary was just making her way upstairs to fetch a shawl for Lady Monteforte when she encountered Menton, who was removing his hat and driving coat at the other end of the hall. Startled, she greeted him with the last shreds of her composure.

"Hello, my lord," she said in a low, shy voice. "Lady Monteforte is in the yellow salon if you would care to follow me—"

"No, I do not care to follow you there at all," he

said unhelpfully. "I desire private audience with you —at once."

She loosed a small sigh. It was as she had suspected. "Then we had better go into the morning room."

"Excellent." He took her arm in his and strode off in that direction. Mary entered the room first and dismissed a wide-eyed maid who was there dusting. He indicated a chair for her, and she sat down in it with her heart performing every sort of gyration but its normal one. She kept her eyes lowered to avoid meeting his. So now he was going to stand here and playact a proposal—for the appreciation of any servant possibly listening at the door, no doubt. She pressed her lips together with annoyance. Going through these motions was unnecessary as well as unfair. She wondered why she had ever been doltish enough to imagine she had a *tendre* for him.

"Now," he said, standing before her and clasping his hands at his back. "There is no need to go into great lengths over this formality." He cleared his throat. "I extend to you the offer of marriage, Miss Clampton."

How could he put it in such a vile manner? She had the strong urge to box his ears, but overcame it. "I accept, my lord," she said with equal flatness.

"Ah." He sounded relieved, as though glad to have it over. "Well, now. I suppose it is in order to make an announcement to the household. As for a kiss to seal the moment . . ." He paused, and Mary's heart sent a near-deafening rush of blood through her ears. "We needn't bother with what is better suited for lovestruck children. This is, after all, no more than an alliance of convenience."

Lovestruck children indeed. Scorn curled her lips. It was just as well he felt that way, for she would never suffer a kiss from him again. No matter that all her life she had dreamed of making a love match. She would still do so—once she was freed from this odious, haughty creature who thought himself above all rules of God and men. He might not be sold out to the

French, but that did not make him any less insufferable.

Lifting her chin defiantly, she stood up and laid her fingers upon his proffered arm, allowing him to escort her to the yellow salon. Lady Monteforte was by herself, still enthroned in her wing chair before the fire. She thumped her cane at the sight of him. "Hah, Menton. I see you're dressed in the first stare as usual. How are you today?"

"Excellent as always ma'am." He bowed suavely over her hand and raised the withered flesh to his lips. "You will be pleased to know that Miss Clampton has done me the honor of giving me her hand in marriage."

There was a long moment of silence in the room, broken only by the ticking of the china clock on the mantel. To her excessive discomfort, Mary found herself the object of Lady Monteforte's piercing gray eyes. There is going to be trouble, she thought, and held her breath.

Menton glanced at his godmother. "Well, ma'am? Do you give your blessings to the union?"

"I do not." She gripped her cane until her knuckles whitened. "Aye, you may gape if you wish, but I refuse to set my approval on such a ninnyhammer affair."

"Oh?" said Mentom with dangerous quiet. "Why do you disapprove of Miss Clampton?"

"I do not disapprove of her," said Lady Monteforte, meeting him glare for glare. "She is all very well in her own way, and has conducted herself acceptably beneath my roof. But she has neither the breeding nor the background to be a countess."

Menton's nostrils flared. "I believe, ma'am, that I am the best judge of that consideration."

She snorted. "And next you shall be telling me this is a love match. Bah! I have never seen you with a maggot in your head, and I do not care to see one there now."

He bowed, his lips set in a sardonic smile. "If that is your feeling on the matter, so be it. But the notice shall appear in tomorrow's *Gazette*."

"And what if Olivia objects? Be sure that she shall do so."

He eyed Lady Monteforte with such coolness Mary caught her breath and was grateful *she* was not on the receiving end of his gaze. "The decision in this matter is mine," he snapped. "I have fixed the wedding date for two weeks hence. Don't allow your disapproval to prevent you from helping my . . . bride with her trousseau. If you will excuse me now, I shall bid you both good day!"

The door closed behind him, and Lady Monteforte thwacked her cane down on a side table with a snort. "Fool." She glared at Mary. "He'll regret this, mark my words. The two of you don't suit and never will!"

Chapter Twenty-seven

MARY MET THE old woman's glare as calmly as she could. "It really does not matter whether we suit or not, ma'am."

"Hah!" Lady Monteforte snorted. "I suppose you are trying to tell me that a love match overlooks all the disadvantages between a couple of different stations."

"I am not trying to do anything of the sort." Mary had had her fill of this biting old woman. "You may rest easy on that head, for his heart is not at all touched by any silly emotions—nor is mine—and this is no more than a marriage of convenience."

"You shan't make me swallow such gammon," retorted Lady Monteforte with a whack of her cane. "I can easily see the convenience for you, but in his case . . ."

Mary stiffened. This whole affair was a lie; why should one more hurt? "Although I am now without family, I am not poor." She forced a hard laugh. "How else could I withstand the dressmaker's bills?"

Uncertainty flickered through the wrinkled face; Lady Monteforte clung tightly to her cane. "You have given no indication of being an heiress."

"Indeed not." Mary produced the coldest of smiles. "I consider it ill-bred to be ever discussing one's financial circumstances." She paused a moment to savor the enraged chagrin her set-down had brought to Lady Monteforte's face. "Say what you like, but Lord Menton made the offer on his own volition. I did not set my cap for him in particular, but I have seen no reason to reject his suit, or his offer." She excused herself before Lady Monteforte could marshal up further argument, and retreated to her room with a splitting headache.

In the days following the announcement in the *Gazette,* all manner of persons from the ton's highest ranks came to call and gaze upon the paragon which had ensnared the ninth Earl of Menton, famous for his expertise in sidestepping the lures of eligible young ladies. She began to feel as though she were entrapped in a glass case, unable to step out of Lady Monteforte's house to go shopping for the merest trifle without being stared at by ladies, ogled by gentlemen, and pointed out to daughters by plainly miffed mamas. She and Lady Menton avoided each other by mutual if unspoken agreement, and that occasioned more gossip. More and more she suffocated in the deluge of activity, longing to run away for even a few minutes just to be outside and to herself for a bit. But there was never a chance between receiving and making calls, or entertaining, or seeing to her trousseau. Lady Monteforte, still disapproving but resigned, persevered in chaperoning her and Arabella to all the functions, though once even she was overheard to remark that "it is like living in the midst of one of those horrid circuses."

Then at last the day of the wedding arrived with the dawn of a vigorous winter sun. Most of Mary's night had been sleepless, and she awoke from her light doze at the faint click of the door opening. Somehow, the sight of Jenny with her plain dress and big pitcher of white porcelain was reassuring. Then Mary recalled that the dreaded hour was almost upon her. With a sigh she pushed back the covers and steeled herself to try to face it as best she could.

Setting down the heavy pitcher by the basin, Jenny gave her a warm, excited glance that made her feel more wretched than ever, and rang for the breakfast tray to be brought up. The nervous fluttering in Mary's stomach made her quite certain that she would be wretchedly sick if she tried to eat the least morsel of food. She knew that she would have need of some sustenance to see her through the next several hours, but when the tray at last was placed before her, she could do no more than sip distractedly at her cup of chocolate with her eyes fixed upon the wedding dress before her on its special fitting stand. Somehow, she told herself, she must strive to maintain her composure. No one must suspect the ache in her heart. No one must know that her precious dream to be wed to Menton was going to be realized today in a manner that was nothing more than a cruel sham. With a wrench inside, she set down her cup.

When the hairdresser arrived, Mary swiftly pushed herself out of bed and donned her dressing gown, eager for any diversion away from her aching thoughts. But other than watching the somewhat effeminate man dexterously pile her dark chestnut hair upon her head in a charming mass of soft curls, she had little enough to distract her. Her eyes gazed unseeingly into the mirror while her slender foot tapped out a nervous rhythm against the floor. It was during this time that the door opened to allow Lady Monteforte to enter. Through the mirror, Mary watched her cross the room stiffly, leaning on that formidable cane of hers, and take a chair near the fire without speaking.

A knock on the door interrupted the proceedings. Lady Monteforte called a response, and the liveried footman stepped upon the threshold. "My lady, the dowager Countess of Menton begs leave to call upon Miss Clampton."

Mary looked up in shock. No, of course she did not want to see this woman. She lifted her head to refuse, but Lady Monteforte was already uttering permission. Mary clenched her hands in her lap, resentfully refusing to rise as the dowager entered the room.

Lady Menton did not miss the deliberate slight, and her eyes burned hatred as their gazes locked in the mirror. She nodded briefly to Lady Monteforte and walked up to Mary. "Aubrey will not see reason," she said without preamble. "So I have come to deal with this myself. Here, Miss Clampton, is a bank draft for seven hundred pounds." She yanked it from her reticule and extended the paper. "This is in exchange for calling off this ridiculous affair."

Even as Mary's cheeks burned in immediate rage and embarrassment, she had to wonder at the dowager's state of mind. How could the woman be such a fool by talking this way in front of all these servants? It would spread over London before nightfall; even the hairdresser's tongue would undoubtedly prove loose enough to recount such juicy gossip as this. Mary clenched her dressing gown at the throat and stood up, ignoring the proffered draft.

She met the dowager's seething eyes with full scorn. "Shall I forget you ever spoke, my lady?"

"Olivia!" Lady Monteforte pushed out of her chair and came stumping over, scowling dismissal at the servants. "What maggot is in your brain now?"

The door closed softly, reluctantly, after the last servant, but Mary had no doubt they were all grouped with their ears to the keyhole. The dowager trembled in futile rage, her light blue eyes filling with tears.

"Oh, Honoria," she wailed. "How could you keep this . . . this viper under your wing?"

"That is my affair," said Lady Monteforte sharply. "And it is Aubrey's affair if he wants to marry her. He is two-and-thirty."

The dowager shook her head as though to escape the words. "No!" she said. "He has been entrapped . . . somehow. All these weeks he has not been himself. I . . . Here!" She thrust the draft at Mary, who seized it and ripped it in half.

"That is my answer, Lady Menton!" She seethed, her bosom heaving. Did the woman think her to be bought off like a cheap bawd? "I—"

"Keep your peace, girl!" said Lady Monteforte. "Olivia, stop your sniveling and attempt to be sensible. You cannot insult the child in this way—"

"Child? Hah!" The dowager was almost screaming. She gripped her head wildly. "A gutter skirt . . . a thief . . . scum! She is a—"

Lady Monteforte slapped her soundly. "Enough! You are acting perfectly deranged!"

The dowager turned away with a choked sob, holding her cheek. She sank down against the bed and began to weep uncontrollably. Unmoved, Mary watched her a moment, then glanced up to catch Lady Monteforte's piercing gaze.

"You do love him, don't you?" asked the old woman softly, her gray eyes boring into Mary's.

Sudden tears blurred Mary's sight. She turned away with a blind nod and gripped the edge of the dressing table. "I . . . I cannot help myself," she whispered, closing her eyes against her inward agony. How she wished she did despise him! Far better to hate than to be obliged to feign indifference.

"This is a most havey-cavey business," said Lady Monteforte, still softly. She paused, and Mary's heart contracted in fear of more penetrating questions. "But I must trust Aubrey to know what he is doing, though I fear he is making a mistake." She frowned. "Very well. I shall deal with Olivia before she weeps herself into a real spasm."

She called back in the servants to take the dowager to a guest chamber, and followed, leaving Mary leaning against the dressing table in relief. Lady Monteforte could have bored the truth from her, yet she had refrained from trying. Why? Mary shook her head and allowed the maids to ease the wedding dress on over her head. It was impossible to figure out now. She found herself trembling, already drained by the morning's events.

The dress was of heavy silk brocade, very stiff, with its full skirts sweeping out from the precisely tailored waist. Its bodice was cut low and filled in with a soft lace fichu. The sleeves were straight to her elbows and edged there with folds of exquisite imported lace. Mary stared at her reflection in amazement. It was a stranger in the mirror, magnificently dressed, magnificently flushed with anger. Her eyes flashed like emeralds and clear amber set out in the sunshine.

The hairdresser was allowed readmittance, and it was his white slim hands which arranged the fine lace over her dark hair like a Spanish mantilla, fastening it into place with diamond-studded pins that winked brilliantly with every slight movement of her head.

Arabella rushed in just as the final folds were caessed into place and gasped audibly. "Mary! You look just like a fairy princess! Oh, how beautiful!" She skipped up to kiss Mary's cheek, her own appearance fetching in a demure gown of palest blue and a necklet of pearls. "I am so excited! This shall be the most fabulous day, all so romantic. You remember I told you that you could catch him—"

A knock on the door interrupted her raptures. "The carriages are ready," announced the footman.

Never had Mary seen two coaches more polished. The paint seemed to glisten in the sunshine, rivaled only by the gleaming coats of splendid Welsh cattle. Such beautiful horses had surely been lent from the Menton stables, Mary decided.

A shout arose from the small crowd of curious passersby as she appeared on the steps. Mary shrank back in instant embarrassment, but already she was being firmly installed into the smaller first carriage. Lady Monteforte—with grim hold of a tottering Lady Menton—Arabella, and Miss Pingleberry squeezed into the second carriage, along with a loudly protesting Harton, who was complaining that his cravat was but half-tied and why must the lovebirds be married at this paganish, unnaturally early hour.

They began the stately procession through the streets, and Mary could hear the clock in the Tower booming out eleven strokes over the city. Alone, with only the steady plop of the horses' hooves to keep her thoughts company, Mary gripped the seat with unsteady hands and thought of the quiet wedding she used to dream about: one with a simple homemade dress of white cambric and a clutch of street-vendor violets. How oddly her dreams had been realized. Today she rode through the streets like a princess in her own carriage, dressed above her wildest imaginings in silk and lace and diamonds, with white roses to carry. And her groom was no stolid, hardworking young man, but rather an arrogant lord of the realm who would never return her love.

The carriage lurched over a pile of refuse on the street, startling her out of her bewildered thoughts. She glanced out the window and saw the chapel just ahead; already they were slowing. Closing her eye, she prayed that he would not be mocking and cynical today before the altar, or she would not be able to bear it.

In an odd daze, she was helped from the carriage and entered the dim interior of the chapel through the gathered company of richly dressed ladies and gentlemen. A rather drawn Rodney Tavers was there with his left arm in a sling; Charlie stood at his side. Serving as the groom's man, Keath was staring at the ceiling with a sulky expression. Mary's breath caught in her throat as she gazed round at the blur of faces; was all the *beau monde* here? She backed up a step, and it was Lady Monteforte who gave her a little nod that somehow steadied everything. Mary lifted her chin with a new show of composure she did not at all feel and glanced toward the altar.

His lordship was standing there in most correct attire of black coat, black breeches, and white smallclothes. His cravat was snowy froth beneath his strong chin, and his black hair was unpowdered. Even as Mary experienced a shot of relief that she too had kept her hair natural, he lifted his quizzing glass at his brother and said in a carrying drawl: "Gad, Thomas was that coat made by a French tailor? I am shocked you have the poor taste to wear it in my presence."

The words, the faint mockery in the drawl, were like a blow. He was unchanged; no miracle had occurred overnight to touch his heart. Mary's own heart seemed to flatten, and she could not move. Why must everyone stare at her? Why could Menton not put down that dreadful glass? And why did he suddenly look at her in such a strange fashion?

From behind, Arabella gave her a small push. "Go on, Mary," she whispered.

And there was no choice left but to obey.

Chapter Twenty-eight

THE PRIVATE TRAVELING chaise was the best-sprung
Mary had ever ridden in. She scarcely felt the jars of
the hard-rutted road, though they seemed to be flying,
so rapidly did the four-horse team gallop. For the past
two hours she had tried to sleep in her corner, without
success, and his lordship had sat on the opposite side
in apparent brooding silence. This did not appear to
be the most promising start for their new union—even
if it was only in name. And everything was suddenly
so different. Now they would see each other daily, and
not whenever he troubled to call. Now her name was
Mary Keath, and now she was a countess. She frowned
over the last thought. She felt not in the least changed
—at least, not inside. She might be referred to as "my
lady," but inside she was still herself—Mary. How
very odd, she thought, and decided it was time they at
least spoke to each other. Even his cynicism was to be
preferred over her restless thoughts.

"How fast are we going?" She blurted out the question.

He looked up in some startlement. "I beg your pardon?"

It was a mistake to have spoken. Now she was beneath that odious gaze of his, like a fly pinned to the
gray velvet squabs. Uneasily she turned to gaze out
the window. "We seem to be going at an uncommon
rate of speed. They must be quite good horses."

"Yes, they are," he said, as though to imply he

would not own anything otherwise. "I expect we are going about sixteen miles per hour."

Mary blinked. "All of that? Then we are indeed close to flying."

He crossed one impeccable leg over the other. "If you are alarmed, I shall order us slowed a trifle,"

"Oh, no," she said, thinking unhappily of how hard his voice still was; as hard as when he had stood before her in Newgate, as hard as when he had said his wedding vows. Since his mood had obviously not altered, she would perhaps be wise to fall silent again. "You need not trouble yourself. I find the journey exciting."

But the polite words hung falsely between them. Mary mentally snorted in self-scorn. Indeed, she looked most excited and thrilled, sitting here in the glummest of moods and not even bothering to look at the scenery. He did not seem to care, however, and so she resolved not to trouble herself further about it. After all, it was hardly her fault the day had been such a trying one, the ceremony such a boring one.

Hot shame spread through her. That she should be bored at her own wedding! But it was the truth. Once she had steadied from her knee-quivering fear, there had been nothing but the long service and ceremony that all seemed to pertain to someone besides herself. She had had to struggle to pay attention and make herself believe that she was indeed standing there saying vows that were going to be made a lie. Under such guilt, she had not been able to leave the chapel fast enough. It was hard to shake off the lowering thought that her duplicity had somehow tainted the walls. But Menton had looked so stern and just as uncomfortable then and all through the lengthy reception following. Mary's lips tightened. He was well-served to be so, for it had been his insistence on going through with this. Perhaps already he was regretting it. If so, she thought darkly, it was too late. They had both cast their dice; now they had to withstand the consequences.

Just at dusk they reached a small village and pulled up at an inn called the Gray Goose. Despite all she could do, Mary could not overcome her nervousness at this first appearance as his wife. In low spirits she picked at her portion of the repast spread before them in the private parlor until he startled her by asking what day of January her birthday fell on.

Astonished and a little gratified that he should remember such a small detail, she replied: "The sixteenth. Why?"

"That's scarce three weeks hence." His eyes narrowed to glinting slits, and he snapped his fingers. "Splendid. I shall throw a ball in your honor, my sweet."

Forgetting her new position, she stiffened at once. "I am not your—"

"Hush." He caught up her hand and lightly kissed the tips of her fingers. "There is a purpose," he murmured.

Of course. She was jolted back at once into remembrance of their mission, and hung her head. "I am sorry, sir." With an effort she tried to mask her mortification by sitting up straighter. "Will you tell me more about it?"

He glanced at the waiter entering with the fish, and shook his head. "Later. And don't look so stricken over a trifle. This has been a difficult day for you, but you shall feel better once we are at the Hall." The faint sounds of rough laughter from the taproom made him smile. "And I instructed the landlord to provide you with a room that has a good bolt on the door, so you needn't worry if any of those rascals start straying about."

She had to smile in reply to that. "Thank you. That is most kind." This first show of consideration from him today could not help but bolster her spirits a bit, and she began to think about her ball with shy excitement.

The next morning they left the Gray Goose at a leisurely hour and arrived at Menton Hall just in time for an excellent luncheon of freshly baked ham and pastries. Menton introduced her to the staff before leaving her to herself, and she gave the entire afternoon to exploring the rambling medieval-Tudor pile that was her new home. Besides the original hall there were three wings, the most recent added by the eighth earl. She found Mrs. Lunt, the buxom little housekeeper, more than willing to show her about.

Then a footman came to inform them that the village children had arrived with holly.

"Good," said Mrs. Lunt. "Now, if my lady will excuse me, I've got to see that the maids put it all up properly."

Of course! How could she forget it was Christmas Eve? Mary pinched herself in vexation at being so shatter-brained and hurried off to watch all the decorations being put up. It did not take her long to learn what all the fuss was about. All of the villagers were to come up tonight!

"It's a tradition," explained Mrs. Lunt between directions to the stableboy struggling to attach holly to the staircase banister. "Whenever the earl is here, he invites all the tenants up and gives the families each a fine eating gobbler and all the new-marrieds a plump ham. It's been done since the days of old Queen Bess. And when the earl ain't here, his bailiff, Mr. Simmons, sees that the food's given out in the village."

Mary nodded slowly. "So tomorrow everyone will have a good Christmas dinner."

"Aye, my lady. Very grateful for it the people are."

That evening Mary sat shyly in the background while Menton wandered easily through the crowd of tenants and their families overflowing the Hall, which was the only part of the original castle still intact. Sitting there watching him rub shoulders with these shy, plain people, Mary was filled with involuntary pride. He was so at ease with them all, acting as much the gentleman as though he were in town, yet treating each in the same personal manner as though they were all important to him. And as his tenants, they were important, but Mary wondered how many fine haughty lords in London bothered to remember that or care.

"Now, ma'am," he said suddenly, startling her out of her warm thoughts, "here are their gifts to us. Would you see to them?"

Mary glanced shyly out at the friendly faces and was pleased that he was allowing her to join in. A footman handed the baskets and parcels to her to open, then handed them away to another underling after Menton's nod at each one. Mary found these things far more delightful than any gifts she'd seen presented in London, more than even the new emerald necklace she wore tonight. They included a brace of pheasants to grace his lordship's table, a basket of brown eggs, some thread and woven cloth, a gray kitten for her ladyship's kitchen, and even a basket of fluffy baby chicks.

In the face of all this, she could not maintain her inner guards any longer, even with Menton standing with one hand on the back of her chair. Laughingly she drew one of the chicks from the basket and held him close to her ear to listen to his soft peeping.

"Isn't he adorable?" she asked of Menton, her eyes sparkling as brightly as the emeralds.

Menton smiled as though in reluctant amusement and stuck out a forefinger, which was promptly pecked. He withdrew the finger hastily. "More savage than adorable."

Mary laughed again, confident by the crinkles at the corners of his eyes that he was not truly offended. "We shall have to keep them in the kitchen by the fire, and I will have the kitten in my room so he shan't bother them."

"What a domestic mind you have," he said dryly, watching her ease the chick back among his protesting fellows. "Are we finished at last?"

This question was directed at the footman, who bowed. "Only this last basket for her ladyship, my lord. It arrived but minutes before, by messenger."

"How odd," said Mary, accepting the wicker basket with a red velvet bow tied round the handle. "I wonder who could have sent it?"

Menton coughed into his handkerchief. "Perhaps the card will say. Excuse me a moment." He wandered off toward a large ruddy-faced yeoman.

Noting that the servants were bringing out fresh honey cakes baked by Mrs. Lunt that very afternoon, and that the men were gathering to sing before his lordship, Mary opened the attached card and frowned

at the message scribbled there: "So you do not forget."
Her frown deepened. What was that supposed to
mean? And how vexing that the sender had forgotten
to add his name. She unfastened the lid and peered
eagerly inside at the bloated body of a dead rat.

At first she was too stunned and too choked by rising nausea to move. Then with a scream she flung
the basket away and ran blindly for the doorway.
Strong arms caught her from behind before she reached
it, however, and swung her around to hold her close.
Mary covered her face with her hands and shook with
silent tears against him.

"Gently," Menton murmured into her ear. "Do not
cry. You are perfectly safe here among us."

Mary shuddered. "H-horrible," she gasped out,
clinging to him.

He took both of her hands in one of his and swung
around to face the rest of the room, from where angry
mutterings were rising. The ruddy-faced man was
holding the basket with a scowl.

"What is in it?" snapped Menton.

"Ain't no wonder the lady was frightened," said the
man slowly. "Look fer yerself, sir."

Menton obeyed, leaving Mary to bite her knuckle
against the tremors still shaking her entire frame. He
glanced in, then shut the lid rather abruptly. "Johnson, have this taken out and burned at once."

The footman obeyed hastily. Murmurs increased in
volume, and Mary struggled unsuccessfully to regain
a hold on herself. She was almost unaware of Menton
plucking the card still clenched in her hand.

"Rather a nasty trick fer the lads to play," continued
the yeoman in rising indignation. "Young scamps
ought to be horsewhipped. The real gift's probably
about somewhere in the shrubbery."

"No." Menton crumpled the card in his fist. "This
was intentional—from an acquaintance of mine who
needs a sharp lesson taught him."

Chapter Twenty-nine

IT WAS ANOTHER morning of sunshine. Mary sat half-dressed on her bed, trying to take her mind off last night by forcing it to comprehend all the luxuries afforded by this spacious suite of rooms given her. There were her bedchamber and parlor, the latter being furnished with a pianoforte, a dainty writing table from the Queen Anne period, and a bookshelf stocked with all the best and newest works of her favorite authors. She even had—much to her astonished delight—a tiny cubbyhole containing a brazier, a screen, and her very own hipbath. As though this were not all overwhelming (even after the comfort of Lady Monteforte's town residence), the walls were all done in wallpaper of the cheeriest yellow satin, and a vase of yellow hothouse roses had been set upon her dressing table promptly upon her awakening.

Mary scarcely knew how to respond to such lavish attention to her every like. She ought to make her delight known to Menton, but dared she? Would he brush her aside as he did so often?

She frowned, rubbing her arms against the slight chill. Of late it seemed he had not been quite so abrupt with her. Oh, he was still his arrogant, overcommanding self, but last night he had not been odious to his tenants or to her—even after that dreadful rat. She shivered and stood up to finish dressing. Indeed, he had seemed genuinely concerned about the fright she had taken.

And she was still frightened, horribly so. She did
not understand why, but the more she tried to put the
incident from mind, the more it troubled her. All night
she had fretted over who could have sent it and why.
She did not know the handwriting, but the suspicion of
Thomas Keath suggested itself over and over to her
mind. He certainly knew the meaning rats held for her.
A vision of sitting in the darkness with only the busy
rustlings of scuttling feet and their high, angry chittering to listen to flashed into her mind with such force
she was abruptly nauseous and had to sit down. She
was certain that if Keath won this he would have no
compunction against returning her to prison.

Menton was waiting for her at the foot of the stairs
with a warm greeting that at once melted all of her determination to keep up a brave front. The horror of it
flooded over her once again, and she looked up at him
in mute appeal.

He flicked her cheek with one forefinger. "You are
still affected?"

His gentleness inflamed her with confusion. She
barely restrained the urge to fling herself upon his
chest, and instead passed a trembling hand across
her eyes with a little nod. "You will think me refining
upon it too much, I know. But I am frightened to death
and cannot get the least ease of mind. Do you think it
was your brother who sent the rat?"

His black brows snapped together over his bony
nose. "It was him. I recognized the writing."

Mary lowered her eyes. "He is very cruel," she
said softly. "Shall he send another?" The thought of
receiving more unnerved her.

Menton reached out and caught her hand. "Do not
be troubled. I have instructed the servants to inspect
any parcel sent to you."

"Thank you." She smiled in gratitude. "But what
are you doing about stopping him completely?"

"We are two miles from the coast." Menton drew a
deep breath. "He meets his man, whom I'm having
closely watched, in Brighton."

She frowned. "Why Brighton instead of Dover?"

"No one expects to find spies in such a gay resort.

Now . . ." Menton seated her at the breakfast table and informed the servants that they would serve themselves. "Thomas makes his delivery—copies of military strategy—to Brighton once every week or so. Upon occasion, he employs a man to do the trip when he is obligated in London—but that is unimportant. What we must—"

"He is paid well for this, is he not?" asked Mary, puzzled for the motives of a gentleman of Keath's position. Perhaps he did it for the risk, but she did not think so. "I mean, he would have to be, to do this."

"Yes, he is paid. That is how he maintains himself in such high rig." Menton's voice was cold, heavy. He carved her a slice of ham with almost savage intentness. "My father's will left him no more than a modest stipend, necessitating his employment in the government, I'm sorry to say. You see, ma'am, my brother lived very high as long as our father was alive, but all of the property is entailed. And Thomas has proved himself unable—or unwilling—to lower his standard of living accordingly."

"But could you not help him?" asked Mary, almost able to sympathize with Keath for a moment—almost, but she could not forget the rat.

Menton shook his head, his face betraying nothing. "We were not on speaking terms at the time of my father's death. I have managed to mend that slightly, but he refuses to be a beggar at my expense." Menton paused. "Indeed, I think it wise of him to have refused my aid, for I certainly would have put a damper on his gambling."

"He plays deep?"

"Very." Menton's drawl was dry.

Mary frowned, trying to sort everything together. Some words of Harton's came to her mind. "Is that how he knows Gilbreath?"

Menton nodded, almost warily she thought. "I believe it may be Gilbreath who led him into the frogs' pocket," he said.

"I seem to be increasingly left with no choice but to distrust the man," said Mary with some irritation. "Everyone speaks so ill of him."

"I suggest that you do distrust Gilbreath," said Menton in his coldest fashion.

She sensed a rebuke in the words and bristled. "I have no expectation of ever seeing him again."

"There you may be mistaken. If Thomas accepts my invitation to the ball, he may allow Gilbreath to tag along." He paused. "With a houseful of people here that Thomas likes to mingle with, he shall surely take advantage of our proximity to the coast. I am counting upon that." Menton's blue eyes bored into hers, and she suddenly thought her heart had stopped beating. "We shall both of us have to make our moves. This is the beginning. Still game?"

"Yes," she whispered without hesitation. A cold thrill ran through her, and she realized with surprise that she really was ready, even eager. She hoped the next two weeks until the ball would pass quickly.

They did, for Menton saw to it that her days were filled with either posing for her portrait in her cloth-of-gold ballgown or learning to gallop and take short hedges on the small mare that she had used at his Brighton estate. The activities exasperated her because she saw her portrait as an unnecessary expense and she considered the prospect of riding in the hunt as the last thing in the world that she wanted to do. But Menton insisted in his high-handed way, and at last she had to reluctantly admit that she did feel more invigorated and confident of herself than she had in a long time.

But more puzzling was Menton's odd behavior in her presence. He was still curt and arrogant with her, especially in the evenings, when he strove to improve her dancing graces, but there were too many moments when she sensed his eyes following her about the room. And he was always producing a rose for her to carry in to dinner or seeing that her box of worked silver was kept filled with bonbons. The days seemed to fly, and she began to rise in the mornings with an unafraid eagerness for Menton's company.

Then all too suddenly the guests began to arrive. At all hours during the next two or three days, carriages pulled up into the drive. Mary was sorry to see the peace of the great house displaced by the bustling of servants, the unloading of trunks and portmanteaux, and the sounds of droll conversation and ready laughter—but within her flamed a heightened spark of excitement and tense readiness when Thomas Keath arrived with Rebeccah Tavers in his curricle.

Chapter Thirty

IT HAPPENED DURING a formal little gathering of the some twenty houseguests in the library for the unveiling of her portrait. She had protested privately to Menton against making such a to-do over it, but he had only returned a quizzical remark and done just as he pleased. So she sat erect in her chair and tried to mask her discomfiture at being the object of so much ostentation while a blushing Charlie read aloud a poem of his own composition and Lucy Thraude shyly sang a short ballad. Then Menton stood, gave an appropriately dry little speech, and twitched away the veil.

It had been set above the mantel, and now as she gazed in some surprise at it she flushed and wished with much mortification that she had prevailed against its being so prominently displayed. For despite the "live" quality that seemed to spring from the canvas, it was not a true likeness. She despised the teasing tilt of the head and the faint smile of confidence to be seen there. It was someone whom she might have been were she not usually so tense and ill-tempered; surely she had not been looking so contented these past days.

But before she could scarcely think all this, they were all out of their chairs, clustering about her first, with effusive compliments, then swarming Menton. Astonished that everyone should like it, Mary was too relieved to do more than smile with embarrassed gratification. At that moment she glimpsed Mrs. Lunt beckoning from the doorway with visible agitation.

Glad for the diversion, Mary went to her. "What is the matter? Has dinner burned?"

"No, no, my lady. Master Thomas has arrived." Mrs. Lunt's face became very severe. "And he has brought a young person with him."

"Oh, dear." Mary sighed, fearing the worst. She glanced over her shoulder, but Menton was in the process of telling a droll story to the accompaniment of much laughter. No, better that she try to deal with this than advertise a problem by summoning him away. "I'll come," she said, following the housekeeper out.

At the front entrance a most disapproving Tyler was directing the unloading of baggage from the curricle while Keath pointed out architectural features of interest to Rebeccah, who was leaning on his arm and proclaiming herself in raptures over everything.

Mary halted on the threshold with a sharp jolt of rage. Had Rebeccah no remaining shreds of decency left to her? Had she indeed sacrificed what reputation she owned just to go jauntering about the countryside with Keath? Mary's lips tightened, and she stepped outside.

"Hello," she said, and made herself sound pleasant, although it was decidedly difficult.

They whirled almost too quickly. Rebeccah tightened her grip on Keath's arm and smiled sunnily. "Hello, Mary. What a grand lady you've become, and mistress of all this besides." She waved an airy hand. "I confess myself green with envy."

No doubt, Mary thought with scorn. But it was time Rebeccah had her set-down. She and Keath might have planned to shock the company, but they would learn now that they must change their plan.

"Thank you, Rebeccah," she said evenly. "How delightful that you have come to pay us a call."

Hatred flashed out suddenly from Rebeccah's face, but Keath laughed faintly. "So thick, sister Mary? I have invited Miss Tavers to join the guests *here*. She needs a rest from town gaiety."

Inwardly Mary seethed at his effrontery, but she pinned on a smile. "You are bamming me with that. I know what it is: the two of you have eloped. How charmingly naughty."

Rebeccah took a hasty step forward, but Keath pulled her back. He scowled at Mary. "No need for any of your rude little jokes. We have not eloped."

"I see." Mary allowed her coldness to show now. "Then Miss Tavers is not welcome."

Keath clenched a fist. "Now, see here—"

But Tyler turned firmly on him. "I know you don't like it, Master Thomas, but her ladyship has said the person is not to be a guest. I suggest you put her up at the inn while we see to your trunk."

Keath went livid. "Damn your suggestion!" He struck Tyler to the ground with one wild punch. "I'll teach you to be impertinent." He bent and struck Tyler again.

Mrs. Lunt screamed, but fury at Keath's brutality sent Mary running down the steps. She seized his sleeve and pulled him back before he could hit the aging butler a third time.

"Get out of my way," he snarled, and slammed her against the curricle.

Mary coughed and struggled to regain the wind knocked from her. Why must that footman stand there gawping? she thought with frantic irritation. Something must be done! Seeing a whip lying on the curricle seat, she seized it with both hands and swung it smartly across Keath's back. He cursed and released Tyler to turn on her. Mary pressed back against the curricle, her heart hammering a hole through her ribs. She lifted the whip to strike him if he dared touch her.

"Thomas!" Menton's voice cut through the air like a sword.

Keath faltered and glanced back, and Mary sagged in relief.

"Get away from my wife." Menton strode down the entry steps, his face thunderous.

Keath stiffened. "Your wife," he said with a sneer, "was beating me with that whip. I've a right to take it from her."

"From what I saw, you were beating my servant." Menton's voice was like a lash of ice. "And never un-

der any circumstances do you have the right to set
a hand upon my wife." He took the whip from Mary
and flung it back into the curricle without a glance at
the shrinking Rebeccah. "Now, sir. You shall either
make your apologies and deliver this companion of
yours to other lodgings in the village, or take yourself
off and be hanged to you altogether!"

Keath's pale eyes gleamed murder. "Then good day
to you, brother, and may you rot in hell!"

In the act of helping Tyler to his feet, Menton did
not even glance at Keath. He supported the half-
fainting butler inside, Mary and Mrs. Lunt following.
As soon as his baggage was restrapped to the rear of
his curricle, Keath whipped his horses away with a
furious clatter of hooves.

Menton eased Tyler to a chair in the hall and gently
smoothed back the man's graying hair. "Easy, man,
We shall get these cuts cleaned up in no time." He
nodded to Mrs. Lunt, who hurried off at once.

Tyler blinked painfully. "I'm sorry to have caused
such a disturbance, my lord," he whispered despite his
bleeding mouth. "But I couldn't have her ladyship insulted by that . . . that . . ."

"Yes, man," said Menton. "Hush now and let Mrs.
Lunt clean you up."

She hurried up with a bowl of warm water, and
Menton stepped back to let her work. Mary tugged
urgently at his sleeve. "What shall we do now?" she
murmured.

He frowned. "I don't understand."

She gripped his arm in exasperation. "Your brother.
You have sent him off. How shall we get to his—?"

Menton swore with violence enough to make Mrs.
Lunt's head swivel around in protest. He paid no heed.
"I'll send a man to follow him." He swore again and
strode for the door. "This has put us in a damnable
coil."

Mary echoed that silently and watched Johnson help
Tyler off to his quarters.

Mrs. Lunt stared at her with a worried frown on
her round, good-natured face. "Are you all right, my

lady? I thought I'd never get his lordship fetched in time. Your hair is all mussed."

Mary hurried to the hall mirror and righted her appearance swiftly. "I suppose I must return to the library before the guests begin to feel slighted." She sighed. Why must she go all weak and trembly now that it was over? "Yes, yes, Mrs. Lunt. Do not fuss, pray. I am perfectly unharmed."

She hurried off to the library and forced herself to be brave against the prospect of playing hostess without Menton's support. But she thought he would return in a few moments. He did not.

Soon Mrs. Thraude sailed up to her. "Is something amiss, my lady? You look pale. And isn't his lordship going to return to us? Why was the housekeeper so distraught? Has there been an accident of some nature?"

"Yes," said Mary impatiently, wondering why this odious woman must grill her so, and why she had bothered to accept an invitation here in any case.

"Yes," piped up Lord Pondestoke with something of a huff. "Aubrey'd started another of his incomparable stories. Why must the fellow dash off so?"

"The butler fell down the stairs and bashed himself up somewhat," said Mary. Now she must remember to tell the servants the same story. Surely Menton would not want it about that his brother had caused such a fracas on the very doorstep, though from the stories she had heard concerning Keath's temper, perhaps the truth would not surprise anyone greatly.

Desperate to think of some diversion, Mary spied Charlie and seized upon him. "Perhaps Charlie and I can serve as guides for a brief tour of the house," she suggested.

From the instant cries of delight and hasty starting up of the guests, Mary discovered to her dismay that Menton was extremely guarded concerning his private domains and never gave anyone a tour of his residences. But of course it was too late to back out of her blunder now.

"Damme if this ain't the very trick," declared Lord Pondestoke, who was seven-and-thirty or thereabouts and handsome in a somewhat limp fashion. He polished his quizzing glass and glided up to take Mary's arm. "Delightful notion, my dear countess. I begin to perceive why old Aubrey married you."

Only later, at the close of the evening, when the guests were slowly parting company to retire, could she no longer contrive to avoid Menton. He caught her to one side. "So you gave everyone a tour, did you?"

Her heart sank to her slippers, and she nodded in guilt. "I did not know better until it was too late. But I could think of naught else to amuse them!"

He caught her hand up in his. "I am not angry. I don't give tours because I find them appalling bores. And you have gained Ponder's approval. Congratulations."

Relieved she smiled in shy gratification. "He is very odd." Then she recalled the more serious event of the day and frowned. "Have you heard yet from the man you sent after . . . ?"

"Yes." Menton sighed, and she eyed him in sudden dread.

"And?" she prompted.

"He lost him. Not the lad's fault." Menton gestured in pure frustration. "His horse cast a shoe. So we are at a loss to know where the . . ." He stopped abrptly and cleared his throat. "I shall contact Rodney at Brighton and see what he finds, if anything. I do not think Thomas will go there, however, until his fellow returns from France. That gives us a few days. He ought to turn up."

The obvious disappointment in his voice made Mary ache in sympathy. It seemed now that his every frustration was likewise experienced in her kindred heart. She looked up at him. "So what must we do if he doesn't?"

"Entertain our guests and hope he overcomes his temper enough to come to the ball." Menton shrugged and shook his head.

Chapter Thirty-one

IT WAS NOT a good situation, and Mary strained her thoughts for the next few days, trying without success to think of some way to get Keath into their clutches again. Menton had sent out men to make discreet inquiries about the countryside, but nothing had yet come of that. She watched him mask his frustration while in the presence of the guests, but at all other times it was apt to show in a quick flare of temper. Lines of strain were in his face for anyone who looked closely to see. But she could not hit upon any solution, try as she might, and it was so terribly hard to pin all hope on the chance that Keath might take a whim to come to the ball. Furthermore, she decided there was no gain if he did come, for he would be a fool to bring the papers with him. And not for a moment did she think him a fool.

"Well?" she asked Menton one morning when he came to fetch her for a ride about the countryside to mark out the course that tomorrow's hunt would follow. "If your brother had stayed here . . . Oh, pray, do not look like that! I know you had every cause to lose your temper. But had he stayed, what exactly was I to do? Yes, I know to take his papers, but how? And which ones?"

Menton frowned and went slowly downstairs at her side. "I had thought there should be any number of chances during the ball. It would be the one time Thomas would leave his papers in his room; he cer-

246

tainly would not mar the cut of his coat with them during such a formal function. Then you should have simply torn the flounce of your dress or gotten faint with the heat and gone upstairs for a bit."

Mary drew in her breath with all the easy excitement one can feel for a danger which is no longer existent. "And I would have searched his room. But what if he had come in upon me?"

Menton looked grim a moment. "That I could have made sure against."

She nodded, believing that without difficulty. "And if they had been locked in his trunk?"

"The poker at the hearth would— Yes, Johnson?" The footman murmured respectfully. "Ah, very well," said Menton, nodding a dismissal. He looked at her. "The others have gone ahead of us to the stables. Let us hurry before they lose patience altogether."

Lord Pondestoke, astride a strapping black hunter, was the first to spot their approach of the stableyard. "Stap me," he drawled loudly. "Here comes the tardy pair." He sent a quizzical glance at Menton. "I suppose tomorrow you shall have the appalling good sense not to try to break your neck on the grounds that you are newly wed." With a sigh he flicked a bit of hay from his sleeve. "I fear, Aubrey old thing, that marriage shall make you dull."

"Care to wager on it, Ponder?" challenged Menton with a gleam in his eyes. He threw Mary, whose thoughts were more on Keath than the chatter around her, up into her saddle and mounted his own rawboned bay hunter.

Pondestoke sighed and glanced about as though to make sure he had everyone's attention. "Done, old man. Now I suppose I shall have to make a tiresome exertion tomorrow to keep ahead of you on the field."

Menton flashed his white teeth and put his riding crop to the brim of his hat in quick salute. "Try it if you can. Let's go."

The following morning brought a heavy gray sky and the lightest of drizzles, but the ground was still firm underfoot and the chill nip of the air was enough to put frisk into the hounds and spirit into the horses.

The ladies in their elegantly cut riding habits laughed from atop their leggy mounts and gracefully gestured with their riding crops; the gentlemen in gleaming top boots and smartly tailored coats pulled down their shallow-crowned beavers and gathered their reins with much laughter and merry talk. Mary was excited and eager at this new experience, until Menton abruptly decreed that the going would be extra fast and that Mary's mare was too short of bone to keep the pace.

The groom obediently led Jewel back into the stables, and panic shot through Mary. She ran over to Menton, now mounted, and tugged at his boot for attention.

"But I have never ridden a different horse," she pleaded. *"Please.* I shan't mind if I fall behind."

"Nonsense," he snapped, his mount sidling out of her reach. "You shan't have the least enjoyment if you are straggled back a good mile behind the hounds."

Mary thought she might enjoy herself far more in such a case. At least her Jewel was more dependable than this long-legged gray mare they were leading out. The horse snorted and rolled her eyes at the others around her, and an icy lump of dread formed in Mary's stomach. She knew she could not handle this creature, and turned back to tell Menton so, but he had moved off to talk to the hunt master.

"Now, don't you be fearful, m'lady" said her groom. "She's a bit more to go than you've been used to, but she'll carry you all right."

Mary stood clutching her whip in both hands, scarcely able to hear him. The mare snorted again, and she jumped.

"Let me put you up, m'lady," said the man. "Her name's Whirlwind and she'll answer to it." He boosted Mary up onto her new sidesaddle and helped fit her foot into the stirrup.

Mary gripped the reins and forced herself to smile, though she desperately wanted to tumble off and spend the rest of the day in the house. The fun and excitement had all been stripped away from her. She was tense and afraid of Whirlwind's slightest movement, and she knew that now she would not have the least enjoyment of the day, even if the mare gave her no trouble.

But before she had a chance to turn coward and dismount again, the horn was blown and with a whoop they all cantered out of the stableyard. In just moments Mary's wrists were aching from holding the too-eager mare in firm control. Far from being quietened by the mounts around her, Whirlwind again and again stretched out her nose and tried to bound to the fore. Mary hung on grimly, with her mouth set in concentration, hardly aware of the bright chatter going on around her. Whirlwind pulled so for her head that Mary was forced to lean farther forward than she liked, and the drizzle fell unerringly down her collar. She thought it an appallingly dreary day and found even the scenery bleak and unpleasing. Mud thrown from the horses' hooves splattered her suddenly as they dipped into a small hollow.

"Charming day, Countess!" called Mrs. Granton-leigh to her. The large woman wiped a streak of mud across her jaw and grinned cheerfully. "We shall all of us be perfect sodden wretches. Isn't it marvelous? I do so love to hunt this country."

Scarcely had she spoken when the horns sounded. Someone shouted: "Right ho! They've sprung the fox!" And suddenly, to Mary's alarm, they were all galloping madly after the hounds.

She was unprepared for the abruptness of Whirl-wind's bound or for the mare's enormous stride, and kept her seat by she knew not what. They were going much too fast. Everything was a blur, and it frightened her not to be able to see well where she was going. Now the group was spreading out as the lesser mounts were checked slightly to save their wind, and Menton, Pondestoke, and the son of a neighbor took the lead.

But she had no chance to think about this, for already they were to the first fence—a stone one. From the corner of her eye Mary saw several of the ladies veer to the right for the gate. That was, she thought in relief, an excellent idea. But Whirlwind had somehow gotten the bit in her teeth and refused to turn aside. The mare stretched her head toward the fence, and

Mary knew suddenly with a chill of fear that she had no control over her mount.

The fence wasn't much taller than the ones she'd been practicing on, but those had been hedge or board, and this was thick solid stone. It looked formidable; she was coming up on it too fast. Quickly she tightened the reins, struggling to keep calm and remember all that the groom had taught her. But the mare did not want to check to a safer speed. The first riders sailed over, and Whirlwind bounded toward the fence with an eager whinny.

Suddenly it was looming right at them; then they were in the air. Mary clenched shut her eyes and kept them shut until Whirlwind's grunt and the jar of landing forced them open again. Without a miss in stride the mare galloped on. Realizing that she was still safely mounted, that they had cleared the fence without difficulty, Mary threw back her face to the wind in a new, almost savage exhilaration. Now she knew why so many riders were so keen on this wild sport. It was reckless and utterly thrilling.

Whirlwind still had the bit in her teeth, and Mary was forced to leave control with the mare, for she was not horsewoman enough to know how to wrest it back But now that the first fence was behind them, she did not mine all that greatly. Indeed, it was much easier to let the mare go how and where she wanted, leaving Mary free to concentrate wholly on keeping her seat.

"Bravo, Countess!" shouted Mrs. Grantonleigh after they had swept over two more hedges. "You're taking your fences in grand style. Remember to slow past this ridge, for the fox may want to double back."

Mary nodded, the wind whipping her loosened hair into her eyes. She hoped the mare would slow of her own accord, for she had no wish to show everyone how out-of-control her mount was.

The fox did not double back. Mary was close enough to the fore of the chase to glimpse a flash of russet fur as it veered for the forest nearby. A lump rose in her throat that could not be swallowed down. Surely they were not going to go whipping through those thick trees. Then in the next moments they were slithering madly down a slippery hillside and Mary had no chance to worry much about it. A slip caused the mare to slow, and quickly Mary seized her chance to tighten up the reins again. Now she was in charge, and she knew she must be careful not to let this wretched mare get the bit again.

But it was hard. Other riders swept on as Mary held Whirlwind to a more cautious pace. The sagging thorn hedge at the base of the hill worried her. She had no idea of how to put the mare at it, and obviously from the actions of the other riders it required some skill. Again some of the ladies turned aside to squeeze through a gap in the hedge, exclaiming at the long thorns which tore at their habits. Mary held back her prancing mount with aching wrists and forced the mare down to the gap.

Whirlwind took it as an insult and protested with flattened ears and much head slinging. She pranced sideways to the gap and balked. Mary's annoyance rose.

"Please, go ahead of me," she said to the two remaining ladies who were waiting respectfully for her to go first. "The others will get too far ahead if you wait."

So they trotted on through, leaving her hot, damp, muddy, and alone. She sent Whirlwind toward the gap once more, and again the mare refused, shaking her head and backing up. Mary lost temper and patience all at once and slashed her riding whip across the mare's sleek rump.

It was a mistake. Whirlwind squealed and half-reared through the gap. Dropping the whip, Mary was flung half from the saddle and just managed to avoid falling by throwing both arms around the mare's neck. Thorns jabbed through her clothing, making her cry out. Still squealing, Whirlwind crashed and kicked a way through the hedge. At once realizing she had her head, the mare plunged and raced away at a wild gallop toward the forest.

Mary could do nothing but hang on, her hands locked by terror in the horse's mane, and endure the pain of her leg twisted beneath her. She was too terrified to even look up, after one glance at the trees, and kept her face buried against the mare's neck. Rigid and aching with stark fear, she knew it was but a matter of minutes until her tense muscles would allow her to fall or until Whirlwind managed to shake her loose. But she could not even summon the strength to cry out for help.

They swept into the trees with a bound through a thicket grown up over a rotted log. As though far away, Mary heard the crash of Whirlwind's hooves over the dead leaves and twigs. Limbs slashed overhead with viciousness. Some whipped across Mary's side with enough stinging force to knock the breath from her. Whirlwind squealed and kicked again, then stumbled and fell to her knees Mary opened her eyes and saw the ground rushing for her face.

There was a dreadful blow to her shoulder, as though someone had knocked it separate from her body. She rolled over and over on the wet ground, at last banging up against a stump, and had one final glimpse of Whirlwind lunging up and galloping away with the sidesaddle all twisted, before falling back into merciful darkness.

Her first coherent thought after that was the sudden conviction that some wild beast was about to make her its meal. With a choked cry she jerked open her eyes and tried to scramble out of the way—only to stop with a gasp of relief as the spaniel sat down and cocked its golden head at her. Mary sank back onto one elbow, heedless of the mud, and stared back at it. She hardly knew what she was about or where she was; only that she was very cold and wet, and that it was near dusk. But if the dog stayed nearby, perhaps it would protect her from the beasts.

Suddenly the spaniel stood up and barked. Moments later a horse and rider came crashing through the trees almost upon her. She shrank away from the man, who flung himself violently off the horse and swallowed her with his strong arms

"Thank God, I've found you at last."

Only then did Mary's dazed senses register his identity. "Menton!" she cried in overwhelming relief, and clung to him with a sudden burst of tears.

"Hush, hush. You are safe now," he murmured, smoothing back her damp hair. "Are you hurt anywhere? Any broken bones?"

She could not answer for her tears, and only sobbed the harder. The dog circled them with a low whine. Menton's arms tightened around her.

"Tell me," he said. "Is anything broken?"

She flinched from the sharpness in his voice and shook her head. "I did not want to ride her," she said wildly, and struck at him with one weak fist "Why, why did you make me?"

He caught at her hands. "You're like ice. Come, let's get you off this damp ground."

He scooped her up, seemingly without effort, and carried her over to his horse. She hid her face. "No! I never want to ride again!"

But he set her up on the horse's back and put his coat around her bedraggled shoulders before leading his mount forward slowly. The spaniel bounced happily along in front. "Warmer?" Menton asked.

His coat did help, but she could not bring herself to answer. Menton glanced up at her, but the twilight hid his features. As soon as they were clear of the trees, he mounted behind her

"Did you win your wager with Lord Pondestoke?" she asked bitterly, trying without success to stop her teeth from chattering. Her left shoulder throbbed every time she moved it.

Menton shifted in the saddle. "It came out a draw," he said in a low voice. "When the hunt ended and you were nowhere to be seen, I assumed you had wearied and returned to the house. But then we encountered your mare on the way back . . ." His arms tightened around her. "We have been searching these past two hours and more for you." His voice was husky "I have been imagining the worst."

Suddenly she wanted to hurt him dreadfully, to make his cold heart sorry. She had been too frightened all day not to be angry now. But none of the searing words would come to her lips, and instead they only added to the ache of her body. He does not care, she thought miserably over and over. He says the words but he does not care.

Lord Pondestoke was on hand with Mrs. Lunt to greet them when Menton carried her inside. "Badly hurt?" he asked softly, laying one hand on Menton's arm. He glanced at Mary, then back at Menton, and his own face paled. "My God, man! Stop looking like that. We'll have the physician fetched directly." He strode away to dispatch a rider.

"Come along, my lord," said Mrs. Lunt, "and bring her upstairs to her own room, where I can get her out of those wet clothes." She bustled away.

Returning, Pondestoke took Menton's elbow. "You're blue with cold, my dear fellow. Wander off and get yourself a stiff shot of brandy, and I'll carry the countess upstairs." He smiled. "Intentions strictly honorable."

Menton shook his head, his black hair curling from the damp. "I'll do it," he said harshly.

But Pondestoke continued to block the way. His face was now completely serious. "Take a damper, Aubrey. She's safe now. You're a fool to blame yourself for an accident no one could have foreseen. Daresay a hare popped out and frightened her horse."

Hot tears burned down Mary's frozen cheeks. She wanted to tell them that it hadn't been a hare but rather a too-spirited mount, but she could do nothing but bury her face against Menton's shoulder and shake in her misery. Pondestoke's soothing words were no more than salt to the rift in her heart

Menton drew an unsteady breath, his heart hammering beneath Mary's cheek. "I'll carry her up, thank you," he said with something more like his normal drawl. "Shouldn't want her to get your Oriental wet." Mary almost thought she heard a break in his voice.

Pondestoke drew himself up. "Damn my cravat," he said, but he made no further attempt to block their way.

Chapter Thirty-two

HER TOUCH OF FEVER was gone by the next day, but her shoulder was still so wrenched and sore she wondered if she would ever use it again. Wrapped in a silk-and-lace dressing gown, she reclined upon the daybed in her private sitting room. Poetry made her impatient today; she could not concentrate upon the lines for the angry whirling of her thoughts around Menton. Everything she tried to force him out of her mind failed. Impossible to forgive, moreover, was his continued absence. He did not even make the slightest attempt to see her—not that she wanted to see him, but it was nevertheless infuriating to be robbed of the pleasure of turning him away.

At last he did come, however, while Lucy Thraude was playing the pianoforte for her. The music was soothing and a welcome distraction as long as she concentrated on it. She did not, consequently, notice his quiet entry. Miss Thraude finished her piece, made a pretty little speech about her hope that Mary would soon be feeling more the thing, and left with a shy greeting to Menton at the door.

Mary raised up in some startlement, gasping at the protest her aching body made. Her eyes met his across the room, and he came forward slowly. His mouth was no more than a thin line, and his finely etched nostrils flared rapidly with each breath. He stopped by the window and bowed to her. As he did so, the light caught on his high cheekbones, and she thought that she had never seen them so prominent before.

She sank back down to a more comfortable position on her pillows and stared coldly up at him. Why had he come? They had nothing of worth to say to each other. "Are the preparations for the ball finished?" Her words broke the silence flatly.

He shook his head and put his hands behind his back. His buckskins and brown double-breasted coat were immaculate, but his top boots were splattered with fine specks of mud. He drew a breath and exhaled heavily. "No," he said, so quietly it was almost difficult to hear him. "But Mrs. Lunt has all well in hand. Some new guests have already arrived." He paused a moment, staring at a point beneath the curved legs of the daybed. "His Highness begs to decline our invitation in lieu of prior engagements. I am sorry. It would have been a great honor for you."

She had not even known that Prinny had been invited. Irritably she opened her book of poems, then stared up at Menton with a frown. "I see no need, sir, for you to continue this pointless hypocrisy. We both know very well that I have no need of the honor from his Highness's attendance at my birthday ball."

Menton flinched and swung his back to her with almost savage swiftness. He reached out and gripped the windowsill. "Can you never put that from your mind?" he demanded, throwing back his head as though to ease tense neck muscles.

Mary flipped a page with violence enough to make the paper crackle. "I do not wish to . . . my lord. Why did you come?" She made her voice impatient.

He glanced back at her over his shoulder. "To apologize for yesterday. I was no better than an unthinking brute."

Mary's frown deepened. She pulled herself to a sitting position. Yes, she thought angrily, you come in and ask forgiveness so easily, my lord. But she determined not to give in. Clenching her fists, she thought of all the time in the past when she had allowed her anger against him to melt away. The merest bit of attention from him had always softened all of her resolves, but it would not do so this time. Inside she was completely cold toward him, and she knew this time his apology was not enough. Yesterday had been the end.

When she did not answer, his hand tightened on the windowsill until the knuckles were white. "The doctor says your fever is gone and that you shall recover quickly." He lowered his head. "I would not have had yesterday's misfortune befall you for anything in the world. You must believe that."

She believed none of it. Let him face her and say that, she thought with mounting fury. She slammed shut her book. How could he think her such a fool as to believe such blatant gammon? She swallowed, hardly able to see the room about her for the rage flaming her blood. "If you had not desired yesterday's accident, you would not have insisted I ride that dreadful horse."

The blood pounding through her brain seemed to be the relentless echo of Whirlwind's thundering hooves, making her voice rise on the last words in memory of yesterday's terror.

Menton pushed himself away from the window. "Surely you do not think I intended . . ." He frowned. "Your brain must still be feverish."

"No, it is nothing of the sort!" she shouted, pounding her fists on either side of her. "And let us not play the game of misunderstanding. You could not have failed to realize that I was mounted beyond my abilities—"

"Have done!" He slammed his fist upon the lid of the pianoforte so that the vase of flowers there jumped. "I have admitted my mistake with the horse. Can you not let it go?"

She ignored the plea in his voice. He would not cozen her this time. "What I find important—and unforgivable—is that you knew the likely consequences and did not care."

He made a futile gesture. "I did not think—"

"Then you should have," she lashed back. "That is what I shall not forgive, sir! Oh, yes, I daresay it is no business of yours to care much for my well-being—"

"Mary . . ." He took a half-step toward her, his voice raw with something she chose not to decipher.

She stared down at her fist, suddenly conscious of how deeply her nails were biting her flesh. "No, my lord. I cannot give any more of . . ." She stopped and bit her lip. Would her stupid tongue even now betray her? "Go. Please," she said in a shaking voice. "I cannot bear this further. There is no more to be said."

His hand shot out and seized the vase. She glanced up swiftly, her breath caught at the wildness in his face. But although the knuckles of that strong hand whitened until they trembled, he at last expelled a ragged sigh and released the vase. Without a word or another glance at her, he strode out like a furious man gone blind, and Mary was left alone to fall sobbing among her pillows with a force that threatened to explode her from within. She had no hope now, for her accident and her cruel words had served merely to madden him and had left his heart untouched.

Chapter Thirty-three

MARY HAD JUST finished the last touches of her toilet and now eyed herself critically in the mirror. Tonight would be her final appearance in English society, for Thomas had not come and she knew that she could no longer bear to remain here as matters stood between her and Menton. She had already told him that she would leave tomorrow, and he had made no demur. Therefore, tonight was her last chance to play the role of a countess, and she must do it, no matter how heavy her heart might be.

Determined to look her best, she wore a ball dress of flaming russet silk, gathered into tiny folds across the bodice and continuing down the skirt. Long white gloves and matching silk slippers completed her appearance, and her hair had been dressed to allow one dark curl to lie coquettishly across her white shoulder. She nodded to herself. Yes, she would do.

The original houseguests seemed so few among the multitude now pervading the house. With an involuntary little shot of pride Mary thought that a full Almack's would not have as many as would be here tonight for her birthday. When the Keath family threw a party, it was an event, she thought with a wry curl of her lips.

But there, she heard the first distant strains of music. And, yes, the little china clock on her dressing table was striking ten. It was time to go outside and take her place in the formal procession to the ballroom. Quickly she glanced into the mirror again and pinched either cheek to create a becoming blush. Then with one last sigh of resolution, she dismissed Jenny for the evening and went outside to the head of the staircase, where Menton was waiting for her.

The crisp tailoring of his swallow-tailed coat molded itself to his form in unwrinkled perfection; his cravat was a marvel of style. But his bony nose jutted fiercely over a face that was almost haggard, and his blue eyes gleamed at her with such pronounced cynicism it was almost a cold slap to the face.

Her own spirit was quick to spark in return, and as she laid her fingertips lightly upon his arm, she lifted her chin in a hauteur to match his. He needn't look at her as though she were a quitter! The guests were already assembled, and powdered and liveried servants lined the entry into the ballroom, where Tyler stood at stiff attention with seeming unconcern about his black eye.

The musicians struck up the opening bars of a Mozart minuet, and she—half on tiptoe and rigid inside with her concentration on being as gracefully perfect as possible in all the moves—swept inside to the center of the festooned ballroom with Menton. The evenings of practice had been well worth the effort. She could dance her part tonight without difficulty, but there was no approval in Menton's eyes. Indeed, they shifted away from hers every time. Mary told herself she did not mind. And she had no right to mind, for after tonight he could wash his hands of her and she of him.

It was a beautiful dance, with silence save for the music and the rustles of silks and satins. When it ended, the musicians immediately struck up a lively reel, and new partners barely had time to catch a breath and find each other. Mary, however, sat out the second dance much against the wishes of several gentlemen and found a chair in a quiet corner to catch her breath in peace. Her bruised side hurt a little, and she wanted to slow her rapid breathing as soon as possible.

She achieved that, but she was not left alone. In but a few minutes Lord Pondestoke sought her out.

"Stap me," he drawled, mincing up to her and making an elaborate bow. "Already without partners, Countess? Never knew Aubrey to be so jealous."

Mary summoned a welcoming smile for him. "No. I merely desired to catch my breath. The minuet was so long."

"Hmm, yes. The dreadful thing is so deceiving." Pondestoke lifted his glass at the dancers, his chin forced rather high by the extreme amount of starch in his cravat. "Looks so slow and graceful, one greets it with relief. But there." He lowered his glass and sighed. "One is forced to drag on and on." Suddenly he glanced down at Mary. "Sharp words so soon between the newlyweds?"

Mary was startled into a false laugh. She shook her head. "Why, no. Certainly not. I wonder you should think so."

Pondestoke was surveying the room again, his lanky form accentuated by the length of his coattails. "Appears to me, Countess, that old Aubrey is looking rather hagged. And *you* ain't the same female that's in the new portrait. Anyone who bothers to think ought to put it together." He took out his handkerchief, polished his quizzing glass, and lifted it again at a young damsel, with a sigh of relief. "Dear me. I ought to polish my glass more often. A speck of dust, and I thought yon lady was afflicted with spots." He shuddered. "Dreadful sort of mistake to make."

Mary sought her mind for some clever way to turn off his curiosity, and thought of nothing.

"And," said Pondestoke with pronounced languor, "Aubrey's off his feed. Looks to be under a strain."

"No doubt he is angry because I could not handle my horse," she said tartly before she could stop herself.

He bowed. "Permit me to disagree. What a bore, these marital spats. You married for love, of course."

"We did not," she snapped with heightened spots of color in her cheeks. She must escape before this conversation went any further.

"Do not leave me yet, Countess," he said without glancing her way. "Aubrey is a friend, and that is why I concern myself." He paused. "How curious. You say no love, and he told me the same thing this afternoon. Yet never have I seen two people more obviously laboring under the pangs of that intolerable emotion."

"You are mistaken, sir," she said in a stifled voice. Several bouquets of flowers were near her chair. Suddenly their fragrances were too heady, the heat of the room too intense. "I . . . he . . . we do not love each other at all."

She stood up, but Pondestoke smoothly blocked her way. "Again I beg permission to disagree." His pale eyes sparked with an expression that made her sink down into her chair again. "To be detestably blunt, madam, your husband is hopelessly besotted with you. If you return his regard in the least way, I suggest you allow it to show, before one of you makes a regrettable mistake."

Mary shook her head. She must not let herself believe him. "You are speaking nonsense, sir."

"Am I?" he asked mockingly. "Very well, my dear countess. Handle this as you like, but I must warn you that he is too proud to crawl to you. And—"

"Excuse me, my lady." Johnson appeared at her side with a bow. "This letter just arrived by messenger for you. I have been instructed to say that it is urgent."

"Oh?" Mary took the letter with a frown. She wondered if it was something else hateful from Keath.

Pondestoke murmured something civil and slipped away, but she took scarce heed as she ripped open the wafer. She wanted anything to take her mind off what he had said. Could it be true that Menton loved her? She glanced out about the room, but he was not to be immediately seen. No, Pondestoke was nothing more than a meddler, saying things he knew nothing about. She snorted to herself. Indeed, if Menton truly felt the slightest affection for her, he would not be allowing her to go tomorrow.

And in the face of that fact, none of the brief moments of happy companionship between them, the attention he had spent here to please her, or the many luxuries showered upon her could mean enough to make her believe what Pondestoke had said. She dropped the letter half-opened into her lap and shook her head. No, if Menton loved her, he would not fly into his rages, or order her around like a servant, or . . . or force her to ride a dangerous horse. There had been so many opportunities for him to give her but a glance or a word, and she would have known without further assurance. But it had never been, and it would never be so.

She bowed her head with a flash of irritation at Pondestoke for stirring her up again when she'd had all of her tiresome emotions under contol. Now she would have to overcome them all again.

Remembering the letter, she opened it and blinked at the signature with a small jolt of surprise. Quickly she scanned the slightly illegible lines, obviously written in great haste, with several blots:

Dearest Mary,

Things are in a Dreadful coil. Grandmama has accepted an invitation to go to Bath and stay as the guest of Lady Hart. So I have run away to escape such an Odious Position as they seek to place me in. Sir Oswald has all but been running tame here since you left. It is Dreadful, and so I have decided to come to you, for I know that you are on *our* side. You, I am sure, will not Hesitate to aid Charlie and me against Grandmama and that odious Fish. I have gotten as far as an inn called the Gray Goose and have run out of money and cannot pay my shot. *Please help,* for the landlord is suspicious, I think, and I could not bring my abigail with me. Some of the people here do not seem to be quite the thing, but I am not much afraid.

Hopeful of seeing you *soon,*
Arabella Monteforte

Mary frowned over the disjointed sentences again, tapping her foot against the floor. Silly Arabella! How like her to run away without the least heed of the consequences. But she must be rescued at once, for Mary did not like to think of her alone and without money. Anything might befall her.

Standing up, Mary stared about the crowded room. Dared she seek Menton's assistance? She glimpsed him flirting with an elderly woman and turned away with near-panic catching in her throat. She could not face him so soon, not until she had shaken her emotions out of their present confusion.

So instead she seized upon Charlie and dragged him out of the room without bothering to explain. He started to protest, and for an answer she thrust the letter at him.

While he was frowning over the lines, she drew Tyler aside and ordered his lordship's fastest horses put to the closed carriage. Tyler hesitated for the merest second, then bowed and relayed the instructions without question. She loosed a little sigh of relief, knowing that in her present agitation she could not have given a suitable explantion of this emergency.

Charlie jerked his eyes up from the paper. "Incredible!" he said. "Can matters truly be at such a stand that she must needs run away in this harebrained manner?"

"I don't know, Charlie," said Mary with a shake of her head. "You know how impetuous she is. But let us go for her at once. I do not like to think of her at that inn alone."

"By thunder, no!" He snapped his fingers. "I can be there in no time with my curricle. Since it is your birthday celebration, you needn't feel obliged to come along."

"Fudge." Mary snatched back the letter. "You may want all the glory of rescuing her from this piece of folly, but I have no intention of remaining behind." How could she possibly tell him that the very thought of receiving any more gifts from a man who cared nothing for her filled her with repugnance? "Let us waste no more time."

She hastened off to her room and whirled through it long enough to seize her dark hooded cloak that was edged with black ermine and the remainder of her pin money left over from shopping in London. Much to her relief, she was able to hurry down the staircase and out of the house unseen. Charlie had donned hat and caped driving coat and was waiting impatiently beside the carriage for her. Mary put up her hood and climbed inside without regard for her sore muscles. "Go at once," she said breathlessly to the coachman.

They surged forward, and she sank down into her corner to shut her eyes with a little gasp of relief. Some of the pressure of the evening lifted from her shoulders as she realized that she would have a couple of hours free of any need to worry about how to cope with Menton. As for what he and others might think about this escapade, in the face of all her troubles she could not bring herself to be overmuch concerned about the gossipmongers. Let them talk. There would be the Montefortes to protect Arabella, and by tomorrow the Countess of Menton would no longer exist, save as a portrait hanging in the library.

Chapter Thirty-four

AFTER MEETING no one on the road save a lone fast-moving curricle which brushed their wheels without the slightest regard of courtesy, they arrived at the Gray Goose just before midnight. Smothering a yawn, Mary allowed Charlie to escort her inside and promptly wrinkled her nose at the mingled odors of cooked cabbage, ale, and bootblacking that pervaded the interior. They were particularly repulsive after the heady fragrance of flowers at the ball and the crisp clean air of the outdoors. She blinked against the acrid, stuffy air and perceived with dismay that the hearth in the crowded taproom was gusting out blue smoke at frequent intervals. Had she not so desperately required a bit of breathing space to sort herself out, she would have wished then and there that she had waited until morning and sent Mrs. Lunt for Arabella.

Coughing, Charlie hailed the landlord, who blinked at their ball regalia but nevertheless led them at once upstairs to the private parlor. The door was standing ajar, so that the arguing voices within could be heard clearly.

Charlie's head came up eagerly. "That's Arabella!"

Mary frowned, thinking that she knew the other voice. "Yes, and . . ."

But Charlie was already flinging open the door. "Darling!"

"Charlie!" With flushed cheeks and snapping eyes, Arabella stood staring an instant, then flung herself

into his arms. "Oh! I have been so terribly, *terribly* frightened."

But struck with a chill that seemed to freeze her limbs, Mary could not turn her attention from Rebeccah, who stood before the window with one hand to her heaving bosom, her eyes very wide. Mary's thoughts began to whirl. Rebeccah's presence meant that Keath was here too. She took an unconscious step forward, frowning. What should she do? Obviously they would not wait here while she hurried to warn Menton.

Arabella raised her head from Charlie's chest. "She is horrid, Mary. And I wish that you will give Mr. Keath a set-down the next time you see him, because he said some perfectly odious things to me before he left, and she laughed." Arabella's eyes blazed at Rebeccah. "She *laughed!* And then she began to talk about . . . about holding me for ransom and——"

"No!" said Charlie, with a dangerous set to his mouth. "You would dare that?"

"Yes!" said Rebeccah in shrill defiance. "Why shouldn't I?"

Rage burned through Mary at these arrogant words, but she could not afford to deal with it now. So Keath was not here. Determination hardened in her. She would make Rebeccah tell where he had gone!

Some of her intention must have shown in her face, for Rebeccah suddenly drew back. "No! No, you will stay away from me!"

She turned with a choked cry and pushed past Mary to flee the room. Ignoring Charlie's call, Mary regained her balance and followed at a run. She was in time to see Rebeccah whisk herself into the farthest room at the end of the passageway. Forgetting all other considerations and praying that there was no bolt on the door, Mary threw herself bodily against it, biting off a cry of pain from her sore shoulder. The poorly constructed door gave way with a crash and a clatter of the falling chair that had been imperfectly wedged against it. Rebeccah jumped away from a small trunk with a gasp.

"Get out of here!" she said. "This is my room. You have no right to follow me here."

Mary looked around at the boots on the floor and the ivory-backed brushes on the shabby dressing table. "You are lying. This is Keath's room, isn't it?"

Rebeccah lifted her chin, her brown eyes hot and filled with hate. "What if it is? Get out!"

Mary set her chin and deliberately gazed all about the room, hoping a little foolishly to find some of those papers. Then she looked swiftly at Rebeccah, who was attempting to slip something unnoticed into her bosom.

"I don't suggest you try that," said Mary with a loudness that made Rebeccah start and drop her hand with the key still clutched in it to her side.

Rebeccah sneered. "I suppose you would stop me."

"I will take it off your person if I must," said Mary with cold determination. Keath must not have taken the papers with him, or Rebeccah would not be acting this way. She must get that key. "Do you doubt me?"

"You bold little slut." Rebeccah locked stares with Mary a moment; then her eyes shifted to the window.

Mary caught her intent and sprang to stop her, but Rebeccah moved with the speed of desperation to fling up the sash and throw the key outside. Dismayed, Mary involuntarily loosened her grip on Rebeccah's wrists and stared outside, where the key might never be found again. Rebeccah twisted away and took up a triumphant stance—eyes gleaming, hands on hips— before the fireplace.

"Now, Countess High and Mighty," she said with a simpering smile and a toss of her head, "what shall you do?"

But a spark of excitement was already quickening inside Mary, for she had noticed the poker and remembered that Menton had said locks could be broken. With a grim smile that brought a line between Rebeccah's thin brows, Mary shoved her aside and seized the poker in both hands. Hastening to the trunk, she bent to examine the lock. It was small and not stoutly made. With a nod to herself she stepped over one of the boots on the none-too-clean floor and slipped the end of the poker into place against the lock.

"No!" Rebeccah hurled herself forward at Mary,

who shoved her back impatiently. But Rebeccah would not give up and kept pushing and snatching and trying to wrest the poker away until Mary lost all patience and called for Charlie.

He appeared in a moment with a wide-eyed Arabella still clinging to him. "Yes, Aunt Mary?"

"Pray come inside and give me some assistance," said Mary, glancing back over her shoulder at Rebeccah, who was standing between them and the trunk like a cornered animal with her whelp.

Charlie obligingly disengaged himself from Arabella's grasp and entered the room. "What's about here? Do you need me to stir up the fire?"

Mary sighed in exasperation and caught up her demitrain off the dirty floor. Full ball attire was hardly the proper clothing for an adventure. "No, Charlie. Just keep Miss Tavers out of the way while I open the trunk."

He frowned doubtfully.

She tried to contain her impatience. *"Please.* Never mind why."

"Is this Uncle Thomas's room?" He glanced around in open distaste. "A bit squalid, ain't it? Not his usual style."

"Charlie!" Mary stamped her foot.

"Yes, all right, though why you want to go breaking into my uncle's luggage . . . Doesn't matter, I suppose." He sent Rebeccah a severe glance. "Step away."

Rebeccah crossed her arms and put up her chin. Charlie glanced at Mary and shrugged.

"You cannot be so poor-spirited, Charlie!" Mary brandished the poker. "She is only a female—no match for you. Move her aside."

"Yes, do, Charlie," cried Arabella from the doorway.

Without further protest he drew a deep breath, seized a furious Rebeccah, and manhandled her, kicking and scratching, across to the other side of the room. Mary pried sharply down on the lock, and after a moment of resistance it snapped with a dull crack. She threw down the poker and knelt by the trunk, without heed for her dress, to lift open the lid. Neatly folded clothes met her eyes; but almost at once she shook free of dismay, for she guessed Keath would not leave his valuables on top.

Without compunction or listening to the others' cries of protest and surprise, she began pulling out the clothes and shaking each garment. At the very bottom was nothing but a pair of slightly worn top boots. She threw down a waistcoat in disgust. Was all this for naught?

"Have you lost your senses, Aunt Mary?" demanded Charlie with some annoyance in his voice. "You can't go through a man's garments in such a fashion . . ."

Mary did not hear the rest. Quickly she bent and seized both boots. One was heavier than the other. Exclaiming in triumph, she dumped out a small packet. It was filled with maps and lists of officers and place names that all meant nothing to her of themselves. But she knew what they were for. Moreover, these looked like originals, not copies. She showed them to Charlie, who had since released a stricken Rebeccah and hastened over.

The annoyance faded from his face, and he whistled. "By Jove, I'll wager my last groat that these are the plans for the spring invasion." Almost reverently he turned the papers over in his hands. "And the originals, too. Damn, this ain't even been sent out to the generals yet. If these are lost, it will put us behind by months!"

Mary drew in her breath with a thrill of excitement. She had never fully realized the extent to which Keath's devilry went. To her mind he had always seemed like the sort who would only sell an occasional document whenever he ran into debt. But she saw now that he was indeed a fiend of the worst order. And why wasn't he here to protect his ill-gained property?

"I don't understand." Charlie frowned at the papers. "Has Uncle Thomas stolen them?"

"Yes, Charlie," said Mary. "This is how he makes his living." She had no notion of whether Charlie was as fond of Keath as he was of Menton, but it must still be hard to accept the idea of having a traitor in the family.

Charlie sighed. "My mother has always said he was born to be a troublemaker. But the plans for the invasion . . . He must not go free for this, even if the family name comes under scandal."

Rebeccah suddenly loosed a scornful laugh. "You think you have won. But you have not. Thomas has gone to take care of his meddlesome brother before we sail for France."

New fear gripped at Mary's heart. Keath was dangerous beyond measure, and his hate for Menton might lead him to do anything. She imagined him pointing a pistol through the window at an unsuspecting Menton and almost fainted. "Quick, Charlie! We must go back at once! I feel sure that was Keath who passed us on the road."

"Then he's got more than a quarter hour's start on us," said Charlie, striding for the door. "I'll order a fresh team put to at once."

Mary hurried after him, scooping along Arabella on the way. While Arabella hastened to fetch her bandboxes, Mary sought out the landlord and impatiently ordered a pistol brought to her. Her thoughts buzzed frantically around Menton. They could not reach him in time to warn him, but perhaps they might yet save his life. Once again her heart nearly failed her, but her swimming senses steadied at the sight of the landlord dubiously extending a pistol to her.

"I've primed it, m'lady," he said, scratching his head with a stubby finger. "Are you sure—?"

"Yes, yes." She snatched it from him, too distraught to be afraid of the weapon. At the moment, it did not even matter that she had never fired a pistol in her life. She must be prepared to do anything to save Menton. Shoving it into her other cloak pocket and thrusting some money at the landlord, without paying the least attention to the amount he named as Arabella's bill, she rushed outside and stood impatiently while the carriage was led round. Would they never hurry?

Arabella came running out, hampered by her pelisse and bandboxes. "Mary! She says she's coming with us!"

Rebeccah followed, waving a frantic hand. "Please! Don't leave me here. I shall have no way of knowing . . ."

Charlie set his hat on the back of his head and deftly blocked her path. "Aunt Mary?"

Mary settled herself on the seat and realized that if she followed her inclinations and refused, there would only be more delay. And it might be wise to keep Rebeccah in hand so that she could be taken to book for her activities.

"I am coming," said Rebeccah, who had not even taken the time to put on her pelisse, "even if I must ride on the coachman's box."

"Let her in, Charlie," said Mary, although determined to put her out anywhere on the deserted road if she dared utter the least sneering comment. *"Hurry!"*

Rebeccah positioned herself on the seat beside Mary, and Charlie followed, to seat himself across from her. Arabella clung to his arm at once. With a loud crack of the whip the carriage clattered forward over the frozen courtyard.

Mary squeezed into her corner and gripped her cold hands together tightly. Her feet were frozen in their thin dancing slippers, but she hardly cared that they had neither the comfort of a rug nor warm bricks for their feet. She was far too conscious of the pistol inside her cloak, and far too afraid of what sort of scene she would find at the Hall. She suspected, as they bounced and jolted rapidly over the iron ruts on the road, that this would be the most nightmarish carriage ride of her life.

Chapter Thirty-five

No ONE IN THE CARRIAGE had the least thing to say to one another, so there was not even argument to occupy Mary's attention. Her whole body willing the carriage to go faster, she bit her lip and closed her eyes against the torment within her. Why, oh why, had Arabella chosen this time to fall into a scrape and apply to her? She should have stayed at the ball and swallowed her foolish pride. If Pondestoke was right, she could have changed everything by going to Menton and just telling him . . . everything. Guilt rushed up within her, and she bowed her head in silent agony. Why had she never been brave enough to show him that she loved him?

Now that she was on the verge of losing him, she realized that the word "love" was inadequate to describe the bond so deeply forged within her. She knew that despite all of her disappointments and heartaches over him, he was the only one who could fulfill her. And if he felt the same way toward her . . . if Pondestoke had not lied . . . Oh, dear God, was Menton to die without knowing the contents of her heart? She must not let it happen. If she could not reach him in time to stop Keath, then at least let her get there in time to tell him what he must know.

A lone tear slipped down her cheek, and she quickly dabbed it away with the iron-hard determination not to be weak and womanish yet. This was not the time for tears. She clenched shut her eyes and prayed.

It seemed forever until they arrived, but at long last the carriage swung to a weary halt before the wide entry steps. Mary strained to see out. Yes, the lights were still blazing from the windows, and there was dear old Tyler appearing at the door. Relief flooded over her. Surely if there were bad news, it would show in his face.

Without waiting for the steps to be let down, she rudely pushed by the others to be the first one out. "Tyler," she said, clinging to him as he seized her arm to save her from stumbling, "is the ball still in progress?"

"It has just ended, my lady," he said. Was it mild reproof in his voice? "Very disappointed his lordship was that you were called away."

She nearly collapsed with relief. Keath had not come here after all! Everything was all right; she had gone through all this worry for naught. How wonderful! She just in time remembered that it would shock Tyler horribly were she to hug him, and hugged herself instead. Oh, that she might have the pleasure of receiving Menton's scold!

"Where is his lordship now?" she asked breathlessly, all aglow.

"I do not believe he has yet retired, my lady." Tyler eyed her dubiously, then frowned as Arabella, then Rebeccah, then Charlie emerged from the carriage. "Good heavens!"

"Yes, Tyler," said Mary with a smile. "You have only to see that a room is prepared for Miss Monteforte. She shall be staying a few days."

Gathering her cloak tightly around her, Mary hurried into the house on light feet. A sleepy underfootman directed her upstairs to the fencing room. With a small sigh she gathered up her silk skirts and hastened up the long staircase. How odd that he should want to practice his fencing at this small hour of the morning! She yawned and shook her head. He was filled with many endearing oddities she had yet to learn about.

Coming to the fencing room, she thrust open the

door and skipped in, only to falter to a halt, staring. Menton glanced up in the act of removing his tight-fitting coat with Keath's help.

He blinked, his bony face suddenly gone pale. "Mary!"

She scarcely heard him as she stared around from a discomfited Gilbreath, to Keath already in his shirt sleeves, to two crossed rapiers lying upon a table. Her eyes widened. She shook her head at Menton, her world crashing down all over again. "No!" she choked out, and ran to fling her arms around him. "No! I . . . please do not . . ." Her voice broke and she could not finish.

He lifted one hand to lightly stroke her hair. "Why did you come back?"

"Come back?" She lifted her head and stared at him in puzzlement, for the instant unconscious of the others in the room. "Of course I did not mean to stay the night in that horrid inn, with not even a bandbox with me. I made all speed to rescue Arabella and return in time, but . . ."

Menton frowned. "I do not understand you." Suddenly he seized her shoulders. "I thought you had decided not to wait until tomorrow . . ."

She froze. Before matters went further, she must explain.

But Keath cleared his throat and pulled her back. "I hate to interrupt such a charming interlude, but we have business to finish, Aubrey."

"No!" Mary struggled against his hold, crying out as he gripped her arm too hard.

"Leave her out of this, Thomas," said Menton dangerously. Mary thought she heard a new vigor in his voice.

"I intend to," said Keath with a sneer. "Here." He thrust Mary at Gilbreath. "Keep her out of our way."

Mary stepped hastily away from Gilbreath. "I trusted you," she said furiously. "You did steal that letter from my reticule, didn't you?"

He nodded and would not meet her eyes. "You don't understand," he muttered.

"Oh, but I do," she said in contempt. How could

she ever have thought this man a friend? He was no better than Keath.

Menton meanwhile ripped off his magnificently tied cravat and slipped out of his shoes. Keath did likewise. Facing each other in their stocking feet, they looked almost of a same height. But Menton had a larger, more powerful frame than Keith, who was almost willowy. Menton selected a rapier, tested the balance, then suddenly frowned in Mary's direction.

"You should not be here," he said curtly.

"I shall not leave," she said in equal manner. Ladies did not watch duels, but she could not bear it if she were made to leave now. She shook her head and retreated to a corner out of the way. Gilbreath kept his stance near the door and shifted his feet uneasily.

Keath seized the remaining sword and shoved the table out of the way. He poised himself, blade at ready. Menton calmly folded back his lace cuffs and took his time about assuming a ready stance. Then suddenly his languor dropped from him like a discarded garment, and he was poised with serious intent in his bony face.

"En garde, brother!" he cried.

As one they lunged toward each other, and Mary shut her eyes. But as the meeting of steel against steel rang out through the room, she opened them again to see the combatants locked together hilt to hilt. Then Menton's muscles rippled beneath the thin white linen of his shirt, and he thrust Keath back.

"Hah!" said Keath, and bounded for an offensive, which Menton seemed to parry easily.

Mary watched them seesaw and circle with held breath, the clashing ring of the swords and the dull thuds of their lunging stocking feet vibrating through her. She was conscious of none else save the combat, and even the occasional grunt or taunting comment escaped her.

The swords seemed to dance and parry with lightning life of their own, blurring in a quick flurry of action, then parting, to poise and leap again. Seemingly in minutes both men were perspiring and panting for breath. She thought they must quit soon, but their arms were of the same steel as their blades. Again and again the blades touched lightly, testing, then trying for the thrust *finale*.

"Damn you," gasped Keath once while they were locked, their straining faces but inches apart. "You have kept in shape."

Menton's show of teeth was more a grimace than a grin. "You should have taken my offer of pistols."

"And stripped myself of all chance?" Keath snorted and leaped away. "Come on, brother!"

With a savage laugh he lunged at Menton with a wild fury that forced Menton back and back and still back. Mary tensed and stood on tiptoe, her whole concentration on Menton's amazing wrist as it controlled a constant guard against Keath's pressing attack. She guessed Keath had been saving himself for this, and glanced back to Menton's face in hopes of seeing some sign there that he had a tactic of his own in store. But grim concentration was all to be read there.

Then suddenly Menton tripped over one of the shoes and stumbled back. His guard slipped, and Keath's blade flicked at his left shoulder. Mary's cry died in her throat, and she thought the rest of her must die with it. But amazingly Menton regained his balance and guard in the next moment and managed a clever parry that sent Keath's sword flying.

Mary threw back her head in triumph, but Gilbreath shushed her with a quick, fierce glance. She did not understand until Menton lowered his sword and waited nonchalantly for Keath to recover his. Then she wanted to scream in vexation. Why must men be so stupid? Menton had won. Why did he bow to this horrifying thing called honor? Why did he allow Keath to recover?

Her eyes flashed back to Menton, and faintness struck her at the sight of a small stain of red hardly larger than the sharp point of a rapier spreading slowly into the snowy cloth at his shoulder. Foolish man, how could he fight with a wound? She knew this could not continue long, though now Menton was making a strong attack of his own. The whiteness about his mouth betrayed him, and surely that last thrust of Keath's passed too close for ease of mind.

Slowly she slid her hand beneath her cloak and grasped the long pistol in her pocket. Even more slowly she drew it out and glanced at Gilbreath. His attention was locked upon the fight. Good.

She swallowed hard, her sweating fingers taking a tighter grip upon the pistol, held out of sight in the folds of her cloak. Biting her lip, she eased back the hammer Then the moment she feared and expected came. Menton's movements had slowed, and the triumph glowing in Keath's face betrayed the nearness of the approaching end.

Suddenly his thrust caught the curved guard of Menton's sword, and with a swift flick of the wrist Keath sent it flying. He grinned, and the sudden flash in Menton's blue eyes showed that he knew there would be no mercy given him in return for his former courtesy. It was what Mary had waited for.

Menton stood pinned against the wall, the blood having now stained across his heaving chest. Keath held him there a moment with sword point at his throat; then a slight shift of his shoulder and a tenseness of his face betrayed his initiation of the final thrust.

Gilbreath took a frantic step forward. "Thomas, my God, don't . . ."

Praying her ball would hit the right man, Mary swung up the pistol with both hands and fired.

Chapter Thirty-six

THERE WAS A deafening report and blinding flash. She staggered back, dropping the pistol to the floor and putting her hands to her ringing ears. The silence now was almost as awful as the noise a moment before. Why did no one say anything? Then she realized her eyes were still clenched tightly shut and jerked them open in time to see Keath turn around with an extremely surprised look on his face before he abruptly turned deathly white and crumpled to the floor.

Mary bit off a cry. "Dear heaven, I've killed a man." She covered her face in terror and turned away. How could she live with his last expression haunting her?

An arm suddenly encircled her "Darling."

She whirled and raised a frantic face to his. "I had to save you! B-but not to—"

He smothered her in a crushing embrace that took her breath away. "Dearest, precious firebrand. You haven't killed anyone."

With difficulty she pulled her face up away from his chest. "I . . . I haven't?"

"No." His kiss sent fire racing through her veins. "And I thought I'd lost you "

She shook her head breathlessly. "Never. Oh, I have been so foolish!"

"No more than I," he murmured in her hair.

"But he is not dead?" Timidly she peeped around

Menton's shoulder to see Gilbreath bending over Keath's form.

"You caught him in the shoulder. And I never knew what an excellent shot I'd married until now."

She dropped her eyes, shy at this new rough tenderness in his voice. "I've never fired a gun before."

"Good Lord!" The startlement in his voice was plain. "Your aim might have gone anywhere."

"I know," she said. "I was very worried that I'd hit you instead."

"I should think so," he said wryly, gazing tenderly down at her.

A sudden commotion at the door interrupted him. It burst open and a frenzied Rebeccah hurled herself in. She stopped on the threshold with a scream.

"My God! He's dead!" She rushed forward, but Gilbreath caught her before she could throw herself upon Keath.

"Calm yourself. He's all right, curse him." Gilbreath almost snarled the words.

Rebeccah looked at him, then shook her head. "No," she moaned "No, you are lying."

"He would not be bleeding on the floor if he were dead," said Menton matter-of-factly.

Mary jerked in her breath. "Your wound!"

"Yes," he said wryly. "And I seem to be smearing my blood on you in a most messy way."

"Oh, pray, do not joke about it," she snapped fretfully. "We must have it seen to at once."

"Hush." His arm squeezed her tighter. "If you do not mind, I certainly don't. Get that infernal woman out of here, Gilbreath."

"With pleasure," snapped the man. He eyed the hostile servants crowding the doorway and pulled Rebeccah back from Keath's unconscious body at once. "Do come, Becky. Let's go while we can."

She slapped him and wrenched free of his grasp. "Do you think I will leave Thomas lying in his blood? They will let him die."

"I hardly think so," drawled Menton. "Might make my mother annoyed." He nodded to Johnson at the door. "Have him carried out." Johnson and another man moved to obey, and Menton sighed harshly. "I suppose we have managed to rouse the guests as well with our bit of a quarrel." He smiled down at Mary. "As soon as Thomas can walk, I'll pack him off to Jamaica, where he can vent his gall on that unfortunate population and leave us in peace."

"Then I shall go with him," declared Rebeccah.

"Don't be a fool," said Gilbreath with a scowl. "He doesn't care for you one jot, save how much he may use you."

"It does not matter," she said, lifting her chin and following the men carrying Keath out.

Gilbreath started to go after her, then jerked to a despairing halt. "I wish I'd never introduced him to this business," he said bitterly. "There was a time when she wasn't besotted with—"

"Never mind, Gilbreath," said Menton. "This is your chance to go. I suggest you take it before I change my mind and have you hauled in as a traitor. And you will leave the country, of course "

Gilbreath looked slowly at him with haunted green eyes. "Not without Rebeccah."

Menton snorted with exasperation. "You poor fool, she will never have you. By now you should know that. Even her own brother has learned how little is her worth."

Gilbreath nodded, bowing his head to hide his expression. Without another word he stumbled out. Menton suddenly grunted and sagged upon Mary.

"Excuse me," he said in a thin voice. "But I believe I really ought to sit down . . ."

Worry shot through her. "Quick, get a chair," she ordered one of the underfootmen.

He hastened to fetch the only one in the room, and placed it just in time for Menton to sink down. Mary knelt beside him, pushing back the stray lock of black hair from his forehead.

"Fetch me water and bandages at once," she said with a snap of authority, and started work as soon as they were brought to her. "The guests need not hang about," she said to Tyler, who was hovering in anxiety. "And have someone fetch the doctor."

"Yes, my lady." He bowed himself out, closing the door against the curious faces.

While she washed away the blood from his shoulder, she told Menton about the packet of papers and how she'd found them in Keath's trunk. "I gave them into Charlie's keeping, since he is a soldier," she finished. "Is that all right? I—"

"You are wonderful." Menton cupped her chin in his hand and forced her to look up too deeply into his eyes. She smiled, then was suddenly shy again and hastened to finish wrapping the bandage around him.

"Mary," he said.

But a little cloud of anxiety was already creeping across her joy. She must tell him; there could never again be anything between them. A warm blush stole into her cheeks. "You must know that I . . . I am the one your father caught in his study and had thrown—"

"Lord, yes, I've always known," he said impatiently, looking a little troubled He drew her nearer. "That is the reason I chose you. I thought you would work well if I held your past over you. But every time you asked me why I was using you . . . I couldn't bring myself to be that ruthless." His eyes searched hers. "I've treated you dreadfully nevertheless . . . frightened you . . . Can you forgive me? Can you . . . love me?"

The warmth in her face intensified, and her utter happiness could no longer be contained. "Yes. Oh, *yes,* Aubrey! Forever. . . ."

Passionately he caught her close, and as she yielded her lips to his with a thrill that ran deep into her very soul, she knew that nothing in the world could be greater than this love—which had come to birth so wildly, and which could never again be quenched.